Playing a Part

Playing a Part

A Novel

Melaney Poli

RESOURCE *Publications* · Eugene, Oregon

PLAYING A PART
A Novel

Copyright © 2019 Melaney Poli. All rights reserved. Except for brief quotations in critical publications or reviews, no part of this book may be reproduced in any manner without prior written permission from the publisher. Write: Permissions, Wipf and Stock Publishers, 199 W. 8th Ave., Suite 3, Eugene, OR 97401.

Resource Publications
An Imprint of Wipf and Stock Publishers
199 W. 8th Ave., Suite 3
Eugene, OR 97401

www.wipfandstock.com

PAPERBACK ISBN: 978-1-5326-6990-3
HARDCOVER ISBN: 978-1-5326-6991-0
EBOOK ISBN: 978-1-5326-6992-7

Manufactured in the U.S.A.   04/18/19

This book is entirely a work of fiction. The names, characters, and incidents portrayed in it either are the products of the author's imagination or are used fictitiously. Any resemblance to actual events or locales or persons, living or dead, is entirely coincidental.

The Poems of Rowan Williams, excerpt of translation of Rainer Maria Rilke poem "Experiencing Death" by Rowan Williams. Carcanet Press, 2002. Used by permission.

Tair Mewn Un, quotation of "Cyfwelliad â'r Bardd" by Gwyneth Lewis, Cyhoeddiadau Barddas, 2005. Used by permission.

The Return of Sherlock Holmes, excerpt of "The Adventure of the Empty House" by Arthur Conan Doyle. In the public domain.

to Larry P.

E nānā i keʻano o nāʻōleloʻano maikaʻi
E hoʻomanaʻo mau wau i kou lokomaikaʻi
E hoʻomanaʻo mau wau i kou lokomaikaʻi

What is the world that art takes for granted? It is the one in which perception is always incomplete.

ROWAN WILLIAMS

Contents

Pretext (before Christmas 1987) | 1
1 Keynote | 29
2 Evidence | 38
3 Peter | 45
4 Dan | 60
5 Rachel | 69
6 Good Shepherd | 85
7 Ariel | 93
8 Clue | 104
9 The Cunninghams | 113
10 Roamer | 133
11 The Game Afoot | 148
12 Edward | 162
13 Further Questioning | 171
14 The Sojourners | 186
15 dal Segno | 206
16 Segno | 212
17 Max | 225
18 Myself | 236
19 Disclosure | 266
20 A Loose End | 293
21 Thanksgiving | 303
Coda | 317

Acknowledgements | 323

Pretext

(before Christmas 1987)

Usually I try to begin with something interesting; Jill says it's better that way. Well, it was almost Christmas, and the tree looked swell, and we were about to have a consolidated family-staff party at Dad's house. I had one concert looming, four nutty jobs, and two maniac fans. Jill also said if you can't catch 'em, confuse 'em.

It had been Rachel's idea to combine our staff party with family. This was mostly because she wanted to have fun with Tonya and Mishael, not because she wanted to make things easier for Peter and me. She also hoped that Dan—definitely not staff and not quite family—wouldn't come. Dan wouldn't come. Tonya planned to but wasn't technically staff; we were *her* clients. Then there was Pastor Felix, neither staff nor family, and coming. But the whole idea could have been called on technicalities: technically, Peter and I were on vacation. A staff party when you're on vacation? And actually, only Peter was off, and it wasn't going to work like that. We had given Mish the present of two weeks off, which meant I had to work every day except Christmas, and Peter, being Peter, was likely to be at work also.

Whoever showed up or didn't, it was still my sister's big chance to play hostess and she had buried the default advance crowd—herself and John and the twins, Dad, Peter, and myself—under a mountain of hors d'oeuvres. They were all exquisite; Rachel had gotten no closer to them than her wallet. I was counting the minutes until I'd be volunteered to rescue dinner, about which I'd gotten a whiff of dire rumors. Dad was busy heckling me about possible gigs. Rachel herself was a little better—if not prying, at least not insinuating too much. She had stopped being mad about the record deal incident and just seemed to be cranky about holiday things. There was an unusual amount of comments about Christmas or the party or about how quiet my place was. I kept saying, "I'm fine at my place." Which turned out to be what she wanted to hear, sort of.

The girls, on their part, were doing what they always did when I was around and gearing for game. They were also, in that uncanny way of preadolescents, sprouting another inch every time you turned around. On Sunday I'd asked John what he was feeding them. "Just good honest sawdust!" he protested. Also in the way of preadolescents, they made to get away with a lot: they had come in their angel costumes from the school pageant, some outsized choir albs borrowed from Good Shepherd. They'd gotten the part of Gladys Herdman one last time; next year, they'd be at Mayhew, and Mayhew did Shakespeare and Gilbert and Sullivan.

Rachel had fussed about their wearing their costumes to the party. "They're getting too old for that sort of thing."

"What, enjoying themselves?"

"They're going to be thirteen next year, Max. They should be acting their age."

"Lighten up a bit, Rach, they've got time now. They'll be thirty-one before you know it."

Now it was later, Mish and Jean-Paul and Felix had arrived, Rachel was simultaneously trying to get dinner going and entertain our guests. All was a spirited holiday camaraderie.

"Mishael, I have some more addendums on the Newrich case I need redone."

"Good luck with them then, Peter. I'm on vacation."

We were there to enjoy ourselves especially by heckling each other any chance we got. The evening ahead was riddled with possibilities. Peter and Mish were already running neck and neck.

"And that's a *paid* vacation too, Mr. Serrev, and no thanks to you. It took the kindhearted Mr. Thompson to get me that. His partner's nothing but a shiftless old skinflint."

"I resent that, Mrs. Chisholm. I happen to be a first-rate cheapskate. Work darn hard at it."

Dad had gotten a head start on them, though. "Dan's stand-in," I called him. Dan jokes went flying, courtesy of John and Lynn.

"Dan wouldn't stand for it."

"He can stand on his own two feet."

"No! he wouldn't stand a chance . . . !"

Dan would have loved it. Jill's threshold was much lower; she toppled over, gagging. "Daaaad, *stop* it!"

Mish, meanwhile, on vacation as she was, could not put work down. According to her watch, Tonya was supposed to arrive any moment. "I predict Tonya will come in five, four, three, two . . ."

Instead there was a wail from the kitchen: "Max, I need you in here . . ."

Playing a Part

Everyone cheered and applauded when I got up, and I bowed.

In the kitchen Rachel was fussing from one counter to another, sniffing, stirring—a chaos of recipe books and spoons. I reached for an apron.

"So Doc, what seems to be the problem?"

"Everything!" she groaned, pushing all the spoons at me. "Why do I do this? I have to call in. Just do something, okay? I don't care what."

Since nothing was smoking or in flames I began as usual by trying to identify dishes or, failing that, ingredients. When everything was under control I enjoyed a few moments' quietude, humming Christmas carols as I went from pot to skillet and back again, correcting seasonings, settings, and forming an estimate of the actual menu.

I had taken five and was leaning against the counter, all spoons in one hand and one ear on the stove, when an angel materialized in the kitchen door, the front of her trailing garb stretched tight under her feet. Her wire halo tilted over one ear and she was hiding something behind her back. It was Lynn.

"They're talking about you," she announced.

"Of course, they can't talk *to* me, can they?" I gestured at her with the spoons. "Guess who they're talking about now?"

A pot burbled for attention and I stirred it.

"Max, what's a bachelor?"

I turned off one burner. "Me."

"Because you're not married?"

"Your dad would not qualify." I grabbed a potholder and reached into the oven for the biscuits.

"She gave this to you, didn't she?"

Lynn produced from behind her back a rumpled, very faded cap.

"Ah, thief," I said, sliding the biscuit tray over the sink, "you've come to turn yourself in."

"Didn't she?"

"Vegetable," I said, tapping one ear. "Sounds like mushroom."

Lynn came closer, studying my cap. "She wanted you to wear it so you would think of her."

I shushed the onions around. "Speculation and interpretation aren't facts, Lynx."

"Is it true?"

"Who knows?" I opened the oven and basted the bird.

"It was a birthday present when you were twenty."

"Not a point of any importance."

"Can you tell me one that is?"

She leisurely pulled herself up on a kitchen stool, wrapping her loose garb around her knees. I turned my back on her to open the oven and spent an entire twenty seconds scrutinizing the turkey, then closed the oven and pulled out a small bowl. I sloshed some vinegar into it and grabbed a measuring cup, picked up one of the wooden spoons, rearranged onions in a skillet. I tugged on my collar, then flipped on the extractor fan.

"After I left the Phil I finished school and got a degree."

Silence. Lynn's face was playing with a few different thoughts and finally she tried out: "You already had a degree."

"So what's a bachelor of music going to do for an aspiring dick?" I stuck a fork in the salt cellar and flicked as much as it would hold into the vinegar.

Looking very perplexed, "I don't know, what would you do?"

"It's the degree, Lemmer. The degree is called a bachelor." I gave the bowl a tablespoon of maple syrup and mustard.

"And you're a bachelor too?"

"Pretty bizarre, isn't it?"

"You couldn't get the other degree at Horton?"

"It's actually a baccalaureate—bachelor's just informal. Try this," I offered her the bowl. "Tell me if it's okay."

She dipped her finger and licked it disinterestedly, shrugging. "It's fine. You always do fine stuff."

"Yeah," I muttered, "thanks."

"Why couldn't you get the other degree at Horton?"

"Dunno." I tossed a spray of mustard seeds in the bowl and whisked the mixture, then pushed it aside. "Something about the board and the charter. You going there?"

An exasperated sigh. "Of *course* not. *You* know I'm going to join the police, remember?"

"Hey, if you can pretend you don't know Horton's full of sonorous air, I can pretend I don't know about you and the fuzz."

"You *could* have answered me."

"Nothing doing. You don't get any points for sloppy questioning. If you want to push a question backwards to get more information, you have to be smarter than just pushing the same point." I glanced at her over my shoulder; she was glaring vindictively at my cap. "Now," I grabbed a wooden spoon and rushed it around the squash, "go and join the police, and I'll give you that cap."

She looked from me to my cap as if surprised she was still holding it.

"You'd do that?"

"Sure, why not?" I turned off the brussels sprouts and watched condensation bead inside the glass lid, then lifted it and tossed in the vinaigrette. "What am I going to do, keep it forever?"

"Thanks, Max."

"You're welcome, sweetie."

Her face was calm with satisfied delight, and for a few minutes she said nothing. After a while she said, hopefully, "I like her name, Ariel."

I looked up at the light over the stove, the knot in my stomach tightening. Rachel was taking forever for a phone call. I directed my gaze back to Lynn.

"Yellow was her favorite color," I volunteered.

"How come she didn't give you a cap in *your* favorite color?"

"Search me." I focused on the stove. "When people are in love, they do crazy things."

"Like proposing from stage during a concert?"

I pulled out a stack of casseroles from the cupboard and turned off the back burners. "Don't snoop too much, Lynn. People aren't the same as facts."

A sigh. Her halo slipped further down her hair and she pulled it off, fretting my cap around it. "But . . . how could someone die like that, just like that?"

"I don't know, Gopher, no one knows." I picked up the bag of pecans and stopped with the fridge door open. "It's one of those things."

For a while we were both silent, Lynn fingering my cap and her halo, and I slicing strawberries into a chipped blue bowl that I had used to dig with in the garden a million years before.

"Does that mean I'll never find out?"

I paused with a perfect specimen of strawberry under the knife, playing with the answers *Maybe* and *It depends what you want to see.* "Who knows?"

Rachel picked that moment to reappear, as abruptly as she had left. "They've got Jeffreys, but they might call later . . ." She plucked a spoon out of my hands and sampled one of the skillets. "Wow! I don't know how you do it." She looked at the bowl of fruit. "What is that for?"

"Dessert."

"Too many cooks," Lynn giggled.

"Exactly," Rachel turned to her. "*Scramme.*"

Lynn slid off the stool and flashed me her best rolled-eyes "Mothers!" look before skulking out. We watched her go.

"What was that one after this time?"

Outside, the crunching of snow as a car pulled up to the sidewalk. "I got interviewed," reintroducing my gaze to the knife and fruit. "Checking out her facts."

Rachel snorted. "Facts, my Aunt Fanny. Practicing, that's what she's doing." She elbowed me over, drained a pot in the sink, and dumped its contents into one of the casseroles I had pulled out.

"Then she'll do very well, won't she?"

Another snort. "So what was the big mystery this time?"

Car doors closing. "What else?"

Rachel paused with the oven door open; I concentrated on the movement of the knife and the red berries in my hands.

"Did you tell her?"

Footsteps outside on the walk. "What's there to tell?" The red berries in the blue bowl immensely satisfied me. It was better than dirt. "There's not much to it, is there? She knows almost all of it." I put the knife in the sink and pulled off the apron.

Rachel nearly conciliatory. "I'll talk with her."

"You already have, Rach. That's how she knows."

"I mean about snooping—"

"I know what you mean. And it doesn't matter. None of it matters." I rinsed my hands and pushed the faucet off. "She'd find out anyways. She's going to be thirteen."

"I'm sorry, Max, I just . . ."

I grabbed a dishtowel and wrung my hands in it. "No hard feelings." The doorbell clanged loudly. "No broken bones." I tossed the towel at her as I slipped out. "No guilt trips."

When I opened the door Tonya blew in on a gust of freezing air, glaring at me out of the woolen globe of tartan that was the rest of her. "So, it's you!" she growled before I could say a word, jerking her scarf down. "I heard what you did about Mish's vacation. Don't you talk to me, buster!"

"My favorite accountant!" I returned. "And at last, a fellow Sojourner. Merry Christmas!"

"Merry Christmas, and you just stay away from business tonight, got that?"

With Tonya's arrival everyone that could come had, and we settled down with the remains of the hors d'oeuvres, waiting for dinner and in no hurry to do anything in particular. Mishael and Tonya and Rachel, who had rejoined us, at once began laughing a riot without any apparent effort or even cause. Jean-Paul and I chatted together in French, this measure at points isolating us on a small island, except for the sharp-eared Tonya, now across the room from us.

"*Comment ça va a l'ouverage?*"

"*Ben, ben. Les temps de Noël sont bon à l'imprimeries...*"

"I hear you talking about business over there, and you better knock it off! This is a party!"

Jill and Lynn were doubled over with the effort of telling jokes to Felix and Dad.

Jean-Paul spoke thoughtfully and carefully as always, his lilting Québécois accent in its Haïtian turns like an exotic rendering of a childhood tune. "I have finally found it, the perfect motto for S&T: '*Je suis donc je suis.*'"

He was still at it. The poor fellow didn't give up easily. "*Oui? Pourquoi?* Is it, 'I follow, therefore I am,' or, 'I am, therefore I follow,' or 'I follow, therefore I follow'?"

Jean-Paul shrugged, grinning. "*Je n'en sais ... parceque ça depende des circonstances.*"

"*Mets-en,*" I pointed at him. "Sometimes, you don't know who's really following who, or who's watching who."

"So, it's a winner?"

Dad, as ever, had been watching me; he came over to us and handed me the November *Flute Talk*. "You see that article by William Watson?"

"Yeah. Good stuff, huh?" I took the issue, my eyes skating over the top of it. "I'm assigning it to some of my students."

"You could write stuff like that, Max."

"Sure, and I have. Something wrong if someone else writes it?" I tossed the magazine on the coffee table, more irritated than I wanted to be.

"Lighten up a bit, Max," Rachel grumbled. "Try taking a compliment like a normal person for once."

Dad lowered himself into a nearby chair and sighed.

I got up to retrieve some pretzels from a tray.

Felix was speaking about the delayed interchange project that was intended to cut out congestion downtown. The conversation was immediately laced with useful perspectives that had more to do with some of my jobs than I liked. Lynn left her sister and came over to flop on the floor beside my chair. As soon as my mouth was stuffed with pretzels, she leaned over and asked, "Max, what's the biggest mystery you couldn't figure out?"

"You," I said through the pretzels, one ear on the conversation.

It would have been quite a contest for my two ears: Lynn's persistence versus municipal issues bearing on business, but in the end, Dad won again, scattering conversation with an appeal to get the music started. It wasn't actually a request so much as a diplomatic order, the polite side of Dad's despotism. As this was what we all expected from him, no one was surprised or offended or thought to object when he began rustling us into formation.

Tonya and Lynn would be at the piano. Jill would play violin. Jean-Paul would play clarinet and Rachel her oboe. Felix, Peter, John and Mishael would listen or sing. Dad would join us on viola. And I . . .

"Well?" Dad smacked his hands together expectantly.

I shrugged. "It's at home."

The news blew him out of the water; for a moment Dad looked completely at a loss, so surprised he didn't even think of volunteering something from his studio.

"I told you to bring it!"

"It's been a busy week, I forgot."

"*Forgot!* You take it to work every day!"

"How about the piccolo?"

Dad was still staring at me as if I'd lost my marbles. "Fine, fine! Go get it! Don't keep us waiting."

I slipped out the front door without jacket or gloves, my eyes watering at the cold. Pale gray night on the neighborhood I had grown up in, the trees looming spiky shadows over the houses, over Mrs. McPherson's house, and Bob's old house now under new management, the illuminated face of the water tower, everything soaked in the persistent yellow of streetlights. The fresh fall of snow—we had been dumped with six inches—newly cleared from the streets and heaped along the sidewalks, dotted with thousands of tiny stars in the streetlights. An icy tingle had gotten under my skin by the time I got to the car and felt under the front seat for my instrument but, despite the cold, I hesitated on the way back.

Darkness and silence, the winter night sky a stuffy gray illuminated by the city; all you could see of downtown from here was the yellow cloud cover. The whish of car tires a few blocks away. Sirens far off. A dog barking somewhere.

I listened as though I had something to listen for, watching my breath escape faintly into the night air.

It wasn't a perfect silence; you could make out the low roar of the freeway some five miles off, and there was no escaping the occasional drone of a jet thousands of feet above. But it was a surprisingly complete silence for the neighborhood, like a hall after the musicians and audience had gone, and it weighed on me like I'd left something undone.

Finally, very small and distant, I caught a tiny sound: voices, somewhere, very sweet, very soft, like a snatch of a choir. The Methodist church six blocks up probably had a service tonight. I couldn't recognize the tune. I had no idea how long I stood, just listening.

"Hey, you!"

I spun around. Peter stood in the screen doorway of the porch, hugging himself and looking frostbitten.

"What are you doing, sniffing the air? Old Blowhard sent me to fetch you."

"Listening." I glanced from him to the street again.

"*Listening?* In subzero temperatures?"

"I heard singing."

"You *would*," he growled, but let the porch door rush shut behind him and stomped out into the night, hands in pockets. He cocked his head and scanned the street both ways for several moments, then shook his head.

"I don't hear a thing."

I tuned my ears to the dark and realized the sound had vanished. "It's gone."

"Huh," he grunted, "why am I not surprised. Well, got your spare?"

I looked at the case in my hand as if surprised I was holding it.

"You know," Peter was gesturing toward the house, "*inside?* We should go *in* now? Remember, dinner? Music? Dad? and it's cold as hell out here?"

The house, the darkness, the sky; I looked down the street again, something tugging at me.

"Alright, Mr. Surly," I said, "shall we go join the club?"

"After you, Mr. Temperamental."

I swung the piccolo case at him. "You're everything that's wrong with our business, you know that?"

"You're no great help yourself," he complimented amenably, adding a slushball for emphasis.

We managed to get back inside without getting soaked through.

The evening's music began with requests of favorites, then, as ever, became favorite interpretations of requests. After Tonya had shown us the *right* way to sing "Go Tell It on the Mountain," Lynn led us through "The Twelve Days of Christmas" in a version where my true love gave me more instruments than found in a Mahler symphony. We hadn't gotten to the flutists—piping, of course—before Rachel came back and announced things were nearly ready. Since everyone was close to mutinously starved by this time, it was no surprise that the music ended right there and the instruments put away at a remarkable tempo.

Dinner was a grand affair, despite the delay. Without too much assistance from me, Rachel had prepared an entire Christmas rehearsal dinner for the lot of us; not bad for someone who had just performed six surgeries and saved a life in the process. We fell to the hard work of passing platters while trying to eat and talk. Conversation made several false starts and then careened into a hodge-podge of amateur -ophies and -ologies. At one end of the table, a discussion bearing some distant relation to theology, or maybe politics; at the other, something about art or philosophy or math, I couldn't tell which, and, stuck between them, was content to devote my attention primarily to my plate, eating whatever my fork found first.

Dad: ". . . That's most of the problem with those selection processes—it just seems too random to be useful."

Rachel, snorting: "Well, good luck. And if you found out everything was random?"

Peter: "I'd check to see if my insurance covered that."

"Wouldn't happen," I said. "Nothing's random."

Tonya, humming, slicing her turkey: ". . . Chances are, your chances are . . ."

Lynn, anxious: "But what about jazz improv?"

Dad, indignant, the selection processes for music teachers suddenly more critical than any other: "What about it? What is that Ms. Nichols teaching you people?"

Felix: "You've heard about fractals, right? Potatoes, Richard?"

Mishael: "I don't really know about randomness, but I do know about patterns. I see it every day at work. I print up a report, and Max decides he has to change something. I turn on the radio, and Max changes the station."

I reached for the dish of brussels sprouts and realized I'd forgotten to put in the pecans, and so had Rachel. "Not quite every day," I corrected. "It doesn't happen when one of us is out."

Lynn, withering in agony: "But what about *improv?*"

"What about it?" I asked.

Jill: "What are fractals?"

Lynn: "You said nothing was random."

"Sure," I said. "Jazz improv's not nothing."

Tonya: "It's kind of like strings, Jill, only in shapes."

Dad, so defensive as to be certifiably unintelligible: "It's the *least* nothing, Lynn, it won't work without it. Even indeterminacy isn't half of that."

Jean-Paul, with his customary gentleness: "What is not random does not stop it from being spontaneous, Lynn. Everywhere there is order, but also freedom."

Rachel to her sprouts, wryly: "Oh, come off it, Dad. You've never been indeterminate a day in your life. You've never even *done* indeterminacy."

Mishael: "I feel like I should be taking dictation."

"Jill loves anything with strings attached," Lynn shared, much relieved. "She's very high—OW!!"

"That's enough please, girls," Rachel directed.

The highlight of the meal did not come with dessert but with Dad. Something on tap must have been working its way through his system; midway through his second plate, the music reached an uncontrollable pitch and broke out. Dad vaulted to his feet, conducting what I suspected to be Handel's *Messiah* with his knife, beckoning with fork for fuller sound. Chaos erupted at the table.

"Grandpa!" exclaimed Lynn.

"Dad!" protested Rachel.

"Richard," John suggested.

"*Stringendo*," I insisted.

The excitement was over soon. He sat down again after a few bars as if nothing unusual had happened, looking disappointed.

"I know," Dad told me, "I try. But what can you do when you've got six concerts to rehearse for, and everyone's mind is in Tahiti?"

Dad had a lot on his mind himself. After twenty-five seasons with the Philharmonic, he was getting ready to retire. It seemed almost too mythological to consider as fact, but the date was set and an enormous to-do planned for the occasion. It wasn't news to anyone by now, only shocking in itself, the way only a megalomaniac stepping down can be. Dad, with an unerring show of dispassion, spoke of it as if it were just one more gig to put on.

"Then what are you going to do, Richard?" Felix asked, with understandable incredulity.

"Oh, a little of this and that; I may just teach," Dad replied, not very convincingly. "And I may guest conduct sometime."

"And you're guest conducting again this season, Max," Mishael glowed.

"Yup." I helped myself to more turkey and stuffing. "Knocks the stuffing out of you, it does. Dad can take it, though."

"I got to go to'hr Chanksgiving conchert at Cay'or Sheater," Tonya negotiated the words with her potatoes. "Yo'hr *fabr'rous*."

"The orchestra was fabulous," I said.

Rachel, lightly and pompously: "Mister Modest Max Mussorgsky."

"When he's conducting, he's always throwing pencils at work," complained Peter.

A compliment after my own heart. This was more like it. "It hasn't happened more than twice."

"Where have I heard that before?" he snorted. "Reminds me of another of your many talents."

Then there was my talent for killing compliments. "You mean asking questions?"

"I mean trouble."

Dessert was another affair altogether. Rachel had experimented with her traditional king's cake recipe to such an extent that it showed distinct signs of a potential to ooze right off the plate, maybe even go on to a degree at Harvard or play Carnegie Hall. We received it with mixed reviews and began searching for the tokens, which, unsurprisingly, the strawberry-studded goo-that-was-the-cake yielded only with great unwillingness.

Felix, in the midst of a mouthful, abruptly shot something across the table into the butter which was promptly returned to him: the pig. "I can live with that," he announced cheerfully. Jean-Paul bit his tongue discovering the magnifying glass; Tonya greeted the bachelor's button with her deadpan, "Well would you look at that"; and on my right Peter extracted a ring and snorted disapprovingly. Across the table Lynn took the other ring from her mouth and laughed. Jill also giggled as she uncaked her prize: the tile with the conductor's baton. Not surprisingly, the crown turned up in Dad's plate; Rachel's contribution ended up on John's, and with the little red heart in his fingers, he leaned over and kissed her. Rachel got the thimble: "What's this??!" Mishael, after some careful excavation, pulled the silver dollar from her cake.

"There's your raise, I'd been wondering where it'd gone to," Peter informed her merrily, forgetting for the moment the ring and Eleanor.

Lynn was eyeballing my plate a little too intensely, and I went through my cake as carefully as I could. I finally found something truly inedible at the bottom: the little golden key that was Mom's immemorial contribution. What was it this year? The key of F# major? A minor?

"Max gets to do the dishes," Rachel volunteered me, spotting it.

That was it, the key of D. It looked like it was going to be D major, too.

The nice thing about dishes was the quiet company—John and Jean-Paul volunteered to help—and the break from questions; I had a feeling it was pick-on-Max night. Sure enough, on my way out of the kitchen I felt a small hand slip into my left hand and looked to find Lynn beside me, her other hand occupied with some of the bulk of her costume. "*You* again?"

"You have a ring."

"You got the ring," I started to say. "Well, yes."

She eyed me doubtfully. "And bachelors wear rings?"

"Why not?"

She let go of my hand and crossed her arms. "Are you just going to keep blowing me off?"

I sighed. "Lynn, don't you know what a *holiday* is? How much do you need to know?"

"I want to know the truth."

"What's *enough*? That's what I want to know."

Playing a Part

"Well, why the ring, then?"

I shook her loose and held up my left hand, fishing for a good translation. "It's like this: the ring says this one's not for sale. *A compris?*"

Again that doubtful frown. "Then it's a lie?"

"Since when is an implication a lie? Try this, Lynn: there are people in this world who choose to remain alone."

"Why?"

If I waited long enough, I'd never have to tell her. "You'll figure that out someday, and you won't even have to ask me. You'll just know."

Looking distinctly unconvinced, her mouth a wrinkle echoed in her brow.

"Then you'll know too why I'm so crazy about you and Jillers and all of you."

"Of course you're crazy," in an embarrassed tone. "You're a musician."

"I'm afraid it's terminal, my friend. But that reminds me." I snapped my fingers. "Wait here, I have to get something."

She waited, and I came back in a moment with my surprise.

"Merry Christmas, Lynn. I have to give this to you before your mom sees it."

Her eyes and her whole person lit up, instantly recognizing the shape. "Max, you can't give me your flute!"

"You think I'd give you *my flute?* Sheesh, Miss Jumps-To-Conclusions, how about you do some homework first? Go on and open it. You might be surprised."

"It's not Christmas yet."

"You know some law I don't about opening Christmas gifts? Go on!"

Her fingers made short work of all my careful taping, and in a moment the brown case lay in her hands. She stared at me goggle-eyed.

"How many directions do you need? Open it!"

She threw it open and sighed, as much in relief as in pleasure. "It's the Gemeinhardt!!" She grinned at me, delighted, and picked up the card I had placed in the case. "'Make it shine like the top of the Chrysler Building.'"

"You'll have to clean it like that, but I'd love to hear it like that too."

"Oh, I will!" beaming like she was the top of the Chrysler Building. "I didn't *really* think you'd give me your regular flute, Max."

"Why didn't you think I could just give you *a* flute?"

"Because it's not the sort of thing you'd do!"

"And what makes you say that?"

"Because you're cheap."

"Cheap!!" I threw in an extra exclamation point in my astonishment. "Explain *that* to me."

"You don't buy stuff, you just give yours away."

"In what state is that a crime? Sooner or later you don't need stuff, do you?"

I got a big hug and a proper thank you before, hugging her prize excitedly, she cannonballed to the living room.

I didn't move for several minutes, prickling with regret, but not for the instrument.

I ought to have gone back to the living room on that note, but I had waited too long; for a moment there in the hall I stopped and let the darkness press around me—the photographs on the wall, the voices filtering from the living room, even the lighting almost the same as it had all been over sixteen years earlier. As if nothing had happened.

In the living room, everyone had broken up into little clusters again and there were no more empty chairs. I spotted Jill sitting alone at the hearth, arms wrapped around her knees.

"Mind if I join you?"

She smiled and shook her head.

I sat and we watched the fire, saying nothing. All the conversations behind us in the room like the roar of surf, coming and going. The flotsam and spindrift washed over me in pieces of budget figures, job cuts, family news, Christmas sales, tax hikes. The primaries.

I rested my elbows on my knees and tipped my head in one hand, studying Jill.

"I don't see how Lynn can go to police academy without you when she's shy as a marmekin."

A shrug, her eyes fixed on the fire. "If she wants to go, she's gonna have to go her own self, 'cuz I'm sure not going there."

"Going to Horton?"

"Yes."

I had no doubt she could get in. "Sure you can get in?"

"Absolutely."

A long pause; the fire hissed and popped. "I'll coach you for your audition."

"Grandpa is going to also, and some of his friends have promised to write letters."

She certainly planned ahead. "And . . . Mom?"

"Still doesn't like it."

"Well," I shrugged, "you can't please 'em all."

She shook her head, biting her lip. "Don't even try."

I fiddled with a splinter of wood on the hearth.

I asked, "You've been writing more stories?"

She turned to me, all brightness and grin. "Yes."

"I'll buy all your books."

"I'll *give* them to you."

"Can I have signed copies?"

The voices of John and Felix comparing the lineup to the NFL playoffs, punctuated with half-informed enthusiasms of Lynn. Dad reciting Nelligan's "Sainte-Cécile" for Jean-Paul. Tonya and Mishael and Rachel engrossed in a conversation I couldn't begin to discern the topic of.

Jill was asking me: "If I wanted to write a mystery, how would I do it?"

"Read any good ones lately?"

"I'm working on *Gaudy Night*."

Gaudy Night! They *were* getting old. At her age I had been satisfied with, well . . .

"Do you like it?"

"Oh yes, it's great. I think I figured out already who it is; I just don't get the stuff about Lord Peter and Harriet . . ."

Well, that would come, and all too soon, it seemed.

". . . I mean, it's *distracting*, and it doesn't really go with the plot."

"You try diagramming the plot?"

"No."

"Try that. Then you can see how it was put together."

"Ahem, what do *you* know about writing stories?"

"Hey, I've read some books. I think I read two whole novels at State. I can figure out the rest."

"Can't you just give me ideas from your work?"

"We haven't even established if you actually *want* to write a mystery, remember?"

"Well, what would *you* do if you were going to?"

"You mean if I were you? 'Cuz I know *I'm* not going to."

"Alright, then if you were me."

"I'd ask my uncle."

I could hear Peter driving a point home and picking up steam; the discussion seemed to be about some hack running for the school board or maybe the DA hopefuls, or the GOP hopefuls. Someone he wasn't peachy keen on. Easily done with Peter.

Jill, as if it were mortifyingly obvious: "My uncle's a monkey."

"Careful there, now, or you'll end up like Lynn. You've got to be persistent first, Jinx. If I didn't do that, I'd be out of business."

"But where could I get ideas?"

"Dunno, read the police reports in the paper and make up stuff."

"How come *you* won't give me ideas?"

"'Cuz you've got a great brain all on your own, and your uncle'ld just get in the way. He's a monkey, remember?"

"But he's a good monkey, the nicest one I know."

"Thanks, Jinx, I'll put that in my CV."

For a while we simply sat and watched the fire again. Dad got up and sat at the piano and quietly—gallingly—began to play selections from *The Nutcracker*. This was all Jill needed; eyes sparking, she jumped up, seized the violin from where it had been left on the coffee table, and joined him. I went and found a chair. Lynn found me.

Everyone else was still chatting up a storm. She leaned over conspiratorially.

"What *is* the biggest mystery you couldn't ever figure out, Max?"

"Celery," I replied at once. "Where are all the good recipes for celery?"

"No, no! I'm serious!"

"Sure, I'm serious too. Where are they?"

"C'mon, Max, you can tell me—I'm trustworthy!"

I yawned and glanced at her, my head swamped with work I was trying to ward off. "Did your sister set you on this?"

"What is it? Was it the one when you called the FBI—"

"Alright, hold up there. Let's backtrack a bit." I straightened and fixed her with my best beady imitation-of-Dan glare, which never fails to not impress her one bit. "C'mon now, Lemmer, what do you think I do all day, live in a crime novel? How come everything has to be a big hairy mystery? How come it can't just be a question of finding things out?"

"What's the difference?"

"Well, you asked for a mystery, you tell me."

That dogged look I couldn't escape. "Was there ever *anything* you couldn't figure out?"

I watched her carefully. "Can you keep a secret?"

"Yes."

"You sure?"

A big nod.

"Cross your heart?"

"*Yes* already, yes."

I leaned over; in my most confidential whisper: "People. Life."

Her face said, "You've got to be kidding."

She said, utterly scandalized, "Is that all?"

"What do you mean, 'is that all?'" my hands imitating her tone mockingly. "You telling me you've got the answers?"

"*People? Life?*"

"*Shhh!* It's confidential, Lynn. Top Secret. What do you want, people to think I don't know everything? Button up, now."

That hard, insistent look so much like her mother's.

"You asked, I answered you. You ought to be tickled pink. Look, I even waived the retainer for you."

"Thanks for nothing."

I sighed. "Alright, alright, enough of that." I rubbed my eyes and propped up my head in one hand, stifling a yawn. "So what kind of farce was that tonight about not knowing jazz from beans? You don't know anything all of a sudden?"

"It's a method of getting information," she said sullenly. "And I read something. I wasn't sure."

I couldn't help a smile. "Yeah, there's lots of stuff out there. So you're still studying?"

"Grandpa's getting me records from the Cardinal Lee Library. I'm working on *Miles Ahead*."

"Good for you. And the old eighty-eight, has it gone Monk?"

"It's still Debussy." She glanced over to where Dad and Jill were hewing away at Tchaikovsky. "Jill and I are going to do duets. Maybe we could perform with you again."

"May be."

We both watched the small concert, but my attention wasn't in it. Lately Dad had kept mentioning getting older. I was so used to hearing the subtext that *I* was getting older, and not doing it as a full-time professional, that the fact of Dad getting older was only really starting to hit with his impending retirement, whether or not it actually took. I had the sudden thought of what it would be like to stand at Mom's grave when it would also be Dad's. Lynn turned to me and frowned. "You don't like it?"

I smiled with my teeth and she banged on my knee.

"Stop worrying so much. You're a bad example."

After the Tchaikovsky, I was up: this year it was my privilege to dispense entertainment. I took my position by the mantel, did some quick archaeology in my pockets, and, after pulling out keys and stray notes at last extracted the folded papers I was looking for. Jill ran and got a candy cane off the tree and handed it to me. "So pleest to amsee foor you ahl toonaite," I spoke into the candy cane. "You ahl well plees leessen clossly foor thees emportant enformacions . . ."

"Sound check!" Peter called out. "We can't hear you!"

"Wood semonne plees to asseest se gentleman oveh thare. Okeh." I shook out the papers. "Listen up. This report is submitted by one Peter

Serrev, 'Four Santas held as Suspects in Burglary of Eggnog and Six Thousand Smackers...'"

Maybe it was having been run down all evening by Lynn's attempts to pin order on the world, but somehow the spoof on business that was our holiday game gave me a slightly better perspective of my life, made me feel slightly more in control of it. I ate up the drama of reading and rereading all the clues, deciphering everyone's handwriting when they had written their answers, and declaring the winners. "Now for the fun part...

"Excellent work, Lynn... No, Felix, Ed does not work at Darby's—that Santa is married to his sister."

"I must have missed that part."

"Very close, Jill, keep up the good work... what is this supposed to mean, Dad? 'They all took a little bit and went home afterwards'? And Pete, I'm shocked."

"What? That I wrote it?"

"That you actually got it right!"

"Oh, you..."

I had to duck quickly to miss kissing one of his size 10s.

"HEY!" barked Dad. "That's my son, and this is my house. If there's shoes to be thrown, I'll be the one to throw them. Give me that," he directed John.

"This is... very interesting, Rachel, but I don't think the robber could have done the burglary *and* attend the benefit gala at Cartensen's *and* be quite so full of Christmas spirits he couldn't walk straight out of the bar all at the same time."

"Well, you didn't repeat things often enough for me to find out what was happening."

"Are you certain you were *listening*?"

During this interlude Dad lobbed the shoe in my direction but Jean-Paul intercepted and threw it to Lynn, who snuck it to Jill, who sat on it.

"This is great, Mish, picture perfect. And you too, Jean-Paul—thanks too for that marvelous interception..."

"Aren't employees of contest supervisors ineligible from playing?" laughed Mishael.

"If it comes to that," I countered, "friends and employees and relations are ineligible. So it looks like you're all ineligible. So just enjoy yourselves, because the winners are eligible for a nice prize."

Everyone groaned in appreciation when I announced the prizes were Philharmonic tickets, which I still received every season. I wondered fleetingly if Lynn was right about my being cheap.

"I'd be satisfied with having my shoe back," Peter announced to the room at large.

"What did you go and give it away for?" asked Jill.

With that excitement past, I pulled out my humble offering, "Two Cars Drove across the State with Four People Right before Christmas." I didn't bother to ham it up this time.

Tonya signed in ASL as I read, making hugely exaggerated facial expressions and taking liberties even with ASL grammar that soon had Lynn and Jill rolling on the floor. "Drove . . . cars two . . . STOPPED LUNCH . . . restaurant CROWDED FRIES . . ."

Rachel, distracted by the laughter, or Tonya, or just by being Rachel, still couldn't keep track of things and kept asking, "Two cars what . . . ? Two what? The people what? They ended up where . . . ?"

Felix: "Let me get this straight—it was a 150 mile one-way trip, and Dave and Marge still ended up where they started, and Becky and Tom didn't? And no one got left anywhere? What happened to Becky and Tom?"

Dad: "And who paid for lunch?"

"This does not sound very economical to me," said Tonya disapprovingly, signing with a flourish.

Rachel, grumpily, "Why didn't they just wait till after New Year's?"

Once again, only Jean-Paul, Mishael, Lynn, and Peter figured it out.

"What am I going to do with all these tickets?" complained Peter.

They weren't for the concert on Sunday, not that Peter would have come. He was due to be in the office while I was due to be under the lights—one last fling for the Christmas season, and in exactly two weeks the Polar Bear plunge, my annual chance to wash up the year and start over. Like dropping a big penny in the water. This year I had only one wish, one resolution.

When I got up to help put together trays for coffee Lynn leapt up too, but I shooed her away. "I need five, okay?"

Rachel had beat me to the kitchen and was setting up the coffee. "What's the vintage tonight?"

"Vienna roast." She tapped the scoop sharply on the edge of the coffee maker and dropped it into the bag. "How come you went and gave Lynn your backup?"

"She could use it." I filled the sugar bowls with cubes one at a time, tossing them in and listening to the *plink* flatten and descend in pitch as they filled. "She likes flute."

"What are you up to, Max?"

I stopped and looked at her. "What am I *up* to?"

"You heard me." She pulled Mom's tea service out of the cupboard and handing it down to me two cups at a time. "I don't see why she needs yet another instrument—she's got more than she can handle already."

"Bright kid. Lots of interests."

"On top of everything Dad's going to give her a trumpet for Christmas. Between you and him I don't know who's worse."

"Take your pick."

"Would you *listen* to me, Max? What's this about? That was your first flute."

"And now it's Lynn's first flute." I stacked the teacups on the trays a bit too testily.

Rachel glowered down at me from her perch on the stepstool.

"Is there a problem with that?"

"You gave away the Haynes too, remember?"

I grabbed the cream out of the fridge.

"And the *Selmer!*"

The distressed clinks of the porcelain pitchers on the counter as I smacked them down. C-sharp, new hairline fracture, just great.

Rachel handed me the saucers and stepped off the stool. "Max, what do you think you're doing?"

"Living my own life."

"How can you go around without a backup? I mean, what if you lose the Muramatsu?"

The cream sloshed into the pitchers and dribbled on the counter and I grabbed the dishrag and slapped up the spill. "I don't need so much old stuff lying around. You know when it's time to pass things on."

"Your backup flute, 'old stuff lying around'?" Rachel snorted, wearing that look of absolute disbelief mingled with scorn she had perfected to a fine art. She unboxed a package of marzipan fruit onto a glass platter, shaking her head. "I don't know what gets into you sometimes."

"*L'espirit d'aventure.*"

"Bullshit. You say *no* to Mensa. You say *no* to every school that wants you to teach. You say *no* to every woman who wants to get to know you. God *knows* how many goddam record deals you say *no* to. Is undermining any possible future the only thing you say *yes* to?"

I picked up a marzipan and ate it, staring at her.

"You know, Max, I just don't understand you, I just don't. I should just give up trying."

"Who said you had to? Are you doing a thesis on me?"

"When you have your rummage sale, let me know. I've got first dibs on those Oistrakh records."

"Why wait? Take them now. Who knows, I might do something crazy like give them away."

Rachel pushed the plate of marzipan at me. "Merry Christmas, Max. Start with this, okay?"

Some Christmas traditions were too time-honored to abandon. The evening went on more peacefully once we rejoined our friends.

On a trip back to the kitchen with a tray of used cups, Jill caught up with me, something in her hands which she quickly tucked behind her back. "Jean-Paul said he saw du Pré in Montréal twenty years ago!"

"Good for Jean-Paul."

More than wistfully: "And you got to *perform* with her." She trailed me into the kitchen.

"Not *that* story again," I yawned. "There must be other cellists in the world."

"Not like her."

"Well, no. They are all different." I set the cups in the sink and wiped the tray, glancing at Jill. "Ready for state finals, two more weeks?"

Huge sigh. She nodded. "Yes." The draping angel costume too big for concert attire, but her eyes burning as they had when I had heard her set Bruch's *Kol Nidrei* on fire. Look out, all you aspiring cellists. Someone was going to get creamed, and it wasn't going to be her. She regarded me fiercely. "Do you think I could be the next Jacqueline du Pré?"

"I don't recommend it. But you could be the next Jill Cunningham."

She gave me an arch look. "I am the *first* Jill Cunningham. I am the *only* Jill Cunningham."

"And a good thing, too. Think of what the world would be like with two of you."

She ducked her gaze, pink and smiling.

"So, what was so great about her?"

Jill raised her eyes to mine, face solemn this time. "She did what you do."

"Okay, I forget. What is it I do again?"

Her smile lit up her face like a flame, spread to her eyes. "You remind me what's possible." Before I could reply, she passed me the gifts she'd been hiding. "These are for you," beamed, and dashed out.

"Thanks," I said, too late. Three wrapped packets thick with folded notebook paper: more of her stories. "Thanks." *Read very carefully*, inscribed on the back of the tag. I smiled, going off to tuck them in my jacket. One of them was bound to be a Christmas story.

In the living room, the talk circled to music again, as it cannot fail to in Dad's presence. With almost no effort, John coaxed Dad into reviewing the performances of the season thus far; Dad feigned modesty and resistance, then launched into a pontification of everything from the guest artists to the lighting to the behavior of the holiday concertgoers. John and Peter stopped short of wrestling me to the floor, but they got me to give my own impressions as well, though I made them work for it. I hadn't conducted for six years and had forgotten how draining it could be. The orchestra had performed beautifully—there had been almost no problems, and except for some irritable brass and a punctured drum, rehearsals had gone well. I tried to return the floor to Dad.

"What about the invitations that have come for you, Max?" Dad enthused. "There're fifteen so far for the next two seasons. Which ones are you going to accept?"

"Look," I said, gesturing to Tonya, "I'm not supposed to talk about business tonight. Our accountant will get mad."

"That's right, blame it on your accountant," Tonya said.

"Besides," I cleared my throat. "I heard you were retiring. What invitations are *you* going to accept?"

"Oh, not much," Dad shrugged, "maybe one or two . . ."

Mishael, with complete authority: "When Richard does 'not much,' Max will be the surgeon and Rachel will be the private eye."

"That'll be the day," snickered John, winking at Rachel.

"And I'll be the monkey's uncle," she snorted. "It's just so hard to believe Dad's passing the baton. I never thought I'd see that happen."

It was pretty much at the far edge of conceivable. I had always imagined Dad would die in harness; it was more than a stretch to imagine someone else running the show at Armstrong Hall. Of course, he was to do far more than "just teach" on retirement; the grand fanfare that would usher him into his next several positions and was set for February twenty-ninth amounted to a celebratory pause between two careers. Most of the details were just being finalized, and everyone wanted to know more. Dad was not shy about filling them in.

"Are you performing, Max?" asked Mishael.

"Of course he will be," Jill decided for me.

"I've invited Slava," Dad told her with a grin, and she sat up very straight, eyes wide. "And you're all invited too. You're getting tickets for Christmas."

"*Quel joie Richard est pas d' police*," Jean-Paul laughed, clapping.

"And all the Sojourners too. I'm expecting all of you."

"Do what we can," I said. "Are you performing, Rach?"

"Ha ha. Do I look like Leon Goossens to you?"

Dad angled, "I'd like you as a soloist, Max."

"You don't have to be Goossens, Rach, and the players would love you to *perform* with them for once, instead of just being Madam Board."

"Dad wants *you* to be a soloist, and *I* don't have to be Goossens? Gimme a break."

"First rehearsal'll be January 5, Max."

"Hold on, lemme think." Mishael smacked her forehead, "You've got interviews that afternoon, Max."

I asked: "Is Rachel performing?"

"Of course she can. Are you coming, Max?"

"I've got to work nights in February!" Rachel protested.

"What are you," I asked, "the most important doctor in the world?"

"Max . . . ?"

I looked at Peter. "Can you cover for me?"

Peter and that old smile I knew so well. "I'll cover you."

"I'll be there," I said.

And that had been it, that had been the last big gathering. True, the Sojourners had met a few more times, and there had been other small celebrations, but that had been the last Christmas party when they all had been there. After everything I had learned it saddened me to think that only five months later . . . But then, that had been the beginning, at least for me; had things not ended, I would never have even begun learning about them. How strange to think that so many things began with a death, both for Max, and myself . . .

I pulled my work out of the typewriter, and turned it off.

No audience fancies corpses. Only when *you* went offstage,
the flats you slipped through let in something else,
a streak of truth: the colour of real foliage
under real sunshine in a real woodland.

For us, the show must go on. All those lies
we learned, struggling and panicky, the stagey gestures
ordered by some director we can't put a face to . . . and then you,
struck off the list, you who are real now a long way off,

Your far-off thereness sometimes overtakes us still, falling
around us like that streak of daylight green, and then
we find, just for a bit, we can play life, not scripts;
not give a damn about applause.

R.M. Rilke, *trans. Rowan Williams*

Of all faces those of our *familiares* are the ones both most difficult to play fantastic tricks with, and most difficult really to see with fresh attention, perceiving their likeness and unlikeness: that they are faces, and yet unique faces. This triteness is really the penalty of 'appropriation': the things that are trite or (in a bad sense) familiar, are the things that we have appropriated, legally or mentally. We say we know them. They have become like the things which once attracted us by their glitter, or their colour, or their shape, and we laid hands on them, and then locked them in our hoard, acquired them, and acquiring ceased to look at them.

J.R.R. TOLKIEN

... The problem, however, is rarely lack of talent, but rather an inability to step back and take a fresh look at the situation. The reason one needs to step back and take a new look is that when you are stuck in a problem, the source of it is never what you think it is ...

WILLIAM WATSON

O edrych yn ôl, rwy'n beio'r cyfieithu

GWYNETH LEWIS

1

Keynote

Three times in my life I have lost everything. The first time, I lost everything I had and nearly lost my life. The second time I lost only my possessions. The third time I lost what gave my life meaning, and nearly lost my mind as well. Artists use such things as grist for their work; I have done as much. It keeps one sane, and can give a perspective that could not be had otherwise. Once—at least once that I know of—it led to something I could never have imagined, and yet the fact remains that I *had* imagined it, and it was still not my imagination. But to explain that, I should have to tell a story.

Looking back, I blame translation—having to move from one language to another, from thoughts to words, from impressions to images, from the music within to the music without. You cannot tell the same story any two ways, and yet you cannot tell the story at all without translating. Some have tried to make art of life, or vice versa, and have fallen for the illusion, but art is always a translation, often a translation of a translation, and there is seldom a happy enough medium.

We have been taught that everything is made of atoms. An empty conceit; everything is made of stories, and even that which is called an atom is only a story that must be told to make sense of something real yet otherwise unimaginable. Who even knows if a story as it is told is seen fully, and isn't missing parts? The only thing no one will let go of is a story.

I could not say how things begin; I can never tell where stories actually start, though I know for a fact this story began a long time ago in another country, at a different time. But this is where I came in, and so it began one afternoon in May many years ago now.

Someone once told me that life is full of clues, that nothing big ever happens without warning. But I never did see this coming, and, after everything, I believe it was for the best. Sometimes, you don't need to know.

On that wet and gray May Friday I was alone in my Thirty-Second Street flat when the door buzzer interrupted a quiet afternoon at the typewriter. I was hardly a week into a five-month lease and had been in country less than a month. Cathy had arranged to stop by at 2:30 and take me out on the town for my research; it was roughly 2:20. Just as I reached the door, the buzzer grated again, and I leapt on the footstool and flattened my face to the peephole.

Two faces damp from the rain floated in the concave pool of the glass, the officiously dressed forms below them curling downward. A burly set of knuckles sprouted out of one of them and thumped the door under my nose.

I stepped to the floor and slid the stool aside, hands on the door. A second of indecision burned a second thought into me; I hesitated, then fumbled with the handle and carefully pulled the door open. The distorted forms of my callers appeared in their customary shape, and registering them more clearly, the first impression not only repeated but reaffirmed itself. The fellow in a black uniform all kitted out, the gruff face and the thinning brown hair, the wry-set mouth and the thumbs hooked impatiently in his belt; the black woman in a gray dress suit, her firm if serene face matched by the unruffled way she held her badge.

They began speaking first, and both at once. They stopped, flashed each other annoyed looks, and the woman began again.

"Are you Ms. Brinsel Thomas?" she asked.

I looked at her stupidly. "I am."

"Ms. Thomas, I am Detective Honey Neilsen and this is Sgt. Stephan Sweigart. We're here on behalf of Mr. Peter Serrev, concerning an investigation under his direction. Do you mind if we ask you some questions?"

I stared at them. They stared at me.

For a long, long moment nothing moved.

In a rush of relief, I flung the door wide and broke out laughing, "Oh, oh . . . how fantastic, oh Cathers, you can come out, the joke's up. Where did you find these two, really, they look and sound just like them!"

Neilsen and Sweigart stared at me.

"Ms. Thomas?" Detective Neilsen was asking, her voice absolutely perfect—smooth, svelte, and tinged with pepper. "Ms. Thomas, may we come in and ask you some questions?"

My grin folded up. Sgt. Sweigart's irritated expression had not changed, but Detective Neilsen's face, serenely professional, nonetheless read "this dipstick's not touching oil."

I looked from one to the other. "She didn't set you up to this? Because it's a fantastic joke."

Sweigart said thinly, "I'm afraid there's no joke, Ms. Thomas."

Of course—why should they admit it? Where would the fun be? There was nothing for it but to play along. "Er, right," I acquiesced. "Why don't you come in and we can have a natter until she shows up?"

I led them down the short passage to the living room and gestured to my two free chairs, perching on my desk chair and shoving papers aside. Neilsen was swinging her gaze round with perfect calm. Sweigart remained sullen and kept frowning, scratching his head.

"What can I get you? No—" I leapt up, "I know just the thing, half a moment," and sped to the kitchenette. I came back in a trice with their preferred drinks and presented them their mugs. "I'm sorry I've not any cake at the moment, though I can fetch you some jam and bread in a sec. So," I began amicably, "what brings two such fine characters to my door?"

Sgt. Sweigart eyed his mug, eyeballed me, and set it down on the table. Detective Neilsen didn't move. Her face was registering intense concentration, and her eyebrows were piqued.

"Ms. Thomas," Sweigart began, staring at his coffee, then directing his glance towards me. "Ms. Thomas, we're here as part of the investigation of the murder of Max Thompson—"

"When's Cathy coming?" I asked, trying to keep my voice light.

"Alright, Ms. Thomas," Detective Neilsen, the gentleness of her voice just touched with steel. "Who is Cathy?"

"Well now, really, 'who's Cathy,'" I laughed gamely. "As if you didn't know." I prompted, "She'll be here any minute now." She would burst in the door and act surprised; there would be laughter, and the game would be up. "I'd never have suspected Cath of a stunt like this." I shoved some tea down my throat in a gulp. "I think it's fantastic, really. Will there be anybody else?"

Sweigart sighed. "Ms. Thomas, we are here for an investigation. This is not a game. We have not been set up to do this. We would prefer to ask our questions here, but maybe you need to come down to the station so you know how serious this is."

"We are here," said Neilsen crisply, her warmth fading, "as part of the investigation of the murder of Max Thompson. *Ms. Thomas*, would you be able to answer some questions?"

My mouth formed the word yes, and I heard myself say it.

Neilsen asked, "Now, did you know Mr. Thompson, Ms. Thomas?"

I met her gaze the way a fryer must view the farmer who comes to collect it—fascinated, clueless.

"Well sure I do, yes."

Sweigart's eye twitched. "Do you know about the investigation we are referring to, the one concerning his murder?"

I answered with difficulty, "Yes . . . I do."

"The reason we are here today is because your name has surfaced in close connection with it."

This was very creative of Cathy. Highly creative. Unusual for her. Why wasn't she showing up?

I knotted my fingers together until they became a tight, sticky tangle. "How do I relate to this?"

Sweigart's grizzly face wrinkled into something approaching a smile. "You can relax, Ms. Thomas, you're not suspect."

This had to be Cathy's doing. This could not be real. And it seemed bizarrely, frighteningly real. There were Sweigart and Neilsen, large as life. Sounding, acting, just as I had always known they would. And they were in my living room. Yes, this was too clever of Cathy . . .

Detective Neilsen was saying, "Your name, Ms. Thomas, appeared in a note written by Mr. Thompson. He claimed that you had information about the case he was working on at the time of his death."

And then the spell snapped. Loud knocking echoing through the flat. Cathy's strident voice, stopping on her Rs to imitate me, ripping through the door. "Brrrinsel, I'm here, dear! I'm *sorrrry* I'm late—" She let herself in, the sound of her wet umbrella spattering on the floor. And bustled into the room.

Sweigart and Neilsen rose to their feet. Frozen to the chair, I stared from the two of them to Cathy, waiting for her act. Ruffled, wet from the rain, in her Marilyn Monroe phase with her short dyed hair sticking out frizzily, her eyes lit on my visitors and she stopped dead.

"Oh my God," she gasped, "what—what—"

This was not an act; the fact hit me like a slap of cold seawater. No, this was Cathy, the real Cathy, the one who couldn't possibly coordinate a dramatic joke or put on an act, who didn't have it in her to be more creative than a printed cross-stitch pattern.

I managed to stand. "Cathy," I choked out, "this is . . . this is Sgt. Sweigart and Detective Neilsen."

They nodded at her officiously.

Astonishment blazed across her face. She gaped at me, then at them. "Well, hello . . . officers, hello." Alarmed, "Brinsel, is everything all right? What's happened?"

"I don't know."

Sweigart gestured wearily. "How about we go down to the station for this, Ms. Thomas."

I looked at Sweigart and Neilsen. I looked at Cathy. I did the only sensible thing I could, without even thinking of it. The world vanished into a gray and winked out.

I came to, to find the nightmare had only just begun.

The room was nothing but blotches for a moment, then three faces materialized out of the blur.

The first thing that came out of my mouth was neither English nor polite. I said it distinctly, enunciating each syllable, and when the faces didn't go away I said it again. Neilsen winced and asked, "*What* is she saying?" Sweigart gawked at me, fingering the radio on his shoulder. Cathy blurted, "For heavens' sake, Brinsel, you don't have to be so rude!!"

"Cathy," I gasped, "what's going on?"

She threw her arm around me, helping me sit up. "Dearest, these officers are here for an investigation, and they want you to come answer some questions." She frowned at them, her face one scribble of worry, but only said, as if they ought to have known better, "It's the uniforms—these things happen with her."

"You didn't send them, Cathy?"

"Did I *what?*" Cathy turned an expression of shocked disbelief onto me. "Oh, my God, no, oooh, no, no, Brinsel, what are you *thinking?*"

"But, but—Cathy—" I wanted to shake her—why didn't she understand? "My *drafts*, you don't remember? You *read* them!—It's not a joke—?"

"A *joke?* A joke, Brinsel, what are you talking about! I don't even know what's going on! We were supposed to go out today, remember?"

No one was moving but the room felt like chaos: irritated officer, baffled detective, Cathy bewildered and babbling over and over, "Oh, my God, I'm so sorry. Oh my God," that only wound me deeper into a panic. I was nauseated and petrified, and when I didn't budge, she pulled me to my feet.

Neilsen jotted something down on a notepad, then pocketed it and stood stroking her face thoughtfully with the pencil. "Are you feeling well enough to come down now, Ms. Thomas?"

Sweigart shifted to one foot, then the other, then back again, and cleared his throat noisily.

I opened my mouth and closed my eyes, then I opened my eyes and fixed on a spot on the floor just behind Neilsen, willing myself to remain upright.

"Let's just go. Let's just go. Let's get this done with."

Neilsen tried to console me in the car on the way there. "Don't worry, Ms. Thomas, this won't be that hard. The captain's a real peach; you won't have any trouble talking with her."

Rolanda Petrucci was five feet two, graying at the temples, and solid as a strongman. She was as solid, stout, and rough as Honey Neilsen was willowy, classy, and smooth, like putting a Brazil nut next to a pecan. She also had a bark like a marine, a fabled knuckle-down, no-nonsense approach to everything, and a gaze and tone of voice that could wither a block of cement. She had never frightened Max, but I had every reason to be terrified of her, for reasons having nothing to do with her clout.

I saw her the moment we walked in the door; actually, she was not hard to miss, swinging through the front office at her full, intimidating height, the nucleus of a small cloud of energy wherever she went. Sgt. Sweigart waited patiently for her to attend to us, signing me in. I hadn't brought my passport nor any identification, and the unfamiliar desk sergeant glowered at me as if I was making a bad day worse.

A moment later the captain came striding up to us.

"Well, sir, I see you've brought her along," and I got a thorough once-over. She glanced cursorily at something Neilsen handed to her and then cut her gaze back upon me, those black eyes glittering through her specs. "Shall we, Ms. Thomas?"

Through the security door. Her office three steps away. She closed the door behind me and gestured to a chair, "Please, have a seat."

I sat, my eyes taking in every detail of her office in horrible clarity. Her desk, cabinets, the pictures, the papers. The family photos. The lumpy clay paperweight her youngest son had made in the first grade. And Rolanda Petrucci in the midst of it. Now she clasped her hands and rested them together on her desk, eyeing me. Her eyes were disguised under the light reflecting off her glasses, and I could not read them.

"Would you care for something to drink, Ms. Thomas?"

Somewhere in my mind it occurred to me she was asking me a question, but in the only part of my mind that I could get at, it was an unreasonable, unthinkable impossibility that she be able to address me at all, under any circumstances.

"Ms. Thomas? Would you like something to drink?"

I just stared at her. She stepped to the cooler and poured a large paper cup cold and brimful, and handed it to me, her expression unchanging. I found the cup in my hand and sat staring at it in sheer horror.

"Now, Ms. Thomas," seated behind her desk again. She glanced briefly at a few notepapers in her hand and then back at me, taking off her glasses and holding them. I held the cup tightly, willing myself not to look into it for refuge, and was surprised by the softness I saw creep into her face. "This is difficult for you, isn't it?" almost gentler than I'd ever heard her.

I pushed the cup to my lips but found myself unable to drink. "I'm not sure what's going on."

"I can understand that, this must all be very bewildering to you."

She couldn't *possibly* understand. Bewildering? Hardly that, no, we had left that behind with *believable,* with *rational,* with . . .

". . . I don't normally work with cases like this, but I wanted to speak with you myself as we begin, especially as I was very interested in meeting you." My face must have answered for me, and I was surprised again as she smiled, somewhat sadly. "I know this has all been very upsetting, but it will be over soon, or at least this part of it. Do you know why you're here, Ms. Thomas?"

"The, the investigation . . ."

"Yes, that is part of it, and you don't need to be anxious about your part, because it's pretty simple, as we understand it." She picked up a folder and drew out a piece of acetate enclosing a small paper, and pushed on her spectacles. "There isn't much point in my reading this to you, as you've heard almost all of it already, so, here we are . . ."

She tipped the acetate towards me; dumbly, I held out my hand for it. The frisson of recognition at seeing the handwriting on the paper was accompanied not by pleasure but by the sense that the ground had abruptly given way, and I was toppling over a precipice, each word an escalation of pressure and panic: *"jinx"* followed by an accented semi-quaver; then *"Riley 8AM wedns re: Davis,"* a long dash, and then, the impossible words, in firm and certain script, *"Brinsel Thomas has all the info I do on this,"* underlined, and unequivocal. This was followed by a scrawl less clear in meaning than legibility, and even less welcome: *"and can help if something comes up."* The paper seemed to float in the air just past my fingers, and just as implausibly, there, there it was, Max's scrawling handwriting, handwriting which had never . . . The words blurred and the world blurred, and I sat shaking, holding that horrible little piece of plastic until Petrucci cleared her throat and held out her hand, and I surrendered it to her.

"The second line refers to the case he was working on," she said, "and the rest appears to be about you." The scraping of tissue being pulled from a box. "Ms. Thomas, please have some of these," very kindly.

Petrucci's chair creaked as she leaned back; she folded her glasses and let them fall on her chest. "Well, Ms. Thomas, and so we've contacted you. You weren't easy to find, I'll admit, and somehow, we missed you overseas. It was quite a stroke of luck that you showed up here."

Here. I sat staring idiotically at the center of her desk, wondering how hard I should have to pinch myself.

"May I ask how you knew Mr. Thompson?"

The impossibility, the sheer absurdity of it all snapped through me like a crack of electricity. I was on my feet in an instant.

"Oh my God," I said, much calmer than I felt. "This cannot be happening. I mean, it mustn't, it simply mustn't, it can't possibly. You . . . you . . ." staring at Petrucci, my voice creeping throatily up the register, "you don't, it can't *possibly*, this *cannot* . . ."

"Ms. Thomas, please sit down. I'm afraid you don't know everything about this yet."

"*But*," I squeaked upwards into unintelligibility, "but you see, this . . . this *simply isn't possible* . . ."

"Ms. Thomas," Petrucci blinked calmly, "please, have a seat."

My throat pinched shut. I lowered myself onto the edge of the chair unwillingly, shaking so hard the water in the cup in my hand leapt about in a frantic boil. I juddered the cup onto the edge of her desk.

"Ms. Thomas, I *know* this is very upsetting, but we do need to clear up your part in this before we go on. Detective Neilsen tells me that you said you did know Max Thompson, Ms. Thomas, is this so?"

I sat there suspended in a sort of lunatic limbo, staring nowhere in terror.

"Ms. Thomas?"

I was strangling, all my seams unravelling. I was about to explode in hysteria.

"Ms. Thomas, did you know Max Thompson?"

The word in my throat was choking me like a stone. "*Yes*."

"May I ask what connection you have with the case he was working on?"

What did I know? Oh my God, what did I know? I opened my mouth and nothing came out.

"This has all been quite a shock for you, and I am so sorry to have to dredge it all up again. How would you feel about setting up an appointment to speak with Mr. Serrev about this? He'd very much like to meet with you, and it would give you some time meanwhile to let all this settle."

Talk with *Peter!*

"Right," I heard myself say, barely audible. "Alright, that would be good."

I scarcely believed what I was saying. This couldn't be happening. I couldn't be here. But what could I do? What on earth could I do?

I wanted most to run screaming out of the building. No. I just wanted to run out. Not even that. I wanted to wake up in bed and think, Oh God! what a nightmare . . .

Nothing happened except that I began to cry again. I stubbornly rubbed my eyes with the tissue. "What day would be good?"

Petrucci was watching me with an expression of great tenderness. "Why don't we have Mr. Serrev contact you to set up a time you can come over? Now that we know where you are, things can go forward. And," she added gently, "a little distance from today would be good for you."

Detective Neilsen gave me a lift back to my flat. We drove in silence through the gray drizzle, and I tried not to look at her. As I got out at the door, she leaned over and pressed a card into my hand with a sweet smile. "Just in case you need to contact us sooner, Ms. Thomas."

In my living room were two untouched mugs of hot beverages gone cold. I poured them down the drain.

2

Evidence

At half past two in the morning I snapped awake.
All the bedclothes had tied me up in a clammy tangle. I was as breathless and perspiring as if I had just sprinted several miles and nearly a minute passed before I recognized that the frantic knocking filling my ears was my heart. The phosphorescent eye of the clock dial and I stared at each other in the dark, its alarm hand still two hours from meeting its hour hand.

Rain was pelleting the world outside with a roar like the sea. I was cold awake, slap awake; I tossed and turned for fifteen minutes, but when sleep would not return, snapped off the alarm, wrapped myself in the housecoat, and put my feet on the floor. Then I stopped.

No one had called on me since I had moved in a week before. But in the back of my mind gnawed a nagging wisp of a memory of two police officers—of all people—standing in the living room, not ten feet from where I was perched on the edge of the futon. In the pre-dawn dark I stared into the dimness and envisioned their forms, their faces—

I hit the light. Wonking nonsense. I wasn't thinking clearly.

I poured myself a cuppa and drank it black. When I could see the dregs in the bottom of my cup, I knew I was fully awake. But the thoughts wouldn't go away.

I poured myself another cup, dumping in more sugar and cream than I wanted, and wandered into my office, snapping on the fluorescent light over the typewriter. The work I had left off the day before was still sitting in it, halfway through a thought. I read the page backwards trying to retrieve it, to think of anything else at all; it was too early, or I was too tired, and my mind flopped to the compositional spectacle of the white paper under the light in the darkness. Two cuppas hadn't cleared my head. I went to distract myself with an early breakfast.

It was nearly five o'clock and the rain had tapered off, the weekend traffic already rumbling out in the street below, when, at last halfway presentable, I forced myself back to my office.

Pale blue light was filtering through the muslin curtains I had chased up over the windows, and the light from the desk lamp had frayed into a small mat of white cast over the typewriter. The pinboard, desk, makeshift easel. The confusion of loose papers, paint tubes, canvas paper, scattered blackleads. The disarray was deeply familiar and grounding and assured me I was somebody and that nothing had changed. I pulled yesterday's work out of the typewriter and studied it importantly, yawned, and set it aside. I picked up a pen and tapped my head with it.

I tossed the pen down and knelt at the filing box, pulling out the papers that had been consuming my thoughts since my feet had hit the floor. There it all was, three files of drafts of stories, notes, scraps of paper, drawings, character sketches, ideas and outlines, a folder of newspaper clippings, photographs, articles that had provided inspiration, pages and pages of written material chalked with corrective marks and criticisms... Here were all their stories, their histories, almost their entire lives. So real to me, more than any of my other work. I was preparing it for publication as a series of short stories and had come here, to the place they were all set, to ensure the details were satisfactory. I had been working on it for years, and how much I enjoyed these imaginary people, Max above all, who had, from the first go off, been the one to go. It had been the first thing I had known about him. He was dead, and I had simply followed the story backwards. I had not at all suspected anything of his story, and it had unfolded before me in a succession of surprises.

I replaced the files in the box and stood up. Beside the typewriter, propped up against the pencil cup, was a drawing of Max I particularly liked, his face partly turned to someone unseen, shining his quiet smile and his eyes sparking. It was an older picture, as he appeared six years before his death; my own copy of what was, on Petrucci's desk, a black and white photograph under the plastic rim of a desk calendar. The very idea that a real photograph existed—outside of my mind—of what was simply a drawing—

And a photograph of Max...

... Max, who had written a note I had never known about, and had mentioned me. Had *known* about me. And if he was *my character*, this simply wasn't possible.

And if he *wasn't* my character?

I came to a standstill and realized I had been furiously pacing round the kitchenette with a teaspoon in my hand. I put the spoon on the table. I sat and snatched a scrap of paper and a pen.

Problem: I am a writer who has met her own characters. Solution: You are barmy, it's simple as that. Solution: They are not your characters, they are real people you happen to know. Solution: You have had a bad night. Go back to bed and try again.

The last one was the most appealing, but so powerful were the scenes in my head that I believed it least of all. There had to be a still better answer. I flipped the paper over.

It was printed; it was a business card. Honey Neilsen pressing a card into my hand. In neat, direct caps it read:

Peter Serrev, CPI
(formerly of S&T Investigations)

For Services please contact
Fordham St Police Station 593.2002 Ext 237

Talk with Peter. Peter was going to contact me.

I wanted to throw something across the room. Hurl the typewriter out the window. Nothing was making sense.

I went to get more tea.

To my relief this cup had a calming effect. I abandoned the idea of bashing my head on every hard surface and stared blindly at the window.

I could go on panicking at every familiar face and voice. Or I could settle down and accept this madness for a while, hope it wasn't permanent, and perhaps find my way out.

And now another idea came to me. It did not require much nerve of me to decide; it seemed I had so little left to lose.

At eight o'clock, as the sun was seeping through the curtains, I pulled on my shoes and left for the cemetery.

I was there by nine. I had forgotten it was so far from the center of town, and I had a long ride on more than one bus. For once I did not follow my usual practice of looking around for ideas for characters. I kept my nose to the window and simply concentrated on getting there.

And then I was there. Three funerals in various stages of completion and another procession just pulling up as I stole through the gate. I kept fingering my jacket buttons and scarf and rubbing my nose, trying to brush off the small cloud of anxieties attracted by everything I saw. The modernist chapel and reception, with the curving drive that was approximately one-fifth of a mile but felt five times that by the time I reached the top. The iron gates with their peculiar green stone urns on the gate posts, and the bronze plaque, spotted with lichen, that announced Mount Moriah Cemetery, 1813. Old beeches and maples, manicured lawns, fields and fields of nineteenth-century monuments and modern headstones dewed with rain. The two stones I was looking for were close to the main road, on a branch that wound along the perimeter. I did not have far to walk.

I was still permitting myself the indulgence of thinking, of hoping against hope, that it really was all merely a bad dream. I wanted to get there and find I was wrong.

And then, I could not hope any more . . .

. . . I was standing at the grave of Maximilian Thompson.

I stood there numbly for what might have been an hour or might have been ten minutes.

Before his stone lay four withered bouquets of flowers left by his family and friends only the previous week; it had been just three years.

I knew it all, the days leading up to his death, his last hours, his last moments. I knew the events that followed. I had written about it. I had made it up.

And this gravestone was saying: You did not make it up. It happened without you.

This, or it was saying: Look what you've done. You have done this.

I was suddenly struck by the idiotic thought that I had not brought any flowers.

I closed my eyes and breathed deeply. Strangely enough I felt no more panic, only a deep, surprisingly gentle sadness.

I opened my eyes and looked at the second headstone. This was the grave of Ariel Chapman, who would, had she lived, have become Mrs. Thompson. Max had been dead now over three years; Ariel, almost twenty.

The stones told me nothing, except that it was all true. I knew every detail on them, names, epitaphs, the arbitrary numerical measurements that supposedly encompassed and signified their lives. It had not really been so long ago . . .

I could not seem to move, let alone think. I desperately wanted answers, to know what was going on. Max had known. Incredibly, unbelievably, he had known about me. There was only one person in the world, the entire world, I could have gone to with my questions. And he was dead.

I couldn't write a thing for days.

At first, I still permitted myself to play with the thought that I really had been mistaken by everything, that it hadn't actually happened. Only the phone terrified me. The idea that it would ring and Peter would be on the other end was almost more than I could take.

The next morning it did ring and I thought I would go through the ceiling. It took an act of heroics to pick it up, and I was rewarded by Cathy's anxious voice. And I remembered. Research. For that story. Sitting in Petrucci's office. Peter's business card. Poor Cathy, convinced something was dreadfully amiss. We arranged, for what it was worth, to get together again in two weeks. I was no longer certain why.

I did try to work on other stories. I made an enormous effort. But it all seemed to be over. The very idea that I was where my characters were—or that they were real after all—gave me a case of writer's block that was more like writer's decapitation. My editor was expecting three drafts of work within a month. I wasn't going to make it. I was going around wringing my hands, not touching the typewriter. I fell into several unhealthily listless habits, and paper and clothes collected in the corners of the rooms.

Then on Tuesday the following week, I woke up again before the alarm and stared into the dark and realized what I had to do. *How* or *why* were well beyond me. *What* was still in my power.

With the strength of this insight behind me, I quietly had breakfast and went to do some chores, for the next few hours thinking of nothing more than following around the broom and duster and bucket of soapy water. And it was there, slowly scrubbing circles in the bathroom floor, that an idea came to me.

I didn't rush; I finished the work to the last detail, had some tea, and let it sit. Then I sat at the typewriter and turned it on.

I took a deep breath, studying the keys. A very long pause. Then I typed, "Hello, Max."

"Hello, yourself."

I bit my lip hopefully, letting my mind gently loosen for the first time in days. There was still one person after all whom I could treat as a character, whose mouth I could put words into. And I had to talk with somebody about my horrible mess, even if it was myself.

"Max, how do you know about me?"

"Is there some reason I shouldn't?"

Yes, in fact. "What did you mean when you wrote about me in that note, Max?"

"No preliminaries? Like, how are you and all that nice stuff?"

"I'd . . . assumed you would be fine in heaven."

"Well, thanks. And how are you, Brinsel?"

A little too true to life. "About the note, Max. The one I never knew about."

"Big hurry, huh? C'mon, you don't begin all your conversations this way."

I hit caps lock and pounded out, "I AM LOSING MY MIND, MAX. I WANT TO KNOW WHAT'S GOING ON."

"Okay, I can see it's difficult, but you still don't have to shout, Brinsel. I can hear you perfectly well."

I stared at the picture of him next to the typewriter, wishing the conversation could be as real as his grave.

After a few moments, "Didn't you want to be here, Brinsel?"

"What is *here*?"

"Here, where I lived and died?"

I hesitated. "Are you mad at me, Max?"

"Mad? This is a new one on me. Why would I be mad at you?"

"Because, didn't I . . . wasn't I the one who killed you?"

"*You*? No, according to what we both know, it wasn't you."

Yes, if all this were real, not only was it *not* I who had killed him, but, like him, I knew who had. And yet that couldn't be what the police had contacted me for, for everybody knew the case was closed and everything taken care of. If all this were real . . .

"You are not . . . my character?"

A small pause. "Do you think I ever have been?"

A week ago, I would have been ready to swear on it. "I have never believed anything else about this."

"And if I'm not your character?"

"Then I . . ." After a moment, "Am I psychic?"

"Could it make any difference if you were?"

Fantastic, an answer that went nowhere. I tried again, "Max, how do you know about me?"

There had to be some sort of reasonable explanation that would come to me. Something had to come.

"So, you think that's the right question?"

Max had built a very successful career out of asking the right questions. But I could not think of anything more important for myself than this.

"It would give me some peace of mind to know."

"You already have all the pieces of my mind. What more do you want?"

This was not working as well as I had thought.

"What more do you want?"

I typed miserably, "To know what is going on."

Nothing. Then, "What if it doesn't matter?"

"How could it *not* matter? I only know you as fiction. You don't exist, Max. None of it is real. I don't understand how you *can* be real, or any of this..."

Silence.

"So, I'm fiction, huh?"

I wanted to say *yes*. It was the only logical answer. But I couldn't reply.

"And fiction means I'm not real?"

It had to. Did it not?

"And you, Brinsel, you are real? I hope so; I mean, what if all my friends were imaginary? Kind of suck, wouldn't it?"

I stared at the picture of him I had drawn. I thought of standing at his grave, the chiseled letters on the headstone hard, cold, and utterly real.

What difference could it make? "Max," I typed slowly, "what must I do now?"

"Now we're talking." A pause. "You are going to talk with Peter."

It was a statement, but I read it as a question. "Well, I might do . . ."

"Do whatever he asks you."

Was I ready to abandon myself to this to that degree?

Had I a choice?

"Brinsel?"

"What is it?"

"Don't be afraid. I love you."

I didn't type but spoke aloud, "Max, please tell me how you know about me."

Nothing.

It was a moment before I realized the typewriter was no longer on. I could not remember turning it off.

I sat there several minutes without moving. Talk with Peter. I had to talk with Peter. And I was beginning to want to.

3

Peter

It was not Peter who rang me but a young officer at the station. It was not, of course, the secretary who had worked with Max and him; Mishael Chisholm had her own business to run, and the closing of S&T had told the end of her career as a secretary. I didn't know Sgt. Joao Pozzobon, but he was very sweet and polite, and all anxiety was disarmed by his heavily accented friendliness. Could I come today at 2:00? At 1:57 I was standing at the door of the station house, not at all sure what I was doing there, but feeling this time that I had to be.

The usual small queue of people at the counter and a cross section of the neighborhood clumped in the waiting area. This time I had brought some identification, and the grouchy desk sergeant whom I also didn't know, didn't have as much reason to scowl at me. She offered a dark look which I took as her most friendly face, and shoved a visitor's pass towards me.

"Where is Sgt. Flo?" I asked of the sunny, buxom officer who usually staffed the front.

"On maternity leave. Next."

I stumbled to a chair to wait.

The buzz of business, which I had only imagined and written about before, was as disorienting as if I were the first person ever to experience it. The worn cyan vinyl chairs, the high laminate counter with the chipped and pen-marked surface, the cracked linoleum. Telephones ringing. The hallway door with its window of reinforced glass and the sign that loudly announced AUTHORIZED PERSONNEL ONLY—ALARM WILL SOUND. Even the lights stupefied me.

Five minutes had passed when a figure that I could not mistake swung through the hallway door and strode to the counter. He leaned over, murmuring something, and I heard the chillingly familiar timbre of his voice. Then he stood up straight, turned round, and scanned the room for me.

You are going to talk with Peter.

And then he saw me; my vacant stare must have given me away.

Peter was not so tall as Max had been, and more solidly built. Flint gray eyes, his sandy hair thinner and grayer in the past few years; an afternoon shadow of ash-and-sand colored stubble around his cheeks and chin. Eyes deeply circled, spectacles characteristically perched on the middle of his nose. Max had been calm and measured; Peter was flippant and tetchy. Max had been deft and witty; Peter was dry and gruff. But there was no gruffness in his gaze as he looked at me, only a kindness grown of sadness. He came over almost shyly, smiling and tilting his head. "Ms. Brinsel Thomas."

It wasn't even a question. That big, hessian voice, bronze heavy and bent indelibly in the patois of the other side of town, I knew as well as my own. I had heard it thousands of times before, but never, never, never like this. Nor ever had that voice pronounced my name. I was astonished to find myself able to stand.

"Well," he said, "well, hello, we meet at last. What a pleasure. I'm Peter Serrev, Max's associate."

He held out his hand and I realized I had to take it. I was shaking the hand of one of my characters. It was like shaking my own hand.

I could just detect, on the edge of my hearing, a horrible, gasping, strangled sound. Then it became a word. "*Hello.*"

"Max must have told you all about me? That I'm a real bear?" The big grin. "Well, don't worry, I don't really bite."

I smiled or I swallowed, not sure where my head was.

"Shall we go up to my office?"

This was Peter Serrev!

He was not a figment of my imagination. He was not imaginary. He was not going away.

Either I was deep in a hallucination of clinical proportions, or he, and all of this, was entirely and unapologetically real.

I was staring at him with what must have been a very impolite intensity. "Alright," I heard myself say at last. "Alright, yes."

He led the way; we passed through the security door, and it fell solidly shut behind us. "Captain says you haven't been here very long," said Peter quietly as we passed her closed office door.

"I've not been." A blank wall, an open door; a radio playing the Latino station and Sgt. Morales crooning enthusiastically in Spanish. The clatter of typing. The clatter of a copier.

Peter nodded. "I've been waiting a long while to meet you, and here you are at last."

The verve that had carried me down the hallway evaporated at the door of the lift. I balked and held my ground.

"It's okay," Peter gestured casually, as though the closed metal box were an open path. "It's only two floors up."

I stared from the back wall of the lift to him, fighting the urge to bolt for the stairs, swallowed and fought for air and made myself step just inside, backing against the corner closest the door.

The third story. We got off, Peter walking and I trying not to dash for it. Peter waved to Detective Riley coming up the hallway.

"Hey, my man," Riley yelled cheerfully at him. "You got that sheet on Louis yet?"

"Like the back of my hand," Peter returned. "Dennis, someone you've been waiting to meet: this is Ms. Brinsel Thomas."

Riley's eyes gave an "*oh*" expression and he stilled, studying me with a solemn appraisal. He bowed slightly, offering his hand to me. "Hello, Ms. Thomas, it's good to meet you at last."

I shook it firmly, hoping the shaking of my own hand was not apparent. "Hello, Detective Riley," I said quietly.

"Oh, so Mr. Serrev did the intros already?" he grinned. "It'll be good to have you working with him, Ms. Thomas. We're trying to convert this old eight-track."

"Know the enemy, I always say," Peter said slyly.

Riley explained to me with a wink, "You know he was a private detective for years? A *privateer*. Now he's gonna be respectable, if we can only unlearn him all the bad habits he picked up out there." He swung a wave at Peter. "Hey Mister V, gotta run, man. Catcha round."

Peter waved after him, then turned and looked at me, eyebrows knitting. But he merely gestured at his office door. Once inside, he lifted a telephone directory out of a chair by his desk and motioned for me to sit, "Please have a seat, Ms. Thomas . . . can I get you anything?"

"Water," I said. "Please."

Max had been painfully neat and orderly, almost annoyingly so; I had often been tempted to take a liberal swipe at all his fastidiousness with something like a tornado or a flood. Peter, on the other hand, seemed to work best in what could be represented by flood or tornado debris. That he and Max had actually been able to work *together*, and with so much success, was as much evidence of their mutual understanding as it was a miracle of logistics.

The absence of Max's example had not inspired Peter to follow it any more than had its presence. His office was a tiny room made even more claustrophobic by an explosion of papers and office supplies, a jumble sale spread of stacked files, directories, manuals, and papers in various contortions of disorder, through which projected suggestions of equipment: something like the deck of a fax machine, what might have been the carriage of a typewriter, the possible arm of a lamp. Across this was strewn a digression of pens, pencils, a tape dispenser, itinerant paperclips, an open stapler, a glass millefleur paperweight, an open day planner bristling with yellow slips and marked with his astonishingly careful penmanship on every line, crumbled bits of paper. As if he had set up his workspace by upending a box of office paraphernalia.

Beside the cabinet a framed piece of paper with the scrawled words: *Lie in Wait—Truth Will Out*. It went back to the very beginning.

The pictures were the hardest part; even amidst the mess, they stood out clearly. On the wall above the desk two carefully preserved newspaper clippings and articles; one large article from not so long ago, with a picture of Max and Peter together, framed.

Peter leaned over his desk to the wall, pushed a reef of paperwork aside, and uncovered a tape recorder. He hit play and record and I heard the machine click into life, its hum throwing a white screen into the air for us to speak on.

"Well, Ms. Thomas . . ." Peter was eyeing me kindly. He had not sat behind his desk but in the chair across from me. "Well, here we are."

His voice still had that thick, accented edge from growing up on the wrong side of town, the careless vowels and the disappearing consonants, so familiar it did not take me an instant to sort out what he was saying. He met my gaze encouragingly and I returned the favor by continuing to stare at him in utter stupidity. *This was Peter Serrev.* I could not get beyond the simple fact. Max's best mate and business partner of thirteen years. A myopic, middle-aged curmudgeon who had spent his entire career to this point in private investigation. No family of his own and long an adoptee of the Thompsons, virtually Max's brother. And I was meeting with him.

I opened my mouth and voiced the most intelligent thought I could find. "It's quite a surprise to see you." A few deep breaths did nothing to make my voice sound less like steam shooting from a boiling kettle. "I don't know why I'm here."

Peter smiled and propped his elbow on the armrest. "Well, Ms. Thomas . . ." taking off his specs, glancing through them against the light, and pushing them back onto his nose. "I know all of this has to be very surprising, to say the least. But there is no need to rush at this point. You've just come into this, and I don't want you to feel pressured." He paused. "You and Captain Petrucci didn't have much of a conversation the other day, and I apologize for how poorly this has begun for you." With a gentle gesture, "You knew Max very well, it seems. But Max never mentioned you, and perhaps you could tell me a bit about yourself."

I was business to him—and to me he was . . . what? Had he not been someone I knew well—even a *friend?*

"Oh, oh . . ." I muttered. I twisted my hands together. "I don't . . . I don't . . . know . . ."

Peter said softly, "I understand this is difficult. You can take as much time as you need."

I took another deep breath. "I'm an artist," I began, as though this explained everything, and promptly ran out of ideas. I stared at my cup of water, looking for inspiration.

"How long have you been in art?" Peter prompted.

"Oh, a long time, for many years, most of my life."

"Really? What sort of art do you do?"

"Well, er, small things. I did illustration. Some printmaking and photography. I have tried composing music too, but it's not my first avocation, and it hasn't done well. As for the rest, I mean the visual art, it's not so important to me at the moment, as I'm doing other things."

"So you have written music?"

"Previously, yes."

"Have you published any of it?"

"Not to any success, but I have, yes."

"Do you do much of that?"

"Very little . . . it's harder to get out there than the artwork."

He tapped his armrest. "I admit I don't have many visitors like you; you have a very interesting accent."

"Is it, now?"

"It is," he smiled, "at least to me. What part of England are you from?"

"Oh, well . . . actually I'm not, I merely live there."

"Ah, so you're a transplant? Where do you hail from originally?"

"Oh, originally? Er . . . from Wales."

"*Wales*," he said with livened interest, eyebrows up over his specs. "Huh, never met anyone from there. So where did you go from there?"

"I was in Cornwall for a little while," putting the words carefully one after the other, and not liking to say them. "I've only been in Surrey a few years."

"Ah . . . you've been around. How long have you been away?"

"Away?"

"From Wales. Has it been awhile?"

"A while," I agreed simply, swallowing.

He nodded. I was afraid he would probe down that road further, but he said only, "What sort of professional work have you done, other than art?"

"I used to teach art. I still work as a writer."

"What sort of writing?"

"Oh, some of everything, what can pay the bills," I said limply, "but mostly fiction. It all amounts to that."

"It does?" He smiled. "What are you doing right now?"

"I have been working for a bookseller for a few years, as well as some writing, mostly for myself."

"Do you still write for publication?"

My face felt uncomfortably tight. "Yes, I hope to get back into that . . . but it may take more time than I thought."

"Any more music?"

I shook my head without bothering to think about it.

"So, no, huh? And what brings you here among us?"

I stared at him stupidly. "I er . . . uh . . . I took some time off to come here to do research for a story which is set here."

"Ah! Wonderful. What was the inspiration to set it here?"

"An American friend of mine who is from here. She is to show me round, so I can get things right."

He smiled, fingering his chin. "You didn't want to invent parts, huh?"

"Er, um," I mumbled, "no."

Another pause fell, the inevitable question dangling unspoken in the air between us. I blurted, "And you, Mr. Serrev? Would you tell me about yourself?"

Peter glanced at his hands. "Well," gruffly, still smiling. "Well, I suppose Max can't have told you everything." His eyes had strayed to the newspaper clippings on the wall. "I haven't done quite as much as you; I've been in investigation for twenty years, and after Max died, I came here. Maybe one day I'll even have a more permanent job here."

I nodded and brought the cup of water to my mouth. Perhaps I could pretend to drink for the next half hour.

Don't be afraid. But it was like writing and not knowing what would happen next. And it *mattered.*

"And, Max," with audible fondness. "We had quite a business, quite a time. I could tell you stories all day. We knew each other quite well." Another pause; a smile crept into his voice. "Do you know why, Ms. Thomas, you are here, instead of at home getting your work done?"

I smiled very small, then swallowed it, then shook my head.

"Well," patiently, "we don't know how Max knew you or how you are connected with the case he was working on. Perhaps you could explain to me how the two of you became acquainted."

Well, there it was. If I told him, they could write me off at once, and perhaps I could get out of this with no further grief. But there remained the question of how Max had known about me.

It was far, far too late to think of saying there had been some sort of mistake. I had admitted that I knew of the investigation, which was surely long finished and resolved, and that Max had been a friend of mine. And whose would the mistake be, when Max had said so plainly who I was, and to contact me? And Peter wanted an answer right now. All they wanted was to know *how*; I could do this, I could invent *something* . . .

"Captain Petrucci showed me the note where . . . Max had mentioned me."

Peter nodded in encouragement. But my mind was painfully, unhelpfully blank.

I'd had days to think about the question and of how to respond and, having avoided it wholesale, had come up with nothing. In that moment, in my panic, I seized on the one halfway plausible explanation my circumstances offered.

I looked up from my cup of water. Peter was regarding me with the same kindness Petrucci had, though I sensed more urgency in his gaze. "Peter, may I call you Peter, Mr. Serrev?"

"Please, Brinsel."

"I don't know why he mentioned me then. It's quite extraordinary to me that he mentioned me at all. I can only think that he did so to be safe, for I had no idea I would become at all involved, and he never suggested that I might."

Peter said, very gently, "Go on."

"I and Max, Max and I, what I mean is—well, quite simply, we corresponded, Max wrote to me about his work. But it was simply presented as ideas, and I didn't understand that it was something real that he was working on. That is how we know each other. It was simply a friendly correspondence, it wasn't anything official. I don't understand why he mentioned me, unless he thought I might be useful . . . I suppose. I don't think he would have mentioned me otherwise. But I don't really know."

Peter had been watching me without expression, his eyes behind his glasses only glinting. He rubbed his chin with his thumb and said, "So he wrote you letters about his work."

"I suppose that would be it, yes."

Peter took off his glasses and rubbed one eye with the back of his hand, then put them back on and regarded me intently. "Let me get this straight for the record. He wrote you personal correspondence?"

And then I remembered. Except for business, Max had never written letters. He had been a horrible letter writer; no, he had been a nonexistent letter writer. Even his idea of a thank you note had been on the cutting-edge of minimalism: "Dear So-and-So, thanks, Max"—or simply "Thanks!" and he would forget to sign his name. *Letters?* The man had never even sent Christmas cards to his own friends. I opened my mouth again, closed it, swallowed, and nodded. "Yes," I lied again, in increasing implausibility. "Max wrote me letters."

The silence was phenomenal, as if the whole room had been erased. I could hear the faint sound of a radio somewhere down the corridor. I could hear birds and traffic outside.

Peter didn't so much as fidget. His face said mere polite interest. "So, Brinsel, how did this all begin, and when?"

It had begun four years ago on a slow and difficult day at a temporary job. Or to go even further back, it had begun with . . .

Music. That was it. Everything, in my life and his, had begun with that.

"About a year before he died, Max wrote to me concerning a piece of music I had written. He wanted to know if there was more of it—the music, I mean. He had sent the inquiry to the previous copyright holder, the publisher, and as it was out of print—the music—the letter was sent on to me. I was able to answer him, and to my surprise he wrote back. He was quite apologetic, he didn't want to be a bother, he was interested in my other work. It was the music he wanted, but he asked about everything, and he continued to write periodically. I didn't mind, you know, sometimes people write you concerning your work; he was innocuous and friendly, and I thought he would, well, give up eventually."

"How often was this?"

"About three times in as many months at first, just asking after my work. Then he vanished for several weeks and I thought I would hear no more of him. Then he wrote back again, only with different questions. He said he had read some of my writings . . ." I took a deep breath. "Then I didn't hear anything for a while. When he wrote again, he offered to give me some ideas he thought would make a good story, if I was interested. I had no reason to refuse and wrote back that I would be pleased to see what he had to offer. Then nothing again for several weeks."

Peter said nothing, waiting.

"When he did write again, his tone was much different. Much more serious. It seemed to me he was preoccupied by something. He asked that I keep all the ideas he was sending me strictly confidential until he would say it was okay to use them. I couldn't make much sense of that at the time, although I did wonder at one point if something wasn't wrong. I had begun to find a friend in him . . ."

"The last letter I got was from the middle of May, in '88."

Peter still sat unmoving. "And then?"

"It was quite strange. I hadn't been able to write to him for some months and was beginning to reply, when I received a parcel from a friend who lives here. She had used newspaper for wadding, and I found the . . . the article about his death in that."

I stopped and, to my complete astonishment, the past week came pouring out right there in Peter's office in an unwelcome torrent of grief. He handed me the box of tissue.

"I'm so *sorry*," I sobbed. I covered my face with tissue, wishing it could blot out the room and the world. "I was shocked to hear that had happened."

"I understand."

A long silence. I tried to mop myself up. I was limp and bewildered, but I had done it—it was over. I had explained how Max had known me, even if it was a horrible and unavoidable and fantastic lie. I would promise never to reveal anything of what he had never told me. I could go home and disappear and get my head put on straight . . .

Peter sighed, "So, that's it. That's it." An intense silence as though he meant to say more. But he said only, "It seems he didn't keep any of the letters you sent him."

"He wouldn't, would he?" I blew my nose. "He probably hadn't kept the music, either."

Now a faint smile. "I found one sheet, folded very small, in his flute case. Nothing else yet."

I stared at him.

"Would you like to see it?"

I seemed to have swallowed my tongue. He leapt up and went to the cupboard, found what he was looking for very quickly, and brought it over to me. And suddenly it was in my hand.

If he had presented me with a giant spider I could not have been less pleased or prepared. Even pressed flat between two sheets of acetate, it was a folded paper puzzle of inconceivable dimensions, as intelligible as something carelessly dropped from another planet. I recognized it instantly. Various sections had been circled in red and the whole of it was scribbled in different colors with diagramming.

"Do you know why he colored the music like that?" Peter gestured.

I knew. I shook my head in horror.

"I didn't recognize it, I can't read music any better than I can read Chinese; it was his sister who figured it out. That sheet there is identical to one of his compositions he was just fine-tuning at the time. It was she too, who had the idea that, whoever you were, this was the reason he had trusted you. That there was some sort of connection between you both that would inspire you with the same music."

The shadow of my thoughts finally crossed my face.

"Are you all right?"

"No."

He stood, his shoes shuffing on the linoleum. "Hang on, I'll be one second."

I hung on, hardly breathing in the aftermath of what must have been lightning. The parti-colored sheet of music lay at my feet, but I couldn't tell if there was a floor under them. Something had knocked the middle out of me . . .

"And some cookies," Peter was presenting me with a paper serviette of biscuits along with a paper cup of coffee. "No fainting here!"

The window mechanism chirped as he cranked it open. The room was coming back to my senses with a feeling like seasickness, my eyes and stomach swimming. The cup of coffee could only be located by the sensation of heat in my hand, and finally I drew a scalding swallow. "Thank you, Peter."

Peter retrieved the sheet of music from the floor and set it gently atop his desk, easing into his desk chair. "I knew this would be disturbing for you, and I apologize if you feel rushed." He rubbed his eyes and tipped his spectacles back on. "There is a lot to this puzzle, and it won't do to dump it all on you at once."

I shrugged limply.

"We'll take our time, okay? Our only concern right now is those letters."

I had already forgotten them. "I hadn't ever told anyone about the letters," I said. "And I shan't, it shall stay with me."

Peter clasped his hands before him on a pile of papers. "That is good to know; that itself is a great help. Would you be willing to help us further, Brinsel?"

Help them? Further? What more could I do?

"What is it I can do to help?"

"Do you still have the letters Max sent you, Brinsel?"

Provided he didn't ask about the music, what did the rest matter? "Yes," I said, my voice sounding terribly far away. "I'm fairly certain I do."

"Would you be willing to give them to us?"

The tiny murmur of the tape recorder sounded suddenly and ridiculously loud.

"Well, surely. If I can find them, you may have them."

He said nothing for a moment, then, very simply, "Thank you."

I realized I had lost my breath and let it out slowly. I took a long draught of coffee. "Do you need them soon?"

His smile was a very worn copy of itself. "It's been three years; but, yes, soon would be good. Three years . . . so I've been looking for you for three years, and here you are."

Three years. They had *known* about me for three years. They had been *looking for me* for three years . . .

"And in case you're concerned about safety you needn't be; I've had tails on you since we found you were here, and nothing's turned up. There is no one who knows who you are, or has even heard of you. Max was very careful, very careful. Not even we knew who you were."

He had been *watching* me. I was being squeezed by stupefaction. I pushed an entire biscuit in my mouth.

"You know, you have a unique place among us here. A lot of people who cared about Max have been wondering just who you are, and what you know that can help us. Your presence here is a sign of hope for us."

And then it sank in, for the first time, why they had called for me. Not simply because they had no idea who I was.

"Peter, his murder isn't still being investigated, is it?"

"Yes, I'm afraid it is." Again the specs came off, and he rubbed his eyes.

"It's not resolved yet?"

Peter regarded me in silence. "No," he said at last. "It's not."

"But—why not?"

Peter shrugged with his hands. "You know, stuff doesn't happen the way you want sometimes. The thing is, Brinsel, we haven't got—well, we haven't got what we need, we don't have the information Max had. We have a suspect in custody, who's more than likely our man, but that's it, and we may not have enough to prove it."

I had never completed that part of the story. I had not wanted to think about it or deal with it; I had simply assumed, however naïvely, that those responsible for the matter would resolve the issue. Above all, I had assumed it had been resolved. I swallowed another biscuit whole, clinging tightly to the serviette.

"Whatever article you saw didn't say everything, naturally. Part of my problem has been that Max's work on his assignment went missing after his death. It's been all uphill for us trying to pull everything back together. There was only that note mentioning you which he had left on his desk, and until now, it hasn't meant much."

The note I had never known about. And his work had been missed? How had that happened? And where were the other records on the case? "Why did he write that note?"

"Well, my guess is because he had written you those letters."

I still could not handle the size of the sums involved. I asked stupidly, "What are the letters to do with it?"

"That's what I would like to find out. If Max told you everything, even what we couldn't find, then they might help us settle this once and for all."

Suddenly the implications of what I had just told him struck home.

And I knew exactly why they wanted me there.

"You've not got, you've not, not . . . *enough?*"

"I would be happier to have more. Part of my problem is that all the work he did on his last case is what imputes his murder, case number two. More information might help me a great deal with this."

The miniscule whirr of the tape recorder had never hummed so loudly, so innocently, so damningly.

"Shall I have to serve as a witness?"

"It depends on just what he told you. If the letters don't give us anything new, they won't be much use. But if they do, it is very possible."

All I could make out of the world was thin contour lines and flat shapes of unvariegated color, everything about me sitting on one plane and much too close to my eyes. I rubbed them until the cage of contour lines receded and shade and dimension returned, but there was no mitigating the blunder I had just made—I, who had been so curious about seeing Peter, had talked myself into wanting to, had stupidly failed to realize they had a *reason* for wishing to see me . . .

I looked at my empty cup of coffee and the last biscuit I had squeezed to crumbs. I was certain I'd felt far more helpless before in my life than I did that moment, but when I finally raised my eyes and saw Peter, *Peter*, with that old, patient smile, the attentive concern that dressed up whatever he was actually feeling, I could not remember when it had been.

"Hey," he ordered, "how about not such a long face? It's not all that bad. We can work something out if being a witness would be a problem for you. We'll just wait and see, right?"

I nodded, miserable.

He grinned again, the harsh gruffness of his features long since softened by age and grief. "Don't worry so much, you'll start to scare me. Besides," he gestured at the articles on the wall. "That one's got the other end of the string, right? How he involved you in this is quite a surprise to me, but then I can't really put it past him, as strange as it seems."

My attention had stuck at a photo of Max and Peter taken in a courtroom, Max's gaze quick and sharp as a burn and seeming to go out of the photo and over my head. I said numbly, "I didn't even realize he was a private detective until I saw the article. I thought he was just a musician who knew a lot about police work."

"Yes, that sounds like Max," his voice the description of wry. "Tells only what he wants you to know. But it comes with the territory." He looked at me over the top of his specs, an old wily glint in his eyes. "You know, letter writing was *not* his forte, and I am really curious about what he wrote you."

My mouth made some shape I hoped was a smile. I cradled the empty cup in my hands, then put it down on a tiny bare spot on the edge of the overflowing desk.

"Brinsel, Max's sister, Rachel Cunningham, would like very much to meet you. Would it be alright if I give you her number, or give yours to her?"

Even supposing I could refuse, what would be the point? "Yes, you are welcome. I'll take it."

He grabbed a clean notepaper and scribbled a number which I knew already, quickly glancing at the clock. "I should let you go . . . it's already four. But first, do you have any questions?"

It was the wrong thing to ask the wrong person. "So, when do I wake up?"

He regarded the floor for a minute, then lifted his chin. "I've wondered that too, many times. I wish I could tell you, for your own comfort, that it's just a dream. If only it really were. But I'm afraid we're all in this, and none of us is dreaming. We are only hoping, especially now, that you can help us, Brinsel."

I was studying the floor myself; when I looked at him again, he nodded.

"We'll do what we can, and then it will be over."

I bobbed my head as if to agree.

"I do have one more question for you today. May I ask how you knew Detective Riley?"

I gestured alongside my face. "The burns. Max had mentioned a police detective named Riley who had burns."

"Ah," again the nod. "I see. I'll be waiting to hear from you, Brinsel. Call me if you have any questions." And a smile I knew very well. "I'll be wondering about those letters."

Home again, I snapped on the desk lamp and stood a long while gazing at the picture of Max.

I turned on the typewriter. I had no idea whatsoever what I was going to write.

*Waterhouse Music Ltd.
Stamford Green Road
Witney
Morrell
Oxon OX14 6UJ
UK*

April 25, 1987

*To Whom it may Concern,
I am writing in the hope you can connect me to Ms. Brinsel Thomas, composer of London Spring & Other Gifts. I would particularly like to know if there is any more from this collection, as I seem to have only one portion of a folio. I have not been able to find her music in this country, or at least I do not know who the American distributor might be.*

*Thank you for any help you can provide. I look forward to your response.
Cordially,*

*Maximilian Thompson
ASCAP*

4

Dan

When Max had written that I had "all the information" he had got, he had not been mistaken, yet it was, incredibly, a matter of interpretation. I certainly had all the information on virtually everything about his life, written or not, but I certainly did not have all the information on the case he had been working on. The worst of it was that I had once known, and had written down the gist of it, with some useful facts and names, in order to understand why things had ended as they had—and that piece of paper, of anything I wanted to find, was unhelpfully missing from all my files. Now I had no more than a vague and sketchy idea; above all, I could not know if I had the information Peter was looking for.

I myself had certainly *not* been what Peter was looking for—he *had* been expecting another professional, somebody with a rational and qualified link to his former associate. Somebody of comparable caliber. Somebody who might have a duplicate file or could at the very least answer some simple questions. Instead he had got a frail, frumpy, middle-aged nobody—clueless, amateur, more or less out of work, quite possibly out of her mind. Clearly, somebody in casting had stepped out at the wrong moment.

I jotted down the content of the troublesome note but got no further than before. Max had meant to see Riley the next morning to turn the whole thing over to him; the cryptic "jinx" perhaps referred to the state of the case, and the semi-quaver simply poorly timed whimsy. But had he meant to tell Riley about *me*? How could he claim I had any information at all? Still worse, what could he have meant by saying I could help?

I had botched it proper and, to cap it all, how I had chosen to resolve it not only played to my vanity as a writer but amounted to something freakishly uncharacteristic of Max: writing letters. And yet it had to make sense. Of course it made sense. How else could he have got any information to me? Through pipes?

I knew a story could take over your life, but this was ridiculous.

I spent some fevered hours racking my brain for ideas and scribbling a sort of outline of what I could remember of the case. It gave me a sense of shape and direction, but it still felt more like thrashing about making random and meaningless gestures than the certain and factual declamation that was needed.

The first letter, which I typed, was not hard. A business letter of sorts, an inquiry between professionals. Easily plausible even for Max: he would be tracking something down, and I was making myself ridiculously easy to track down—he had only to write to my music publisher, and they would find me for him. But this was also on the assumption that he had had all of the score at some point, and *that* I could not know. At least that much didn't matter, and at least it was not difficult to imitate his careless, scattered penmanship when I came to his signature. I had only an instant of satisfaction, for the next thing I recalled was that same handwriting in the note Petrucci had shown me, and it took all the rage I could muster to keep myself from subscribing to despair then and there.

Rachel's phone number sat atop the papers on my desk, like a buoy stubbornly resurfacing no matter how much I tried to smother it, and recognizing defeat, I picked it up. Trying to muster up the courage to get as far as picking up the phone as well, I leafed through the papers on the desk and found the conversation I had written with Max—or rather with myself.

Until I had been driven to it by desperation, I had never before tried speaking with one of my characters. But once I had done so I discovered it was altogether a doddle. I knew Max best of them all, and what he might say and how he would think presented no challenge but came as spontaneously as my own thoughts, in fact with less effort. It was a game, I knew, but . . .

I turned on the typewriter anyway.

I put a fresh sheet in and typed, "Hello Max yourself."

"Hello there, love."

"I went to speak with Peter, Max."

"Good for you."

Silence.

"Max, if all of this is real, why must I write the letters which you supposedly wrote to me?"

A slight pause, then, "Did I say I wrote letters to you?"

Irritated, I typed, "No, *I* said you did."

"Well, then, there you go."

No surprises, really. But perhaps some blunt questioning would jog my memory.

"Max, I don't understand any of this. I have nothing, nothing, to explain why you mentioned me."

"You have these letters."

"The letters don't exist!"

"So, something's keeping them from existing?"

"I don't know all the details of the case you were working on. Could you not tell me what they were, so I can write them?"

"Okay, help me out here, Brinsel. If you can say that I wrote you those letters, is there some reason you can't say what was in them?"

Well, there it was; I was blunt, he was pointed.

"Because this is real. It involves a real investigation."

"And my investigation wasn't?"

"I had thought it was fiction."

"Was it?"

"Evidently not . . . If it's all real, then why is it I can change things?"

"I would be more surprised if you couldn't change things."

"I don't understand."

"You are real? Well, then, you can change things. If you're not real, you can't. Makes perfect sense."

I wanted to clobber him. "But I'm just *making it up!*"

"Are you making it up?"

"Yes, I *had* made it up. I can't just write what *is* anymore. I don't *know* what is. I invented these letters, and I don't know how they are going to turn out. I have to tell Peter the truth, and I don't know what he needs."

"And that's stopped you when?"

Why did this conversation have to be so infuriatingly real, when it was the one thing that wasn't?

"Brinsel, when I asked you to go to Peter, did you know what you were going to say?"

"I had not."

"And did things turn out okay?"

"Not at all! Things turned out horrid! Look where I've got by listening to you. I've talked myself into doing something I don't think is even possible!"

"What if it is?"

I sat and stared at the words I had just typed for almost an entire minute.

"Will you let me help you?"

"Help me? Do something impossible? What are you going to do, Max, play flute?"

"Will you let me help?"

"I'd like to see you try."

"I can't help you if you don't let me. And I would like to."

It was such a relief to openly rage at him that those patient, predictable replies only enraged me further. And while his offering to help was horribly, bitterly true to life, while I clearly would have loved his help, it was perfectly useless of me to make him offer it.

"You have helped sufficiently by involving me to begin with. What do you intend to do, rewrite history?"

"I intend to help you do what you need to do."

What I needed to do was get out of this, and as quickly as possible, but there wasn't a way out that I could see.

"Brinsel?"

The exercise had become exceedingly unhelpful. "Please don't let me regret this."

"Do you regret knowing me?"

"I regret . . . I regret not writing down the entire case when I didn't know it was real."

"And now is where we can begin to redress that. Brinsel, do what you *can*. When you can't do any more, I will do the rest."

I covered my face with my hands and sighed. That was what I got when I at last wrote what I wanted to hear. I couldn't even be realistic. I flipped the paper over and scrolled it back in, shaking my head. "Thanks for nothing."

"Well, we haven't got there yet. You have to do your part first. You going to call Rachel?"

"I suppose I might."

"Good. That's somewhere to start. And take it easy, there's nothing to be afraid of."

"Thank you for making that perfectly clear."

"Give it a try. I'm right behind you."

I began to type a suitable retort but stopped; once again, the typewriter had turned off. If I was going to ring anyone before too long, it would be the repairman. I sat staring at the paper, then at the picture of Max, that smile that went somewhere I could no longer see.

"Right," I muttered. "Right, let's go."

It was the following evening before I could work up the nerve to ring.

I was half afraid of getting the answerphone; I was trying to think of what I could say to it, when the ringing suddenly stopped and a familiar, heavy voice met my ear.

"Cunninghams, this is John."

John—good heavens, what had I been thinking? I stammered out something incoherent that included my name and Peter's name and for all I knew my National Insurance number as well.

"Oh, yes," his voice lightened to a friendlier pitch. "How nice to hear from you, Ms. Thomas. I'll go get Rachel, she's been waiting for your call."

Several moments of faint humming. I stared nervously at the picture of Max, simply trying to breathe.

"Hello, this is Rachel."

Rachel. All my nerve evaporated and my throat pinched to a point. A thousand memories of her leapt at me. Which was I to speak to? How did you address someone you knew very well but . . .

"Hello?"

"Er, hello, Dr. Cunningham, this is Brinsel Thomas. Peter—"

"Oh, hello, Ms. Thomas, it's so good to hear from you." She would be sitting down slowly, brushing her hair behind her ear. A slight pause, then: "I've been hoping you would call—Peter mentioned you might. We've been hearing about you for so long, and I thought we might get together sometime, if that would be okay with you?"

"Thank you. I—I've been hoping to speak with you as well."

"Oh!"

"I had, I . . . had wanted to meet the sister of Max Thompson."

I was horrified at what was coming from my mouth. One didn't speak to strangers like this.

But Rachel didn't seem to notice. "Well . . . well, how about we make a time to meet? You could come over to our place. When are you free?"

I was free just about any time. Rachel went to check with John for a good day, and I listened to the empty line, still trying to swallow my heart.

"Ms. Thomas? How is this Saturday at 6:30 for you?"

It was good. There remained only getting me there.

"Peter can swing by and drop you off. He sometimes comes by here, and it'd be fine by him. Would that be okay for you?"

Peter. Yes, it would be okay.

"Great! I really look forward to meeting you, Ms. Thomas. We'll see you on Saturday then."

Her voice rang in my ears for hours. And on Saturday, not only would I hear it again, but I would have to meet her myself.

Before that, however, there was still the outing with Cathy to be muddled through. It seemed ages ago now that we had arranged to go out so I could do research for . . . this story. It no longer seemed remotely necessary, but I was happy to see her when she appeared at my door, much happier than the previous time. This time she rang the bell and waited, and her sheepish smile greeted me when I opened the door.

"Hello, dearest, I thought I'd ring this time, just in case." She handed me a ceramic pot wreathed in opaque lavender tissue. "And I brought you a friend, someone you can look after."

The "friend" turned out to be a sturdy little aloe vera. "Oh, I haven't got to water it, have I?"

"Say that again!" she laughed, giving me another hug. "I love to hear your squashed vowels."

"Oh, they aren't squashed, they only grew up different than yours. How *much* water?"

Cathy's presence was an immediate salve; she was still the same vaguely scatterbrained postgraduate, still overtaken by pop-culture manias, whom I had taught years before, now sweetened with age and a sprinkling of maturity. Everything about her pinpointed a safer, saner moment in my life, and I happily swept the specter of unpleasant realities under a rug at the back of my mind. And no sooner had we got into the car and got underway than Cathy, with a sleight of mind I found unjust, pulled the unpleasantness out of her hat.

". . . *You* have certainly had an unenviable welcome to our fine country. Welcome to the United States, and what a welcome for your first visit. And who's going to keep an eye on you, since I'll be out of town for a while? You never did answer that when I wrote you."

"Dai said he'd ring me." I squirmed in my seat.

"Well, that's good," her voice slightly distant. "Especially considering this mess that's found you. What about that investigation thing? Is that still going on?"

I made an affirmative mumble.

"That's just nuts. I mean, who knows who you are *here*?"

We glided onto the slip road to downtown. "Well, you do!"

A laugh. "That's right, but still, all this is very weird. Shades of international intrigue, you know? Dave would get a kick out of it."

I fixed all my attention on the scenery. "Is it difficult to find parking at this time of day?"

We left the car at a multi-story close to the courthouse and set off on foot. Cathy steered me to her favorite bookshop, educational supply company, ice cream parlor and, because she thought I would enjoy it, a fine and very familiar music shop which happened to be in the same precincts. Cathy's garrulous company was a pleasure after my bewildered solitude of past days, something to distract me, and someone I could enjoy. I needed this; I was haunted by the thought of Max's presence, walking these same streets, of his *having been* here and no longer being so, as though his absence had displaced the whole meaning of the place. I shied as much as I could from the specters of all-too familiar landmarks, avenues, atmosphere, as if I could hold what I had previously imagined and what I now saw at sensible, even logical extremes. But it was rather like walking on a beach and expecting not to get sand in one's shoes. By the time we sat down at a café, I was exhausted from the effort of being in one place and trying to pretend I was in another. There was not much respite for me at the café, either; the words on the menu kept disappearing into unsummoned recollections, and I had to put forth great effort into deciphering an item that began "Pastrami, Swiss . . ." and ended somewhere in a lunch meeting of Richard Thompson and the Philharmonic's artistic director planning his retirement.

We were served our drinks quickly; though it was inching towards noon only a few chairs held customers. "We're here just ahead of the lunch crowd," Cathy observed with satisfaction, flashing a glance at her watch, then another at the compact in her handbag, fluffing her fringe. "We've made good time." She put down her handbag and propped up her elbows, glancing at me pointedly. "I think that's just the strangest thing, that investigation. I can't get over it."

"It is strange," I acquiesced, but Cathy could not detect that nuance.

"You just get here, and bam! Someone's looking for you."

I tried to turn down the unhappy memories of when both Richard and Max had worked for the Philharmonic. "H'm."

"You don't think . . ." her face pinching a little. I stiffened. "You don't think it has anything to do with . . ."

"No!"

"I'm sorry, Brin, I won't ask about it. It's just so weird."

"Don't worry," I brisked, flicking the thought away with my hand, "It's nothing, it will be over soon. How have you been doing? Tell me about work."

Our salads and sandwiches arrived during her recital and we tucked in, Cathy continuing her story undaunted. "Now tell me about *your* work, Brin. I want to hear more about this story you're working on."

"Well, it's sort of autobiographical," I fibbed wildly.

"Really?" Cathy almost choked on a mouthful of lettuce. She looked shocked. "You're writing a book like *that?*"

"Well, not really," but no longer certain if I was lying or not. "It's not like that, it's, you know, just got bits." I did some massive and extemporary revising to give her something to snack on, but this only whetted her appetite, and she needled me with questions until I was ready to collapse in an exhaustion of "ums" and "I don't knows" and quite unfictitious anxiety.

"It's going to be fabulous. You haven't done any work in so long. I'm thrilled you're writing again, I can't wait to get more drafts. I propose a toast," she raised her iced coffee grandly. "To your next book—what was it called again?—may it become a bestseller. I'll be looking for it on all the bestseller lists."

"Now you're making fun of me," I growled, but returned the toast.

When the bill arrived, I reached for my satchel, but Cathy shushed my offer. I turned politely, and I even enjoyed an entire untroubled instant of observing the passers-by, but within seconds whipped my attention back to the table, my hands trembling and everywhere. I fumbled with the water glass and clanked the spoon and saucer and sprayed sugar across the table agitating a teaspoon of sugar into my empty cup. Cathy glanced up. "What's wrong?"

"Nothing, nothing."

"You're white as a sheet, Brin. What is it?"

"Nothing, Cath, nothing." I hid behind one hand. "I just . . . had a flashback."

She twisted in her chair to peer down the pavement, where Max's first investigative employer, friend, and musical collaborator Dan Malcombe could still be glimpsed hunched down and rolling away amongst the noon crowds. "Did someone look familiar?"

"Sort of."

She clucked in sympathy. "Nowhere's safe, is it? How about we get you back so you can rest?"

Rest, in the midst of all my stories about Max? Before the typewriter, with a blank sheet of paper in the carriage?

Suddenly it was harder to let Cathy disappear back into her own life than it had been even to come researching. I spent the ride back to my flat babbling incoherencies about inadequacies real and imagined, all of which she cruelly and glibly pooh-poohed. My problems were not so unique. I was not the first person. I had done this before. At the door of my flat I ultimated, "Cathy, I don't think I can do this!"

"Sure you can!" My objections were squashed in a bear hug. "Hey, you're gonna be fine! You'll make some friends and the time will fly. Piece of cake, right? Give me a call before I head off to the boonies next month. I'll want to know that you're doing okay."

I must have stood staring at the door for half an hour, completely unable to think, after she had finally gone.

In my office again, I tried to hold my brain to the task of what to put in the next letter. After everything I had seen in town, after Dan . . . It was all there, all just as I had written.

Could I not sit down and write a few short letters just as Max might have written them? The idea was looking as likely as my being able to remember the case I had long ago spent scarcely two minutes jotting down on a piece of paper I had since lost.

I went to bed with a headache. It was a bad sign.

5

Rachel

Saturday. Peter had arranged to come at 6:30 on his way home from work. At 6:20 I was sitting anxiously in my office, wondering what on earth I was doing.

Talk to Rachel? To John? I knew every room in their house. I knew where all their lost socks were. How would I be able to pretend I didn't know a thing?

Six-thirty came. Nothing. Six-forty.

I fiddled with some papers and drank some water and untied and tied my shoes. And the door buzzed.

And there was Peter standing at my door. "Ready, Brinsel?"

Two weeks ago, I should have fainted dead away. Or slammed the door in his face. Or laughed at what could only have been a hilarious joke.

I locked up, and we went down to his car which, for all practical purposes, was double-parked in the fire lane. Inside, it was not shandivang like his office; there was almost nothing within or without to distinguish it as the car of anything other than a middle-aged bachelor who was not too fussy and not too sloppy. Peter took a mild satisfaction in the thought that no one who might glance into his vehicle would be able to tell much about him. I comforted myself with my knowledge that he was a safe if overly defensive driver as he blasted the horn at another car and bolted into traffic.

"So . . . how have you been, Brinsel?"

"Er, better. And you?"

"I'm doing okay." His voice curled up on the word. "Life . . . keeps me busy." Then, "How is your work going? Your research and all that?"

"Er . . . Okay, I think. Good days, difficult days."

"That's the way it goes." Nodding and smiling, not taking his eyes from the road as he spoke. He cleared his throat. "I'm glad you can get together with the Cunninghams while you're here. It's good for them, especially as I haven't been able to let them in on a lot of my work."

"Oh." I clutched my hands together to stop from hiding my face in them as he swerved and shouted out the window.

"Have your people had any luck looking for those letters?"

"They haven't, not yet."

"You know, we can try to help move things along by other ways. We've got connections with several government and private agencies over the pond. If you want, I can get someone over there to look for you."

I nearly panicked. "Oh, Peter, thanks, that's dear, but I don't think it would be necessary, you wouldn't want to bother them . . . and all my things are in such a mess as it is, I don't think it would make any great difference."

He shrugged, giving one of his half-smiles. "Well, it's up to you." He reached for the thermos of coffee and took a swig. "We're just holding out hope for something." Another sidelong smile at me. "So many possibilities. I'm happy at least that who you are in all this is a puzzle piece that's at last falling into place."

Who I was in all this . . . who *was* I in all this?

As happy as I was for the ride to end, it was over all too quickly. We were entering a large residential quarter, the street branching into a boulevard canopied with plane trees. Even from the turn of the lane, the Cunninghams' arts-and-crafts kit house was already the most visible residence halfway up Washington Avenue, a quiet side street with large trees and older, picturesque houses.

And then we were there. Peter stopped in front of a beige brick house with dark trim and a large porch cascading white wooden steps. The narrow walk that led up to it passed between a small strip of lawn and careful borders of perennials. Welcoming yellow light shone through the curtains.

"Well, here we are. House of Cunningham."

"Oh, no, oh *no*."

"Is something wrong?"

"I can't, can't do this," I babbled. I shook my head insistently. "I can't, I just *can't*, I can't *meet* them."

"Well, sure you can," Peter said slowly. "Sure you can. Look, you met me, right?"

I stared at him for a minute that seemed to last an hour, until I was quite sure he did not mean it the way I heard it. By then the real absurdity of my refusal sank in. "Right," I whispered. "Alright."

"Okay? Shall we go up?"

He jumped out and hurried around to open the car door for me. I was touched by his care in wanting to walk me up, but it also comforted me no small measure not to have to face the Cunninghams' door alone. If I had been trembling to speak with Rachel over the telephone, at this moment I thought I might shake to pieces.

Footsteps inside. The click of the latch, and the door swung open.

John. "Hey, Peter! Good to see you. And this must be Ms. Thomas."

Thank goodness it was John, a buffer in every sense despite how startling it was to see him. That tawny head and round, utterly genial face, the big nose and the lines etched across his forehead. Max would have greeted his brother-in-law like an old pal, hand-shaking, name-calling, one of the fellows. I gaped up at him as open-mouthed as I had greeted Peter, immobile as a stone on the doormat until he extended his hand. "Pleased to meet you, Mr. Cunningham," I squeaked.

"Well, hello there, Ms. Thomas, it's good to meet you at last." Gentle, affable, even-tempered. I felt like a gerbil meeting a golden retriever. "I'm glad you could come over. Rachel will be right down."

Movement in the corridor. Tall and slender, a dark head of hair.

Peter was talking to John.

A figure walked up to the doorway and ducked under John's arm.

Rachel. Max's sister. That kindly, composed face so like her brother . . . and so unlike. Her mother's fine straight hair and clear eyes and strong chin, her father's height and wiry build.

She was a foot taller than me.

"Hello, Ms. Thomas." Very gently took my hands in greeting.

"Hello, Dr. Cunningham," I said, dazed.

Rachel. Rachel the sweet, the sentimental, the snide. She had won the spelling bee two years in a row at her grammar school but it had taken her almost a year to learn to ride a bicycle. She had narrowly escaped with her life from a road accident some ten years before. She had looked after her brother following their mother's death, and rather annoyingly for much of the rest of his life. Rachel, generously endowed with the Thompson intensity and sensitivity, deeply and inextricably loyal to the lost dream of Max's glory, plagued with regret for having been the only one never to accept her brother's chosen profession and with guilt for always letting him know it. I had all of Max's memories of growing up with her, and I still knew things about her even he had not.

John and Peter came back from logistics and noticed we were there.

"Well, hello, it looks like we're all here."

"And it looks like my work is done for now." Peter gestured smilingly, "Rach, this is Ms. Brinsel Thomas, of Max's collaboration. We've *finally* got her here. Alright Brinsel? I'll see you around. Glad to be of use. Let me know if you need anything."

I needed to defer being left to my own devices. My mouth acted before my head could object. "Oh! Happy birthday, Peter."

The faintest blur of surprise piqued his brow and was gone. "Well . . . thank you, Brinsel. How did you know that?"

My own surprise pulled my face into what must have been astonishment, if not outright embarrassment. After a moment I shook my head.

"Sounds like a leak in the department," he sighed, smiling and lifting a wave to John and Rachel.

And there I was, at the house of Rachel Cunningham. The entry with its taupe and burgundy braided rug, the worn trail through the middle. The framed print of Sargent's *Carnation, Lily, Lily, Rose* over the table. The hallway with family pictures: the twins as four-year-old matching peas at Hallowe'en; Rachel and John's wedding, the groom just slightly shorter than the bride; a small photo of the entire Thompson family in grainy color, taken when Rachel was a spry five and Max a bug-eyed infant, and Richard looking shockingly young. They could have all been drawings pulled from my files, but they were photographs, and I had to stifle the sudden urge to weep at the sight of them.

Then the living room, the burgundy print couch and chairs. The wooden rocker that had been her mother's. The glass-topped coffee table made from old printers' trays, their boxes filled with retired type of the letter C and a whole score of musical signs in various shapes and sizes. The glazed tile fireplace. On the opposite wall a poster of the cheerful, colorful nonsense of de Stael's *Musicians*. The low wall connecting from the hallway sported a tall ceramic vase of pink, white, and gold spears of fading glads, surrounded by a cloud of birthday cards taped all over the wall; the twins' birthday had been only three days before. The room full of warm colors, pillows with tangled tassels, braided rugs that lapped over each other. And everywhere that faint, stale bouquet of burnt biscuits, of furniture polish and painted plaster that Max had always associated with his sister's house.

And there stood Rachel and John, John with the aura of petrol and Rachel with the aura of hospital. Both looking as though a meteorite had fallen on their doorstep and smiling as though they intended to be pleased about it, and hang the expense. "Well," Rachel said in a rather bright, watery voice, "well, it's good to meet you, Ms. Thomas."

I had almost stopped shaking and flung about for something to say disarming and not too foolish. "You must like music, Dr. Cunningham."

Rachel laughed, nervously. "It's in the blood! And you can call me Rachel, Ms. Thomas."

"Please, call me Brinsel."

She turned to John, one hand on his arm. "Honey, would you go put on some coffee? And maybe some cookies or something."

"Coffee and some cookies or something, coming right up!"

With a delicate gesture, Rachel invited me to one of the chairs, perching rather stiffly on the edge of hers. Mine surrounded me; I was not large enough to fill it. I felt smaller and more misplaced than ever, inserted into a scene that didn't know how to accommodate me, the entire room growing larger in misgiving. Rachel was enormous, enough to make two of me, and even when seated remained taller than I. She pushed behind one ear a spray of hair escaped from her French knot. "How long have you been here, Brinsel?" The warm, self-possessed note of her usual self creeping back into her voice.

"Er . . . I think over a month now. I keep losing track of time."

"Peter was so pleased—that's really not saying it—when they found you. So were we. We've all been hoping . . ."

I mumbled, "I hope I shall be able to help in the way that is needed."

A grateful smile. Then, to my surprise her gaze withdrew like a mouse down a hole and a shadow passed over her face; but she only wrapped her hands together and asked, "Have you ever seen a picture of Max?"

She took my silence as a negative and, rising, indicated a photograph hanging by the rocker: a large black and white print of Max seated before a music stand, grasping his flute in one hand and gesturing with the other. A faded Liebmann University sweatshirt and reading specs perched on the middle of his nose. He had been about thirty-five but looked years older; it might have been the lines across his forehead or his insomniac eyes, or simply how far his face was from the handsome energy of his youth. But he was smiling radiantly. Rachel explained, "This is him . . . it was taken during a rehearsal for a children's concert some years ago. He was there as a soloist." Even with the stiffness in her manner, the pride in her voice unmistakable.

I knew the incident well, yet the photograph had distilled it like a well-turned sentence. "Oh, he looks exactly as I thought," I blurted. "I mean, he looks the way he sounded . . ."

Rachel bit her lip, half smiling and, for the moment, relaxed again. Something in her uneasiness perplexed me; it wasn't quite like Rachel to be so chary about talking.

John rejoined us just then. "Pictures! Yes, I remember that concert very well. He tried to talk Al into joining him on a similar one years before that. You remember that, Rach?"

"Yes, I do," Rachel said, the slightest tone of frost in her voice. "Quite a few years before."

"You know about Al, don't you, Brinsel?" John asked.

"Er . . ." I cued myself to look inquiringly at Rachel.

But it was the wrong moment. Her eyes were fixed on her husband, misgiving freezing her features. He was staring at her insistently, his eyes unflinching, hers hissing the *John!* she didn't voice. Standing there caught between them, I again had the dreadful impression of the room and everything in it swelling enormously, larger than I could bear, and squeezing me into a tiny space at that moment beset on either side by two towering figures staring each other down.

A violent flush rose in Rachel's face, but she turned to me. "Al," her voice a few tints too bright. "Do you know about Al? Max didn't mention anything . . . ?"

"No, he didn't."

"Well, we can introduce you," John said cheerfully. "Go on, Rach, I'll have the coffee ready when you're done."

Rachel shot him a look he deflected by turning aside. "Well, let's go to my study," she said. "I can show you the pictures."

Rachel's study was down a small hallway in a room facing the rear. A tall window with drawn drapes. Warm earthy colors, neat bookshelves, scatter cushions on wing chairs, an open secretaire with stacked files and papers in pigeonholes and little gewgaws. A bookcase of medical volumes and binders. A framed print of Bearden's *Out Chorus*. She pulled a photo album from a shelf.

"I guess," she said, pausing with the book in her arms, "I guess he didn't tell you much about his history, did he?"

"No, he didn't."

She nodded. "He wouldn't, that's true enough. Well," a slight smile, now shaking her head, her eyes ranging off momentarily, "I think some of it might surprise you then, especially knowing him as you do, with his business and all. It's not the background you'd expect. But we've all had our share of surprises lately, finding out about the letters, and your music and his . . . and all this about the investigation must be quite a surprise for you as well."

"Assuredly, quite."

"You don't mind, do you, if I tell you about Al?"

"Not at all. Who is he?"

"She. I'm sorry, her name was Ariel, and she was someone who was quite close to us, for one." She lay the album on the desk and opened it unhurriedly. "Ariel was his fiancée, ages ago," her gaze crossing my face as though looking for a lost line, then returning to the pages. She passed without comment over black and white photos of a young boy giving flute recitals. Her words came haltingly as though unused to speech. "They were at conservatory together; he discovered her when he was fifteen. She thought he was the scum of the earth, and he thought she could do no wrong." She searched my face again, but now was elsewhere, distant. "They both came around, eventually."

She stopped at a page of small square photos in grainy color. I knew they were there, that I would see them, yet I still stiffened, stifling a gasp, when the photographs of Ariel appeared before my eyes, as though Rachel had shown me there in her study not Ariel but a picture of myself. Rachel's voice softened. "He proposed to her several times, but she wouldn't say yes for the longest time." Another faint smile. "He just lost his head. And she—she had a lot to—overcome."

Rachel's face still betrayed the sudden discomfort it had in the living room, and I was caught between wanting to adjourn the matter there and simply letting her speak.

"They were saving for their own place before getting married. It would have been a bit tight since the Phil didn't pay so much in those days, and he and Ariel were both going to school to boot; he was helping pay her tuition on top of everything. Ariel convinced him to go to school, she felt he should think about more of the world than music." Rachel's voice was without bitterness.

I knew everything; it was so hard to cue myself, not to speak for her. "The Phil?"

"The Philharmonic. His first career."

"Of course, the picture you showed me. You mean he was with the symphony then?"

"Oh, yes." She couldn't hide her pride. "He was seated as principal when he was sixteen. He was the youngest player the orchestra's ever had."

"He must have been a prodigy."

She nodded; for an instant she stiffened again. "Yes, he was that. He was all about the flute and music. Then there was Ariel, and he didn't seem to know there was a world for a while, or other people in it. His world was Ariel and the orchestra." A small, intense silence. "The two things he never talked about. So . . . I'm not really surprised he didn't tell you about this."

It puzzled me that Rachel was taking such a circuitous route to telling me Ariel had died; then I realized she didn't want to think about it, she simply wanted to remember Ariel, like her brother, the way she had been. And she had been lively, dramatic, no quiet cutout. Even in a picture near the end of her life, the self-possession in her face was so severe it was frightening, sharpened by a defiance that made the softness and warmth of her eyes appear more, not less, vulnerable. She was relaxed on the Cunninghams' sofa beside her fiancé, at ease and smiling, yet her countenance an open argument with the world, its glimmer of trust reserved only for him and those closest him. Max was twenty-two, an esteemed and successful professional, a very young face full of grand unbroken dreams. The happy eyes, the grin, his posture all speaking not a little of the casual arrogance of youth, in his self-confident air the presumption that his own grasp of things would always be sufficient to parse the world. Thus far, it had seemed to be working.

"Dad was so thrilled. He was music director at the time." An edge of irony had slipped into her voice. From the twenty years she had been gazing across, she pulled her gaze back and met mine. "I guess you've heard a little about Dad?"

I shook my head.

"Well, that's alright. He's a composer, and he just retired from directing the Philharmonic a few years ago. He's gotten quite well known."

"What was his name, now?"

"Richard Thompson? You know, he composed the *Bow River Suite* and the *Piano Variations on a Theme of Marchand?*"

She hummed a few bars helpfully, but I thumbed my lip and shook my head once more, and she laughed. "How about that. I guess it's only the past few years he's been at all well known, but things did get hot very quickly. It was just after Max joined the Phil that the ball really got rolling." After a slight pause which I didn't miss, "Max loved it, but I sometimes wondered if he wasn't there just as much to . . . well, prove something to Dad. But it was that one, though," nodding at the pictures of Ariel, "that one that made him so great, and that one that he stayed for. He could have gone off as a soloist after Horton, but he wouldn't move away from her."

We were looking at a picture of Ariel, about twenty, accompanying Max on a concert tour. They were standing in the midst of a bevy of post-performance excitement in the green room of a concert hall somewhere, Max in tails and Ariel in a black dress that said *look at me*. He was looking at her, with great satisfaction, great tenderness. Rachel gestured at her brother, "Just look at that goofball. You would never guess he had just gotten a ten-minute standing ovation and three encores."

I asked as gently as I could do: "Why did he leave?"

Rachel pressing her fingers across the plastic over the picture as if she could touch what was in the images. "Ariel died very suddenly when she was twenty-one. It was just one of those things; they weren't sure then, but it seems she had an undiagnosed heart condition."

"Oh, my dear. I'm so sorry."

"She was such a sweet girl . . . Not a lump of sugar, she had bite to her. But great charm, great liveliness." Rachel let go of the album. When her voice came again, she had retreated once more, but three years this time instead of twenty. "When she died, Max was . . ." She closed her mouth firmly, her eyes going flat. "It was all a mess," she mumbled. "I'm sorry."

Her head dropped, and she dabbed her eyes. Then, almost too quickly, she turned to me, at once composed. For the first time, her face had something in it more than calm or stiffness, more than the glimmer of friendliness, and something so like her brother that I felt myself shrinking inside. But unlike Max, she was staring at me with unapologetic curiosity, and being able to guess the shape of her interest I was frantically manufacturing an arsenal of answers. But she simply said, "You know, I have Max's flute."

"My word," I stammered, all thoughts abandoning me.

Every object in the room quavered like a drawing whose paper had moved beneath it. Max's flute. The flute he had played almost every single day, that had been by his side for almost thirty years.

Which, until almost that moment, I hadn't quite grasped really existed.

Rachel slid back the doors of a glass-paneled cabinet beside her desk and drew out a scuffed black leather case embossed with a scrolling silver M, set it gently on the desk, and flipped the clasps open.

The light of the desk lamp leapt on its silver the instant the flute appeared, but it was as if another light had suddenly blossomed in the room. There it was: Max's offset G concert flute, its three silver pieces nestled in a threadbare bed of velvet Prussian blue. A professional Muramatsu—I had never seen one in person—solid silver, with open holes and French pointed arms and a B foot, and the tone holes soldered. Rachel was assembling it with studied attention, deftly, and there it was in her hands, a long beam of silver light dotted with the magic buttons of its keys. She held it to me with reverence.

A frisson of something like terror shot through me the instant the metal touched my hands, all coolness but presence like something alive. In one sense, nothing could have been more unremarkable than that slight instrument; yet, even silent, the significance and beauty of it were all out of proportion to its heft and size. No one will get very exercised about a writer's pen, and visual artists are so motley a lot, the only tool they definitively have is the urge to make, but a musician is an interpretive artist and almost without exception, identified with a particular instrument, a particular sound. This flute was the unique instrument that had borne Max's genius and was now charged with his legend.

In my head if nowhere else, I had heard the light pour out of this, out of *this*. "Pure gold ore out a silver shell," the critics had gushed. "A wealth of spontaneity and personality; he speaks direct from the heart with utter candor." "A magician of sound, he has perfected the alchemy of air and spirit, spinning from nothing masterpieces of incandescent glory." "We have not heard anything like him since Barrère." "*Die original Zauberflöte*." "Nothing short of genius." How could one describe such a sound, and all that lay behind it? There are some things that bear no words. *This* instrument, in his hands, had prompted no end of acclaim, and after Ariel the acclaim had ceased to mean anything at all.

"He had a few others," Rachel broke into my thoughts. "A very fine Haynes, an alto and a bass, and one of Boehm's first flutes, and ... others ..." The wistfulness, and the loss, forming the words so that her voice seemed secondary.

"I don't know much about flutes," I apologized.

"He had some of the very finest that are made, and he gave them all away or sold them." Rachel brushed her fingers in the case lining. "He'd been going to have a career; he'd started to tour when he was with the Phil," her voice a jumble of pride and regret. "He had a great partnership with a pianist from Horton, but *everyone* loved to work with him, he just had that charisma, and especially the chops. So many works were written for him ... He was always wanted for something, even later on. We always expected he would go back to performing for good," her gaze resting on the long beam of light in my hands. "He never gave up his business like I hoped he would. He was just a weekend concert artist, which was pretty crazy ... and he never stopped playing."

No one had played it in over three years. It was burning in my hands, white fire, wanting to be played. No one was going to; no one could do.

"Thank you," I said, handing it back to her. "Thank you."

She received it as carefully as she might an infant, holding it close for a moment. "Sometimes if I close my eyes," she said softly, "I can still hear him. No one ever sounded like him!" The small gesture of taking his instrument apart was, in her hands, a secret dialogue that took far longer than necessary; at last the case disappeared back into the cabinet. "We have Max's music, too. I bet you'd like to see that!"

Between the marriage that hadn't happened and the career that hadn't happened, there was almost too much vicarious regret in the room to budge an inch. I greedily agreed to look at something chancier.

Gratified, Rachel pulled from the cabinet a large, sloppy folder bound with an elastic band, and spread it carefully on her desk. Handwritten notes and sheets, published folios, manuscript pages of jotted notation scribbled with comments. "It's not all of it, Dad's got the rest, but this is the bulk." She quickly sorted the papers and drew my attention to a draft score thickly worked over with scribbling and corrections.

"This is it, the one that has the same music as what you wrote."

Yes, this was it. As I had once thought I alone had written it; they did not know that my entire piece matched his, and not one section only. I had called my piece *London Spring;* Max had originally titled his the same but had canceled it with a few decisive strokes, leaving his work nameless. Was that when he had found my music?

"I wanted to show you this in particular. We could talk about it some other time, but since you're here now, well, I needed to show this to you, because we've hit a bit of a problem. Dad and I spent several months working on it after Max died . . . It gave us something to accomplish, because nothing else was happening. It wasn't until after we'd gotten the proofs back that Peter was finally able to tell us about you and the music he had found. He didn't know it was the same, but when we looked at it, we recognized it. So we decided to stop press until we could talk with you about it, because of the legal matters that have to be cleared up. What our publisher would really like is proof that Max didn't take from your work, and for that, they'd like to see a notarized copy of your composition. We can already attest to the date of these drafts. Your dates would settle the matter for them."

"My composition . . ."

And with that, I knew, I knew as though I had known from the first, what I needed to do with my work. It was not complicated; it appeared to be the only avenue open to me, but not truly having a choice in the matter did not simplify it.

"It's quite out of print. I suppose I could look for one at home, but you want this soon, don't you? I can contact the publisher. I'll . . . I will have them send you a letter with the date and whatever else they have got."

"Thank you so much." Her eyes brightened in gratitude. "That'll be a big relief. The only thing left is how similar it is to your work . . ."

"Oh no, don't change it, that's not necessary. Please do go ahead and publish it. It doesn't matter to me that it's the same music, there is no question in my mind that he wrote it on his own inspiration."

She was beaming. "We would like to put you down as a composer."

"Please, you needn't do that, he wrote it himself and he should receive the credit for it. That the music is the same—don't worry about that. Mine has been out of print for so long I doubt if anyone even knows it exists." But whose music was it anymore, his? Mine? Nobody's?

And then I realized what was happening. It was not only one piece of music I was giving up. It was the entitlement to call anything I had ever made my own work and mine alone.

For a dizzying instant, the world vanished into swirls of darkness so intense I could not tell where the earth lay or which way I might fall, like balancing on a chair with two legs too short. It felt like hours before I knew

I was still breathing and I gasped a few deep breaths until I could see the music in my hands once again.

Rachel clasped my hand, not realizing the earth had jolted beneath me. "Thank you, Brinsel."

"It is no problem at all. If someone raises trouble for you, they'll have me to deal with." I lumped the words quickly together, fixing my eyes on Max's handwriting. "I would love to hear this, I've never had a chance—I've never heard it, I mean . . ."

"That's just it! There's a special concert to premiere some of Max's work this summer, and we wanted to include this. So now you *should* get a chance."

But did I truly wish to hear it? What would that cost me?

Everything was happening five and six paces beyond what I could manage. I had once had all the leisure of private discovery to write about these things, but now objects and information were thrust upon me at a speed that was all too much like the rest of life. Rachel was probably satisfied—tiresome business out of the way. I was giddy and overwhelmed, neither able to direct matters nor handle them, and unable to communicate that I most wished the world simply to slow down for a bit.

In the living room we found John with the newspaper pulled apart in his lap. Rachel leaned over and kissed him. "We're back," a small ire in her voice. "Coffee not ready yet?"

"Oh," he waved towards the kitchen, returning the kiss. "Everything's all set."

Rachel gestured to me to make myself comfortable. "Have a seat, Brinsel, I'll get you a cup."

One of the Cunninghams' wing chairs all but swallowed me as I sat. John grinned at me, and I half-smiled, half relaxing. After the bewildering upset with Ariel's photos and Max's music, John's presence was a solid and dependable landmark, safe and doggedly friendly. He was as enormous as his wife, but where she had height he had brawn, burly hands and a bulbous nose and a frame that more evoked an American footballer than a career mechanic. He could fill half the room without meaning to, unlike Rachel who could fill more than half by height and nerviness and sheer domination, both of them unlike the even taller Max, who had given life to a room like a plant, so quietly he could have been present and remained unnoticed.

John folded up the paper and tossed it on the table, a crimp of black grease on one sleeve cuff a signature of his livelihood. I remembered when he had worn his hickory hair in a shaggy mane to his shoulders; it had been cropped short for some time and now I noticed how thin and grayed it had become. I had been thinking of him as the young father of two little girls, but he had become a middle-aged man well in his forties with two teenagers to leave home in a few years. "So, Brinsel, did she educate you about Ariel, life, the universe?"

I unhooked my attention from the sound of dishes tinking down the hallway. "Yes, she showed me the pictures of Ariel. I had never . . . It was like seeing a whole different part of Max, especially as he never mentioned her."

John nodded thoughtfully. "Yes, he didn't talk about her. I'm glad Rachel shared all that with you. Ariel was someone important to us." He smiled. "I always remember Rachel saying she made it easy for me because Ariel made it so hard for Max."

"Hard for him? How?"

"Well, the story is she didn't really like him in the beginning . . ."

Rachel brought in a tray with three cups and saucers, and a plate of sugar biscuits. "I've got some for you too, hon, your usual." She set the tray lightly on the coffee table and handed us our brimming cups, perched on saucers with a scrolling rose trim: her mother's china. "We went through Max's music," she reported, dropping into a chair. She brushed her flyaway hair behind her ear with one hand and pushed her cup to her lips with the other. "And about the concert this summer."

"Wonderful," John brightened, turning to me. "You could come with us."

"Where do I ring for tickets?" I asked.

"Tickets!" Rachel, her cup jumping scandalized on her saucer. "You'll be our guest. We've got a box we'd love to share."

"Thank you." I cradled my cup in both hands. "I am so looking forward to it."

"And," Rachel lowered her voice, addressing John, "we can present the duplicate piece. Brinsel has given her permission for us to publish it."

"Thank you for that, Brinsel," John said at once. "We haven't known what to do about it."

"You're welcome." I flushed the same rose as the décor on the china. Rachel took some biscuits from the plate and passed it to me.

"Peter told us about the correspondence you and Max had." Rachel smiled small and wistful, the stiffness flickering across her face. "That in itself is phenomenal to me; the idea of Max having a correspondence is just wild. No one ever knew about you. My brother was very good at keeping secrets."

"Did he ever share with you any of his music?" asked John.

"I'm not sure anymore," I pressed my thumbs on the saucer's rim, trying to breathe a bit slower. What would be the most foolish thing to say, and how could I avoid it? "I believe he might have. He did mention that he composed. I wonder what I should have thought, if I had known of *London Spring*—that is, I mean . . ." I fiddled with the teaspoon.

"He never did tell *us* about it," said Rachel. "All we know is what he wrote on your music. Peter showed it to you?"

I nodded. I thought of the creased, colored sheet Peter had handed me. The only thing that clearly connected it to me was a pencil scrawl in Max's handwriting that had read *"from LS © B? 1987 composed by—Brinsel Thomas."* How had he known what publisher to write to?

"You ought never have heard of me. My work is too insignificant by half." I frowned. "I don't understand how he came by it."

Rachel brushed away the topic with a nod. "Well, I'm glad it turned out to be a quiet night here. We're not known for being the quietest house on the block."

"That's because," said John, "the double-trouble aren't here tonight."

Rachel explained, "Jill and Lynn are at a friend's house for a graduation party."

"Jill and Lynn?"

"Our daughters, they're a matched set," John, very cheerfully. "Two for the price of one."

"What would *you* know about that?" Rachel teased him. To me: "It's a friend's party, not their graduation just yet; they have two more years to go. They've just had their sixteenth birthday this week."

"They must be twins?"

"From day one," John nodded. "And can't seem to do without each other. They are always helping each other out of trouble, and into it."

"It's either music or trouble right after the other," added Rachel. "Since school is out next week, it'll just get worse around here. But we get a reprieve later on; they're both off to orchestra camp at the end of July. They'll be back in time for Max's concert in August."

"You have family, Brinsel?"

John's voice was utter friendliness and courtesy. We were talking about family, and this was common polite conversation; they had certainly seen my ring and wanted to be courteous. But I still flinched. Something caught in my throat and I burst out coughing. I let go the spoon and it shouted on my saucer. "I'm sorry," I said instinctively, rather pointlessly.

I diverted myself with some coffee, trying to hide my flush behind the safety of the cup's rim. Fantastic! Embarrass one's hosts. And what *would* Max do in such a pickle? Subtly change the subject. And I wasn't Max, and could see less and less how I ever could have pretended I was.

I had spent all of two grueling seconds arguing with myself in this way, my insides setting up into intricate knots, that it was desperation, not impatience, that made me set down the cup and blurt, "They do have the suspect in custody, do they not?"

Rachel visibly paused and glanced from John to me. "I believe so."

"Peter knows most about it," said John. "We know enough."

"Please," I said, fraying in pitch, "believe me, I shall do everything in my power for you."

Rachel straightened, her face pinching. "Of course we believe you!"

"You don't know what it would mean to me. I mean, it would mean so much to me for you to have justice. If I can do the smallest thing to achieve that conviction, I shall do it!"

John said gently, "We are so pleased you want to help, Brinsel."

"Just the same," pressed Rachel eagerly, "I'm relieved you're a normal person! We kept thinking you were something like another detective until Peter found you."

They had snatched back the conversation so quickly that it took even less time for me to realize I had been approaching inhospitable decibels. And something—Rachel's tone, John's kindness, the scramble of topics—was sounding warning bells for me. I pushed the feeling aside.

If I had hoped for the evening to accomplish anything, by the time it came for John to drive me back all I could think was that I had succeeded in forfeiting one copyright, derailing the conversation at least twice, and alarming and embarrassing my hosts. I was so absorbed in my failures, and John's presence, however new, was so overly familiar and unthreatening, that I spent several minutes of the ride home ignoring him entirely.

"It's good that you've come tonight, Brinsel," John said kindly as he turned onto the highway. "Rachel has needed to talk about Max. She hasn't talked much about him since it happened."

"Ah, yes." And for a moment I cringed as though something had been my fault.

We drove in silence for a while. Then, "Rach is quite taken with you," he said. "She is convinced that you have an innate connection with Max."

"I hope so," I said, cringing further. "I hope she is right."

Ms. Brinsel Thomas
Bwthyn Stella Maris
Strand Lane
Wimsey
Bristow Surrey
RH7 9JP
UK

May 28, 1987
* Thomas Moore (1779)

Dear Ms. Thomas,
Thank you very much for your letter. I was very pleased—well, I was thrilled to receive the music you sent, and your courteous response. I'm grateful my letter was sent on to you, for I was hoping very much to contact you personally. I have already played all the music you sent several times and I am itching to take it to some friends of mine who would really like it. It's too bad there is no American publisher yet, as I think this music could do very well here; perhaps we can come up with something.

May I ask what inspired you to write the title piece of London Spring? I can hear the whole city in it, but I can also hear the sea.

I admit I am curious about all your work now. In your letter, you mentioned some prints you were working on. May I ask what these are? I would be very interested in seeing some of your other work; I am assuming it is also published by Waterhouse, at least I will start with that. I apologize if my inquiring isn't welcome, but your music has really intrigued me. (I was especially taken with On Caernarfon which was so jaunty and catchy I had it stuck in my head for a week, and made me go look at a map.) Am I correct in guessing you are from Wales?

I just can't say how pleased I am to have some of your music at last. Music is my lifeblood, and what a privilege to be able to play such beautiful things. Thank you so much again; I hope, if it is not too importunate of me, you will reply again.

   con guibilazione
   Maximilian Thompson

6

Good Shepherd

Art must be believed in absolutely to be done at all. No religion—political, scientific, or otherwise—requires more unquestioned faith, demands more blind obedience or brooks less doubt and waffling than that tremendous mystery known as the creative process. That I was now stuck in the midst of something I had previously only recognized as art, was tempted to disbelieve all of it, and nonetheless was compelled to play along, did not go far towards helping me deal with it.

Somehow, I had let Rachel persuade me to come to Good Shepherd with them on Sunday. I had wanted to visit anyways for research, but I was having doubts, and they were much more practical than anything to do with art.

In his life Max had been at Good Shepherd for two reasons: unquestioned routine and questioning struggle, and it had become a joke between him and Felix that he was there to conduct an investigation. The struggle was not to do with any tenets of faith, unless forgiveness was one; his greatest challenge had been not allowing himself an exception to that. My problem, of the moment, was not forgiveness, as practical as that was. The first problem was worshipping in such a distracting place: every boss and spandrel and everybody's hat or the chips in the tile or the nicks in the pews were suddenly new simply for being real and tangible, and claimed far more of my attention than anything of the spirit. Even the music was as I had known—Richard having prevailed upon the previous music director that the Mass settings in the hymnal were "insulting to the ear and spirit," and imposed his own, and no one had been able to dislodge them since. They were all lined up in the bulletin for me to gape at, and I quite forgot to prepare for Eucharist.

Then there were hazards of another sort.

Midway through the processional hymn, a voice made me glance up, and I nearly lobbed my hymnal into a woman in the next pew. There among the altar party strode Richard Thompson in a surplice, his eyes fixed on the open hymnal in his hands and his booming tenor carrying over the rising sound of even the congregation. I lost my place listening to that voice. All I could think of was a voice I never would hear, which nevertheless had sounded remarkably like it.

I completely lost all pretense of worship after that, however, for as I scanned the faces in the choir, my heart jumped: the twins.

The last time I had imagined them, they had been no older than thirteen. When I had written about them, they had been five and seven and ten. Somehow I had neglected to imagine them as the two giants I picked out in the choir. The two little girls I had known had become two tall young women whose identical faces, still girlish, were beginning to fill out: in their choir albs, only the style of their hair distinguished them. Lynn with her tawny hair pulled into a French plait, somewhat frayed. Jill, content with tying her hair back in a ruffled scrunchie. They had grown nearly a foot each in the past few years; they were now a few inches shy of six feet and still not done growing.

I spent the rest of Eucharist obsessing over my presence, pretending no one could see me.

Somehow, we arrived at the last hymn, and the altar party processing out. The organ recessional. Richard returning to snuff out the candles. The recessional ended and the congregation applauded, the pews creaking as people gathered handbags and papers, put away prayer books, began filling the aisles. Rachel leaned over smiling. "How did you like it, Brinsel?"

Peter had sat with us also, to my surprise. I could not remember him coming here more than once when Max had been alive; like Ariel, he had never had any use for faith. He had gone ahead with John, talking. I had to sternly check myself from giving the impression I knew how to get to the fellowship hall and followed Rachel meekly as I could do, unwisely trying to make conversation. "I noticed your father was acolyte."

"Why, yes. How did you know it was him?"

"Ah, er . . . well, he looks very much like Max."

"Yes, he does," she admitted. "I guess you saw the girls are in the choir?"

I nodded, dreading what was next.

"I want you to meet them before they run off to class." She paused in the hallway near the sacristy door, and we let people swirl past us. The sight of so many familiar faces dizzied me, and I was doubly unsteady when the twins stepped out of the sacristy one after the other. Lynn swung her gaze round and spotted her mother and me, smiled, and pulled her twin's arm.

Seeing someone in your mind's eye or in a photograph is always quite different from seeing or meeting the person. What I had never grasped about the twins, especially now that they were sixteen, was that they had inherited the Thompson stature. I had seen them towering in the top row of the choir, but now I had to contend with the fact that if they chose, they could comfortably rest their chins on my head. Both were already nearly as tall as Rachel. I was a nymph among the three Graces.

Rachel presented them with the smile only mothers can have. "Brinsel, this is Jill and Lynn." And to them, "This is Brinsel Thomas, who wrote the same music as Max and is helping Peter with the case."

Those two identical faces, the two heads with their father's toffee-brown hair and their mother's dark eyes and slender nose. They were like a repeated word, side by side, and yet even in a glance I could have so easily read the subtleties of tone and emphasis between them: Lynn the verb, Jill the modifier. Lynn smiled shyly with a touch of sweetness, gentle and affable like her uncle. With a definite air of subtlety. "Hello," very quietly, taking my hand with some hesitation.

One of the Graces, however, had mysteriously traded off with a Fury. Jill blinked and said nothing and did not respond when I reached to shake her hand, her gaze cutting coldly across mine and then fixing on some point behind me. Her usual warmth and casualness nowhere in evidence, her mouth set in a fine line, and the air around her slightly frosted.

I was perplexed; this was not the vivacious and self-assured Jill I knew. I caught a thin, sharp sigh from her mother: it was not the Jill she had intended to present, but, it appeared, the one she had unwillingly expected.

"It's such a pleasure to meet you," I ventured. "I saw your pictures when I visited yesterday, but now I get to see you. You're much taller than I thought."

"It runs in the family," said Lynn. "I don't think we'll grow out of it."

I smiled, Rachel laughed, and Jill bristled.

Lynn asked, "Did you know you were in Max's seat?"

"No," surprised, not because I had not known, but because it had not occurred to me. "I am sorry."

"Oh, don't worry," Lynn assured me. "He wouldn't mind."

But it seemed Jill did; she did not simply stiffen, she froze rigid as flint. Her face went from unwilling to adamant.

"All right, go on you two," sighed Rachel. "We'll see you later. Try not to be so *cheerful*, Jillian."

Rachel was stung with embarrassment and tried to smooth over any I might have. "This isn't like her at all, I hope you'll get to meet the *real* Jill another time."

I didn't know where to situate Jill's coldness on the map of my bewilderment and, overwhelmed by confusions closer to hand, pushed the question entirely aside. In the fellowship hall I dutifully took a cup of coffee and a piece of cake. Rachel steered me back through the chatting groups to find some free chairs and moored me safely in one. "I'll be right back, I want to get Dad."

With so little time to brace myself, I spent it scrambling for distraction: the bookcases against the western wall; the rogue's gallery of previous rectors dating themselves by spectacles and cut of hair; all the milling parishioners of today. Then my ears caught a voice echoing from down the corridor. Footsteps. And Richard Thompson entered the room, followed closely by his daughter.

He was speaking to Rachel but trailed off when his eyes lit on me. Almost bashfully—not ever a trait I could associate with him—but with his habitual command of presence, he approached me at once and extended his hands. I stood, utterly self-conscious, letting him take my hand and surprised to feel in his trepidation and a slight trembling.

Richard was where his children had got their stature, and I was just truly discovering it. My crown scarcely reached his shirt pocket, and I had a front-row view of the bifocals clipped to it. *This* was how tall Max had been. "Oh, my God," I gasped. "Oh, my God."

"Oh!" he laughed nervously. "I'm just a composer, really, nothing grand! I've been wanting to meet you for so long, Ms. Thomas, and it's a pleasure to make your acquaintance at last."

I managed to get out: "Please, you can call me Brinsel, Mr. Thompson."

"Thank you, Brinsel, and please, call me Richard." A smile that was literally a much older version of Max's. The hair on the back of my neck prickled wildly.

Max had had more of his mother's softness of voice and visage, to say nothing of manner, but had still possessed his father's edge. I could see in Richard what Max might have become—authoritative, a venerable old master, an exuberant and influential icon. And I could see in Richard something of what Max might have looked like had he lived longer—much weathering, the brown flop of his hair graduated to silvery gray, the deep lines in his cheeks. They both had the same intense eyes and the same dark sleepless rings around them. And I could see in Richard what Max had not been and never would have been.

I couldn't seem to absorb the fact of his presence. He was a giant of the music world, a tireless and inspired composer, an inspiring and energetic leader of more than one orchestra. He had more successful recordings to his credit, several of them his own compositions, than my typewriter had keys. He had nurtured the Philharmonic from its undistinguished beginnings and ushered it onto the world stage. He had garnered dozens of national-level awards for his work as well as honorary degrees from a handful of prestigious universities happy to be associated with his name. He had worked with most of the greatest artists in music of his day. He was as big as the cinema, and I, a mere patron who happened to be in the theater.

"I've been wanting to meet you, Brinsel, and it's good to have you here with us at last. Peter told us about your correspondence with my son."

I nodded to acknowledge the lie, ignoring the request behind it. "I saw you were acolyte. Rachel had said you were a musician, and I had imagined you might do something musical at Eucharist."

"It's my day off today," he returned happily, hooking his thumbs in his belt and swelling up like a robin. "I do work some with music here, but mostly I try to keep my hands off."

"What is it you do?"

"Well, in theory I'm retired, but I like to do a little of this and that, nothing too much. I've mostly been teaching, and I do a little conducting still, and give recitals now and then."

"You conduct? You're a conductor?"

Now a grin. "That was how I made a living for many years. Can you imagine?" He lifted his hands, and it was too easy to imagine. "This big acolyte, waving a stick around?"

"Oh, you were with an orchestra?"

"Yes, I directed our Philharmonic for a good many years, and then they had enough of me and I retired." He crossed his arms jovially. "What is it you do, Brinsel?"

I explained myself as an unknown writer and artist who had vague delusions of being a musician, and he laughed.

"That's right, you and my son wrote the same music . . ." He rubbed his chin and gazed at me with the same air of deliberation he would give a puzzling score.

I sensed Richard, for any desire to meet me, didn't know quite what to do with me. The investigation which had announced my existence to the Thompsons further deepened the mystique of my presence. I stood in the curious position of representing to him—and to all of them, and even to myself—a part of Max none of them had known.

I spotted another familiar face come into the room, glance round, and come at once over to where I had ended up by Rachel. Pastor Felix, large and affable and utterly familiar . . .

"It's so good to meet you, Brinsel," he said warmly. "I've been hearing about you from Rachel for months, and now here you are with us."

"Ah, it seems everybody knows me!"

"Well, a friend of Max is a friend to all of us."

Felix's character had always intrigued me. His was a very solid presence, yet quite unlike Richard's. Felix radiated a sensitivity and peace and serenity one wanted to find in the clergy and seldom seemed to. He sat comfortably with divine mysteries, including all the mystery of people, and uncomfortably with theories and talk and excessive liturgical bother. I wanted to stay and speak with him, but the parish closed in on me.

As I had feared, every other mildly cultured extrovert wanted to speak with me about a place called Londonoxfordcambridge, and every mildly cultured introvert, to mention their travels in England or even Eire, if any. From behind the typewriter such characters had been under my thumbs; it was all very well to smile at the spoof when I didn't have to be subject to it, but there was no escape now. Trapped, I made myself listen to the extroverts tell me all they knew about Oxford, etc., and the introverts tell me all I didn't know about England or Eire. I'd read at Cardiff, not Cambridge, and in past years spent as little time in England as I could, but these were facts that never got a chance to pass my lips. No one had been to Wales and no one asked me about it, and I congratulated myself on being disillusioned that no one seemed to care it existed, either.

Some wanted to discuss politics, a subject I never fail to maintain total ignorance about no matter what or how assiduously I read on it. The very well-read Allen Clark tried. "So, how are you finding John Major?"

"I'm not, really," I admitted. "Who is he, now?"

Then there was the parish administrator, Vicki, an older British woman who had come to read for chemical engineering at a local university years before. A job had been waiting for her back home. She met and fell in love with Henry Price at Good Shepherd. Got married and the rest was history. Rachel made the introductions, making me wish I'd had the wits to say less the evening before.

". . . And she is a Reader," Rachel raved, in complete innocence. Vicki's eyes widened.

"Oh, how wonderful. We can have you preach!"

"I'm not *licensed* to work in this diocese," I lunged at the first excuse. "And you know how these things go, it would take months to get, and then I'd have gone."

"Oh, you wouldn't have to take any services. If you're going to be here it would be lovely if you could be a part of the parish somehow. It just so happens we're needing someone to read the Epistles this summer. Don't you think you'd like to do that?"

I didn't rather and looked to Rachel, but she thought this was a fantastic idea too and didn't grasp I wanted rescuing. "Oh, no, my accent is *so* . . ."

"Nonsense, it will do beautifully. You see, I've still got one, and they take me just the same."

"No, no, *quite* honestly, truly, I *couldn't* do, you see I . . ."

Laughter. "There you go, I know you Celts! You yes your nos and no your yeses. You'll do splendid, really, and it will be a great opportunity for the parish."

Vicki, her radiant smile and businesslike efficiency enough to charm a nun into heels and to stupefy me into acquiescence. I wondered if she could do anything for my editor. "I'll see Ellen about setting up the schedule. It'll be a treat for the parish and a good change. We just found yesterday our regular lector shall be away for the summer and been wondering what to do."

How convenient of me to appear. A parish of 780 souls could not cough up a secondary lector in the presence of an exotic visitor. When Vicki turned aside, I anxiously plucked Rachel's sleeve. "Rachel, are you quite certain I should do this? Is there not—I mean, I had thought, I mean, is this sort of thing not done by the parishioners on rota? I don't want to interfere with the parish's arrangements."

"Oh, it's no problem! And you'll be fine, it's no intrusion, really. We love having guests, and it'll be great to have you a part of things here."

Being a part of things whether I wished to or not was becoming a lamentable theme in my life.

Perhaps it was her transparency, the unconscious transparency of them all, that blackly underlined to me that, among them, simply being myself was not an option. I had to play the role they had called me for, both for my own sake and theirs; in order to let *them* be real, I couldn't be the real Brinsel Thomas, the one I had known. I had to be the one Max had singled out—who, paradoxically, was both.

The classes had let out. At the door to the hallway, flooded with children of all sizes, a striped-shirted crot of a boy tugged at my shirt and gravely asked his burning question: "Are there really WHALES in your church?"

"Whales?"

"Mrs. Cun'ham said you come from the Church of *Whales*. Do you really got whales in your church?"

"It would be fantastic if there were, wouldn't it? We'd get to have our service on the sea. But we aren't that lucky. Wales is only the name of my country."

A very perplexed look. "But Mrs. Cun'ham said you came from *England*."

"Well," I said unconvincingly, "well, yes, and no."

I had taken the bus earlier but agreed to let the Cunninghams take me home. Jill had not changed her mind about the intense displeasure I gave her; she slouched in the back seat and glared, engrossed in a fit of pique so intense I almost rolled the window down to let in some fresh air. Behind me her mother kept up a stream of insouciant chattiness with John and myself that only partly defused the atmosphere.

At my building Rachel let me out and piled into the front seat. "Take care," she called after me, "and have a good week."

I watched them drive off, feeling very odd, as though I were still watching them through someone else's eyes.

7

Ariel

After a night dreaming of whales and churches, and of Jill, surly and adolescent, nightmarishly encamped in my office, I decided Good Shepherd was no place for research. If it was the only place here that had any actual connection with the world I had left behind, this was all the more reason nothing there could possibly help me find what I needed.

I had come for research, and research I would do. Investigation was to do with gathering information and making sense of it. Finding out facts. That had been, more or less, my original intention in coming: to explore the actual places I had set a fictional story. Things were not working as planned.

Even my diversions were going awry. When packing for my months' long sojourn, I had included a handful of things that experience proved I should not have and which made themselves useful by being concrete aide memoires of what not to bring. Ironically, this inconvenience also inspired me with a wild hope. If the critical piece of paper I was missing was not with me, then it *had* to be somewhere back at home. I could ask Dai to go look for it. I telephoned him at once at work; he was away, but I left a long, detailed message on his answerphone and begged him to ring me. The thought of the paper I needed being *somewhere* versus simply missing, and the possibility of getting it, was heartening. And Dai could find almost anything.

Tuesday morning dawned clear and mild, the early June sky brushed with cirrus. I pushed open the windows and let the morning inside, the sound and smell of traffic flowing in with it. I was going out.

Jackson was one of six streets in a northern district laid out with trees and wide pavements. Like those in the middle of town, the buildings were older but well kept, predominantly apartment blocks and small businesses, a few hotels and restaurants. The block of flats where Max had lived for eleven years stood two buildings from the corner, four stories high, surrounded by other blocks of varying heights. Number 3A, 1612 North Jackson Street. Somebody else was living there now; I had to be content with looking up at the windows.

That was when I saw the sign. FOR RENT. I looked down the street, then back at the sign with its red telephone number.

Dominique Perez came over within half an hour. Dark and buxom and all dynamite, constantly flashing her gorgeous smile of white teeth as though I could not do without seeing them one more time. She unlocked the door to 1612 and led me up to the second story without once stopping to take a breath.

". . . long did you say you will be here Ms. Pierce we've just had this apartment renovated nicely I think you'll be *very* pleased it has a nice view of the park the neighborhood is so *nice* I would live here too if I didn't live over . . ."

The door to Max's flat. Dominique snapped it open, excitedly beckoning. I followed, hesitating every step.

It was like walking in on him on a typical evening. He breezed into the small entryway carrying a bundle of post, passing the boot crate, slinging his jacket and brolly on the coat pegs, flipping through the post, up the narrow passage which opened on the left to the sitting room with its windows overlooking the street . . .

". . . you can see the trees over there Ms. Pierce I always thought the stairs were worth it for an apartment like this we have had the windows reglazed also and over here is the kitchen isn't it a *peach* . . ."

. . . to the right into the kitchen, with its windows looking out on the rear of the block on the next street, and a glimpse of the thin green sliver that was Beaumont Park, quickly sorting the bills and junk mail before leaving these on the kitchen table, then straight ahead to the two small rooms of the flat with the bathroom and toilet sandwiched between them.

". . . we've even had the bathroom redone it used to be gray and blue tiles and I think the green is much better don't you think this is the master bedroom it's also been repainted the walk-in closet is *ten* square feet and you can see the window gives a lot of light . . ."

In his bedroom and studio he dropped his briefcase on the floor and his flute case on the bed, pulled off his shoes, and paused for the first time; he selected from the small bookshelf a legal handbook, two folders of sheet music, and his tabbed and worn Book of Common Prayer, and sat in the rocking chair with one ankle propped up on a knee, books spread out in his lap and reading specs pushed down on his nose like his father. Seated, he was now beneath my gaze, and regarding him like this, I suddenly had a quite different grasp of scale: his shoes on the floor as big as boats, his hands as big as cabbage leaves—he had truly understood little of just how large he was, and I saw I had not, either. After a while, he put the prayer book on the bureau by Ariel's clarinet case and tossed the handbook onto his bed. He gathered up the sheet music, pulled a tie out of the closet and draped it over a hook on the closet door, and slapped the sheet music on the music desk by the window. Stacks of music sat on the shelf under the window; at times, if he was working on something that bothered him, a file from work would end up here with the music, incongruous but at hand, though only music was there at the moment.

His character didn't permit useless decoration; in every room, everything on the wall was a sign, put up in order to read over and over. Near the window was a framed picture of Ariel from the time of their engagement, which sometimes would be propped against her clarinet case. *Whose I am.* A crucifix on the wall by the bureau. *I am everyone*—a sign he had often argued with. By the door was a particularly precious gift: a small, framed drawing of himself playing flute, done by Lynn when she was three. She had come only to his knee and so had rendered her six-feet-four-inch uncle with a tiny head and big button eyes and a scribble of hair, enormous hands and feet, his figure wonderfully elongated, perhaps wearing tails. The flute a rod almost as long as the figure was tall and covered with thumbprint-sized keys, his long fingers curving over them. *Who I am.*

". . . and the second bedroom also has a walk-in closet this window has just been replaced and the finish is also redone . . ."

In his work-room, he snapped open the briefcase on the desk chair and began pulling out files and papers and pieces of equipment. It was going to be a late night hunched over his ledger and going through work brought home from the office, with his industry overseen by a small picture of a staid-faced Saint Maximilian Kolbe. *You can give everything away.* I leaned over him as he sat at the desk, trying to see what file he was looking at, but it was nothing I needed to know. In the closet, he went rooting through another box atop the safe, pausing to push back onto the shelf a winter scarf curling down over the garment bag of his formal blacks. He straightened the framed poster of de Stael's *Musicians*, a happy dash of color and noise and the gift of another friend, hanging on the opposite wall. *Friendship and music are gifts.*

I followed him down the corridor to the kitchen as Dominique chirped nonstop about the *all-new appliances* and that the kitchen had once been *beige* and now it was *mauve*.

He pulled a cookbook, stained and paper-stuffed, from the neatly-arranged shelf beside the refrigerator. The post lay where he had left it in the breakfast nook, and he lay the cookbook beside it and drew back one of the four chairs. Above him on the wall hung an intaglio of Saint Francis Bernardone, the handiwork of a friend, attired not in his tunic but in the clothes of one who lived on the street, rendered in raw, challenging lines. *Souvenir*. The eyes blind, intense and burning as those of an early icon, the hands holding a book of the Gospels upside-down, with the upside-down words: The Gospel of the Lord. Once only a blur of scenery, the image now had the sharpness of a presence, and I shied away. Max did not look at it but went quickly through the post, chose a recipe for dinner, snapped on the small radio by the telephone on the end of the counter, and with a pencil scribbled down a grocery item on the notepad that sat on the telephone directory, then went for some garlic in the hanging basket, pasta in the narrow pantry, a liquid measuring cup, a pot, a knife. A glass, blue plate, no china. Everything always in its place, cupboards and drawers always shut fully. Nothing ever just slapped down, the newspaper at the end of the table always left folded even if he were in a rush. Everything where it belonged, as orderly as a museum, only the labels and glass cases missing.

". . . *isn't* this light beautiful Ms. Pierce this good southern light is the best place for plants and with those three windows you could grow anything I bet you could grow a garden . . ."

Cooking was one thing, but as for plants, he simply couldn't handle them; they never survived here. After dishes he headed to the sitting room opposite and set a disc on the turntable—Emil Gilels, I guessed—from the cabinet crammed with cassettes and LPs, virtually something of everything. He flicked a lamp on and pulled one of his old textbooks off the bookshelf, flipped through it and put it back at the top of a shelf of humor that descended to an ensemble of jacketless biographies, a few pristine gift volumes of poetry and several tattered tomes on psychoacoustics. No art nor literature, but shelves of music and sciences with little consistency of language; the bookcase must have held books in a dozen languages, only half of those he knew. There were pictures on the wall, friends, family; Peter and Eleanor in better days. *We are made by our choices.* A black and white print of a woman at a piano, a face of sharply defined features, clear, prominent eyes, and smiling graciously: his mother Elisabeth. *You must do what you love.* It hung above an upright Kimball Whitney that stood against the stairwell wall, the lid stacked with sheet music, scores, and hymnals, and accompanied by two music desks. He had half an hour before he had to leave to teach a class of his students; he pulled out the bench, tilted up the fallboard and hesitated; he slipped on his reading specs and flipped through a stack of manuscript papers, found the ones he wanted, and began to play. He grabbed a pencil, struck out three lines, and sat with the pencil in his teeth, staring up at a beautiful calligraphy on the wall: *Make me an instrument of Your peace* . . .

When he had last walked out and not returned he had left working drafts on the piano bench. He left an umbrella unfurled behind the door and his mac slung like a second thought on the last coat peg in the entryway. He left his razor on the bathroom sink and a towel folded on the edge of the bath, and various files from work and his checkbook and ledger spread out on the desk in his workroom. He left a balled pair of socks tucked in his work shoes at the foot of his bed, a pressed shirt hanging on the closet door, and a dark blue tie with tiny white print lying across the bureau. He left a schedule of music classes and drafted syllabus on his bed and correspondence from the Philharmonic's artistic director with a calendar of national music festivals tucked in the day planner on his chair. He had forgotten to lower the blinds in the kitchen. He left a spoon in the kitchen sink and his empty mug atop the folded newspaper with the opened post on the kitchen table. He left his reading glasses neatly folded beside the post.

Nothing was left. The flat was empty, there was nothing to look at. Nothing existed to prove that all was as I knew it had been, except the walls, the windows, the wooden and tiled flooring, as sad and richly empty as a Hammershøi interior. I might have walked easily from room to room without opening my eyes, knowing exactly where I was, and only the echoing barrenness would have surprised me. Only my memory held what had been here before, and the memory of the place itself.

He hadn't returned here that last night; as for myself, however I managed to get out of the mess I had landed myself in, there could be no going back to where I had begun, either.

The branch of the state university where Max had spent three-and-a-half years occupied a few blocks just west of downtown, where the grand trees had been blighted years before. A planting of new trees had restored some of the old cachet but failed to redeem the campus; the architecture was, euphemistically, uninspired—it was frankly ugly—and the atmosphere depressing.

The interior of the administrative building corresponded to this dreariness, in spite of the briskly cheery face put on by fluorescent lighting and quasi-institutional décor. Between terms, the flood of students was at ebb tide. I walked slowly, picking out familiar doorways.

Peter had been here also, the socially-slow if quick-witted kid from the inner city. For people, connecting absurdly incongruous points to intelligible ends is called genius; for the universe, it is called a fluke. One had led to Peter's becoming friends with Max, the professional musician who had four sets of black formals in his closet and no social life on campus. They had shared a few classes in common, as well as a mistrust of politics: both had spent those years of the war in Vietnam with their heads down. It was Ariel, angry and unintimidated, who had protested, taken part in marches, and, after her twenty-first birthday added a night in jail to her CV. It was in her character: she had certainly seen enough of unthinking violence and injustice in her life. But it was just as true that she would never have had the courage to do those things without the change Max had brought about in her; and her protesting had been as much against the issue of the war as against the faceless and heartless threat it represented to her newfound security. The fear that came with such powerlessness had been part of her life for as long as she could remember; this was the first time she could object to it, the first time she was strong enough to.

Ariel. All these corridors and classrooms were heavy with the memory of Ariel. As though Max had just walked out the door here for the last time, as though I were still writing about it through his eyes.

In a way, everything had happened because of her. "You should try doing something different," she had told him. "Music doesn't challenge you."

In one sense it was true: music was entirely too easy for him. On the whole, it was a great deal of work, and he worked obsessively at it; there was no question of his potential nor that it fulfilled him, but overall, it did not stretch him very much. His imagination seemed to extend only to music and then drop off into a formless void. Except for musical and technical publications, he was not a great reader, either, a deficiency which scarcely expanded his horizons.

I had reached the library, a lofty box of a room at the end of one wing. Stacks, carts of books, periodicals and scattered chairs, by reputation one of the most inviting rooms, but somehow dull, dusty, lacking a sense of life. The tables spread out by windows looked onto a bald concrete terrace peopled only by a few lonely arbor vitae in pebble dash pots; within, not many students, and most of them older. But there were two young ones: Max and Peter, textbooks spread about untidily. Peter was leafing through a large volume of law, sermonizing in full youthful flood on the necessity of private investigation, and Max was dutifully taking notes—Peter, the earnest performer; Max, the amused dabbler. Peter had found a career, Max a pastime.

That Max had found something to interest him other than music thrilled her; whether or not he did anything with it was beside the point. Certainly nothing was going to become of it; he was innocent of the popular literature and entertainment alike that the field inspired. To him it was a joke, and part of the joke was that the topic merited serious study; it was more interesting to help Peter, the enthusiastic student. Investigation was crosswords, casual puzzles; even his degree work was intended only to help him navigate a future in music. His work and his life was the Philharmonic and Ariel, and as hard as he worked in music, he had never worked harder at anything than to win her.

"For her he would have moved the world," Rachel had observed; and "she had a lot to overcome." Two points on a trajectory that had irremediably plotted the courses of each—perhaps the only two points that mattered. Ariel's history, when she had finally entrusted it to him, was his first encounter with the sort of violence he had hitherto only met on the safe, indifferent ground of hearsay, and the first time he had faced outrage in himself of the kind her history provoked; the outrage, and the impossibility of an outlet for it.

Ariel had found a small and inadequate outlet for herself in her antiwar efforts, her opinions on the call-up and the war in Vietnam colored entirely by the shadow of her father. Max's struggle to forgive Richard for being overbearing was pennies beside the devastation Ariel had inherited, and he would carry her inheritance with him for the rest of his life. His patience and respect had won her trust more completely than anything else ever could do; she had become someone quite different from the defensive girl he had first known. Max, who had never taken to using the words *hard* or *easy*, had admitted Ariel could be *difficult*—and yet they had been absurdly happy, with an unusually adult, mutual trust. Both so inexperienced and with such challenges, they had, by some miracle, become that contradiction in terms, the extraordinarily mature young couple. The world was exciting, full of possibility and potential, his life and future fantastic and secure and in his hand. They had ambitiously set a date for their wedding: it was to be late December, something to temper the bitterness Christmastide had accrued since his mother's Christmas death. They had been ready for anything but what had happened next.

Ariel's, I had forgotten, was the other significant face I would not be meeting; time had erased her so effectively that only a handful of people remembered who she was. This made her voice one I was free to affect if I chose. But I could see no point in writing a conversation in Ariel's voice; it was Max's work I needed to know about, and Ariel had not known of that.

I pulled out a chair at one of the small library tables and, reluctantly, drew a piece of scrap paper from the pile in the middle of the table.

For a few minutes I wrestled with the urge to jump up and walk out. I took a pen out of my satchel and grasped it as if it might do as much, then put the tip to the paper.

"Hello, Ariel."

Nothing, then, "Hello, Brinsel."

I hesitated, then wrote, "How is it you know me?"

"Well, I know Max, don't I? And he knows who you are."

I didn't need reminding. What could I say to her? And what *would* Ariel have said about this?

I pictured her sitting there across from me, elbows on the table and hands unconcerned around her neck, that gorgeous honey-colored hair washing over her shoulders. Sharp hazel eyes, unflinching, quicksilver attentive—they picked up everything about, weighed and measured it, seeing straight through one—and a face surprisingly, for all that she had been through, always rather girlish. But then she had been very young; as with Max, it was her eyes that were old. Their brazen cast echoed in her leonine carelessness, repeated in the challenging thrust of her chin; she had the air of one effortlessly cunning, yet shrewd enough not to show just how cunning. So much strength and resilience hidden under that wry twist of smile, and so much mildness and sweetness, a butterfly shyness no boldness could undo. This was how he had remembered her—almost—the strong one, the fragile one; she was light, and all that such an identification entailed. The person who had at one time known Max better than anyone else ever had. This person who had meant more to him than anyone else in the world, the one person he had been certain he could never live without. The one after whom, there could be no other.

"I'm sorry we haven't spoken before."

"That's alright, there wasn't a need to."

Was there one now?

"Ariel, what do you suppose I should do about Max's case?"

"I would ask him about that."

"I have asked."

"Well then, do what he says. That's his work, he's the one who knows about it."

"He's being rather evasive."

"He's like that, you should know. If you know his tricks, though, you can get through them."

"I find his tactics quite frustrating, and I am supposed to be doing something useful."

"Yes, he's *like* that. But I don't think he'd do it without a reason, not now."

She *would* defend him. But she was still more reasonable than he was. I tried again.

"It's all so muddled. I cannot make head or tail of anything."

"Yeah, and then you have to work with someone like Max. Still, you can trust him. He knows what he's doing."

"And won't breathe a word of what that is to me."

"That's because you're part of it. Think of it like teaching art or music. You can't give *answers*. You can only say so much, and then your student has to discover the rest."

I put the pen down to mull on this, but at once had to pick it up again.

"Brinsel, you did come here to learn something, right?"

"Well, yes, but it wasn't going to be this . . . it's just that I hadn't planned for any of *this*."

"That's life for you."

A jaded twenty-one-year-old. And she was right.

I persisted gloomily, "I cannot see how any of this even can be possible."

A pause. "Why shouldn't it be?"

I couldn't tell her; if I suspended belief in the middle of the conversation, I wouldn't be able to write a word.

"Try to think in terms of what's possible. And think that *anything's* possible."

Perhaps not so jaded. Or in reality, somewhere well beyond jaded. On the other side of disillusion and illusion alike.

"Well, what did he say to you? Didn't he give you any clue?"

That was the other part of the problem. He hadn't said anything to me, because I hadn't been speaking with him. No more than I was conversing with Ariel herself now. "Well, not really . . ."

"I can't believe he wouldn't say *something* that might help."

"I can't remember."

"Try talking with him again."

I cringed. "Easier said than done. It's like talking with a roundabout."

"I know exactly what you mean. But if you keep after him, he'll slip something somewhere. Just listen closely. He's not doing it to be an ass—not this time, he's just got something up his sleeve."

"Yes, a funny bone and a hidden agenda."

"You do want to help with this, right?" The blunt, stop-this-nonsense tone she had used often enough on her fiancé.

"It seems I've not much of a choice."

"But you want to help?"

"I do, if I can help. I just don't know how."

Silence.

"Don't be upset, Brinsel. It's not impossible, no matter how things look."

"I rather wish I had your confidence."

"Well, perhaps if you were standing where I am, you would see it differently. But even if I can't help you, I know Max can."

It seemed too much to ask. Only his memory could help me.

"I wish I could have that in writing," hating the irony.

"If he doesn't, then he'll have me to deal with. But he will, I'm sure of it. You don't think he'd *like* to help you with all this?"

In desperation, "What *is* all this?"

A pause; the words seemed to be fighting with a smile I could not understand. "Maybe that's something you're here to find out."

I couldn't say anything. I sat there with the pen pressed to the paper until a large black dot appeared, and I lifted my hand.

Nothing; neither of us had anything else to say.

I scrawled "thank you" on the bottom, folded the paper and pushed it into my satchel.

I didn't pass a soul on my way out; instead the hallways, at first empty, quickened with memory. The university's barren corridors unfolded in a hall of mirrors: everywhere flashed Ariel's disappearing figure, retold from a thousand sides. I walked faster, breathed faster, but every wall or corner looked cruelly, obstinately identical, even small variations repeating the loop. A posted directory turned out to be nothing more than a long list of *Whys* to every direction. A row of frames in one corridor were all empty. Blank metal doors went only to classrooms. I pelted down another dead end, then staggered to a halt, giddy. Where had I been? Ariel—Ariel—one contorted maze of loss. Had I been nowhere else before? Frantic, I picked over my thoughts. Books. Where? An image of stacks and tables. Max, and Peter. *Peter.* He had offered Max the most unlikely lifeline. Round the next corner a white square of light announced the way out, and I ran for it.

Outside again, I collapsed in a corner of the front landing to pull myself together. I was so occupied with being in one recognizable place and finding I still could breathe, that I spent several moments emptily staring at an array of jackets and backpacks and untidy shirts disappearing before me, at first not recognizing these as a small procession of summer students that had poured down the steps, shouting to each other. I watched the group slowly unravel down the street; then, as though light had slid across my back I suddenly felt that I too was being watched, and turned. A young woman who had not joined the students stood at the other side of the landing, near the door. She wore her dark blonde hair unconcerned on her shoulders, her hands shoved in her pockets and her attention fixed on the unseen horizon with an enviable air of conviction, and something about the sunlight describing her figure in such clarity that the concrete building behind her seemed no more than a haze of memory. After a moment, she glanced down and met my gaze, and gave a very sweet smile and a small, shy wave. I waved in return and, dazzled at the shine of amber aureole the sun made of her hair, for a moment buried my face in my hands. It was the last I saw of her, for when I looked again, she had gone.

8

Clue

Liebmann University was the next box I wished to tick, but to set out required an extra cuppa and a series of short pep talks—circling the kitchen insisting aloud "Yes!" "Alright!" "Certainly!"—and a lot of wishful thinking. Yet after the drabness and urban ugliness of the state university and its torment of memories, the densely greened grounds of Liebmann with its Edwardian buildings were almost like salve on a burn.

Term was long over and summer courses were in progress. The administration building, a grand opus of red brick titled Folks Hall, hummed with a quiet busyness and polish the state university had patently lacked. I dawdled as much as I could, busying myself with a pinboard of upcoming courses and events, taking in a large display case of historical images and vintage scientific paraphernalia, and finally, entering the wide double doors that led into the library. Straight to the opposite wall by the windows, to a long maple table holding a few plants, little piles of pamphlets and prospectus, and in the center a large binder filled with back issues of the university magazine *Exemplar*. What I had come for would be here, and I half wished that it had not been so easy to find.

I turned back the pages several years, the paper becoming successively thinner and cheaper, and stopped at the 1972 summer issue. The fashions of the era appeared much older and further away than simply nineteen years, with an exuberance almost sadly comic. I found Max's name. *Mr. Maximilian Thompson (BS) Business Administration.* A tiny graduation portrait showed him eight months after Ariel's death: hollow-eyed, his smile only perfunctory and paper thin. The biographical remarks concluded cheerfully, *"Good luck, Max!"*

The rest, to me, was all too familiar: sporadic accounts through the issues presenting sketches of his life chiefly in terms of work. Then the necrological note in the autumn 1988 issue, like a door to a busy passageway shut without warning and sealed. I turned to the latest issue, spring 1991, and was surprised by an article for the upcoming concert. *An Alumnus' Lifework Remembered. The Compositions of Maximilian Thompson in Concert.*

I read it through closely, but knowing him as I did, the whole thing made me impatient; they had got him all wrong, stressed all the wrong points. All to do with awards he had won and youthful virtuosity and "son of renowned composer and the Philharmonic's Music Director Emeritus, Richard Thompson," performed at *this* concert hall and *that* festival. S&T Investigations, mentioned almost as an afterthought, was cited as an example of his "diverse interests." Diverse! I could have counted his interests on one hand.

A second photograph, this time of Max at a rehearsal during one of his conducting stints. He was speaking to the players, holding the baton forward, flat in his fingers. Rumpled gray Liebmann sweatshirt and hair that followed its own whims. His reading specs pushed down on his nose underlining the dark shadows under his eyes, but his expression intent and alive, his entire person communicating enthusiasm and urgency. Unlike the words, I recognized him there; I flipped past it busily.

I spent some time poking round the library, searching for any sign of him—or even of myself that he might have seen. But there was nothing more. He had been here scarcely five months, only long enough to graduate; he amounted to little more than a nominal, retrospectively illustrious accretion to the university's glory.

I found more evidence to support that view out in the hallway. Along the wall ran another long table, this one piled with information on admissions and courses. I flipped through an open prospectus; in the back, interspersed through the long index, were photos of renowned alumni—high-level bankers, business persons, economists, journalists. And there, of course, was the photograph of Max I had just seen in the recent *Exemplar*. The tiny caption: *Maximilian Thompson (BS '72) Conductor, composer & music educator (1988†)*. Music educator: it was an apt designation if grand for someone who had taught inner city students in his spare time for the most token of fees. And *composer*. Very prestigious, that. Do something, do anything, and you were given a title, yours for perpetuity, an identity of one dimension. Once again, no acknowledgement of his profession; on the slick paper the omission read like an embarrassment. This time the attentive face in the photo tore at my heart before I could turn past it. There was energy there, and strength, but unlike the pictures with Ariel there was no more youthful arrogance—only the gently quizzical, deeply-pained mien of someone who never stopped asking questions. Any presumption that his own understanding ever could be complete was gone, replaced by a vulnerable openness no longer satisfied with the tawdry luxuries of indifference or dismissal. It was a patience able to live within contradiction, but where it had once been merely incomprehensible to me, it was now unendurable, and I searched those eyes that could not see me, begging him for an answer.

Rather than answers, suggestions, or even ideas, I left with a fresh batch of anxieties. The accessibility of so much trite information had pulled into focus some more worrisome practicalities of the problem at hand. As I had found when speaking with Peter, if my relationship with Max were based *only* on letters we had exchanged over the course of a single year, I could not risk giving away more than could be expected from that. Worse, I could not be expected to remember the contents of letters now three years old that I had hardly deemed important enough to keep track of, and anything I might suddenly "remember" that had been in them could only seem false coin, if not plainly counterfeit.

The week didn't improve from there.

All sorts of things went inconveniently awry. The dryers in the basement refused my quarters. I wrote pages of schlock because I could think of nothing else. Three local youths who had been at the bus stop took up the sport of loudly and coarsely imitating my voice whenever they saw me and enjoyed it so much, I took to walking to the next stop.

Saturday evening I hit black bottom. I could neither write nor concentrate on trying to produce the letters I had promised. No art was happening. Music stayed away from me. When I tried to read the words fled off the page. I went to put on the kettle.

The tea helped as always, but one cannot sit around slurping tea forever. I contemplated the typewriter, Max's picture beside it, with sunken heart.

It no longer felt so easy or comfortable to put words in Max's mouth, and yet I had no better method for sorting out my thoughts on the matter. I didn't think I could put on a conversation with Ariel again, as comforting as it might have been; it wasn't comfort that helped me think. Clearly, exasperation did.

I turned on the typewriter.
I typed slowly, "Hello, Max."
"Hello there, Brinsel."
"I'm in trouble, Max."
"So soon?"
"I really don't know how I am going to write those letters."

"I'm sure you'll manage quite fine. If I had thought you were a poor writer, I wouldn't have bothered engaging you for this."

"Writing is nothing to do with it. What am I doing here? It's all impossible. I can't *do* anything."

"Okay, first question, Brinsel. Know what *revision* means?"

"I know I surely can't do that now!"

"Whoa there, Nellie, let's back up a bit; what does *revision* mean? You know, like *review?*"

After a moment, with great resistance, "To see again."

"Try *revising*. You can do that. You can even improvise."

I bristled and winced and tried to pretend I was someone else, somewhere else.

"Does that give you a reason to be here?"

I sighed. "You are patronizing me, Max..."

"I prefer to think of it as helping you use your own head."

Two could play that game. "Now I have a question for you."

"Fire away."

"Tell me, Max, did you know you were going to die?"

"Why do I try so hard? All that work, down the tubes. Brinsel, what kind of a question is that? Yes, I knew I was going to die. Everyone knows they're going to die."

"No, not everybody knows! And you know I meant that May. Did you know you were going to die just then?"

"Why do you ask?"

"Because it would answer for me why you mentioned me in that nonsensical note that sent everybody looking for me."

"And as you know already, the answer would still be no. And it wouldn't give you any kind of answer one way or another. C'mon, you can think better than this. For instance, suppose the *reason* you are here is not as essential as the fact that you *are?*"

"Why *am* I here?"

"Alright, I'll bite. If it comes to that, why are any of us here?"

"Listen to me!"

A pause. "I am sorry, Brinsel, but I asked a real question; I wasn't being flippant."

"What is any of us being anywhere to do with any of this?"

"Do you think I would have asked you if it weren't an important point?"

I grumbled, but had only myself to grumble at. "We're here because we were born."

"Good start. Keep going."

I huffed shortly. "Because we were created."

"Go on. Tell me why."

"Tell you *why*? Why should it matter?"

Silence.

I bitterly rued my own lack of focus, consistency, and point; then typed, "Because of love."

Silence.

"Max? What is that to do with my being here?"

"Do you love us?"

I stared at the words. "Do I *love you*? Of course I love you. Why would I have wasted four years of my life writing about all of you otherwise?"

"That sounds to me like a good reason to be here."

I bashed the top of the typewriter with my fists. I yanked out the paper and whipped in another, crumpling both in the process. I pounded out, "I am perilously close to hating you. I am this close to wishing you had never existed. Why am I here *now*? *Here*? Where you lived and died, you idiot whistler, remember?"

Silence.

I was stung to my hair roots with embarrassment. Alone in an empty flat hurling abuse at typewriters and dead men, neither of whom could speak with me. *I* was the idiot whistler.

I picked up my empty mug and slunk out of the office. Perhaps I was going about this all wrong. I emptied the kettle into my mug. Surely there was a better, saner, more logical way to approach my problem than cuppa after cuppa or pretending to carry on a conversation that went nowhere. I glanced across the room to where the typewriter sat humming to itself. Perhaps what I had to do was start over, go clean something again, actually get a clue, a *real* clue.

After a few minutes I sidled back to the desk, peering over it as though there were no typewriter there and nothing I didn't want to deal with sitting in the carriage. I dropped myself in the chair, tossed back the tea, and hurriedly read through everything just typed. Equivocation, impatience, and insults—small wonder I'd got nowhere. What had I been thinking?

Finally I put my hands back on the keys, and typed, "I'm sorry, Max, this isn't your fault . . . But I cannot see what loving *anything* is to do with why I am here, right now. Right now, it appears to me that I am here because of those utterly ludicrous imaginary letters that Peter believes will help solve your case."

"Brinsel, did you ever do any research for your story about me before you wrote it?"

"No, I hadn't, I just wrote." Just as I was doing now.

"You didn't sit down and think about it?"

"No. I just enjoyed it." What I was *not* doing now.

"So, you're saying you didn't know anything about what you were writing about? Nothing about what Americans are like, say, or what it's like in the States, and so on? Nothing?"

"I knew *some* things."

"Well, great. So how did you know the rest?"

"I don't know! I don't know, I just wrote, whatever came into my head, I just wrote."

"Did you . . . happen to ask any questions?"

"Yes, yes, I asked questions, I got answers. Are you happy now? That's how I wrote."

"So, that's all?"

"What is that to do with my being here?"

"You're saying you didn't do any research to write about all of this—you just sat down, asked questions, and you enjoyed it. Maybe even you *loved* it."

"I suppose you could say that."

"Does it surprise you that all of it was true?"

"Immeasurably."

"Are you so certain those letters are imaginary?"

If I was meant to draw a line between the two, it was beyond me. "You must admit they are certainly preposterous."

"*Think*, Brinsel."

I thought. "Am I here because Peter can't finish your case without my help?"

"What am I, your answer man?"

"Well, whom else am I supposed to ask?"

"I said I would help you, not think for you. Small, important distinction."

I sighed and tried thinking again. Nothing.

"Suppose these letters are real. What do you have to do with it?"

Whatever was going on in my head would have to pass for thinking. I typed, as if each key were a reluctant promise, "If there is a chance the letters may be helpful, then perhaps . . . I am here in order to get those letters to Peter."

"Go on."

"And, consequently, letters I have still to write. And I don't know the details he is looking for."

"Didn't I say I would help you? Come on, full speed ahead. You've never been afraid of writing before."

"Max, it was never REAL before!"

"I beg to differ. All the time you had been writing about me, you wrote fearlessly, and you have seen it is all true. You don't have to be afraid now."

"Oh, so now I know what to do, thank you so much. Why could I not think of it? What fantastic help. Just smashing. I hope you'll enjoy dealing with Ariel. You'll deserve whatever you get."

A pause. "Been talking with Al, haven't you?"

"Yes. Why can you not be like her? She's at least straightforward."

"Because I'm not her, for starters. It's good you could speak with her, she's an important part of me. But my work here is to help you do what you need to, and I can only say so much. If being direct is to risk sacrificing your autonomy, I can't do that. I can only guide you."

"My—my autonomy! You—you—you're the one that got me involved! This is all your fault to begin with!"

"Yes, I can take responsibility for that, at least partially, it was I who got you involved. But understand you're not doing anything wrong by how you've chosen to respond to that."

"No, not wrong, just plain illegal!"

"I would not encourage you to continue with this if it were illegal."

"But *you* wouldn't even have done this."

"If it were illegal, no, I wouldn't have. It's your integrity that will be most useful here, Brinsel; I value that, and I am not about to ask you to compromise it."

First autonomy, now integrity. How nice that he refused to interfere with my integrity after shanghaiing my utility. I scrolled out the paper and cranked in another, pronouncing colorful Welsh blessings on my integrity. "Max, how am I supposed to do this?"

"The way you always do it. By letting it come to you. Without fighting it. *Con amore. Con brio. Galante. Intrepidamente. Abbandonno.*"

"And if I make a mistake? A mistake that ruins everything?"

Silence. The faint ticking of the clock in the kitchen. Traffic in the street.

"And if you don't try?"

I looked down at the keys and couldn't seem to remember how to type. It was *idiocy*, it was all idiocy, for there was nothing I could do, yet I had to do something.

I reached for a key and hit it. Nothing. The typewriter was off.

The whole world was becoming unruly and incomprehensible.

Look at things again? My face stared at me upside-down in my teaspoon, but the frown was still a frown.

Ms. Brinsel Thomas
Bwthyn Stella Maris
Strand Lane
Wimsey
Bristow Surrey
RH7 9JP
UK

June 18, 1987
* Paul McCartney ('42)
* Ignaz Pleyel (1757)

Dear Ms. Thomas,
Thanks so much again for your reply. I was deeply pleased to receive the set of cards and the print you sent, as well as the little bit of information about your other works. Thanks too for cluing me in on Open Windows Press; what a way to size it up, "publishing out of a hatbox!" I guess that explains why I've had such poor luck. I've been to the library looking for some of your writings and have proved that our municipal facility is not so broadly stocked as they believed; they have had to go fishing for your books on inter-library loan, and I'll hopefully be able to get them later.

I haven't had any more luck in looking up your art, and I am guessing this means you have no catalogues printed of your work. Or if there are, could you tell me where I could get one? We are out of touch with the European art scene. At any rate, my line of work keeps me out of a lot of that, and I have to be content with dribs and drabs here and there, and mostly music. But you can guess this is not a great hardship—I mean the music. And I am still taken with your music and still looking for more. It's such a pleasure to find new music that speaks so powerfully and plays so beautifully.

So, I was right, you are from Wales. I bet you are familiar with the music of Hoddinott (I had a friend who deeply loved his *Clarinet Concerto*), and Mathias—maybe even the musicians themselves? I confess I don't know much about Wales at all, except that it's in England.

I think I may have a lead about getting an American publisher for your music, if you are interested. It's still in the information-gathering stage, but I think it's promising.

If you would write again, I hope it would not be too much trouble, but if not, then please know of my deep gratitude for your work, and for sharing it with me.

with every blessing
Maximilian Thompson

9

The Cunninghams

Some distractions are good and helpful, and some are just proof that you cannot keep your mind on the job. I couldn't tell which the problem with the typewriter was, probably the latter, but uselessly worrying about it continued to preoccupy me.

I was at least able to work after a while on my other stories. I gave myself high marks for producing anything at all and added a note of approbation. Then Samantha rang up and I got a hefty dose of disapprobation for the missing drafts for *this* particular story. I dodged the issue, barely. Of course everything was fine. I simply had some culture shock and a typewriter that kept turning itself off. Why wouldn't everything be fine? I believe I only confirmed her suspicions that I was working very hard at nothing at all.

In the middle of the week, Rachel rang up to ask if I would like to come over Sunday evening for dinner. More willing to oblige than wanting, I said yes and almost immediately wished I hadn't. I had a feeling she nursed the hope of showing me the "real Jill," and for her sake, I hoped it could be muddled through. For my part, I was still wondering how the commitment of letter writing I had got myself into could be muddled through.

Then there was the commitment of letter reading I had let myself be looped into.

On Sunday morning I spent my bus ride and the subsequent walk gloomily congratulating myself on this development, and as the liturgy began, had a flash of pique—at myself, at Vicki—for having let it happen. On one hand it was rather nice, and extremely flattering, to be embraced by a parish that had never met you as soon as you stepped through the door, a comforting alternative to being ignored back onto the street. And on the other ... to inveigle a visiting guest with a parish duty, simply because the guest happened to be there and happened to be, of all things, a *Reader*, was impolite at best and an imposition at worst. And yet once again, I hadn't the gumption to say *no*.

The lectern stood across from the pulpit, on the right side of the congregation; it was some five feet above the nave floor, a footstool thoughtfully left for me adding another dozen inches of altitude, and when I at last reached the summit and looked down, I was nearly giddy. Over the edge of the open lectionary, I could see Peter and the Cunninghams sitting where I had left them. Rachel beaming and John smiling with his quiet regard. Peter with his chin in his hand and his gaze tipped down. The congregation of Good Shepherd spread out below me as I had never seen them before because it was I and not Max ... And who was I to them?

I reached into my pocket for my reading specs, blushing every hue from beet to cherry.

"A reading from the second letter of Paul to the Church in Corinth ..."

It was over and I was back in my seat beside Rachel before I could get any more existential about it. I let the rest of Eucharist wash over me in soothing familiarity, with even the small differences less conspicuous.

My accent must not have been as conspicuous as I'd feared, either, but that was more to do with painfully deliberate diction. On the way down to coffee Rachel commended me, "You read so cleanly, Brinsel. I understood everything. That's quite a change from our regular fare. Martha's got such a passion for making scripture heard, you lose the syntax in her ardor."

"Thank you," I said, grateful I had not been duped into joining the choir.

At a door just off the administrator's office Rachel paused and beckoned me after her: the music director's office. While she went for a bookshelf, I stayed in the safety of the doorway, gazing at the pictures lining the walls. Rachel found me studying the prints and smiled, pointing out one of the choir that I hadn't looked at too closely.

"Here's my brother with the choir; that's just the way he was."

The photograph was of the choir some Easters ago, arrayed in the white linen used for Christmas and Easter. Richard, the parish music director's bane, in the topmost row, bearded for a season. I couldn't find Max at first; it was only the sloping shine of his flute which gave him away. He stood off to the left in a gray suit, flute to his lips and eyes attentively on the director.

Yes, that was just the way he was: he hung back, off the side, not asking to be seen; you had to look for him, and his flute gave him away.

"You see him?"

"Yes," I gave her one of my by now customary half-truths. "I see him."

I wished, fleetingly, I could really see him for a moment, then snuffed the thought. If I saw him, I would probably try to knock off his block in my overwhelming gratitude that he had landed me in this mess.

After coffee the Cunninghams dropped me off at my flat; in the evening, John was back to pick me up, and Lynn was with him.

"My chaperone," he grinned, pointing with his thumb at her in the back seat as I settled in the front. "To keep me from getting lost when I go out alone."

"This one's been known to raid the florist's on the way home," Lynn informed me as we crawled into circulation. "We have to keep an eye on him."

John said innocently, "I only raid the florist on Saturdays and before special occasions."

"He has a habit of *making up* special occasions."

"I'm good for the floral industry," he replied. And to me, "She's practicing for the police. She'll give you my entire profile before we get home."

She didn't; instead, by the time we pulled into their drive, I knew more about your average Japanese-built combustion engine than I ever wished to. Lynn had taken apart and reassembled one in her auto mechanics class at school and was all on fire to do the same to an entire vehicle. John was delighted with her recital and I was simply stupefied. I tried not to dwell on the details as we drove, especially now that I understood what was meant by *combustion* engine. If I hadn't felt before that I was quite justified in having abandoned my driving license, I now felt sufficiently armed with an excuse.

Being at the Cunninghams' once more was beginning to feel more like being at home. I was known—a little—and knew nearly everything there. Rachel bustling around in the kitchen humming something Gershwinny, and John with his reading glasses nearly hanging off the end of his nose as he pecked studiously at the computer in the corner of the living room— "He's doing an article on some new kind of turbo-whatever-thingumajig for *Mechanic* magazine," Rachel explained, "It's well beyond me"—and Lynn prepared either to entertain or interrogate me for hours, and Jill . . .

The only evidence offered for her presence was the rhythmic ascent and descent of scales on a cello, golden and unalarmed, drifting down the stairs and into the kitchen.

"Is that your sister?" I asked the ceiling.

"Yes," replied Lynn, tossing her gaze over her shoulder from where she stood at the sink, her hands buried in sudsy water. "Playing her fish music. Every day, three hours of this."

"Scales," translated Rachel, setting down a mug of hot tea before me. "Some cream with that?"

"Yes, thanks." I tilted my head, listening. She was working around the circle of fifths; she pushed the notes downscale like vanilla silk, opulent and liquid, luxuriously languid, laissez-faire; she touched the tonic like a swimmer kicking off the bottom of a pool and floated up, now honey-bright but amber strong, now more pensive, someone in a thoughtful mien ascending a stair. Each note slid off the strings round, rich, and resonant, bounced lightly down the stairs and corridor and rolled around the kitchen doorway, the vibrato lingering sweet on the air. Her tone was brilliant, shivering with light. She was well on her way. "It's ravishing."

"That's just warm-up," said Lynn approvingly. "Wait till she really gets going."

Jill came downstairs only when Peter arrived, late; she joined us as tardily as she could and the polite cheerfulness in her mother's voice sounded on the thin side of tolerant when she called her to the kitchen to help carry dinner to the dining room.

The flowers John had picked up yesterday filled a square glass in the middle of the table: ruffled red glads and yellow gerbera daisies, Rachel's favorites. The table was set for "company"—her mother's rose and ivory china rather than their usual white set. I sat with my toes suspended inches from the floor, trying not to remember that this seat had been Max's and that his knees had unfailingly cracked into the table leg every time he moved. Once, he and Richard had often come over for Sunday dinners; now it was Peter who came, at least when he wasn't dating or working. Tonight, he sat across from me and smiled and passed the greens and rolls and looked exhausted; he spoke very little. He asked me how I was, not remembering I had told him that morning at Good Shepherd, and promptly forgot once again, nodding into his asparagus, "So, been doing a lot of work . . . ?"

Beside him, Jill tucked in briskly, talking and looking in every direction but mine.

Remembering how I had embarrassed Rachel and John at my last visit, I was determined to be more congenial to conversation, but the extra number of players created an extra hazard. While John chatted about work with Peter and Lynn, Rachel tried to draw me into a conversation on my work. It was hard, however, to disregard the pile of mechanical jargon collecting on the table from the parallel conversation, and I took a small gap in the talk as an invitation to be politely inquisitive.

"I fix sick cars," John explained to me.

"John's an auto mechanic," expanded Rachel, serving herself with asparagus and passing the bowl to Lynn. "He's got a garage down on Marlow. He's the useful one around here."

He went at his asparagus like a mechanic, too. "I would never have been able to stand just a desk job."

"No," cackled Lynn, passing the bowl to me, "you would have had to sit at it!"

"I love working with my hands and with people," he admitted. "I get to do all that." Gesturing at Rachel with his asparagus, "But there's the useful one, Brinsel. She's the one holding up the fort, with what she brings in."

"She fixes people," said Lynn, with just a trace of sulkiness. "She's an ER surgeon."

Rachel snorted. "With what we have to pay for malpractice insurance these days, it's a wonder I can bring in anything. Next subject."

"What is a monkey wrench?" I asked John of one of the terms he had thrown to Peter minutes before.

I got exactly the answer I expected—a spanner—so I laughed and admitted it sounded like something to use on a monkey puzzle. Now it was their turn to look blank.

It was Jill who spoke. "Clearly, it's a kind of tree," her voice crisp and dry and on the downslope to sarcasm. "Mechanics doesn't have that kind of relation to dendrology."

Before Rachel could leap on this, John said easily, "Well, it depends what your monkey puzzle's gotten into, then, whether you use a monkey wrench on it or not."

"Unless you've thrown a monkey wrench *in* it," quipped Lynn.

I heard Jill kick in her sister's direction under the table, but if she struck home Lynn gave nothing away. Instead she asked me, "Have you ever seen *Blackadder*?"

"What is that?"

"You know, the British sitcom, with Rowan Atkinson? On TV?"

"I've not seen it," concentrating on my asparagus. "I haven't a television."

Jill gave an exasperated huff and sharply scooted her chair so that it made a curt barking sound.

That became the theme of much of the rest of the meal. Lynn would ask me a question. I would confess ignorance or supply information or make an amusing remark if I could. Jill would contribute a small reaction indicating her apparent disgust of my sovereign right to exist and to speak.

Rachel tried firstly ignoring the problem, then threw herself all but bodily into the conversation. John joked and talked and did his best not to notice. Peter grunted and made polite affirming noises and asked the twins a few questions about school and their various projects, but unless spoken to directly said very little. Had I not been the root of the problem, I should have found the whole thing rather comic.

John wished to know what I'd seen about in town, and I briefly mentioned a few places I had been, specially noting my recent adventures and misadventures and discoveries in the automotive department: nearly hailing a learning driver for a taxi, not being able to queue up at the bus stop—the buses that had the driver on the wrong side, of course. I made much of the yellow school buses.

Lynn perked up. "You don't have stuff like that in England?"

"Not really. The students I know go by city buses."

"Did you do that?"

I pulled my roll apart and reached for the butter. "I didn't have that growing up. I went to a boarding school."

Jill, her tone a bit hard, "I would like the *zucchini*, please."

Once, in the midst of one of Jill's coldly diverting comments, I saw Peter glance over to her, then, quietly, at me. He returned his gaze to his plate, his face saying nothing.

It took neither a genius nor a detective to tell that Jill hated my guts, but one or the other would have been useful to work out why. I was neither, and Peter, worn out and sitting practically between us, was not volunteering anything if he had any clues.

"So, my fellow gumshoe," he addressed Lynn, "you still giving your teachers a hard time?"

"Yes," she dropped her gaze, suddenly shy.

"Good for you." He glanced over his glasses at Jill and asked roughly, "And how is our old friend Jüggen?"

"The world's only known performing fossil?" she replied in a bored voice, downing a mouthful of courgettes. "Ripped up the flutes at finals, as usual. Still plays like Moyse on steroids. We took bets on whether he lasts the summer, but you know he'll be there next fall."

"Huh. Some things don't ever change, huh?"

"Nope."

After a few minutes, Peter checked his watch and crumpled his serviette. "Time to fly," he announced, standing up and pushing in his chair. "I'll be seeing y'all. Take care. And you, Brinsel."

We heard his footsteps in the hall, then the front door swing shut, his keys jangling distantly.

"He's a great one," commended John, turning to me. "He's a piece of family."

"We adopted him," Rachel explained. "Sort of unofficially. He doesn't have family; he was an orphan, and since he got divorced, he's pretty much been alone. He and Max were always tight like brothers."

"He's another uncle," appraised Lynn. "He just doesn't know anything about music."

"Well, we ignoramuses are useful people too, you know," her father grinned at her, piling more potatoes on his plate. "Got to have someone to appreciate all that noise you make. What good is a musician without an audience?"

My interrogation continued, much to Jill's displeasure.

"When you wrote books, what did you do about the book critics?"

I tried to regard Lynn in the way I had been accustomed. Beneath all the glib curiosity she could be alarmingly crafty, but I couldn't yet pick out any pattern in her thinking. And from where did that *when* come? From Peter? "Should one do anything?"

"Well, did you *ignore* them?"

I shrugged. "It's a bit of ephemera, isn't it? One of my friends always says that publishing is like preparing a dish in one's kitchen and sending it to the zoo, where it is thrown to the lions. It doesn't matter how good it might be, people are more interested in what the lions do with it."

John's good-hearted laughter and Rachel's knowing snort were interrupted by a crash of cutlery—Jill's—all but hurled onto the floor. Her mother shot her a look, but she had ducked under the table. Lynn appeared not to notice the sounds of apparent demolition erupting beneath us as Jill went klunking after her cutlery. "But what did you *do* about what they said?"

"*Jillian!*" Rachel hissed.

"Nothing much, I'm afraid. It's not a terrible thing necessarily; I've written them myself. In the best of worlds, it's a bit like collaboration between artists. But one isn't asked to do anything; the only thing reviews can actually prove is that universal appeal does not exist. And good or ill, it's largely a matter of exposure. If you want, take what's good and constructive, and rubbish the rest, and go write something even better."

"But what if they don't understand you? Then what do you do?"

I offered her another shrug. "Have a good cry if you must, and carry on. And if you wish to be understood, don't publish." I paused and took a sip of water. "Are you planning to write?"

"Oh no, but Jill writes some. I was thinking of the reviews Max used to get, you know, for music."

Rachel, who had been listening to our exchange with attention, said, not quite nonchalantly enough, "He never read them, remember?"

John glanced at her. "They didn't really figure on his scale of values. That's not such a bad thing."

Lynn looked from her mother to me—unless my eyes deceived me—calculatingly. "He especially didn't read the purple ones."

"That would be all of them, wouldn't it," Rachel's voice so blunt even I could hear the hurt. Then to me, flushing, "But I guess it doesn't really matter..."

Jill had reappeared in her chair, her face set stonily and her hair slightly mussed; she made an elaborate show of wiping her cutlery on her serviette, which irked me for some reason.

"But what are the critics that *you* read?" persisted Lynn. "The kind you prefer?"

"The kind I prefer? Well, I suppose I prefer those who don't indulge in clever cruelty. But children, too; they have a way of seeing through cock-a-hoop, and with great economy of expression."

"Do you have any children?"

"Lynn," said Rachel quietly.

My breath caught in my throat, but I smiled and said, in a way to explain all, "I'm an artist."

"What was the last book you wrote?" she drove on.

"It was some years ago." I took up the rest of my roll with the half-formed thought that I could use it to ward off questions in this vein.

"Are you going to write anymore?"

Rachel responded more to the look on my face than to her daughter's persistence. "Lynn, for heaven's sake—"

"It's alright," I said, pressing out a smile. "I don't mind an interview." And to Lynn, "I am going to try."

But something about our exchange struck me as odd. I could not put my finger on it, but something did not feel quite right.

Lynn, however, was oblivious to her effect; she drove on full tilt. "What was your favorite review ever?"

This was easy, and easier to talk about. "Well, it wasn't a single review, but I think it must have been the ones for the book I said I had begun by accident, and all the reviewers agreed that it was that."

Laughter around the table.

"*I* hadn't believed it was an accident," I added, and they laughed even harder.

During this conversation Jill had been shoveling food into her mouth like an engine driver slinging coal in a speeding train, and I feared she would hurt herself with the fork.

"What about your first book?" asked Lynn.

"It wasn't much loved." I set my fork down on the plate, quickly wiping my mouth as though I could hide the flush. "There was one review I never forgot, it was titled, 'How Not to Write a Novel.'"

"They didn't!" exclaimed Rachel.

"They did, and I had it framed and hung on my wall."

"I bet you laughed best," John winked. "Because you're still writing."

"I am trying."

Jill's fork screeched across her grandmother's china.

Lynn wanted to know about my friends and their occupations, and Jill appeared about as thrilled with the ensuing exposition as with an out-of-tune ensemble mangling Beethoven.

On my part it seemed a harmless enough exercise, but I ran into a bit of trouble when trying to describe the idiosyncrasies of one of my neighbors back home. A very small, elderly woman congenitally shy and incurably reclusive; I reached for a word my friends and I used for such characters. "She's a real marm—"

I stopped myself just in time. There were several words Jill had invented that I couldn't risk saying—*noof*: a hopelessly daft individual; *frah*: stuff in general, or stuff and nonsense; *marmekin*: a reclusive, imaginary creature that hid in small round pots, or, somebody prone to withdrawal and hyper-shyness. If I dropped a word like *buzzle*, her term for the racket of woodwinds warming up and the like, who *knew* what scene might ensue. The terms had been common parlance between herself and Max, and most had entered the vocabulary of the Cunninghams, and this clearly wasn't the place or time for me to employ them.

"—marmot," I fudged, rather ridiculously adding, "That's not an impolite term here, is it?"

The titbits on my background had the awkward effect of making my hosts more curious still and, as once before, John gamely took up a thread I had rather left alone.

"And you're from Wales?"

"Originally, yes."

"And you speak the language too?"

"Yes." I nervously reordered with the fork the bits on my plate.

"Was that difficult to learn?"

"No, no, it was my first language. It was English that I learnt at school; that was difficult. It's rather a messy language." The bits on my plate weren't any closer to getting on my fork. "But I've always done languages well."

"My brother was like that," Rachel smiled, her eyes holding a bruised look I recognized. "I mean, you know, good at languages."

"He was good at all sorts of stuff," John said, adding with a nod at me, "and you seem to be too."

I nodded, at last pushing a forkful of courgettes into my mouth and trying to smile at the same time.

Rachel suddenly brightened and submitted with an expressive air: "Well, you know, anyone who speaks Welsh can surely do other beautiful things."

I came as close as I hope I ever shall to swallowing my fork.

"Good heavens," I sputtered, coughing, hastily shoving my water glass, asparagus, serviette at my mouth.

Rachel took this small drama for a show of modesty and beamed. "Isn't that nice?"

"Er, well," I coughed, "I suppose it could be said of almost any language."

"Max used to say that. No idea where he got it from. Probably some musician!"

Max? This time Rachel read my stricken expression as self-consciousness.

"Oh, he must have meant *you!*"

But even supposing he had suffered a fit of quixotic bunkum, what had Max known of *Welsh?*

Without a word, Jill pushed back her chair, stood, and stalked out of the room.

"Pesh me th'potatosh, pheath," said Lynn.

John looking uncomfortably at the door. Rachel glaring at her plate, not moving a muscle.

A door slammed upstairs.

I passed Lynn the potatoes.

The upshot of the evening for Jill was that her mother consigned her to the dishes; John took himself after Jill to try to contain the fire to the kitchen. Lynn was appointed to keep me company while Rachel excused herself to make a few unavoidable phone calls regarding work.

"It's okay, Brinsel," said Lynn kindly. "Jill gets upset about things, especially anything about Uncle Max." We had settled in a corner of the living room near the hearth, the hiss of running water and the clink of dishes only very faint. Lynn curled up on the wing chair, hugging a tasseled pillow. "She's been very uptight about the investigation ever since Mom told us about the note that mentioned you."

I frowned. "How long has this been?"

"It was about a year ago that Peter told us about it. That was after everyone had been apprehended, they think . . ."

"She doesn't think it was anything to do with me, does she?"

Lynn tilted her head thoughtfully. "Oh no, I don't think it's that. They were just very close, you know?"

"I am sorry," I said. "She might have had a better evening had I not come."

"And then what?" Lynn shook her head. "Don't worry about it, she'll be fine. She gets a tiff and goes off half-cocked. It happens. It'll blow over."

Yes, as soon as I disappeared from her life. "You're good friends."

Lynn acknowledged this with a small nod. "Do you have any brothers or sisters?"

"I was alone quite a bit as a child."

She regarded me quietly. "Artists are alone a lot, aren't they? Mom says Max was like that growing up. You paint too, don't you?"

"Aren't *you* an artist?"

"Oh sure, a titch." She shrugged. "Sure, I can do stuff. Mostly, though, I like studying people."

She was studying me this moment.

"And music, of course. Oh shoot, I've got exercises to do. Have to work on sight reading. Would you like to hear me on the eighty-eight?"

"I would love to. That's not a bit simple for you?"

"Oh, you can always learn more," very patiently. "It's important to exercise, and you can never sight read too well, Max always said. We've got buckets of possibilities for unfamiliar works, especially Jill, since she goes to Horton." She flashed a rather shrewd, friendly smile, and I was startled at the resemblance to her uncle. "C'mon, let's go look."

I held my ground, half mortified, half puzzled. "Really, it's quite alright if I wait here."

"It's okay," she insisted. "C'mon, I've got to look after you, right?"

I hesitated, but she had struck my weak spot and I followed, still circumspect, as she swung up on the banister and leapt the stairs two apiece in her long lope. I felt the carpeting on each stair, worn in the middle, and the polished wood of the banister, with the same tingle of discovery and awe one finds when visiting a famous place. Upstairs, she breezed through the door to Jill's room and beckoned me, untroubled. "Come on in."

I sidled in and stopped by the desk chair, gazing at everything without surprise.

Jill's room—this, too, as I had once painted it in my mind, and never before had it felt like trespassing. The dolphin-blue bookcase casually crammed with books, scores, knickknacks, a few stray toy animals. The maple bureau and mirror that had been her grandmother's, the wood nicked and glowing with age and the glass freckled with mercury. She still had the yellow and white quilt on her bed, more brack and spotted than I remembered it. The room smelled just as I had imagined, of wood polish and a whiff of floweriness that came from a basket of potpourri on one of the shelves.

Lynn was already riffling through a few boxes of scores she had pulled from the closet. Behind her stood her sister's violoncello, propped in its stand. The lustrous amber soundboard, as vivid as Jill herself, hurled the accusation of trespassing at me from across the room, and I nearly turned to go wait out in the corridor. I stepped closer to the desk, eyeing the instrument with the same caution one greets a potentially rabid animal.

Jill's desk was a study of an artist at work: parts of scores and exercise books, a block of rosin, a cloth and a loosened German bow; but slightly safer because here she also wrote stories—if such a thing were at all safe. Her writings were not here, though, but secreted somewhere away from both Lynn's and Rachel's prying.

"What is it you're looking for?" I asked.

"Oh, I thought of something of Uncle Max's I wanted to show you. I think Jill might have it, since she's got a load of his music. Mom let her get it from his stuff after . . . I think it might be here."

Above her desk hung a framed picture of Mstislav Rostropovich, and one of du Pré with her burning eyes; above these, a photo of her uncle performing, attired in the formal black kit he had called a "clown suit." Every image was an icon of her hope. Lynn, as her uncle had been, was—and always would be—content with relatively little. Jill didn't dream a little; she dreamed enormous. She thought enormous. And she agonized enormous. I wished I could have said something to her, but then perhaps that wasn't for me. As things stood, it seemed she wished the earth out from under my feet, and I had no outstanding lines to offer her anyways.

"Oh shoot," mumbled Lynn. "It's not in here."

The scraping and shuffling of boxes being quickly reordered and she swung round the closet door with a handful of sheet music. "I've got to look in my music." She gestured with the papers.

Obediently, and with relief, I followed her out.

Lynn's room was directly across from her sister's. She pushed the door wide and, without further introduction, went for a box under her bed.

Jill's room had been none too tidy; Lynn, while not so neurotic about order as her uncle had been, nevertheless preferred things neater than her twin. Everything in her work area was conspicuous for being neatly in its place. A notebook lay open on the desk, a pen resting on a page embroidered with her slack cursive; so many tidy perpendicular shapes were arranged about it that it took my eyes a minute to disentangle them all. I smelled paper and acrylics and paste and silver polish.

I didn't see any photos of her uncle.

The Gemeinhardt flute lay assembled on top of its case on her bureau, accompanied by a stack of exercise books and scores. She was studying it seriously; I was pleased and unsurprised. She wasn't about to become a flautist, yet being like her uncle had always been a point of honor to Lynn. From him she had learned how to *look*, and he had obliged her to think more critically: "Pay attention *now*, or you pay for it later—your choice!" At times he had simply answered her queries with a terse admonition of Saint Bernard: "*Non scrutatio, sed admiratio.*" Or his own "*Voyez et au revoir!*" and once, "What does Mark 7:16 say?"

"That's the one he gave me." She glanced up again and spotted me studying the Gemeinhardt. "His first flute. Go on," she waved magnanimously, "take a gander."

I did, and more than that; I drank it in like the relic it was. After having held the Muramatsu, it seemed this flute ought to have been anticlimactic, yet there had been so much wrapped up in this one, the one he had waited for until he thought he would burst, the one whose arrival almost made him split with joy. It was incredible how many memories a thin silver pipe two feet long could hold.

"He must have got into conservatoire with this?"

"Yes." She sounded unsurprised that I should ask, the trace of a smile in her voice as though charmed by the term's idiosyncrasy. "Did you go to . . . conservatoire also?"

"I did my postgraduate reading there."

"At the Royal Welsh College of Music and Drama?"

Now I looked at her closely, both amused and, once again, with the disquiet sense that one of us was saying too much. "That would be the one, wouldn't it?"

Lynn smiled winningly; she gestured at the flute in my hands. "He had others, of course," shrugging off the aside. "It wasn't his principal, he just used it for backup. Have you seen his regular flute?"

I nodded. "Your mum showed it me." I gently set the instrument back on its case, noticing now that the exercise books were those he had used as a child, and the scores, those of music of which he had been particularly fond. Lynn must have advanced quite rapidly to tackle all that.

The famous yellow cap, faded and edges nibbled by the years, hung on the wall by her desk, and seeing it I understood why there was no picture of Max here. She was too much like her uncle; she needed the "sound" that something concrete gave. One photograph felt like another, but a cap or a clarinet that had belonged to somebody—these spoke to more than the eyes. Here was her uncle's picture, and the Gemeinhardt with the scores and etudes . . .

Jill had pictures of cellists; Lynn had only one other hero to hand— Earl Hines grinning in the corner of her bureau mirror. A photo of a lynx in a snowy scene perched commandingly nearby. A few pieces of her artwork here and there, and on the bookshelf, the most beautiful print of her maternal grandmother; it was black and white but resembled a silver print, so transparent and penetrating the light, the contours of shapes limned with the same transparency. There she was, Elisabeth, the French-Canadian pianist Richard had lost head and heart to. The first one to disappear from Max's life, the first one to fail him. She sat in a windowsill, gazing out into a rectangle of overexposed light, chin in one hand with the other hand lying across her lap. She was about twenty-eight. "Who is this?"

"That's *Grandma!* the one who gave Max that flute." Lynn came over and stood beside me. "We never knew her, she died of a brain tumor when Mom and Max were kids." She reached up and brushed a thin scrim of dust from the glass, and I was startled again at how tall she was; as with her mother, I had to look *up* to her. "The negative was damaged, that's why the window is so bright, but I think it's beautiful."

We gazed at it in silence. "Yes, it's just as she was," I heard myself murmur.

"What?"

I started. "Oh, well, very much like your mum. One can see the resemblance."

"Yes," but I could hear the hesitation in her voice. "You know, she talks about Grandma, but until now, she's never talked so much about Max. I mean, these last few years..."

This time I did blush, twisting away as though she had flashed a light upon me.

"Is something wrong?"

"Well," I admitted, coloring what felt five possibilities of red, "you are all so open with me. We have only just met, yet you have opened your house to me. It's, well, rather a lot to give to a perfect stranger."

"Are you so strange?" she grinned. "I'm a good judge of character, Max always said so. And besides, you're not such a stranger if he trusted you with his case. You don't know about how rare that was for him; that makes you as trustworthy as Peter."

As trustworthy as Peter... and if she knew that I had lied, to cover for her uncle?

Downstairs, Lynn peered a swift appraisal in the direction of the kitchen and turned to the Whitney that had once been her uncle's, dropping herself on the bench.

I lowered myself into a nearby chair, still puzzling over the ruse of sight reading practice. Lynn had been playing piano almost since she had learned to walk. "You've been playing for some time?"

"A few days, Dad would say." She patted its low top affectionately, flipping open the fallboard. "Dad would also say this one's short a few keys. Grandpa's got a Big Softie," using her uncle's beloved pun.

"A big what?"

"You know, a *grand piano*. That's what Max called it . . ."

Over an improvised chromatic exercise, she treated me to a flood of musical puns learnt from her uncle, qualifying this with a precise recitation of the pun license he had awarded her, and finally accompanying with the music she had brought down. "As long as I'm careful," she concluded, "I can keep it."

"There's prudence, that, to use language responsibly," I commended her. "Not many can."

"There is some fine print," she admitted sheepishly, "and a line about not driving Mom crazy."

I heard voices from the kitchen hallway and then Jill's footsteps on the stairs; John's footsteps descended the basement stairs, then after a few minutes ascended and returned to the kitchen. I glanced at the clock and was astonished to realize it had been scarcely fifteen minutes since dinner had finished.

Lynn was still chatting animatedly over her practicing. This one was puzzling me unduly; among her uncle's friends, Lynn was sociable to a fault, but strangers—and I surely qualified—were another matter. I knew she was slippery, she had picked up many of her uncle's dodges. But I couldn't tell what she was up to this time. I had lost Max's perspective that had given me a shrewd inside angle of her machinations, and I had lost the omniscient author's license of knowing and inventing whatever I pleased. All that was left to me was things to remember, and one could only remember things that were past or that did not change. People changed; I "remembered" them at my peril.

"Hey, is this a private party?"

We both looked round to see John had come in. Lynn brightened. "It's about time!"

He picked up the sheet music she had left in a chair and settled into it. "It's not about music?" he grinned. "This one been giving you the royal treatment, Brinsel? Mussorgsky and Hutch . . . ?"

"Not yet those, but yes, I've been enjoying a concert."

"I couldn't find the music I wanted," Lynn said. "It's too bad 'cuz I really wanted you to see it." She laughed. "I mean hear it!" She drew herself up, regarding me cunningly. "Can you see music?"

Would it be fair if I understood what she meant at once? I nodded.

"I'll play something, and you tell me what you see." She glanced at the ceiling. Out of her fingers came Mozart, *Rondo alla turca*.

Lynn perched on the bench reminded me of nothing so much as a porcelain teacup balanced on a saucer, delicate yet solid, everything just as it should be. Her eyes swept over the keys in a single gesture of both command and surrender, and for a moment, seeing her in profile, another comparison struck me even more forcefully: she was almost the image of the maternal grandmother she had never known, sitting at another piano. All she lacked was that one's command of expression. Lynn had been playing Mozart for more than a few days to be sure but, when not improvising, the chief character of her music-making was a mere virtuosic nonchalance: she tossed off the music exquisitely as a card trick, but no more than that.

"What do you see?"

I drew serrated scallops in the air with my finger. "And it circles over and over right here. There are little rosettes and bunting."

John contributed, "I see dots, lots of dots!"

"There's no hope for you, Dad."

I asked Lynn, "What do you see?"

"On the piano, I see the ocean. When I play it on flute, though, I see the beach also."

I smiled. "Some psychiatrist would have a field day with us."

Lynn shrugged disinterestedly. "It's music. It's just doing what it's supposed to."

"What is that?"

She glanced at the score propped on the desk. "Max said it reveals the truth of things."

"What do you think it does?"

After a pause, "I think the same. What do *you* think?"

What was it I believed music did? I hesitated, but Lynn was watching me with open curiosity; I was aware of John, head tilted attentively. "I don't know how to say it, I'm not so good with words."

"What a line!" Her voice shot up like a bell and she laughed. "You're a writer!"

"My dear, being good with words and being a writer aren't synonymous. And besides, I'm not writing, I'm speaking. I don't think well on my feet, I'm a dreadful speaker."

"But you can say something, go on. Even if it's awful."

"Well, it's not being awful, only inadequate . . . It's a matter of translation, really. How do you express something that is what it does? I think music . . . communicates other forms. Like all art."

Lynn's expression was quite still and unreadable. She dropped her eyes to the keys and finally said, very low, "That's interesting, I never thought of that."

"Huh," appraised John. "That's very nice, Brinsel. I'll have to remember that."

It was another ten minutes before Rachel was able to rejoin us; Lynn took her mother's entrance as her cue to exit, gathering up her sheet music and sliding the bench under the piano so that all the visual lines remained neatly perpendicular; we listened to her footsteps on the stairs. Rachel closed her eyes and rubbed her forehead. "Well, now that you've survived an evening with the Cunninghams, you can consider yourself a native, Brinsel. It isn't always like this, but then perhaps we'll get another chance to clear our good name." She tugged out the comb that was pinning up her French knot, her fine straight hair sighing over her shoulders. "I'm sorry things weren't ideal."

John brought in a tray of cappuccinos, and handed me one on a saucer. "But I'm glad to be here, and I have enjoyed meeting your daughters. They are both quite remarkable young musicians."

"And you don't seem to have much trouble telling them apart," John smiled.

"It's not as if they're making it difficult at the moment," Rachel said resentfully. Her hair swung in her face as she sipped her cappuccino, and she brushed it behind an ear. "You've met at least one of them. I'm still not sure when the other one will turn up. She seems to have skipped town and left her evil twin."

"Not Lynn!" John laughed at my expression.

"Surely not," I agreed. "I have a friend who says *each* of his twins has another set that comes to the table after the meal and must eat again. He calls them the déjà vu quartet."

"He's got two boys, hasn't he?" Rachel grinned. "Yep, each set come with their own unique spares." She gestured to John. "Remember when the girls used to be in school plays and understudy for each other? We were never sure who really had the role."

"Playing themselves, Max called it," John smiled at some memory. "And getting more authentic all the time."

"Ugh!" Rachel turned to me. "Would you like to borrow some twins?"

"Which set do you prefer?" I quipped, and in their laughter felt I had redeemed my former gaffes.

I found Rachel considerably browned-down at Good Shepherd the following Sunday. When I appeared, only John glanced up and smiled at me; he was holding his wife's hand with both his own, and she was leaning on him as if headached through. Not until I sat down with the bulletin and noticed the date could I hazard an explanation. It was 23 June; the previous day would have been her brother's birthday.

The choir was ended for the summer and Lynn sat with us, legs crossed and posture very straight and attentive; Jill, her perfect double, sat in the sanctuary with her cello, accompanying the music director in the prelude—*Song without Words in D, Op 109*, bending over her instrument with the single-minded absorption of an artist over their work. She was a "stringed soul," Max had said, she vibrated very high, deeply sensitive. Someone with an ear for cellistic prowess could have said all sorts of lovely things about her playing, but all I heard in that beautiful sound was a tightly coiled violence, a purplish, almost bruising undertone and biting edge that had nothing to do with the Mendelssohn and did not belong there.

Richard, not serving this morning, also sat with us, one arm propped up on the armrest at the end of the pew, fingering the ribbons from his tattered prayer book open in his lap. I did not have to guess what page he was at; every Sunday for almost twenty years, he had prayed the collect "for a person in trouble or bereavement." The page was marked by small pictures of his wife and of his son's fiancée, and now, of his son.

I gazed at him, that long frame in an old gray suit, sagging in the corner of the bench, the lined face and the tired, ringed eyes, the worn hands and the cloud of silvery hair. He looked reduced and weighed down; feeling I was intruding, I turned away.

The prayer book at the end of the rack by my knees had the soft, rounded corners that told much use and handling. Resisting—in name only—the same sense of intruding, I pulled it out and leafed to the Order for Marriage. It was still there, rescued from the old prayer book and inserted by Max into the 1979 edition: the torn piece of bulletin dated February 1971 on which, in a flush of literary swank, he had scribbled Spenser's Sonnet 75; Ariel had leaned over, taken the pen from him, and twice underlined *vain man*. I left it there; the book could keep its secret. I slumped in my seat and listened to Jill hating me with her cello.

There turned out to be another, more immediate reason for Rachel's gloominess. She had been deeply embarrassed by Jill's behavior, and at coffee covered me with apology, regretting that she did not feel free to invite me to dinner again until Jill had got over whatever malaise was afflicting her. I suspected both Rachel and myself privately diagnosed the malaise as adolescence and the duration as another two years on the inside, not very promising for the prospect of dinner again that summer. She chatted distractedly about the weather, her work, my work, General Convention, music...

Music. I had something for her in my satchel I had been putting off. When she paused, I drew out the envelope and thrust it at her. "This is for you."

"What is it?"

"Go on, it's for you."

The letterhead made her brow wrinkle up, but the letter itself, legalese as it was, made her jaw drop and a gasp jump out. "Oh, my God!"

"Mine, too."

"Brinsel, you can't do this, you can't just transfer your copyright!"

"Shh, not so loud, dear," I said dryly, "or everybody shall want to do the same."

But my one chance to use the joke meaningfully was lost on Rachel, and no one else was there who could appreciate the awful irony of it.

"How did you do this?"

"The copyright reverted to me. It was mine to give away." I gestured at the paper. "Will it be sufficient? Will your publisher need anything more?"

She was still gaping at the letter. "Dad, come look at this," she said, and Richard, who had been sitting not far off, came over to us. She handed him the letter. "Look at what she did."

Richard's dumbfounded expression was even more satisfying than Rachel's had been. He looked from the letter to me as though unable to make the connection. "Brinsel," he said, first command and then distress in his voice, "you can't do this."

"But I have done," I replied, my poise drooping. "I wanted to give this to you."

"But this is your work, Brinsel," he insisted.

"Yes, but I have other work, too. It is not important, truly it's not. This way, there should be no further legal questions. Oh please, I want to do this for you."

"But you didn't have to *do* that," persisted Richard. "There was no infringement since it could have been proven he never saw your music before he wrote his. It wouldn't have been a problem."

"Nobody had ever noticed it, and it couldn't have lasted forever, anyway," and then realizing this was precisely the wrong thing to say, "Nobody ever really knew the music as mine, but it shall be known as Max's."

Richard was shaking his head. "You're a classic copyright law case, Brinsel. You had every right to the music you wrote. I am sorry it was destroyed. I would have liked to see it."

I had no wish to be a classic anything, and the fact that I represented a textbook illustration of copyright impossible—and thus unimpeachable—had no appeal to me. "I couldn't have done it for anyone else," I said desperately. "There is no one else I would have done it for."

"It's true," and this time his tone was almost reproachful. "No one else wrote what you did."

I was getting a lot done at Good Shepherd. I only wished my work on the case could be so productive.

10

Roamer

Seeing all the Cunninghams each Sunday made me restless to get out and see anything else. On a gray day that had poured early and was picking to rain more, I followed my nose to the public library, sensing, or perhaps just wishfully thinking, some non-directional research might get me somewhere.

I had long admired the neoclassical building, the reception with its glass dome and mosaics—Cathy had sent me pictures, and so it had been particularly easy to imagine Max there. Today, however, I had no energy for admiration; I was haunted by the thought of Max, in this same place, searching for my books. A small fiction, and at least I knew for certain he had come here in search of other things: information, recordings, and all of them nonfiction. I crawled over the stacks for over an hour in search of ideas but in the end capitulated to cowardice and emerged with an anthology of shorter detective fiction identical to one I had got Dai for Christmas, and a few volumes of Shel Silverstein, not to revisit something loved but to stupefy an ache with something familiar. By the time I left the library the weather had turned unfriendly and it was raining old ladies and sticks; my empty flat welcomed me, wild-haired and wet through, with a stillness of stale warm air. I kicked off my shoes and put on the kettle, and turned to *The Missing Piece* over my tea. After five minutes I tossed it aside and drowned my sorrows in some poems instead.

Rain and the muted twittering of the radio accompanied me through supper, but as evening fell into night, it was replaced by the silence of my rooms and the somewhat self-important, stuffy voice of Dr. John Watson narrating, with an ironic aptness to circumstances, *The Adventure of the Empty House.*

I ought to have stuck with the Silverstein and "Hug-O-War." Adventure! Insanity and denial was more like it. What had I been thinking?

"... May I ask how you knew who I was?"

"Well, sir, if it isn't too great a liberty, I am a neighbour of yours, for you'll find my little bookshop at the corner of Church Street, and very happy to see you, I am sure. Maybe you collect yourself, sir. Here's *British Birds*, and *Catullus*, and *The Holy War*—a bargain, every one of them. With five volumes you could just fill that gap on that second shelf. It looks untidy, does it not, sir?"

I moved my head to look at the cabinet behind me. When I turned again, Sherlock Holmes was standing smiling at me across my study table. I rose to my feet, stared at him for some seconds in utter amazement, and then it appears that I must have fainted for the first and the last time in my life. Certainly a grey mist swirled before my eyes, and when it cleared I found my collar-ends undone and the tingling after-taste of brandy upon my lips. Holmes was bending over my chair, his flask in his hand.

"My dear Watson," said the well-remembered voice, "I owe you a thousand apologies. I had no idea that you would be so affected."

I gripped him by the arms.

"Holmes!" I cried. "Is it really you? Can it indeed be that you are alive? Is it possible that you succeeded in climbing out of that awful abyss?"

"Wait a moment," said he. "Are you sure that you are really fit to discuss things? I have given you a serious shock by my unnecessarily dramatic reappearance."

"I am all right, but indeed, Holmes, I can hardly believe my eyes. Good heavens! to think that you—you of all men—should be standing in my study." Again I gripped him by the sleeve, and felt the thin, sinewy arm beneath it. "Well, you're not a spirit, anyhow," said I. "My dear chap, I'm overjoyed to see you. Sit down, and tell me how you came alive out of that dreadful chasm."

Until that moment it had never occurred to me quite how horrible the scene was; it had always been merely amusing—was it not the classic British understatement? Holmes's dispassionate, theatrical reappearance and Watson's painfully realistic reaction? This time, though, I wanted to leap up and shriek, "Fantastic, Holmes! you had NO IDEA Watson would be so affected, when he had every reason to believe you were dead! It's not even FUNNY!"

There, too, was the entire problem with literary characters. You could do next to anything with them. You could revise until you were black in the face. This trait rather than that trait. This plot twist rather than that one. Holmes, by a conceit of fiction not dead after all—the *conceit* of it! The irony of it was unfairly brutal too, and even in less ironic particulars, it still struck a little too close to home. Not least the bit about fainting.

If Conan Doyle had truly hated his character so much that he was compelled to finish him off, he had done himself no favors by settling for unwitnessed theatrics versus verifiable efficiency. Only a dance of muddy footprints and a farewell note—no body, no grave, no proof. Sherlock Holmes, doyen of deductive logic, had been *deduced to death.* Quite clever, oh yes, *too* clever by half, but hardly very thorough. Conan Doyle hadn't even *wanted* to bring him back, but his carelessness meant that, when pressed to, he could do so.

And I, who had not hated Max, who would have given my every talent to be able to speak with him and find out what he had known, to be able to explain this somehow, had no such opportunity for revision. His murder had been complete and witnessed and terrifyingly real. There could be no bumping into him on the street, no appearances on my doorstep. There was only the typewriter.

This was going to need more tea. Not until I could sit down with another hot cuppa wrapped in my hands did I begin to feel one degree less anxious. I studied the typewriter from over the rim of my mug.

Max had said I knew everything he did. I hadn't dared to contradict that. And yet I didn't know *why* he had said that, could not yet remember what he had known about the case, and had no certain way of finding out either. And through a series of unavoidable admissions had got in too far to get gracefully or credibly out.

And I had chosen to respond to it by fabricating a series of letters from somebody who had never bothered writing any.

And the only way I could think of to get myself through that process was to pretend to talk to a dead man.

It was a good exercise, on the whole. It forced me to loosen up, and Max was someone I could be honest with. And he had a way of making one think.

But that was also the problem. He didn't give answers to questions, he only asked more questions.

To make matters worse, not only did he make me think, he was consistently and infuriatingly right.

I turned on the typewriter anyway.

"Hello, Max," I began, throwing the words out without thinking.

A pause. "Hello there, Brinsel."

"I need to ask some questions, Max."

"Got a lot on your mind, huh?"

"I have. Such as, what am I going to do about those letters?"

"How about *write* them?"

"And you might tell me how, as they are supposed to be from you?"

"You don't have to be anxious about getting it right if you would just let go of having to control things."

I had a withering sense that this exercise was going to be even less undemanding than the previous one.

"Right. Next question. What am I *doing* here, Max? What on earth am I here *for?*"

"You're not going to decide that?"

"I *had* decided. And nothing is what I decided because everything is as I *knew*. And there must be an explanation for all of this. There must be a *reason* that would tell me what to do."

"This isn't like you, Brinsel, you're all out of sorts. Try to aim a little higher. Pay attention to what you're saying. Think of the most important question."

Impatiently, "What *is* the most important question?"

"What you make of it."

"If I don't know what it *is*," very testily, "how can I make *anything* of it?"

"Look at it this way. When you know what question to ask, what are you going to do about it?"

"Is *that* the famous most important question?"

"I'll leave that to you."

It was worse than talking to myself. And I could have sworn I was doing just that.

I imagined him leaning against the windowsill, tall as the lintel and chin in one palm. That long-suffering, dogged expression on his face, with just the trace of a smile he was politely trying to swallow. The mental picture was all I required to sharpen my ire.

"Brinsel, I want to help you be able to approach your situation a little less emotionally."

"I'm not being emotional!"

"And a little less rationally too. A little less analytically. A little more gut level. The way you normally work, isn't this so? The way you do art?"

"Max—Max, what good is that? This isn't to do with art. The furthest thing, if possible."

"Try it. *Look* at it that way for a moment. It's okay not to think for one minute."

"Two weeks ago, you were telling me I wasn't thinking! Now you're telling me not to think! While you're at it, please tell me why one question being more important than the others is so ruddy irrational!"

I whipped out the paper and cranked in another.

"Since when does *less rational* mean *irrational*? Tell me, when you do art, are you faced with a 'most important question,' call it an overriding concern?"

Even more snidely, "Yes, the authentic ontology of what is to be made."

"Leaping lizards! Okay, whoa, *whoa* there. Time out. Time out. Look, hey, Brinsel, this is just a civil conversation, there's no need to drag that kind of equipment in here. I don't inflict all my jargon on you, so you can do me a favor and leave all the fancy artsy mumbo jumbo over in left field, okay? Try talking to me like a normal person. Now, come again?"

"It's *not* a blinking mystery, Mr. Musical Genius. It's ensuring that I create a work according to its own exigencies, not mine."

"There, now we're on the same sheet of music. And how do you respond to that?"

"By removing myself from its path and letting it happen."

"Whoa, we're not thinking very rationally all of a sudden. So how do you manage that?"

"Well, by trusting the process!"

"And you can't do that now because?"

He had just drawn a circle around me. And made me walk on the line.

"How can we get you to that level of dispossession in all this?"

I picked up my tea, staring at the page. Sighed deeply. I put the tea down. "I can't do that now, because it's all real after all, and I am part of it."

Silence.

"Brinsel, what did you just do? If you are concerned for what you call the authentic ontology of the things you make, doesn't that mean they too are *real?*"

"Yes, but not the way all of this is. That sort of *beingness* is intangible. I *make* those things, but I didn't make all of this. This isn't art. This isn't writing. This is out of my hands."

"How is all of this different from the rest of your life then?"

"Max, you are not even being SOUND. First you say, treat it like art! Then you say, treat it like life! I cannot possibly do both; I would go mad."

"Listen, *listen*. If you see either of them as things to be controlled, yes, you would go mad, but you don't force the things you make, according to what you just told me. And your life? Do you force that?"

"This is irrelevant!"

"Do you force your life?"

No, it was far easier to talk with oneself than to write in another's voice. One argued with oneself much less obstinately. "I make plans, and things . . . unfold."

"And you can't let all of this unfold too?"

I looked away from the paper as though there were a gaze to avert from.

"Doesn't music happen in *time*? One part following another? Can you jump to another part without a sign?"

I held my head in my hands, wincing, but had to put them back on the keys.

"When you are working on art, or something, and it's not moving for you?"

"Max, this isn't to do with art."

"What do you do?"

I fiddled with the mug handle and brushed the top of the typewriter with the heel of one hand. I rested my head in the other hand. Leadenly, with one finger, "I wait."

"You will try, Brinsel?"

How long could I wait? How long could Peter wait?

"I can do no more than that."

"I am not asking for more than that. I promise I will do the rest."

I sighed in disgust. I was at it again—outrageous rubbish. Unpardonable fantasy. When I wrote what I didn't want to hear, I was infuriatingly realistic. When I wrote what I did want to hear, I couldn't *manage* to be realistic. "I'll believe it when I see it."

"*Try* to let go a little. I would be sorry to have had you come all this way, and then see you go back without discovering anything."

"If only," I typed, abandoning suspension of disbelief, "I could really talk with you, Max. If only I could *really* ask you what is going on. But this is pointless—you're dead and you can't help me, or talk to me, and I'm sitting here talking to myself because I've not any better ideas."

"As you just said, it is real after all, and you are a part of it. It must seem impossible to you. It must seem unreasonable. And you probably think you're putting words in my mouth. But don't be afraid to try to talk with me. I just might be able to help you that way."

Not without sarcasm: "What are the chances?"

"Well, a lot better than if you didn't bother, I'd say, though you'd have to ask Peter if you really wanted to know. He's the one who talks odds. But give me a chance, at least. Give yourself a chance. What else are you going to do?"

"Go home and try to forget all this ever happened."

"Perhaps today isn't a good day for this, Brinsel."

I let my eyes close, listening to the silence of the room. The *sotto voce* grumble of the refrigerator, the typewriter.

The keys repeating their endless mantra under my fingers, far calmer than I felt inside. "No day would be good for this. No day would ever be good for this. This is insane, absolutely insane, and if I get the chance I am going home—letters, investigation, writing notwithstanding. I don't believe this, *any* of this. This is simply beyond belief, plain and simple."

It felt wonderful to write it. It was almost the first completely sane thought I had had in weeks. I stared at it for long minutes, a warm surge of satisfaction filling me. Yes, that was it. I had hit upon the solution at last.

Silence, quite long. For a moment I thought nothing else would come.

Then, "H'm. Alright. Let me just stick this out there. You talk with Dave about this?"

The bottom of the page. I scrolled it out and wound in another.

"That I'm crackers is only a family joke, Max. What do you want me to do, give him *proof* I'm out of my mind?"

"Just asking."

Silence.

"Will you do something for me, Brinsel?"

The rich satisfaction of only a moment before was already gone like a dream. "What is it?"

"Will you go see Roamer and give him something for me?"

I stared at the words.

"Brinsel?"

What was the point of refusing? "I will go."

"Give him this. R: The things I owe you. I'll get back to you. Don't think I won't, I keep my promises, you know that. -G.

"Tell him whatever you need to. And if he asks who you are, you're Badger. Got it?"

"*Badger?*"

"Okay, fine, how about Sunshine?"

"No! No, Badger is fine."

"You with me, Brinsel?"

I looked at the drawing of him beside the typewriter. "I suppose."

"Do *this* as soon as possible. If you wait on this job, I know you, you won't do it."

I resented that; he didn't know *me*, I knew *him*.

"Brinsel?"

"Yes."

"I love it when you say that. Thank you."

I don't know what I should have said next, or if I was even going to type anything, because a moment later I realized the typewriter was off.

I was too tired and deflated to react; I sat staring at it for a few minutes, then at the message for Roamer. Then got up and went to find the right kind of paper.

He didn't make himself easy to find. I looked in all his usual places around town and drew blanks. I had to go into the inner city. Mile upon mile of tedious and all-too familiar poverty was horrid enough but by the time I reached 130th Street I was close to tearing my hair out over my own infernal irrationality in having come at all. Why on earth had I thought of going to see Roamer? What had I hoped to find out? Roamer was as cunning as Max had been, and I could expect to get just as much information out of him, too. At the very least, I could prove he existed, and that might do some trick for my memory, but still, it was not on the wide end of rationality.

At last, after almost three hours, I found him lounging with a companion at a gazebo in Washington Park, both of them leaking smoke like mosquito pots. A third companion huddled just out of the way at the top of the stairs, beetle-like in the shadows. They stared at me dully and threw out a few compulsory unpleasant remarks.

When I did not reply, one of them asked softly, "What you want?"

"I have a note for Roamer, from Gopher."

Roamer didn't move. I held the slip out to him.

"Who sent you?"

"Rig," I said.

He uncurled like one with all the time in the world, rose to his feet, tossed aside his cigarette and approached. I handed him the note, and he took it.

Max had sometimes written him notes regarding his work when he could not reach him another way. They had all been on a certain kind of paper, written out by hand with certain abbreviations. The paper Max had always used was a tiny strip of worn cotton rag, about a quarter of a inch wide and usually at least four inches long, not quite white and usually rather tattered, with minuscule blue and red threads scattered through it, sometimes with a line of black filigreeing on one side. The messengers who brought these tiny slips had been known to Roamer. If not, they had to know Max or Peter, and by the names Roamer knew them.

He read the few short words quickly, then again.

"Shitass," he muttered. He stuffed the scrap in his pocket and motioned to me. "You, I want to talk to you."

We walked a short distance from the gazebo, then he wheeled and fixed his eyes on me, his voice very low but commanding, "Who gave that to you?"

Roamer had the full strength of the accent for this part of town, of which Peter had lost the hard edges. It took me a moment to register what he was saying, and probably took him some time to sort out my own voice as well.

"Rig," I said again. This was Peter's tag. "He asked me to apologize this took so long to reach you, he found it with some old papers."

Even lower, "How you know me?"

"Gopher told me about you."

"You seen Gopher lately?"

"I haven't, he's dead." I added knowledgeably, "It's been three years."

Roamer was a youthful picture of what Peter might have become had he not scraped off the streets when he had. Now he was casting an eye over me uncannily like Dan Malcombe's. Hands on his hips, he glanced away quickly, then back at me, raptorlike.

"So, who are you?"

"I am Badger."

His eyes, slightly glazed, snapped and cleared. "You're shittin' me."

"I would not do that," I said simply.

"YOU are Badger?"

"Yes," I said, wondering who I was.

"Shit!" he announced, head jerking. He repeated himself a few times as though to ensure he could still say it.

"Had Gopher told you about me?"

He sputtered, "He knew I wouldn't tell no one." He stared at me. "And shit, it's you! What are you doing here?"

"Taking care of some old business." I tried to smile.

"Rig know who you are?"

"Not the way you do."

He whooped and jerked his head sharply, his face registering an awed triumph; he looked back at me, shaking his head still with that delighted incredulity.

So Roamer knew something—but what did I know? My mind was clicking frantically over the word *badger*. All I could think of was that it was local slang for a journalist or someone after a story, but Roamer would never speak to me if that were the connotation here. "So why did Gopher tell you about me?"

Roamer squinted and responded with a series of unhurried gestures. The scratch on the back of his neck. The run of hands rapidly over his hair. The hands on his hips. The arms crossed across his chest, contraposto. The sharp flick of his head. "He told me not to say."

"Not even to me?"

As soon as the words were out of my mouth I knew it was the wrong question; the illusion that I was in any way in charge of the conversation was sticking out like a wallet begging to be appropriated, and Roamer needed no cunning to pinch it. "But he did say why you're called Badger."

I shrugged, smiling to say I knew everything.

"You use a typewriter."

I tried not to swallow my tongue.

"You gonna see Rig soon? Sooner than three years maybe?"

"Next week," barely holding onto my smile.

"Tell him this for me. Just like this." He held up one hand and pulled down his fingers as he spoke. "Wednesday, fourteen, seventeen, bridge." He stopped at his thumb and held onto it, then put down his hands, matching my gaze. "He'll know."

He broke his gaze, looking towards the gazebo. His companions were drifting off. He glanced back at me, pointing meaningfully with a wild gesture of the streets. In a moment I was alone.

I was alone, and wondering how much more absurd the irony could get: of everyone he had known, Max had apparently spoken of me to the one person who, in the event of his own death, would do nothing for anyone. Whatever Roamer knew about me—and for whatever reason Max had told him about me—it was not knowledge he would be willing to surrender.

I wondered for a while if telling Peter that Roamer had known about me would be a breach of Roamer's trust. Then I wondered what the point would be anyway, since I was here now and it didn't matter what they had or hadn't known before.

And there was not really any point to such ideas. It had been a simple enough matter to talk myself through giving a note to someone I would not see again. But my next trick involved giving a message to Peter I hadn't ought to have been able to receive.

I had my opportunity on Sunday at coffee.

For any inconvenience offered by its members, Good Shepherd was a good place for me; it was, on one hand, completely familiar, and on the other, still new and embracing enough to make me pay attention. The parish was in fact so embracing, it was difficult to find a moment to speak with Peter that wouldn't be made awkward by the self-invitation of a third party.

And then, there I was, and what could I possibly say?

"Peter, I realize this may sound odd, but I have a message for you from somebody named Roamer."

Peter was unconcerned. "Well, let's have it."

I held up a hand and gave the message just as Roamer had dictated to me, feeling self-conscious and clueless and that I had reached the apogee of absurdity.

"Huh," grunted Peter. "Well . . . thanks, Brinsel. I'll put that in my pipe and smoke it." He scratched his head. "I hope it wasn't any trouble?"

He wasn't surprised. I shook my head.

Offhandedly, "Not to worry, it's probably in the bag." He stuffed his hands in his pockets. "By the way, how have you been doing? How's your work going?"

"Er, very well, thanks," swallowing my bewilderment and relief all at once. "And you?"

"Good, good, yes. We're just winding up some business that's been bugging me all year . . ."

And, watching his face, I understood. This was how he worked. He was doing nothing that should have caused me any surprise. He was handling me as part of an investigation; I was a player he was watching, on a field he would not step on. He would do nothing to influence me one way or the other; I would give myself away. It was the principle he operated under: things would reveal whatever hidden truths they had, what they were, whether they wished to or not, and no matter how much anyone tried to suppress or deny them.

And I was trying to carry on a normal conversation as if I had nothing to hide.

"Tell me, Brinsel, do you remember very much about Max?"

I shook my head, hoping I actually did not nod, and immediately unsure. "Not a great deal, although being here, and finding out it is still going on—the investigation, I mean—certainly jogs me at times . . . What I remember most is how much affection he had for his friends."

He nodded, the light sliding off his specs as he tilted his head. And it was then that I realized what a scrape I had just had. I had given Peter a message from Roamer, whom I could not possibly know except by Max. And just how, Peter wanted to hear from me.

"Yes," he said gruffly after another moment. "Max had a big heart."

I said feebly, "I am learning very much about him from Rachel."

"Yes, Rachel loves to talk," he admitted. "And she's needed to talk. She's hardly talked about Max at all, since all this happened. It's good for her that you're here. And, actually, Brinsel, I'm glad we could talk today, because I've been meaning to call you. The date has been set for the trial. It will be November ninth. I can't get it pushed any later, I've done everything I can about that."

He had done everything he could, with every resource he had available . . . and what was I doing?

"Hey," he said gently, placing a hand on my shoulder—and to my surprise I did not flinch, when once I would have torn violently away. "We'll do what we can. If we can't get the letters, it's not your fault, Brinsel."

I said miserably, "I don't know what I could have done with them."

"If you'd like to go back and look for them yourself, we can arrange that."

"If I go back . . ." I couldn't finish the thought.

"Is money a problem?"

"It isn't that," I lied again, feeling more horrible by the second. I didn't have my own house, nor hardly a job, I was living hand to mouth, I was traveling on Dai's generosity; of course money wasn't a problem.

"It's a visa problem, huh?"

I shook my head, wishing I could use that excuse, and offered a worse one. "I'm terribly bad at flying." As though there were no such thing as airmail.

Peter's face was a perfect mask that read only patience and concern; behind it he was renegotiating his lines. *Peter's the one who talks odds.* What were the odds I was telling the truth? That I could actually help him? I imagined the numbers growing further apart in his mind, one in ten thousand, in ten million. After a long moment he dropped his chin and crossed his arms, taking off his specs and rubbing an eye with the back of one hand.

"Well, we'll do what we can, Brinsel," he repeated, pushing his spectacles back on. "I have a few good leads and a lot of reasons to hope. We're not alone in this. Hey. It is not your fault."

It wasn't my fault. How often had I been told that? I wanted to believe him. "Max wrote that note because he wanted you to have something to go on, didn't he? And I'm being horridly useless to you."

"We don't really know why he wrote it." He clapped my shoulder again gently. "And you're not so useless, your presence means a great deal. It tells me Max had everything lined up."

I looked up at him. He nodded.

"I am certain of that. He never said something for nothing. Anything's still possible. It would be great to have one of his tidy exposés, but if we can't, well, we can't. I don't want you to feel this whole thing is hanging on you."

I couldn't meet his eyes. "Thank you, Peter," I managed finally. "I'm—I wish I could be more of a help."

"Hey," more familiar and cheerful. "You do your job, I'll do mine."

"My job?"

"You look, I spy..."

Ms. Brinsel Thomas
Bwthyn Stella Maris
Strand Lane
Wimsey
Bristow Surrey
RH7 9JP
UK

August 15, 1987
* *Johannes Nepomuk Maezel (1772)*
* *Marion Bauer (1887)*

Dear Ms. Thomas,
It was a great pleasure to receive your last letter. I'm gratified too that you don't mind answering my questions, for I wouldn't want to be a bother. Whenever I get a chance to speak with an artist about their work, I always discover more than when simply peeking at things. So, you're not really in "the European art scene"? Well, I'm glad at least to have afforded you some amusement. It's more enjoyable to be on the periphery anyway.

    Thanks so much for explaining about your address and the name of your domicile in Surrey. I was moved by the story of this name and the significance it has for you. It's like one of your little prints you sent me: distance, opening, "points to view," beautiful shades of blue.

    At last I've been able to appreciate some of your other *work. Would you believe our library had to get one of your books from a private collection, and another had to be obtained from Canada? The library system was not too cooperative, but fortunately, I know how to pull strings. You were right when you said you were hard to find! But now that I have been able to enjoy some of your work, you are a smidgen better known. And I did enjoy it; you have a wonderful touch and I found some of the short ones very fun. I liked* After Dark, *and then the whole series with the very endearing and Dangerfieldesque Sgt. McCloskey, who had me in stitches with "The Basket Case," "The Hopeless Case," "The Brief Case," "The Flute Case" (!) "The Case of Hiccoughs" . . . Boy, did that bring a few things to mind. I'm familiar with some of that work, so he had all my sympathies. Talk about nothing going right from front to back and yet, I don't know how you did it, things turn out in the end. (I'm sure you intended it, but he has a rather humorous way of going about business. I'm* not too familiar with some of the slang you used . . . I'll have to go researching. And your detective—very interesting fellow, unique, never met one like him! I am guessing you drew your inspiration from someone you know, which if true, gives it all a nice realistic color. Or am I out in left field?). You say you are (to quote your letter) "a teller of tales, a scribbler of featherweight fiction," but I don't think, as you also remarked, that this makes your work "irrelevant." You don't have to retire to the ivory Tower of Theory to write something cogent and meaningful, and, I can add, very enjoyable too. As one to whom the golden doors of fiction have always been firmly shut, let me say that I found your work a great deal more accessible than a lot of the classics that got thrown at us back when. Fiction is actually starting to make sense to me now. How's that for a review?

Thanks so much also for clearing up for me some of the history and geography of Cymru. You can see why I am a musician and not a cartographer (but I do my best).

You asked about my music. How did you guess that I compose? I haven't been able to publish very much, but maybe it will happen someday. What is really happening is that I am off making music with friends; I'm part of a small ensemble called Sojourners. They are a fantastic lot of talent and friendship. It's mostly a weekend thing, though we will have mid-week engagements at schools, churches, etc. Though my work, and teaching (music, privately) keeps me up to my ears in doing-ness, I so value our sessions of Sojourners because music for me is less doing than being, or rather it's where the being is the doing, and vice versa. A chance just to play. I'm excited about sharing some of your music with them, but I have to wait. We each write regularly for the ensemble, and at the moment we're in the middle of an ambitious project for Christmas. Dan is very strict; no new music in mid-season, but I am a handful, and perhaps I can sneak it in somehow.

Your letter arrived at a good time—right before a rare week-long vacation. I spent it visiting with friends and listening to music around the country. My business partner will be taking his vacation in another month and then I get to hold down the fort while he heads for the beach somewhere. His idea of time off. À chaque son sienne.

I'm enclosing a very funny little picture of myself and a fellow musician taken while I was at a concert on vacation. (I am an incurable concert-goer). You will be able to tell which one is me because I am not Rampal.

With every blessing and gratitude,
Max Thompson

11

The Game Afoot

I had come to the end of the initial correspondence, four rather awkward introductory letters. The point of receiving letters from a readership, a snooty colleague had once remarked, was merely to boast one never replied to such things. I had never received a letter, let alone a word, and that *these* letters carried the implication I had rushed to respond made me wince. Uncharacteristic, amateur, back to fore the worst sort of cheek and blundering and somehow, the next letter would need to come level with the less frivolous subject of his casework.

"He never said something for nothing," was Peter's characterization of his business partner, and I knew how true that was. Everything I had ever known Max to say had always meant *something*, and often several things. But mentioning my name in the context of his investigation? Had he wanted that to mean something, it could only have been because he had given me the information in question. But I had nothing. How could he have got me anything? And just as importantly, *why?*

On Monday, 8 July, I set off to research the places where Max and Peter had had their offices. There had been two in their history; the first one on Mitchell Avenue in a small and downtrodden collage of businesses. The second, downtown on State Street, in a decent-sized suite on the fifth story of an office block—actually, the fourth story by my reckoning, but in this country, it was the fifth.

From the file of everything I had ever written about their work I drew out two cards they had filled out at an investigators' convention years before.

Even now, the answers they had written captured their characters with an accuracy that dazed me.

Name: Max Thompson	*Name: Peter Serrev*
Agency: S&T Investigations	*Agency: S&T Investigations*
Position: In-charge/co-owner	*Position: In-charge/co-owner*
Specialization: surveillance/reconstruction	*Specialization: security/ legal*
Experience: 10 yrs	*Experience: 10 years*
Background: music	*Background: the street; college*
Expertise: depends on who you ask (interviewing)	*Expertise: see above*
I look: everywhere. again. geeky in a fedora.	*I look: like a million bucks*
My IQ is: a number	*My IQ is: nobody's business*
Advice: look again. listen closer.	*Advice: Lie in wait—be persistent*
Pet peeve: people who don't read or follow directions	*Pet peeve: pointless questions*
In my spare time: a fascinating concept. tell me more	*In my spare time: who wants to know?*

Max, witty, wily, geeky in a fedora—he had never owned one—Peter, prickly, blunt, gruff. They had made a business. Peter's "legal" specialty had grown into fraud investigation, and Max's "surveillance" had eventually discreetly umbrellaed a specialization in investigation of domestic violence. It had begun so inauspiciously, and as an entirely provisional arrangement—to Peter at least. Perhaps it oughtn't have worked, yet it had, and quite successfully, for almost fifteen years.

I got off at the stop on Franklin and walked the two blocks up to State Street. Three blocks to the north, and I was there. I took a deep breath, studying the high glass and cement façade, and pushed through the door.

The same scene that had greeted Max every morning: the reception stretching into the building about twenty yards and ending in a high wall hung with a large abstract painting that dated itself as Seventies. The maroon carpeting with faded weave pattern. Artificial trees in baskets, their disordered ticks of green relieving the dulling geometry of perpendicular lines. The stiff, dry smell of conditioned air, and people in polished shoes and business suits importantly striding about. Here, as at the Philharmonic, he was one formal suit amongst many, only here the cases everybody carried were all the same. He walked quickly, disappearing in the gathering waiting by the lifts, and I hurried after him.

The listing of businesses on the wall near the lifts had seen a few adjustments, but nothing significant. Or at least, the only significant thing to me was that it no longer listed S&T Investigations at Suite 541. After Peter had closed up shop, I had not given the premises a second thought. The new listing was for something called Silver Lining Design, and I had no idea what this might be.

I took the stairs.

The fire door opened onto the floor of their offices; I had missed him and the corridor was empty. Dulled linoleum glazed with the light from fluorescent ceiling lamps. Another board listing the businesses on this floor. Some nondescript framed prints punctuating the walls. And then I was at the door. Suite 541.

I bit my lip and, barely breathing, pushed open the door.

I could still see just where the chairs had been. The formal, unadventurous décor; Mishael's desk, her colony of paphos vines, spider plants, jade plants. The small dustbin just inside the door, labeled *Preconceptions*. The bank of windows shining through the second doorway to the inner office.

I found in the former premises of S&T Investigations an interior designer who specialized in wallpapering.

A client meeting with a consultant and the secretary gummed to the phone, her glazed eyes fixed on the computer screen before her. Pictures of model homes on every wall, oversize binders of wallpaper styles and design motifs stacked hither and thither. I took advantage of everybody's inattention to scrutinize everything and, standing there, it hit me so powerfully that I was *there*, that I had to put my hand over my mouth.

He was sitting at his pin-neat desk, and in one of the chairs in front of it perched a rather nervous chap. While Max prepared some forms for him, the man bit his nails and ran his hands over his neck and could not keep his eyes in one place for more than five seconds. He kept darting anxious glances over Max's desk and finally said, "You know, that's just the funniest thing, your name."

"My name?"

"Yeah, it reminds me, you know, there was this kid way back when, like some kind of prodigy and all, in the symphony and all that. He played something, I don't know, like a clarinet or something. I played clarinet in school. This kid was real good, I mean *really* good. Like he did gigs and all. He had the same name as you."

"You don't say."

"Yeah. And then he got out, real fast. Like just split, disappeared. Real young kid, nineteen, twenty. Don't know where he is now, haven't heard a thing about him in years. You ever get confused with him?"

"Not really."

"Huh, well that's probably a good thing. It's those young hotshots, you know, things get tough and then they can't take the heat. Those child prodigies that get all pampered and spoiled and then they get surprised when they get older and no one notices them, and then they find out they're not so special. You ever play anything?"

"Flute."

"Oh, really? Not many guys play that. But it seems everyone played something once, and you get over it, like kids in a garage band. I heard this kid's dad was some big shot musician too. You at all related, maybe?" He laughed nervously.

"Who knows?"

"Yeah, yeah, I hear you. Well, it was all a long time ago. It don't matter anymore."

"Probably not." Max passed him the forms with a pen. "If you would read this carefully, and sign there, please . . ."

I could remember any number of their jobs as I stood there, but the majority of their work was nothing that would make a good detective fiction; their standard repertoire, Max had dryly noted, was mostly the work of hacks, not great composers. This didn't render them uninteresting or without challenge; people were always the center of concern. They were never simply problems, they were faces with names.

Davis had come with a problem. Then, unusually, he became one. It had been Max's purely accidental discovery of information that made him look at his findings again and at Davis's involvement, that had prompted him to begin a secondary investigation on Davis himself.

Davis knew nothing of this, his face piqued, not seated but standing by the desk, trying to appear as tall or at least as assertive as he could as he spoke with Max. Max said he would have to reject the job. Davis wanted to know more.

"There isn't more," Max said simply. He hadn't altered the calm of his voice in any degree, yet I could feel everything inside him, most of all the hot steel of his fury, and the casual lean of his height was suddenly so intimidating that I took a step back. "We reserve the right to refuse a job without prejudice. Understood?"

If Davis had trouble with plain speech, he could read subtext easily enough: Max had discovered far more than Davis had intended him to and this investigator would not quietly pretend nothing was happening for any amount of money. And had not the nature of what Max had uncovered so infuriated him, he might have been less terse, but he could barely restrain his anger. Max had known Davis too would be angry and that he might try to retaliate; but he had expected Davis to disappear, not to commit murder.

"Everything comes from somewhere, caused by something," he once admitted to a ruthlessly inquiring Lynn. "One thing builds on another until someone does something. Sometimes you have to pick up the signs after the fact, and it helps to know what they are. Study your music," and he left it at that.

The signs after the fact . . . Signs such as *copyrights*. My heart turned to lead and dropped to my feet—investigation of intellectual property theft had been part of their work.

That had been the issue with my music—Peter, and then Richard and Rachel, had been faced with the peculiar matter of Max naming me as the possessor of important information, and then the discovery of a piece of music of my composition, exactly matching Max's. Would he have given information to someone whom he believed had stolen from him? The music dated from the same time as the information in question, yet from what he had written on the music they could not have concluded that the theft had been his. That they believed there had not been any theft on *my* part was evident from their expressions of trust, but just how it could be possible apart from theft had to be as puzzling to them as their reality was bewildering to me. Even Max had been stymied by the music, or he would not have diagrammed it to bits.

From what I knew of his work and clientele, it could not have got much more bizarre than that, and they had seen plenty of weirdness in over fourteen years.

The secretary still attached to the phone. The consultant still chatting with the client. I drifted towards the open doorway that led to the inner office.

Peter and Max's desks had been in the inside office space. Max's desk was to the left; my eyes picked out first a framed picture of the Cunninghams taken when the twins were about three, and another picture of the twins by themselves—older, dressed in matching outfits, two sticky notes labeling them "Clouseau" and "Cato." A tiny framed sign which read, CAUTION: *"The facts we see depend on where we stand and the habits of our eyes."* Walter Lippmann. Everything orderly and identifiable, tools and papers tidily arranged. Peter's desk about ten steps away, nearer the door to the storage closet. No photographs or mementoes, and always looking as if a burglar had just jumbled through. Files, papers, equipment, books, boxes, everything juxtaposed with the arcane logic of a David Jones painting—in Peter's case, of the archetypal mess—and nevertheless, Peter had understood it.

They had had a handful of full and part-time employees as well as several less attached staff, while their most permanent staff consisted of one woman whom they both acknowledged as a miracle of management. Mishael Chisholm, officially the secretary and unofficially the company encyclopedia, had kept the outer office. She was like a honeyed version of Captain Petrucci: authoritative, efficient, ingenious, gregarious, office mother and office police. She and Peter had a common background; certainly, they both had the same accent, and on some days Max could complain he was being accented out of usage.

"Excuse me, are you *looking* for someone?"

I was zapped nastily to the present. One of the design consultants stood at the door of the storage room, a forbidding wrinkle working its way from her nose to her forehead. Very young, very sprauncy, brisk and brushed as a model on a runway, and there I was, shabby as an old broom; she concluded in an instant I had no business there and was pinning me to the wall by a look anything but welcoming.

I decided to play Utterly Clueless Foreigner. "I'm *so* sorry," I gasped out. "I thought—I mean . . . this *isn't* the consulate?"

Her expression relaxed: I was foreign and I was, really, quite clueless. She strode into the room and stood imperiously near the desk. "No, this is Silver Lining Design," indicating a sign on the desk and speaking slowly and carefully. "Are you lost?"

It wasn't a question so much as a hint to get more so, and I lacked the spirit to press my case. With a last glance round at the former offices of S&T Investigations, I went out.

Visiting what I had thought would be the most promising place had not corresponded with my hopes; bruised them, if anything. I had to hold out hope that going to the less logical places might do a better job. So much for Persius's stoical *ne te quaesiveris extra*—I went out looking for any sign of myself in Max's life, trying to follow his steps, and making notes as I went.

I went everywhere I could go—I popped into bars and pubs and cafés and fast food places all over town, peered in businesses and police stations and libraries, wandered past county administration buildings and other places to which I had no access but which he had, loitered at the DMV, admired the outside of the courthouse, sat and sketched the architecturally uninteresting Public Works Building. I walked miles through the inner city and under flyovers and through subways and up and down streets I would never have set foot on for no other reason than that he had worked there. Anyone following me would have thought me either a curiously selective seeker of fresh air or someone with an offbeat taste in tourism. I was following him and he was always ten steps ahead, his long stride never slackening.

Apart from the investigation, music was the one other thing that connected the two of us, and I once followed him through the doors of the Performing Arts Center where he had worked on and off for most of his life. Newly rebuilt not long before his death, it was enormous, a very modern, very fashionable complex: everything still crisp and clean and saturated with newness, as if the entire facility were freshly unpackaged. The soaring glass front split into panels of opaque facing and glass showing within a quiet atrium of miniature palms and a pool. It was a quiet place on the surface, but the tumult of intense emotion and energy beneath made me stop short of the security desk. I needed a better ruse than curiosity to get past the guard.

After a walk through the city I ended up at the library and dropped myself into a chair far in a back corner. The library had nothing on Max's second career, but it had a treasure trove of historical data on his first. I sat staring at the microfiches of those early accolades, slide after slide of information I knew almost by heart, nothing failing to correspond with what I had written. It was uncannily, exactly as though someone had got hold of parts of my files, tidied them for film, and catalogued them without crediting me. Had the rest of the world not agreed so precisely with my files as well, I might have had cause to be enraged at an apparent theft. And there it all was, all those flowery, foaming reviews. Nearly six years of breathless praise followed by a sudden silence for eight.

I waited only another day before deciding to storm the Performing Arts Center. It had been harder to charm my way into the Philharmonic's offices and then archives—I had spontaneously invented a project of writing an article on local flautists, and then had hurriedly to phone Samantha with a desperate plea to corroborate—but I had done it, and there it all was, if rather tersely recorded, all the black and white in a pattern that could not fail to betray the living color behind it. Even a handful of articles generously tinted in the direction of the facts as I knew them. And there were photographs. After ten years away, Max—simply to be able to grieve—was performing again. He had thought one season would quiet the impulse, yet from then until the end of his life he worked as a soloist every year but three. He had no rivals; he had nothing to defend, nothing to prove. Not even to Richard. But he was still in a class by himself and everything he had feared would happen, did.

Through with the archives, I was just rounding the corner to the reception when I walked in on the argument. Two towering, angry men. Richard and his son eye to eye and glaring each other down.

"You could be doing so much," Richard was pitching. "You could be so much more, and you're settling for so little."

"I happen to think," Max retorted, "that the people I work with are worth the time and effort."

"But what about *you*, Max? What about *your* needs? What about your life, and your worth?"

"Are you referring to your son," replied Max coldly, "or are you referring to the grand personification of your son's talent?"

I looked away, embarrassed, turning quickly down the corridor, but Max turned down it too, and Richard followed him.

"I heard there's an opening at Cardinal Lee for a woodwinds coach."

"That's great, I've got some friends who would love to do that, I'll let them know."

"You could apply, Max."

"I'm busy, thanks."

I quickened my pace, but they tailed even closer until I had to scurry to keep ahead.

"A lot of good flutists could become spectacular under you."

"Thanks, Dad. They could become spectacular under someone else, too."

"Max, you can do what other people can't."

"What am I, God's gift to the flute? They'll learn well enough without me."

"But you have a gift!"

"To hell with it. I have a life, too."

I flattened myself against the wall by Richard's office; they stormed past me through the door, but a few moments later stormed back out, Richard still ruthlessly hurling compliments after his son. I ran. They walked.

"So, you planning on getting back into music full time?"

"Maybe when I retire."

"Why wait, Max? You can do so much meanwhile; you can't just let it rot."

"I am not letting it rot. I am making good use of it, and I am quite happy."

"But you're not out there *showing* it. The world doesn't even know you exist. When are you going to make something of it?"

"Why must the world know I exist?"

I darted into an empty studio, hoping to lose them, but Max marched in and Richard blew in after him, not stopping for breath.

"Max, you could be teaching at Horton. They would bend over backwards to take you on staff."

"Oh yeah? On whose merits, yours or mine? Look what I've added to my frickin' CV—diddlysquat, that's what—"

"Being a goddam soloist is not diddlysquat, for God's sake!"

"I've got a job and career I love and on top of that I'm out where there isn't anyone, *teaching*. That doesn't make you happy?"

"Would you listen to me, Max? Look at what you're doing! You could be teaching master classes for the best artists in the world, the *world*, and what are you doing? You're teaching for peanuts, for crying out loud. You're teaching kids who are never going to get anywhere or amount to anything—"

"Don't you talk about my students like that!"

"Max, *listen* to me—"

"Just suppose I *like* what I'm doing. Just suppose I'm *happy*. Did that *ever* occur to you?"

"You weren't made for this!"

"Oh, I see, you, *you* of all humanity, you've got the master plan, don't you? So, what was I made for? Tell me!"

I clapped my ears, crashing from one wall to another like a bird trapped inside and desperate for the door.

"Max, there are thousands of other talented people out there doing even more than what you're doing. Thousands! And they still can't get as far as you've been, not even half as far. They don't have the gift *you* do for this. You don't have talent like that just so you can go and blow your life on something else."

"I am *not* my talent!"

"Dammit, Max, your talent makes you who you are!"

"So that's it, is it? I'm nothing but what my talent makes me? Have I got news for you."

"Max, would you *listen* to me? That's not what I said! I just want what's best for you."

"Then leave me alone."

The door slammed after him.

"Are you okay, Ma'am?"

I opened my eyes to see a custodian, one hand on the pen over his ear and the other hand grasping a clipboard, eyeing me with a mixture of uncertainty and concern. I was standing before a studio door at the end of a corridor, hands clapped to my ears.

"Oh, quite," I said hastily, letting go of my head. "I'm alright, truly. I was just—thinking of something."

"Heh heh," he smiled. "I was *hoping* the music wasn't all that bad. I thought you might be one of those drama students running around today trying out parts. It's like a *madhouse* down in the lobby."

It was either that, or a midsummer rag week; the atrium end of the reception had been taken over by college-age students paired off doing little sketches. Outside in the sunlight I stopped to catch my bearings. I needed to clear my head of all the arguing and my heart of all its hurt, and was headed for Fordham Street, intending to find a phone box to stake out the police station and possibly jumpstart my memory, but instead my feet took me directly to Good Shepherd. I glared at the church ungratefully and, feeling it futile to go elsewhere for the moment, went looking for an unlocked door.

To my surprise the parish hall was open, and I wandered down the cool hallways, catching snatches of conversation from office doorways and the clatter of dishes and equipment from the kitchen. So little had changed here. The same pinboards, perhaps even with the same tired scalloped borders. The painted cement block walls cold to the touch. The dim, steep stairway to the basement kitchen and dining room that each day saw hundreds of feet descending, ascending. The stale odor of yesterday's chicken dinner. I stood at the head of the stairwell mired in a dozen memories that had nothing to do with Good Shepherd, or even Max.

"Excuse me, hey, hey there, serving doesn't start until five o'clock."

I looked up, startled, and found myself almost eye to eye with a stout younger woman, her voice all authority and her jaw set in business. She jerked her thumb towards the door. "C'mon, you can come back later. The parish hall's not for waiting in."

"Brinsel?" Out of nowhere Rachel's voice cut across my stupor. The young woman and I turned to see her coming up the corridor, toting her enormous handbag and an armful of folders. She gave the young woman a slight smile and beamed at me. "What a piece of luck to find you here. Have you got some time today? I was hoping to call you this week to look at some music."

The young woman's mouth dropped open. "Oh, I'm sorry, I thought—"

Rachel's voice had recalled me to myself. "I was homeless once," I said flatly. "And suppose I still was?" I turned to Rachel. "It's good to see you too. Shall we go to my place?"

It was an offer meant only to drive a point home; my flat was not actually ready to receive Rachel, and my stomach flopped over when I unlocked the door and remembered the pictures scattered around my office, one of them of her brother. "Oh, it's all but *cwtyn y saint*." I rushed ahead of her. "Don't mind the mess, really!" I pushed the offending drawing over and dropped a handy file on top of it, then tore about shoving papers into piles, no doubt only giving her the impression that I lived in conditions not too far removed from Peter's workplace.

And there was Rachel standing in my living room, enormous and inscrutable as an apparition and gazing around with a small smile. With someone else in my lodgings I was suddenly conscious of its peculiar odors—staleness, paint, cheap soap. Yesterday's overdone turnips and the morning's tea and scorched porridge. How had Rachel ended up here, in my world?

From where we sat at the kitchen table I could see—across the room near the window—my typewriter, the selfsame at which I had first written about the person I now saw by shifting my gaze to the left. She sat tall in her chair, the brown sweep of her hair loose over her shoulders in the idiom that signaled she was off work; she cradled her teacup in one hand, the small half-smile still etched in her face. She had dark circles under her eyes today. "These are tasty little morsels," she addressed a handful of cake. "You made them?"

"Oh no, these are from the bakery," I nodded at the platter heaped with butter-yellow cubes each the size of a conker. "The only thing I can really cook well is porridge, and I didn't want to inflict that on you."

She laughed, leaning over and gently pinching my wrist between her finger and thumb in a very doctor-like gesture. "Well, I just hope you get enough, you're almost skin and bones. We'll have to fatten you up before you go back."

I hastily bit back the frown, hoping Rachel did not see the anger pinking my cheeks, but she merely brushed her hair from her brow and picked up her cup again. "So, this is where you're staying while you're over here." She swirled her tea and peered over the rim of her cup from one end of my flat to the other, a glance of an instant. "Home away from home."

Home. My gaze followed hers from the kitchen to the opposite wall, cataloguing the dingy linoleum, drawing tablets, stacks of typed sheets, a lost stocking by the desk . . . almost like a picture from my cottage, but all this was still a long way from home. "I had been hoping to invite you over sometime," I lied, "but I hadn't thought it might be today."

"It's lovely, nice and cozy." Her brow wrinkled up. "And you were homeless once?"

I held my cup in both hands, listening to the traffic in the street after her voice. "Yes."

"I'm sorry," she said simply, and I shrugged. She nibbled at a cake and set it carefully on the edge of her saucer. "Max did that once. I don't mean that it happened, I mean he *did* it; he went out on the street because he wanted to see what it was like." A resigned sigh. "He wasn't made for that. He paid the dues for it, too."

"What time of year had he done this?"

"Um," she swallowed a mouthful of tea. "April, I think."

"He would have been alright. He wouldn't have frozen to death."

She looked at me, but her attention was fixed in the fear of the possible past. "I suppose not." She gestured away some invisible lint on her sleeve, shrugging. "It's funny, you know, both of us got into professions where you have to care, but you can't care, if you know what I mean. But nothing was ever enough for him. Did he tell you about his students?"

"His students? Had he taught investigation?"

"Well, he did that, but I mean music; he taught kids in the inner city for next to nothing. His idea of a hobby, but he did a lot of good by it, and some of them even got into the arts."

"There's lovely, that." I broke off bits of my cake as if intending to eat it smaller still, but the pieces remained on the plate.

"I told you he gave his flutes away, except for the one." She pushed her teacup into her mouth, staring at a spot on the table near my hand. "He gave them to his students, and to other musicians. *Thousands* of dollars' worth. I always thought he was on his way out of music completely, but he never explained himself." A huge sigh. "That was his way."

"I rather wish it hadn't been."

She laughed, taking another little cake from the platter. "His letters were clear as mud, huh?"

"I mean," I said hastily, "I don't know how he first found out about me, he had never explained that."

"Well, your music, of course." She nibbled at her cake, unconcerned. "I don't suppose the rest really matters, does it?"

"Perhaps not," I acquiesced, squirming at the thought of the letters.

"And that's what I wanted to see you about." She brushed off her fingers and busily dug in her handbag. "I saw our music director today about this, but I really needed to see you. Do you recognize this?"

Rachel unfolded and spread out on the table two sheets of music from the same composition, one sheet from near the beginning and one nearer the end. Except for the music itself, neither had any identifying attributions. I stared at the sheets helplessly, my heart a fist beating inside me. "What is it?"

"I don't know yet. Dad found it in some of Max's papers the other week; they were mixed up with some unfinished works. The reason I wanted to ask you was because it matches another of his unfinished compositions, at least a part of it, since this can't be the whole piece of whatever it is. I wouldn't be at all surprised by now if it *was* yours."

The title, which would be on the missing first page, was *April for Winds;* if I said it was mine, they would not publish his; if I said I did not know whose it was, still they would do nothing.

"Of course, I've seen this. This must be his own music. I believe this is some of his work that he sent me."

"But this is published! We have his drafts, but Four Winds didn't publish it, and they don't have any record of it, either."

The lights in the room were glaring too intensely and my appetite was finished then and there. I blinked hard, my eyes roaring in pain. "Perhaps this was published by somebody else?"

"I don't know why he'd do that, but I suppose it's possible." She knit her brows. "You're sure this is some of the same music he sent you?"

"Positive."

Rachel's face had become a doubling blur, but I could see her eyes suddenly glisten brightly. "There's so much oboe in this, I wonder if he wrote it for me. You know," her voice at last cracking, "he played oboe incredibly, so much better than me. But then he did everything better than me—he was an amazing violinist, and pianist, he was a better cook, and . . . he would have made a better *parent*—"

"Oh, my dear," I struck my hand on the table just to stop the room from tilting so much, "I am certain you've done quite well."

"Thank you, I'm sorry," She dropped the papers, dabbing her eyes and nodding. "It's just, you know, all of this . . ."

Somehow, for another half hour I managed both to keep upright and to keep Rachel from sliding to the far end of the flat; at length she rallied as though to cheer me, and in my less sick and vertiginous moments I enjoyed the company. But after she had gone I slumped in a corner and let the room tumble about me and cursed myself black and blue in Welsh and then Cornish and Scots Gaelic. First the letters, then music I could not promise. I was stripping myself of copyrights left and right and getting nowhere. It really was starting to look like my mind would be the next thing to go.

I had gone across the city and his careers and back. From where I stood looking back on it all, everything had a place, everything had a rationale, except where I had come in. Not a hint of how he had learned about me.

And why should that have surprised me? It should not have been any more possible for him to know of me in his world—this hectic, urban zoo where he had lived a reserved and extremely busy life—than I could have known of him in my own world—rural, and small, insular and thousands of miles across the Atlantic. There existed only one way I had known of him, and that was as a character. I was not a character, and could not imagine where he had learnt of me. It would have asked an inside job to find as much as my name. Who had mocked my writing?—not *The Times Literary Supplement*, but the arts page of an insignificant Welsh rag, whose critic had no better way to employ his wit than in derision, and whose indictment would have required more than one sympathetic translator simply to untangle the idiomatic abuse. Who published my music, my books?—not any major house, but two microscopic publishers who had taken me on merely out of convenience, whose range of distribution scarcely totaled a hundred miles together. It all asked too much of Max. The man who didn't care for fiction, go to the lengths that would be needed to search out and read my stories? The man who "couldn't carry a correspondence to save his life," as his own sister had once put it, who had had as much interest in art as he did in literature, write *letters*, and inquire after art? There was no rationale anywhere in his life that I could see remotely to suggest the notion. There was nothing in his character to support it. He didn't write letters. End of story.

My music appeared to be the answer. But it had never occurred to me to do such a thing as put it in his possession *as* my own music until that panicked moment in Peter's office when it seemed the best idea I'd ever had—until I found it was true. True, and even a fact.

I had been walking for days and days and had got almost nowhere. I stopped on a corner within sight of Good Shepherd's spire, wishing the private detective agency existed that could find out what I needed to know.

12

Edward

Searching is hard, but remembering is always the hardest part. Like grief, it comes when you don't want it to—all the things you'd rather didn't come. I lay in bed the next morning staring at the ceiling, remembering until I was sick with it, then at last pushed myself to my feet and began another day remembering someone else's life.

The Horton Conservatory of Music stood only two blocks from the Performing Arts Center, yet I had not stopped there on my other visits, putting off as long as I could what seemed least promising. It was strung along the riverside just north of downtown proper, six acres of trim grounds and sandstone and windows topped with Ionic pediments, all flagged paths and elite professionalism. The main building hugged a narrow porch buttressed by Ionic columns, the entrance atop a mountain of stone steps smoothly scalloped by a century of service. I stood catching my breath at the door, a masterpiece of woodwork and frosted glass. Each large pane was etched with the cipher of an H stylized as a lyre, held in a mandorla banded by the conservatoire's motto in transparent gold uncial lettering. *Servus Musicae nunquam peribit.* A grand promise, and not what Max would have called a fact without sarcasm.

At the open Dutch door to the administrative office, I signed myself in and was granted a visitor's pass. Bright walls, modern lighting, but the high ceilings and dark dado, the thick transoms, the checkered tiling silky with age, all breathing an old-fashioned air into halls at this moment echoing faintly with the excitement of a student rock band in a distant studio.

Several glass cabinets in the main hall showcased relics of the school's past and portraits of its stars; my attention drifting just above these abruptly lit on a photograph of Max. He was standing on stage at Richard's retirement concert, a spotlighted figure between the orchestra and the dark hall, his flute a telescoped blaze of light in his hands, and his eyes and expression rapt as though in the midst of an intense conversation. It was iconic, mythic, remote as a glossy image in a concert program; the photograph had captured a mystique and power neither of us would have recognized—a portrait of his sound, not of him. After a few moments, I lowered my gaze, and realized the case below was filled with memorabilia—photographs, articles, every award he had ever won, the honorary doctorate he had been awarded the year before his death. Items he had filed away and largely forgotten, here assembled as a portrait of renown. Even his piccolo was here, lying in its open case like another trophy. Horton had more cause to remember him than any other school, and, on its own terms, it did. No other alumnus had been awarded such a generous share of Horton's recognition; he was their brightest star and these were the effulgence of his glory, what they would not permit to be lost or forgotten. Nobody had to find it, or look for it; students who had never known him walked past it every day. Jill walked past it every day...

I shuddered. It was her family history, here in public—all the things Max had always refused to tell her about. They had lost control of so much at his murder, and here I was, a stranger upsetting their control further. Was that what angered her about my presence?

Halfway through the building I came upon a carefully decorated demi-lune table guarded by gangly pot plants and stacked with papers on applying and auditioning. An open prospectus was crammed with descriptions of courses, the back part thick with faculty biographies. The names had changed considerably since he had studied here, but a few senior members dated from that time. One was Alfred Jüggen, a local flute luminosity who had been one of Max's professors, and a character in any context. Perhaps as rehearsal, I ingratiated myself into a brief and doomed "interview" with him—he had as much desire for a lunch of mothballs as he did for speaking of the once-star pupil who had abandoned a promising career.

I had better luck, if just as predictable results, with another faculty member who had been one of Max's instructors. Victoria Rivers had some time between classes and, in her endlessly gracious way, made of my request for a spontaneous interview a chance for "a quick chat before I have to go harangue." My recital of the article I was writing on local flautists excited her; she had a trove of stories on the very topic. She invited me to accompany her on the walk to her next class, and offered a sympathetic smile when I explained my interview with Professor Jüggen had not been very productive. "Well, Ms. Sumner, you found our fossil-in-residence! Alfred was one of the stars of his generation who went into education . . . and he's gotten very comfortable where he is."

Victoria was as round as S&T's onetime accountant, Tonya Farr, but with a character just as cool. She had a musician's meticulous posture and it gave her large figure a finesse and grace she would not have had otherwise. Like Jüggen, she was a local flute talent; she had been teaching at Horton for almost forty years, and at eighty-one was one of the most senior faculty members. Also like Jüggen, she recalled the younger Thompson without any prompting, but with warmth and affection.

When we reached her classroom it seemed time for me to go, but she invited me to stay and observe, and not having other plans to appeal to, I consented. The class she had to "harangue" turned out to be a summer course for beginning flautists. When after some minutes of instruction they began to play a little, I learned again the ambiguous nature of the term "beginner." I could only surmise they were beginners compared to someone of Victoria's experience; if these were beginning flautists, I realized I should have to reappraise my own skill level at subterranean.

Though he had been playing only three years when he entered, Max's proficiency had been much closer to Victoria's own. Somewhere on campus, back in the main building, was the room where he had auditioned, aged eleven, exactly thirty years ago. He had been filled with suppressed grief and bounding excitement, certain of the way he was going, wanting nothing but music and innocent of fine technicalities like faculty politics. He was given twenty minutes to warm up in a practice room and then appeared before the audition committee with his Gemeinhardt.

The sound of a flute yanked me firmly out of my thoughts and dropped me with a jolt into a chair in Victoria's classroom—not any flute, but the same I had held in my hands in Rachel's study. Even when I had located the source, all the hair stood up on my arms, and an electric prickle flashed over my scalp.

It was one thing to have "heard" Max's flute in my mind for four years—*this* was the sound of the flute itself, of Max himself. The music flew, arced, spiraled into the air, slid into a stream of quicksilver, flung into a thousand liquid droplets, chime pure, deep as sky. Now he made it sing like an oboe, now a dulcimer. Now it was blue a thousand miles long, now amaranthine, now meteoric white, now high verdure. He loosed one untrembling note and it opened like some cosmic rose into a thousand dimensions of sound, each vaster than the last, then retracted it to a scatter of pebbles. It was a shimmering whip of Northern lights. It feathered air. It sparkled, blew bombast, turned itself on its head with sweet tenderness. Now it was a nightingale, a cricket, it was cheeky, sobbed, cracked jokes. It was distinct as a fingerprint; I could have singled it out from any of a thousand other master flautists, the way one could not mistake a van Eyck *Annunciation* for a van der Weyden.

A hundred reviewers had exercised themselves to magnificent effect to put that sound into words. All rubbish, absolute rubbish. One might as well dam a waterfall in order to observe it, or dissect a flower to see what made it so lovely. It wouldn't bear that sort of translation—it deftly escaped rational grasp, laughing. Was it Bach, Franck, Bolling? It almost could not matter; it was Max translating himself into sound and amplifying as he did so the power and energy of the music itself, Max stretching himself to the very limits of his expressive power and skill, and his limits had been so far above any *conception* of limit, no comparison was possible. It was a sound that would only age with the decay of the tape, and never again could it be heard, except by means of this ...

Victoria stood with her hand on a cassette player, the light glinting off her glasses as she leaned over. She snapped the pause button in the middle of a phrase.

"Now, that's the second subject ... can anyone identify the major second and the dynamic ... ?"

Had she said "We shall now play Twister according to Robert's Rules of Order" I could not have been knocked for more sixes. I went mad with impatience for the class to end; when at last all the students had gone and she turned to me with a great smile, I was still so giddy with that sound that had lit up my soul from end to end and left it ringing in glory, I almost blurted, "He has set the air on fire, and you talk about technique??"

"That music you were playing—that was—who was that?"

"That, Ms. Sumner, was Max Thompson. Didn't I tell you he was one of the finest there was?" Her smile deepened, this time in memory. "How did we ever teach him? He was always one step ahead." She shook her head, her voice as sad as her eyes. "I still wonder what more he could have become. I think about it every day."

"But did he not have a career?"

Victoria looked at me critically, the no-nonsense instructor Max had both admired and argued with. "A career," she sighed. "Yes, he did. Depending on who you talk to, it lasted six years or most of his life." Again she shook her head, this time with a note of impatience. "All those flutists I told you about—let's call what they did conventional. It's what I myself did. We worked hard to stay in the game. We didn't disappear. But Max wasn't like that," a sudden emotion interrupting her voice. "If there's one thing you should know about Max Thompson, Ms. Sumner, it's that he didn't do conventional very well. He had too much innate authority, and asked questions no one else did. He was easily the best of us all—and he had certainly worked hard to be that. But he wasn't interested in being the best, only in being of service. It was really what made him tick, and if anyone could have had a career doing that, it was him. But he didn't."

This time I wanted to ask fifty more questions, but she had a meeting to get to.

"Good luck on your article, Ms. Sumner. Be sure to send us a copy! I'll be interested how it turns out."

The front hall was much quieter than before; not even memories interrupted my exit. On the way out I paused at the doors again, this time from within, studying the gold-tinted slivers of shapes peeping through the design in the frosted glass. The school motto defining small discrete portions of the world outside: *The servant of music will never die.* "No," Ariel had scorned, "just go stale, or calcify, or get frozen in vinyl. For God's sake! What's all the screaming about?"

Horton had seemed to turn up nothing; I put off my search for a day and did nothing more than errands to try to clear my head, completely moithered as to what to do next. In the morning I went out walking just to see if I could find a clue.

I did, at last; it wasn't the one I wanted, and I didn't care for it at all.

The Fifty-Sixth Street jail stood smack on the pavement, a block of concrete and wire, and seeing it in person I felt my stomach coil into a knot.

Max had stopped here as well, both as part of work and off work for visitation. This was only by appointment, and I had nearly forty minutes to check in and be brushed down. The officer at the desk took a double take at my passport and identification and momentarily walked off with them, but soon came back nonchalant and gestured me to wait. The waiting room was filled with spouses, friends, a few suits and professional-looking people, but most of us had the tatty, frayed air that comes from life on a small income. I amused myself, as did a few others, watching a young woman in heels and a tight blue dress decorating her face; her handbag, her portable cosmetic counter, propped open in her lap and an open compact cradled in one hand. She drew all over her face with any number of little implements, making marvelous expressions in the little mirror, either unaware of the performance she was giving us or reveling in it like a diva. I appreciated the diversion; the voltage of my nerves was cranked so high my hands scarcely kept still. I fiddled so much with the strap on my satchel it detached itself in my hands, and I spent the rest of my wait clumsily trying to tinker it back together.

My name was called.

The procedure was not too different from what I had known years before in another country, and the flat-painted walls, the bars, the security glass and the unpromising starkness all the same. The chair at the counter I was shown to had cracks in its black vinyl seat, but I hardly noticed it because Edward Davis was sitting on the other side of the glass.

Of all the characters I had written about in Max's story, here was one I had spent very little time on, despite that I had been aware of him almost as long as I had been aware of Max. I had begun with Max's death, and here was the person responsible for it.

He was slumped on his chair in his plain jail duds, hands clasped in his lap. His face older than I remembered, heavier, and pink as if he had just been rubbing it, his round jaw pricked with the thought of a beard. The brown hair receded to a thin fringe around his head; a loud purple bruise on one arm. Features remarkably like those of one of my cousins, worry-eyed, thin-lipped, a wide forehead—in other settings an intellectual's face, certainly on my cousin. Davis at least had the brains for it, though he had spent them sliding around in the scum of pseudo-philosophical rot and worthless recreations that made up his narrow understanding of the world and which he called his life. He was not large by any measure but had no sharp edges; he was all soft bulbousness, round nose, round shoulders, round knuckles and elbows, round fingernails. An air of boredom as though it were all one to him if he sat before an empty chair or another human being, and my presence, known or unknown, of no more significance than an advertisement to be weighed and discarded in less than a glance. It was his eyes that gave the lie to this appearing ease: unhappy and edgy, his attention seeming to wander between the world outside himself and some private inner screening. Had everything ended as I had believed, he would have been long since convicted and moved on to prison. But here he was, and, impossible as it seemed, there I was, too.

In a story, a murderer is a tool, if with a history: elderly parents living in another state, an increasingly disenchanted girlfriend and a child from a previous marriage, a perfunctory education and an erstwhile career in marketing with high ideals—he believed anything could be marketed, one had only to create a demand or meet one, and he had lucratively met a demand by selling women and girls. He had amounted to an extra, the less time spent on the better. For the first time, I had to face him as a person, and one I couldn't edit away or reduce to a passing mention. I had two reactions on meeting his gaze. The first was a wooden and somehow alien sense of pity. The second was a violent urge to be sick on his shoes, and to turn and run straight out.

He spoke first.

"So, who are you?"

I had not heard that voice—never mind only in my imagination—since I had first written about Max's death. The sound of it shattered the wooden pity in me.

Here, in this whitewashed and echoing place, I knew who I was. I was someone who had seen too much and had lost even more. I was the witness to a murder that had had no witnesses.

"My name is Brinsel Thomas." I could not lie about myself here. "I . . . I was a friend of Max's."

No reaction; he tilted his head. "I'm sorry about that," after a moment, his voice flat as the white paint on the metal doors. "He was a good guy." He nodded. "And I am too, Brinsel. I got framed good."

There he was, one of the last people who had seen Max alive, the one responsible for killing him. I had thought about this sort of encounter before, but I had never imagined it might be possible. I was prepared for the fear, the contempt, but not the punch of nausea and the manic tangle of thoughts trying to devise a way to catch him out.

"I guess you've heard about how they did it," he said, omitting to make it sound like a question.

About how the missing file had been used to frame him. "I've not heard much of anything."

His eyes darted between my face and the shelf at the bottom of the glass partition. "It's not what you think." He shook his head. "It's not what you think. It's real hard, Brinsel. When everybody is saying, it's like this, it's like this, and you're the only one saying, no, it's *not* like this, and no one believes you, it gets awfully hard sometimes, it's awfully tempting just to give in, just to go along with it, and say yeah, I did it, just to get it all over with . . ." He shook his head. "But I can't, I'm innocent and I know it, even if no one else believes it."

I swallowed hard, quickly, my stomach twisting in revulsion. My mouth was so dry there was nothing to swallow.

"You don't believe me either, do you?"

It wasn't a question, and I didn't answer it.

"So, what are you doing here, Brinsel?"

"I wanted to see who you were."

"Well, here I am."

I was unprepared for the words I spoke next.

"They don't know who killed him. They may never find out."

Davis gazed at me flatly, remorse for himself or its phony twin for me deepening the lines in his face. "Geez, I'm real sorry, Ms. Thomas . . ."

I am certain it was that suddenly courteous *Ms. Thomas* that made me blurt, "They don't even know why."

"Well, sure they know why . . ." he began, then stopped. He repeated, "He was a good guy, a good guy. He was doing some work for me. Bad things happen, look what happened to me."

"They may never find out why," I said, and this time there were tears in my throat.

Silence. The dull background rumble of other conversations around us.

Finally, "Well, well, don't you worry too much about that, Brinsel, things'll get straightened out. They'll find the right guy, and I'll get out of here, and we can all go home and forget this ever happened."

"You never forget," the words cracked out of me. "You never forget things like that."

He lowered his eyes. "No, I'm sorry."

I wondered for which of us the effort of his pretense was more painful.

"I really wish it hadn't happened." He was staring at the glass where it met the counter. "I can't tell you how much. Things weren't supposed to happen like this."

No, they weren't, he had intended something much different, and then Max had found out too much and got in the way. From first to last, the blame was entirely his, and yet once, once, I had believed I had caused it myself. I had believed it was *my* fault.

There he was, *there he was*. At last, at long and horrible last, an enemy I could see and hear and speak to, one whom I knew with unequivocal certainty was guilty. Nothing had ever prepared me for this. Every inch of me howled in pain I had long passed by. I did not even want to forgive him, and knowing Max had not only hardened my intent.

And there too was the fiendish irony of it all. Here sat the one person who had known all that Max had known, all that I needed to know, and not only would he—could he—not say a word about that, but I could not ask him, and it could not be tricked out of him.

"The trial . . ." I began, and couldn't finish.

"Yeah, the trial." He would have a resourceful lawyer; he could certainly afford it. He scratched his knee, uninterested, his gaze lowered. Another long pause. "So, what is it you do, Brinsel? How do you get by in the world?"

For an instant a furious silence seized my tongue, then I chose something. "I am a musician."

At this he lifted his chin slightly and ran his fingers around his mouth with one hand, the handcuffs flashing another reminder of where we were. "You make music, huh?"

"Yes," I pushed the word out. "Like Max Thompson. I play flute."

"Huh." Davis evaded my gaze, flexing his hands and studying them instead.

I thought of what he had done to Max's hands because it had amused him to wound a musician that way.

"Was he an old friend?"

"Who?"

A small gesture, dismissive. "Thompson, Max Thompson. Was he an old friend of yours?"

My breath was coming quite short. I held my mouth shut and nodded.

"How long did you know him?"

I swallowed hard again, avoiding his gaze. "A while."

He gave a small grunt. Evidently not long enough.

I asked, "Did he say anything?"

"No."

The word came out as a noise of disgust, but it was a word.

"What do you mean, 'did he say anything?'" He blinked, his eyes coming back from somewhere and his doughy face flushing an ugly purple. "Did *who* say anything?" He leaned back in his chair, his stare not leaving my face.

"Do you find it amusing, playing with people's lives?"

"I dunno. Do you?" He snorted. "Look, I'm the other victim here, Brinsel. I just asked him to do a job. What happened after that had nothing to do with me."

"I suppose murdering somebody who had discovered you have too much to do with sex trafficking would count as nothing."

"Like I said," his voice icy quiet, "I got framed good."

I said nothing.

"My whole life's been messed up by all this. I am an innocent man."

The words made their way out of me with great effort: "It's hard to live in a lie."

"I bet it is." He leaned forward. "And I think you're done here. It's not like *you* care what happens to me."

The one thought that filled my mind as I stood on the pavement again was that somehow, some way, I had to write those letters.

13

Further Questioning

Seeing Davis had brought back a tidal wave of memories and reactions, none at all helpful to my task. Weeding through them was like thrashing through a bramble of thorns. I typed up the brambles and the thorns and the flood that had come with them, but when I finished, nothing new had surfaced; if anything, only more questions that left me raw and incensed.

If seeing anybody could help me, it should have been seeing Davis, the first problem and the last. Why was I the one who had to have so much conscience that it paralyzed me, and Davis so little that he could so blithely act as though he had not committed murder?

Paralyzed by conscience on the most important job, I somehow found a way to keep more trivial work poking along. The writing I wanted most to work on next, however, I didn't have the files for—they had been left behind at home. It would be necessary to ring Dai again.

This time it seemed best to have him where he could find things. It took some careful planning; after nothing short of a logistical pièce de resistance, on Sunday afternoon he was sitting in the family summer cottage at Wimsey where I had been living for the past several years and I was sitting in my Thirty-Second Street bedsit early Sunday morning, and his familiar voice crackled over the lines. "David can't say here, or rather can't say *why*, but here I am!"

"*Cefais Ddafydd fy ngwas.*"

"You have indeed," he replied cheerfully. "That's in the *prayer* book, isn't it? A psalm? One-hundred-something—verse, er, one?"

"Eighty-nine, verse twenty."

"Yes, of course! You see, I know where to find things. And at your service."

"Good, I've got some things you can find for me."

"Well now, *really*, Suhl, if you've got them, why must I find them for you?"

We started off all in Welsh; after so many weeks of bombardment by American vowels and volume, it was a delight passing expression to rest my ears and warm my voice on such comfortable sounds again, and I let Dai go on about small bits of nothing and family news. Mur was going batty with the end of the school term. Kyffin was going through a Welsh-only phase, not even responding to English; "I seem to remember his dad doing the same thing at that age," I commented. I grilled him on his apparently erstwhile search for the paper I was missing, and he sighed and sputtered and objected, and promised to keep trying. The file I had called to ask him to find was not making itself known, either. I was losing hope that anything I needed could ever be discovered. I thanked him for making an effort.

"It's rum of you not to call every few weeks," I added. "You had mentioned you would, so I was a bit surprised when you didn't. But the time has been flying, and I've been doing well."

"Oh, well, that's wonderful, Suhl. And about not ringing you, I had thought of it, but then I figured Cathy'd be there if you needed anything, so, you know . . ."

"Cathy is away on holiday," I reminded him. "And then she's got transfer work around the state for a few months, remember?"

"Oh, that's right. Well, I thought you'd be fine, you know, been a while and all, and you have a way of making friends."

I was amused, though it didn't seem like Dai to be so lackadaisical about me. At any rate, the rest of his conversation assured me all was the same with him; he amused himself and entertained me by making an uproarious palaver over pinches of nothing, mimicking his colleagues, tarring the NHS, and working up a melodrama over anything else going not quite according to plan.

It was then that one useful idea finally hit me. After having just praised my own miserable integrity through the roof, I could do no worse than actually ask him to look around for the idiot letters so that I could at least for *once* be telling the truth. "Dai, that reminds me, could you please take a quick look in my correspondence file? I'm looking for anything from someone named Thompson."

"Correspondence? Which one is that?"

I directed him.

". . . let's see." The grinding of the cabinet. "Coooorespondence . . ."

Static and rustling. Silence. David's funny little "h'm-h'mming" noises. Papers.

"Nothing . . . nothing . . . wait—not that either, that's . . . Timson . . . and, not Tomlinson . . . Travis . . ."

Silence.

"You're certain it's Thompson?"

"Quite certain."

"Thompson . . . ha, odd. And *you* know somebody named Thompson?" More shuffling.

"I have good cause to believe I do. Think of all the Thompsons in the world. Are the odds not on my side that I would know at least one?"

"I'm just fooling, Suhl *fach*, I'm sure you know heaps of Thompsons, entire populations . . ." The scraping sound of transatlantic papers. ". . . But none here, don't see nowt."

"You're not certain there's anything on the desk?"

"H'm, h'm, let's see . . . biros, lots of blackleads, doodles, some artwork just *horrible beyond*, oh my God, someone could get hurt . . . piles of papers . . . heaps of books . . . what are you reading, what is this, *Foolproof Tricks for Failed Writers* . . . ?"

"Very funny, Dai."

". . . a dish of marbles . . . so, you left these here? A cotton reel, some conté bits . . . yeuch, what is *that?*"

"What is what?"

"Oh, it's a . . . it's this big gloppy thing . . . it looks . . . *yeuch,* it's all slimy . . . *ach-y-fi* Suhls, what did you leave out here? . . . shit, it's got tentacles going . . . it's got—oh, *shit*, help—!"

"Dai, you clot," I couldn't help laughing. Desperate Dai noises, the sound of a forced struggle. Oaths and shouting. Something large crashing.

". . . My goodness, Suhl, I didn't think I'd make it, you grow some nasty mold when you leave your cup out for months. I had to bash it with the chair."

"My prize specimen. Now what can I take to the Chelsea?"

"I don't believe they accept fungus at the Chelsea, Suhly. Try the British Museum."

"You alright?"

"Cracking, you know me. But I don't see any Thompson letters anywhere, sorry."

"Bother. If anything shows up, do let me know. But it's not terribly important."

"All *that*, not terribly important? I come all the way out here to turn your digs upside down, and nearly get eaten by the fungus, and it's not important... Oh, I should know better, you artists. By the way, how is your *ditectif* doing, the one who plays a flute? I think that's just the funniest thing, however did you come up with it? Rye kept asking after you when I saw her last month. Really wants to hear this story you're working on."

"Oh *diws*," I groaned, "well, don't give away too much, I've had to do so much revising."

"Lots and *lots*, of course," too cheerfully for comfort, "it's all quite different when you actually get there, is it? Give you a job good, does it? That whole cultural bit..."

I couldn't say anything.

Warming to a theme, "And then all those bits about what the work is like..."

"*Dafydd.*"

Catching on a bit, "Sam getting after you again?"

"Not Sam, just life," unable to hide the catch in my voice.

"Oh," gently, this time. "No worries, Suhly. I know this story is important to you. I'm sure it will be fantastic."

"*Diolch yn fawr*," not at all gratefully. "When is it you are leaving?"

"Two weeks. It's been nothing but Mallorca Mallorca Mallorca around here, you'd think there was nowhere else in the world. Kev's at full fuss and Nate is beside himself with anticipation, just frothing at the mouth. I'll be glad to get it over with, you know how I am with sandy beaches and the grockle set. Would you like us to get you anything?"

Some peace of mind. "Could you get me that file before you go?"

"Well, I'll try. Anything from Mallorca?"

"Send me some rain."

"Gloomy, Suhls!"

"I happen to like it. Give Rye my love when you see her, and to Mur and my two favorite critics."

I rang off feeling more foolish than ever. Why on earth had I asked Dai about the letters, the *nonexistent* letters? Thank goodness, for whatever professional sensitivity he had, Dai could be so cluelessly dotty and so endearingly familiar. If he were to suspect I was being artistic with the truth, it would lead to no end of trouble, and I didn't need his help with that.

Sunday afternoon I had a welcome diversion: luncheon with Rachel and John. With the twins away at orchestra camp, Rachel felt it was probably the only time I would get to come over again. "You know," John warned me when he came to pick me up, "Rachel's going to want to talk some more, so be prepared for a lot of it."

"Oh, it's no trouble," I said, "I'm glad she can talk, and I'm prepared to listen."

"You seem to be very good at that," he said warmly.

I didn't bother contradicting him.

The afternoon was sweet and mild and we ate out on the back patio, enjoying the taste of a curry concoction of John's and the sight of the rich colors of Rachel's flower beds. Two terracotta pots of her floral handiwork perched at the end of the patio, each overflowing with blue lobelia trailing onto the ground and crowned by a hat of golden pansies. I was staggered by the vividness of the blue, the same flowers I had in my window boxes back home; the sight of them made me ache, and I concentrated on the rose pattern on the china. I thought of Max sitting here with the two of them on summer Sunday evenings, the twins tumbling in the lawn, and the fourth empty chair. Easier than thinking of all the broken things, all the empty chairs in my own life.

Afterwards John brought out a carafe of coffee and three cups and saucers on a tray, and we basked in the green quiescence of the afternoon. It was like being on holiday and I thought of the Cunninghams' vacations; they would have gone before orchestra camp, but they hadn't been away. Was this because of me? Then there was the worrisome fact of Peter being at Good Shepherd—was *that* because of me? I was puzzling over these, my attention fixed on a row of fuchsia pinks, when Rachel turned to me.

"Brinsel," she began, "when you and Max wrote, did he . . . well . . ."

I involuntarily tensed; it was sure to be about music. My mind went into high gear, throwing all associated thoughts crazily in a heap until I could not tell them apart.

"He wasn't sweet on you, was he?"

"Sweet—Max? Oh, no!" I did a sudden and violent imitation of the pinks, forcing a small laugh. "Not a bit of it. He was a perfect gentleman, very friendly, but all professional, sweet not at all." I pushed my teacup into my mouth, taking too big a gulp and then sputtering on it. "I rather had the sense that he was trying to find out something, though he never said he was a detective, and I never found out until later."

John nodded. "That does sound just like him."

"Yes, Max did that sort of thing, he was a sneak," agreed Rachel. "It's just the letters. You see, Peter didn't tell us *why* Max wrote you, just that you had corresponded, and that that was how you had the information on his work. As for the letters, well, it's not what we'd've expected of Max. My brother almost wouldn't have written a correspondence to save his life."

"Ah, I see." I tipped half the sugar bowl into my cup and stirred sloppily.

"Well, it's just this," studying her own cup and swirling it gently, "when we heard about the music you wrote, and when Dad and I looked at it, I don't know, I guess it was crazy of me, but then I just had this idea that he was interested in you, on account of the music. Because the thing is, Brinsel," beginning to smile guiltily, "and this is why I asked, before any of this, the only other person my brother *ever* wrote to was Ariel."

Had I been tipping the chair even ever so slightly, both it and I should have gone crashing spectacularly over. Why could I not have remembered *that* in Peter's office two months before? First I idiotically claim Max would write me personal letters when he never wrote letters, and then I forget the only personal letters he ever wrote were love letters. Fantastic, just *fantastic*. "Oh my, oh good heavens. There was nothing to it. He was just sending ideas for stories, that I understood, and he didn't talk about much else than his work, or to find out about mine. I'm certain any romantic interest was the furthest thing from his mind." It certainly had been furthest from mine.

Rachel was nodding to herself, her eyes far away now. "I believe it, it makes sense. He never did get over her, and he didn't try."

The phrase annoyed me, as though Ariel had been merely a bad cold. I said woodenly, "He must have hurt very much."

Again the nod, but her gaze impossibly distant. She began to speak of the past and I was suddenly lost; I sat and watched the bands of sunlight slide across the ground under the chair opposite me and listened to Rachel babble about her brother, he had been magnificent, he had been superlative, he had been like etc., etc. And somehow in this recital she missed Ariel, Ariel shining like a streak of solder down the glass of his life—Ariel who had surprised him, had revealed him, uncovered all the lies of his life and *ruined* him. I wanted to object, "You never spoke this way when he was alive, you never left him alone for one day," to protest, "No, no, you don't know what it is you're saying." I just sat there all idiotic smile and polite attention, smarting from the added difficulty I now had with the letters and dying from the disclosure of so much intimacy. And cap it all, I was intensely piqued: why had a man and a woman corresponding to equal an item? Was there no such thing anymore as a genuine friendship? Did *everyone* see only what they wished to see?

I could scarcely keep my hands still and clutched at my cup and picked up and put down the spoon. Neither of them seemed to notice what a frantic shambles I was becoming. I couldn't seem to finish my coffee.

As pleasant as the diversion of dining with Rachel and John had promised, I was relieved when the visit drew to a close; unfortunately, it was also at that point that the ordeal took another twist. Rachel excused herself to fetch something and returned clutching a large packet, her face lit up like a little girl's. "I have something special to share with you, Brinsel. It just came last week." She peeled the packet open and pulled out a folder, finally sitting down but fidgeting with restless energy. She spread out the folder on the table so I could see it clearly. "Look!"

Inside was a stack of sheets and I very slowly picked up the first one, a bead of some intense emotion stuck in my throat. Across the topmost edge of the sheet ran the words *Master Proofs, Conductor,* and the title, sheet number, page number, printer's marks. Max had left it untitled; Rachel had titled it *This Gift* after a line from one of his verses.

There it was, there it all was. It was *London Spring* published as *Gift*, and every single correction, alteration, or omission from the drafts had made it more exactly like my own composition, not less. Rachel and Richard had even incorporated the interweaving of *Ash Grove* that Max—like myself—had written in, canceled, written again, rubbed out, and rewritten still. He had been undecided; Rachel and Richard had decided for him. And there it was, exactly as in my work. Every single note, every rest, every direction. It was Max's.

And someone else's. I had transferred my copyright to his estate; Rachel had retaliated by listing me as a co-composer. It was a kindness, a noble magnanimousness, painlessly within reach of their means, and it neatly scrubbed my own generosity in having turned over the copyright to begin with.

"I want you to have this copy, Brinsel. You see, you wrote it, too."

"Thank you, Rachel." I thought I said it; I was fighting a terrible urge to shriek at the injustice of it all, that to be recognized as a composer I had to have *his* name before mine. "I don't know how to thank you."

She beamed. "Where did your work premiere?"

"It hadn't," I told my lap. "It never got anywhere. None of my music had."

"So now you'll get to really hear it! How wonderful is that?"

I smiled facilely at my shoes.

"I don't think we've asked you about your other music," remarked John. "We've been preoccupied with this one piece."

"It's not much different," I objected, hoping he would not understand it the way I meant it. "I mean, I'm not yet a good enough composer to break out of the same sound, all my works sound much the same."

Rachel laughed as though I had told a howling yarn. "I wouldn't have thought it, you compose like Max, and he's as good as Dad. But that will come," she assured me. "Just keep at it. It's like cooking. The more you do it, the more you can branch out. Or it's probably even like writing, I don't know." She picked up her cup, noticed it was empty, gestured to both John and me with the carafe before emptying it into her cup. "What sort of books do you write?"

I told her.

"You don't write mysteries?"

"Well, almost anything could be a kind of mystery, and many things are."

"There's a wonderfully direct answer," twinkled John. "You sure you never met Max?"

Rachel held the empty carafe in midair. "He sent you all that stuff, and you don't even write mysteries?"

"No," I said this time, "surely not detective fiction!" Mysteries in general were one thing, but though I had once read murder mysteries, the idea of writing one repulsed me, and murder was what most detective fiction was to do with. The excitement of all so-called mysteries—no real mysteries at all but merely problems to be solved for which one was not responsible—all this seemed to make people forget the human implications of murder; Rachel had become someone who could understand the grotesquery of that. "I'm not at all interested in that kind of story. I am simply interested in people. Quite honestly I find them all the mystery I can handle."

All this information seemed to puzzle Rachel even more. "I wonder what he was thinking?"

"It could be that he believed what he sent me would be useful some other way, for a different kind of story. At any rate, he offered, and I did not refuse. You never know what might be useful."

"Did you ever use it for a story?"

I shook my head. "I was too busy with other things when I received them . . . And then I was ill for a long while and forgot them. They ended up, I'm fairly certain, in a box of correspondence in my loft. That's one reason why it is taking so long to get them back. I hadn't labeled anything."

John nodded kindly, addressing the quaver in my voice, "It'll be alright, Brinsel, I'm sure of it. Even if you can't have them found, I'm sure Peter will be able to do something. You know, Max always had something up his sleeve; he was just one to inspire confidence, even when he was full of mischief."

Rachel's voice had become calmer. "I think John's right; we really don't need to worry. Max knew what he was doing, and, you know, when I think about him, I'm not worried about the trial, or any of it. He always said that things unmask themselves in the end, that they can't help being whatever they are. That's given me hope for all this."

I had to wonder which of us would be unmasked first, myself or Davis.

On the feast of Saint Swithun, a blazing July Monday, I set out, yet again, to be someone else, and pretend I knew much less than I really did.

Frank Giantomas, the large Italian-American who served as the principal archivist at the historical society, greeted me effusively when I arrived. He wore a grizzled chestnut beard and a Mickey Mouse tie, and his enormous, heavily lined face was as jolly and cheerful as the subsequent interview, at least for him. It was all painfully familiar for me. The date of the installment of the tram lines. Did I want them taken out? Out they had gone. Did I want built three Presbyterian churches and ten light industry factories in 1867? Up they went. The rector at Good Shepherd in 1916 instrumental in founding Saint Thomas's Hospital? All a done deal. I was a blinking expert and by no discernable means. I dutifully did my bit of laughing on cue and asking my questions attentively and acting, in general, appreciative and inquisitive. Act! It seemed that was all I did anymore. Was there nowhere I simply could be myself?

I had a chance—of sorts—the next day, and played myself so well I succeeded at doing nothing else. On Tuesday, the Philharmonic had its first rehearsal for Max's concert. I was invited. I debated ditheringly whether or not to go, arrived late, presented my pass to security, peeked in the hall, and buckled. The guard was nonplussed to see me creeping back moments later, clutching my copy of the score as though ill. I was unable to so much as sit quietly in a corner and listen to the realization of music I had composed; it was the wrong place, the wrong time, and worse, I couldn't bear the sight of so many familiar faces and the assault of memories that accompanied them. The concert was going to be much harder than I'd imagined.

It was back to changing hats and names promptly thereafter; there were three other interviews scheduled that week, this time with former employees of S&T. Two of them had got out of investigation, one was still in it. I fed each a different line about writing an article for a periodical, gathering information for a thesis, researching for a novel. They were all friendly and cooperative, unsuspicious of my curiosity and unanimous on the quirkiness of their sometime employer—"He played flute every day in the office," "Every other day he was playing it at work," "I remember he was really into, like, symphonies and stuff"—and his keen business canny—"I don't think we ever lost a job when it really mattered," "He was sharp as a tack, almost never missed anything, he especially really listened to people," "Wasn't perfect, but from what I've seen one of the best." They made no references to any one case they did not denude of particulars or confuse by conflating with references to another. Their remarks on his methods did not signpost for me any of those he had made use of in Davis's case. I had three colorless and unsurprising interviews that, tallied up, led me in only a despairing little circle.

It may have been useless to vent my frustration on Max, yet of any option, this was still the sole way I could address the real matter—and I needed to vent.

I turned on the typewriter and scrolled in a clean sheet of paper. I stared at it for a long while, then turned a frown on the drawing of Max. That eternal smile. And so often lately I had wished I could pop him in the nose or box his ears or . . . or . . .

It wasn't about to get better.

"Hello Max."

"Ah, I thought it would be you. I had a capital hunch."

"You and your capital hunches. Could it have been anyone else?"

"Good question. How can I help you today?"

"What am I doing here, Max?"

"This question again, huh?" A pause. "I'll walk you through this, so you may figure out something yourself, okay?"

"If there's an answer at the end, I'll do anything."

"You'll have to trust me."

"Fine, fine."

Another pause. "Alright, here goes. How many beats in common time?"

"What?!"

"Would I ask you a question that didn't mean something? Now, how many?"

I ought to have known better; this was his method for teaching recalcitrant students. "Four. Max, I *don't* understand what that is to do with *anything*."

"Come on, Brinsel, you're sight reading this. Follow me, okay?"

"Right, Mr. Thompson. Fire away, Maestro."

"Thank you. Now, can you have more than four beats in common time?"

"Not without changing the time."

"Good. So, suppose I had six? Then what would it be?"

Apples and oranges, Max. And you're driving me bananas. "You would be in 6/8 time."

"*Superbe*. Now tell me, what do those numbers signify?"

That you are a git. "The denominator is the kind of note and the numerator is the number of them."

"So if I have a measure in 6/8 time, what could it look like?"

"It could look like anything!"

"Okay, no panicking now. I was inviting you to be creative; I didn't expect the opportunity to provoke abject terror in you. Let's shoot for the simplest variation."

It was like being ground down by pumice. "You have got six eighths, a beat each."

"Good. Doing swimmingly. Still with me?"

"Yes," I lied.

"Now, next drill. I'm writing fiction. Can I put nonfiction in it?"

"Good heavens, Max, what kind of question is that? You are always going to put some in, unless you intend to write pure nonsense."

"Look, it's a warm-up, Brinsel. Let's say it's fiction and I throw some nonfiction people and stuff in the mix. Am I kosher?"

I pulled myself forward and sighed. "You are fine. Fine. Use all the nonfiction you please. It only depends what kind. And how you handle it."

"And if I'm writing nonfiction? Can I put fiction in that?"

"You cannot."

"So what's the difference? What does each signify?"

"One you are presenting as facts. The other does not have to be facts, it simply must be true, most of all to itself."

"Could I ever present fiction as nonfiction?"

"What is this—where do you get these maggoty questions from, Max?"

"Humor me, Brinsel. Do I ask questions to no purpose?"

I ground my teeth. "It would certainly depend just what this fiction consisted of. It is not impossible under certain conditions, but the first requisite will always be that it is *known* to be fiction; otherwise it's not generally recommended. It's a common method of abuse, the most extreme and infamous sort being the scientific or artistic hoax."

"Any special reason why that wouldn't be good?"

"Reason why! It wouldn't be *true* for one thing. And if you are particularly unscrupulous, it is one of the best ways both to dabble in illegalities and destroy your own credibility."

"But if it can still express truth, isn't that good?"

"What is good about destroying one's own credibility? What is the point of that?"

"So you couldn't tell the truth by doing so?"

I had wasted an entire sheet of paper already. I yanked it out and scrolled in another. "I cannot see how."

"Are there any circumstances in which you could?"

"I don't want to think about this, Max, I just want to know what to put in those letters."

"That's what we're talking about, Brinsel."

I could feel a migraine coming on.

"Alright. How about presenting nonfiction as fiction. Bad for you?"

At the window, dusk had already dissolved into the streetlamp-yellow night. I thought of all the normal, sane people being lulled to an oblivious stupor by glowing televisions this evening, untroubled by the question of what to put in fictitious letters that had to be factual.

"Well, you can write historical fiction and you can write fictional histories; again, you simply must ensure everyone knows it *is* fiction. Beyond that, don't trouble yourself."

"Why?"

"Because you cannot sell facts as if they were something you had invented. You simply can't do it. Nobody has that kind of authority, the only authority one has is interpretive. And if you are talking about nonfiction that involves people and their lives, it could trounce on all sorts of privacy rights to which you have no privilege; in fine, another good, fast way to ruin your credibility. And depending on the material, your career."

"So there's nothing good about it?"

"Not under any circumstances I could imagine."

"And you couldn't tell the truth with it?"

"I cannot see how."

"Why not?"

"Max, this is insane. Ask me a sensible question."

"Please answer the question, Brinsel."

I wished there were someone to smack other than myself. "Look, facts as facts are one kind of truth, nonfiction. And then there are opinions and suchlike; write an essay and say all the rot you please and it's still nonfiction. But fiction isn't facts, it's another form of truth. If you try to give the one as the other, without qualifying it as fiction, the likelihood is they shall cancel each other, and you shall not be believed. Your fiction won't be true, and no one will trouble themselves to take your facts seriously either."

"But why *is* that?"

I almost grabbed the typewriter and shook it. "Because if you must have it put simply, you fatuous windbag, fiction is telling lies to tell the truth. Nonfiction cannot do that. Try it, and see where you get."

"So you're absolutely certain you couldn't do any good by it?"

"*Diws*, I can't credit this." I slammed my head and fists on the typewriter.

I sat there stewing and fuming, head smarting, not knowing which of us I was more enraged at, and too infuriated to want to know. I had no intention of writing any further, but the words came to me anyways.

"Would you ever do that?"

"I would not."

Another silence. I glared at the typewriter as though it were meant to tell me something.

Then, "Okay, enough. Why did you come here, Brinsel?"

"Max, I don't . . ."

I stopped. I had come, as I had been telling myself over and over, to do research for this story. And I had found the research was unnecessary. I already knew things just as they were. If I hadn't come, if I had simply been content to publish what I had written, when in fact it was all real . . .

I typed, "I can't publish what I have about you."

"That's a start. It would not be common time."

No, it wouldn't. It would not have sounded good at all. There would have been legal questions, questions of attribution, questions of privacy. But that couldn't be all.

"Why else am I here?"

"Didn't we go over this already?"

We had. And yet there was more . . .

"And if your fiction is *nonfiction*, if it's just as you knew . . ."

"Have you no idea how bewildering and frustrating that is for me?"

Silence, of almost the same shape as a word—almost like a sigh. I didn't wait for a reply to come.

"I never expected *anything* like this. I never expected, never dreamt, you were all *real*. I don't know how to tell you how hard it is to know all about all of you, and not to let it show."

"You do have a unique position. It's a lot of responsibility to know all that, yes, and it takes a lot of patience."

"Don't talk to me about patience," I exploded. "It wasn't supposed to be real! It wasn't supposed to go as far as it did! I didn't *want* for you to have a history, to be someone! You were only a detective so you could *do* something! Because nobody could do anything, because nothing was happening! And now you've *ruined* everything, I can't even—years of work, wasted, lost, just because you're *real!*"

Silence. Then, gently, "I'm sorry, Brinsel."

I buried my face in my hands. I couldn't even justify myself without cutting myself to the heart.

After a few minutes, the words came, "Okay, let's try this."

Then, nothing. I sat there staring at my hands, wondering if I had heard wrong.

I typed, "Try what?"

Another pause; then, slowly, "We're two different people, right? You don't control me. But there is a connection between us. Try to see it like that, Brinsel."

"How is *that* supposed to help? I cannot even speak for you anymore."

"Well, what is a connection? And can you have it with something you simply control?"

"How is that supposed to help me with this mess? Is some connection with *you* supposed to help *me* to be a detective? Because that's what I'd have to do to complete those letters."

"It's much simpler than you think, Brinsel, you don't need to change what you're doing. You don't need to be a detective."

"Right, of course, now all my problems are solved. And you're going to be the detective?"

"No, I'm not that anymore. I didn't take that with me."

"What did you take with you, besides your penchant for unhelpfulness?"

"This is your work, do what *you* do best. Let go of the rest. Look, I'm trying to make this simple for you."

"Well, it's not working!"

Silence. "Alright. Think of this, if you want it in more analytic terms: do we have a connection? Can you control someone you have a connection with, and would it still be viable if you could? And what is there saying you *cannot* speak for me?"

"I don't recall *you* ever saying I could do."

"*Brinsel,* you wrote about my entire life! Why do you need my permission now?"

"I'm nothing, I'm nobody! I've got no authority to do anything here!"

"You have the authority of someone who is loved."

"All the good that does me!"

"Alright, try this on: you can still speak for me."

"But what of the investigation?"

"What about it? As far as everyone else is concerned, I granted you complete authority in that note I left. Keep doing what you're doing—keep writing."

The anxiety tightened round my neck. "You are asking the impossible of me. How is all this going to work?"

"Like life. That's what it is."

"Like *life?*"

"Yes. You don't have to break your head over it. You don't have to know everything at once. You can let it come to you. A little bit at a time. Try it."

It would be so much easier just to be a writer. You could make outlines and plot things out.

Sometimes. Perhaps. If you were lucky.

"Brinsel, what's the worst that might happen?"

"The worst. If you really must know, then that would be my going to prison for lying and impeding an investigation. And you can also include hurting everyone who was counting on me, as well as making you look pretty foolish for having mentioned me to begin with and making myself look idiotic and unprincipled for having covered for you. And while we're talking worst case scenarios, let me throw in giving myself away by revealing that I know everything about everyone, and causing complete chaos by my utter inability to explain any of it."

"That is quite a list. Do you know what's going to happen?"

I all but snarled, "I can make a remarkably good deduction, entirely in the realm of possibility."

"Do you know what's going to happen?"

I wound in another paper and abandoned suspension of disbelief, not caring if I could continue or not. "If I did, I wouldn't be sitting here pretending to talk to you."

Silence.

"Brinsel, you trust me, right?"

"You have already asked that once today," I typed tiredly.

"Do you?"

I looked at the typewriter. I could feel every key as I typed. "I trust you."

"Good. I trust you, too."

I closed my eyes. Why could my life not be simple and straightforward, the way it had once been? Well, alright, so it hadn't been simple and straightforward. Then sensible? Intelligible? If not all that, then perhaps a good sight less bewildering and frustrating?

When I opened my eyes, the typewriter was off. It was only then—before I could even form the thought, as unambiguously as a hand laid on my own—that the air of the room declared another presence, that I was not alone. I couldn't move for several minutes. And of course, when I at last looked quickly round, no one was there.

14

The Sojourners

The 28 July dawned oppressively sultry, the heat intensifying as the hours and the sun ascended; in mid-afternoon the humidity congealed into clouds and the clouds dissolved into a shower. When at four o'clock Rachel arrived to pick me up the brunt of it had steamed off and we drove through rain-blacked streets to the old urban neighborhood where she and her brother had grown up and where Richard still lived. Huge, torn pieces of cotton rag floated in a sky scrubbed transparent cyan and the sun seared the wet road in a glare of light. I was a bag of nerves and butterflies, and Rachel, spouting away as usual, did not notice if I was particularly silent. And then we were there: the enormous oaks and maples, the colonial kit house down the street that belonged to the forbiddingly dour Mrs. McPherson, the gray and tan gingerbread on the next corner where former sheriff Raymond Jakes lived. The water tower, turquoise and bulbous and obvious over the leafy summer skyline. Then Rachel was easing along the curb across from 2632 Amundsen Street, and had to ask me twice if I was coming.

I was coming, with a show of pleasure and a curiosity I hoped could be taken for the real things, to the annual barbeque of Max's musical ensemble, the Sojourners—six amateurs with day jobs who got on with or without him like an orchestra in miniature—who wished to meet his famous mystery friend. This year the gathering was at Richard's house, and I had spent days bracing myself for the familiarity that could be my salvation or my undoing.

The Thompson house might as well have been my own home, yet following Rachel I became tangled in a bight of sadness and loss. It was all someone else's: Elisabeth's tea roses on either side of the wooden stoop scattering damp damask petals that stuck to the wet grass, and the screen porch with the decrepit rocking chair. The front door painted white, its scrammed brass handle and three narrow, beveled windows. Rachel rang the bell and stood back smiling and for an instant she was twelve again and coming home from school and Elisabeth would open the door . . .

But it was Richard, aged and beaming. "Well hello, my favorite doctor! And my favorite author! Come in, come in, John's already here with the two terrors."

The foyer, the hat tree and coat rack and the bench with the umbrella stand. The stairs to the first story ascended to the right, and beside them a door that led into a small sitting room and out to the garage. A narrow hallway angling off to the left ended at the kitchen, and I followed Rachel and Richard into it.

The room was wide and well-lit by the broad window over the sink, and daylight cast a sateen glow on the black-and-white checkered linoleum that had been there since Richard had bought the house. The white baker's rack, its glass shelves stuffed with cookbooks and tins of recipes and cradling a few dusty bottles of wine. The antique maple table and set of battered maple rush chairs in the nook by the door. Dishes piled in the wooden drying rack beside the sink; I recognized a blue glass bowl, chipped around the rim, still intact after so many years. Max had been two or three and had brought Elisabeth the bowl filled with his excavations from the garden. "This is for you!"

"Oh, how exciting, you did a dig! What did you find?"

"*Je trouvai la terre!*"

"No bones? *Tu ne déracinais aucun des os?*"

"No, I only dug up dirt." He was distracted by some insects crawling out of the earth and around the rim of the bowl. ". . . And bugs." He repeated, "*C'est à toi! C'est une tarte au chocolat.*"

"Would you like some tea, Brinsel?"

"Oh, a bit of that coffee should do just nicely, thanks."

Rachel poured me a cup and I received it gratefully, glad for something to hold onto as much for the fortification. This house and the evening's company were a field mined with possibilities of things to remember. I did not have to go far: on the wall outside the kitchen hung a display of pictures and small pieces of memorabilia of Max's second career, all neatly framed. A clipping from an old telephone directory. *S&T Investigations: "Let us look for you."* One of his several certifications. A photograph from the year he died, at his desk before a typewriter and surrounded by papers, thumb to his nose and wagging his fingers at the camera. There was the original of the card Max had filled out at a convention: . . . *Specialization: surveillance, reconstruction . . . Expertise: depends on who you ask (interviewing) . . .*

Richard spotted me examining the display and beckoned. "There's more of that sort of thing down the way, Brinsel. C'mon, I'll give you a small tour."

The first part was brief: down the hallway to the right, the small guest room still as Elisabeth had decorated it, and at the end of the corridor, the door opened on his study, a long room that ran almost half the length of the house, interrupted by three tall west windows crossed with mullions. Then we reached the door closest the main corridor. "The best for last," he smiled. "Take a peek in here," opening the door with a bow: his studio.

It was one of the largest rooms, as broad as his study but with the atmosphere of one of the practice rooms at Horton: long effort and accomplishment, dark trim, the scent of old papers, polish, wood. At one end, like some enormous beast, presided his Steinway, its lid pinned down by stacks of scores and sheet music. On the wall closest to, surrounded by various strings, and polished and preserved rather like a bronzed infant shoe, hung the quarter-size violin with which Max had begun a life of music. My eyes skipped over recording equipment, keyboard and computer in a nest of cord, shelves of scores, books, manuscript sheets with papers sticking out everywhere, and the walls positively blotted with photographs and memorabilia of both Richard's and Max's careers in music. It was as familiar and cluttered as my own rooms. I couldn't take it all in.

Framed posters of articles and concert announcements. A press photo of Max in formal black, smiling, eyes avoiding the camera. *"Renowned flutist Maximilian Thompson will appear as both guest conductor and flute soloist at select concerts in the 1986-87 season . . ."*

"Read this." Richard singled out a small frame nearer the door. "The rest is just commentary."

There were two windows in the mat; one showed a photograph of Max in concert from late in his life, but it was the contents of the window beside it that Richard wanted me to see: a review from that same period during Max's black depression, given by a high-profile reviewer when he had been a visiting soloist with another nationally acclaimed orchestra. It was almost not a review: chock-a-block with vertiginous praise, it dissipated into a smear of adjectives and dragged on for five overpainted paragraphs.

"The rest" consisted of souvenirs of his illustrious career with the Philharmonic. Photographs of famous artists with Richard, collages of printed encomium on the Philharmonic's ascendancy under his direction. The images spoke for themselves, and Richard was content to let me gawk.

The main corridor was more fraught: a study of family photographs I hoped we would pass by, but in vain; Richard flipped on the light, convinced I should be as interested as himself if not more, and I endured a recital of exhausting familiarity. At last we made it through the gauntlet; then the doorway of the dining room through which I glimpsed the great walnut table and its eight spindle-backed chairs. Another short corridor, and at once the living room with the settee and chairs and hearth and piano and the French doors that opened onto the patio, the afternoon light sliding through the squares of glass and checkering the parquetry and creeping up a chair. That faint odor of the hearth, of floor polish, the warm scent of something comforting like linens or old stuffed furniture and the antique-wood smell that had always told Max he was home.

The beautiful Quidoz baby grand, Elisabeth Thompson's piano. Elisabeth had first taught him music; she had been practicing Chopin's *Variations* the day her son had run in speechless, suddenly overwhelmed with the hunger that would eat at him the rest of his life. He had been nearly five. Max had been listening and watching his parents and sister at the piano since he had opened his eyes on the world, but, forbidden to touch it by Elisabeth, who feared Richard's lack of moderation in his regard, he docilely complied, apparently disinterested; and until that moment, the sound had never moved him. When she placed his thumb on middle C and struck the key, he could feel the sound vibrating from somewhere in the massive instrument before him, and the realization that the key he touched was connected to something else which produced the note jolted him like a stab of lightning.

"*Ces sont les touches*," Elisabeth had been saying. "Do you know why they're called keys?"

"No. Yes." He knew what keys were. *Les tons.* His mother was always speaking of them to her students; they wrote their names in such a way as to decode whole series of sounds. *Les clefs.* Richard had a big ring of them that, like this instrument, he wasn't permitted to touch, jagged shapes hard with reflected light. They looked like shiny, bared fangs, and made small crashing sounds against each other when shaken; they unlocked the car engine, the house, and many other things he couldn't imagine. "They make noise, they open things."

She asked him, amused, "What do these keys open?"

He shrugged. He was still leaning on middle C like a skipped record, now soft, now hard, listening intently to the resultant vibration and tracing the subtle breathings of it, the whispered swishing and the muted *thuff*, becoming more and more aware of the incredible mechanism that had to produce it. *Les touches;* he understood—keys connected to something hidden. *Cache-touche, cache-cache.* He would have to find a way to look into this machine. Touching the key, he at once realized that the sound he heard was not one single sound but hundreds, even thousands, layered upon each other in a towering column until they exploded in that clap of uncoiling energy that he could not see but could hear and feel in more ways than one; in a moment he calculated how many sounds it must be that he heard. "This, this sound." There was something else he grasped they opened, too, but he kept the thought to himself like a secret whose novelty frightened him: *himself.*

"*C'est le ton d'ut,*" she guided his hands over the eight ivory bars, and something clicked in him with such authority that he shut his eyes, overwhelmed, hearing the sounds within himself like an object he could see and touch. A domino cascade of remembered sounds fell out of his hands and found the keys they belonged to, the key of C, the key of D, the key of F, listening on some level deeper than hearing, to the peculiar shape made by each and arranging them accordingly. The logic of it fascinated him; he was numb with admiration and discovery and after a moment shook off her hands and hewed out a rough version of what she had been playing. With the memory of the music he had just heard brilliant as daylight in his mind, both intervals and rhythm flattened themselves into an easily traceable pattern into which he could drop the notes without a second thought. It was awkward and not as clean and dancing as he had heard it but the sounds came together as easily as his wooden puzzles with the little red pegs, and with each note played the awareness sank deeper into him. He felt alive as he had never felt before; he knew himself recognized and had recognized in turn, and somehow, he did not question it, he knew what to do. Elisabeth laughed and said, "Oh, my, you've been practicing, haven't you?"

"No." His eyes slid intently over the black and white bars, concentrating on connecting the individual sounds to the keys. They were stacking up together inside him the same lithe way he assembled the binomial and trinomial cubes at his school, and just as unconsciously.

"Did Daddy show you how to do that?"

"No."

"You like it?"

Richard was standing by it, his image with his fringe of silvered hair reflected in its gleaming jet surface, smiling at me with his head on one side.

"This old heap of tinder," Max had affectionately called it, but I didn't dare say that.

"You have lots of these," I said instead. "You've got a collection."

He laughed. "Of course, you play?"

"Not very well."

He chuckled and slapped its shiny top appraisingly and his wedding band clinked on it. "This was where my son started out when my back was turned one day. He was just a squirt. Then I had to undo all the cheap tricks he taught himself."

The piano took up most of one end of the room; in the midst was the old maroon settee and wing chair, the octagonal glass coffee table. It was altogether too easy to remember Max growing up here. As though we had walked in on a lesson, stuffed folders of sheet music and instrument cases lay on the settee, the chairs, the floor—a violin, a saxophone, a guitar and a flute, and against the far wall what could only be a double bass. I was suddenly conscious of the muted sound of voices coming from outside.

"Shall we?" Richard gestured to the French doors and swung one open for me.

A wooden deck had been built onto the patio in the last few years; a few steps led down into the lawn, and against the railings stretched two narrow benches. The benches and steps were filled with sitting figures, all talking and laughing. The four Cunninghams and six others, and everyone looked up expectantly as we came out.

"This," Richard made a grand sweep of his arm, as though I were a soloist, "is Ms. Brinsel Thomas. And these are the Sojourners, Max's ensemble."

I was welcomed by an effusion of "hellos" and a "hiya" and a jury of friendly if curious stares. I smiled and nodded and made some noise like "pleased to meet you," but what I wished to do was dive behind the nearest piece of paper. How could I have ever got them in one room when writing? It wasn't even a matter of logistics; it was rather like throwing one's pencils into the air and having an Escher land on the canvas.

Filipo Albedo-Sanchez, tenor sax, had been busking when Max first stumbled across this sly and quite shy talent; his brown face still youthful and perky, though his dark hair was threaded with silver. The only one of the group who had worked in theater—he had once owned his own company—a slyly sardonic curl of mouth that might suddenly pour out Calderón or Bloch or, just as likely, a jolly yarn. Then Tonya Farr, harp and piano, the single mother of two deaf boys, bull-in-china-shop businesswoman, flip comedienne; her deadpan face, "incurably sage" as Max had characterized it, lit up with a smile that read "Cheshire cat" to me. Apt to speak her piece either verbally or bodily, and either way conspicuously. Paul "Beanpole" Sheffield, double bass, bald as an egg and taller than Richard, his dark, sculpted face that of one who worked outside in all weathers, and filled with lines. An immense, steadying presence, an aura of stability and great strength and also heavy and buried grief. The client who had become a good friend. And Penny Marshall, flute and pennywhistle—"Their other flute," Richard introduced her—small, thin, nervous, ash blonde, spectacled, perched robin-like on the edge of a bench; "Hello, Ms. Thomas," with a small wave, her voice as always a bit loud and her face preserving a wide-eyed surprised air, and she had a natural fluster that got up Dan's nose. Beside her, Patricia Chevers, guitar, older and stockier and filled out, more solid than her younger companion in every way. A delightfully aged soul, a warm presence, with whom it would have been a joy to sit down to tea. One of those souls who also had never quite got the hang of clothes, attired as though she had got dressed by falling into a wardrobe.

And here was Dan Malcombe, violin, and charter member with Max, large as life. As with seeing the Cunninghams, Peter, and all the others, what startled me most was seeing them without the words or drawings that had previously been their only vehicle. This was especially true in Dan's case; like Richard, he was so sharp and mobile he bore no semblance to being retired, and Dan, nearly four years older than his contemporary, was by now a very youthful seventy-five. Despite all the mishaps and danger he had crammed into those years, it had been nothing more dramatic than a slipped disc that had won him his wheelchair, though he had handled the crisis with all the voluble, foul-mouthed drama of which he was capable. Dan's first quality was bellicose bombast; his second was a very delicate, very patient attentiveness that usually disguised itself as distraction or, more commonly, blazing disregard. The slant of his smile and the glint in his eye said everything; like Max—whom he had taught—he picked up stray details and remarks the way a magnet picked up iron filings, could distil unacknowledged facts from the utterly disparate, and would bluff his way to making you confess next to everything. I wondered how long I could forestall a cold sweat.

"Dan founded the Sojourners with Max," said Richard. "He's the one who helped get them off the ground."

"I've found lots of things in my time. And I didn't have much else to do after I retired." Dan regarded me the way he might examine a violin of unknown provenance, the eyebrows withholding judgment but the smile forming some hypothesis. "So, you are the musician who wrote the same music as our old friend."

My tongue tied into a dozen knots, terrified of what my face might be saying. Five more hours in Dan's presence? I felt even less reassured moments later when Peter arrived, tardily as was his custom, and smiled at me in the exact way he had been doing for months, some fusion of friendliness and detachment. Rachel and John were obstacle enough, the Sojourners still several more, but add Dan and then Peter, and I had grossly overestimated my cunning.

And then there was Jill. The discussion had drifted into the plans for the evening; she had contributed not a word, and I was startled when she pointedly turned in my direction and asked, "Have you ever gotten so deep into a lie you couldn't get out?"

This non sequitur had the effect of pinching off all talk for an exhausting two seconds. "Jill," said Rachel coldly, and I hoped I was not coloring according to the violent flush I felt creeping up my scalp.

"Well, actually, yes," I replied, "everybody's got a history, even me, and I've got a story to go with it." I looked appealingly at Rachel, who did not look convinced this could help. "When I was in grammar school, there was a day when some kids were to be let out early on account of an activity. You had to take a form to your parents and bring it back signed. Well, I brought it back signed because I wanted to get out early, but my aunt never saw it. So there I was out of school early on that day, and I didn't dare go home, for I wasn't expected, and I didn't know where to go. I just hid on the grounds until school ended for the day! There's resourcefulness for you, and I was shaking like as jelly too."

Laughter in the group, but Rachel had been right; if I had thought Jill would be mollified by getting an answer, her face showed plainly not. She was white with rage and her expression so closed no light came from it.

There was Jill, Jillian Elisabeth Cunningham, whom I had decided had been born 5 June 1975 but who had been born without any help from me, whom I loved as my own child, who was one day to be a remarkable cellist, an author, a linguist—loathing for no apparent reason the least atom of my being and finding a thousand and one ways creatively to tell me "I hate you! you are nothing!"

To be in the company of someone who as good as wished me not to exist was a discomfort only slightly ameliorated by the goodwill and courteous interest of the rest of the company. The adults took no notice of Jill's sulk; even Lynn seemed cheerfully unconcerned by her twin's glowering atmosphere.

The group was exchanging stories; everyone had some little story, and, without exception, I knew these stories. And the people they had happened to still had so many of the idiosyncrasies that I remembered them having: Patricia's tendency to wander into vague anxieties, Filipo's goofiness at awkward moments, Penny's straight-laced idealism. Dan's weakness for arguing with anything that moved. They were swapping old stories of musical mishaps. The time Dan—or perhaps it was Paul, they could not agree on who, and neither would admit to it—had forgotten to bring his bow to a performance, and so they had switched back and forth when one of them came to his part, to great comic but not musical effect. The time the lights had gone out while they were playing, and none of them had really noticed. The time—one of the times—Penny and Max had lost it completely during a performance because one of them had started giggling, and that was the end of them both. "Damn giggling flutists!" snarled Dan, and everyone howled with laughter.

I too tried to smile and laugh on cue, but my attention was everywhere, too conscious of being crowded by the bodily presence, the faces, the voices, of all those names and characters. Everyone was quite at home—even Peter blended in like family—and worst of all, everyone was genuine, even as they performed and commented for their captive audience of one.

By the time we had moved inside from the patio, I was ready to write off the evening as something merely to endure without hope of discovery. I had gone to the toilet momentarily to escape, and was on my way to get a glass of water when I heard voices from the kitchen. Jill and Rachel. Rachel growing in volume.

I stopped in the corridor.

"Jill, this is sheer childishness! What's gotten into you?"

Muffled muttering.

"It's more a measure of your trust in Peter . . . I don't know *why* you're doing this, but you're going to stop . . . I will *not* tolerate this behavior."

Muttering.

"I never said you had to like it. Do you think *I* like this? Do you? Do you think Max did?"

Muttering.

Rachel exploded.

"That is *bullshit,* Jill, this is *not* Max's fault!"

Stony silence.

"Do you actually think that your uncle would have mentioned her for *nothing*? As if because we can't explain this, he couldn't either? What on *earth* do you think you're trying to prove?"

Embarrassed, I stared at the photographs on the wall. The large portrait of Max and Ariel, young and radiant and oblivious to the world.

"Jillian, you are being a *child*. She didn't steal anything . . ."

A picture of the Sojourners assembled in Richard's classroom at Mayhew. Dan with his instrument in his lap, jabbing at the music with his bow and speaking with great expression, quite cross. Max holding his flute upright and laughing.

". . . You will *not* do this, Jill . . . *NO* . . . Jill, don't, don't talk to me like that, young lady . . . for crying out loud. I don't care *what* you think of her . . . you are not going to treat a guest . . ."

A photograph of Max with his nieces; he was about thirty-three and they, eight. One on each knee. The girls grinning very silly at the camera and strangling the uncle with hugs. His eyes pained.

"Young lady, you are *going* to whether you want to or not..."

Sharp and agitated adolescent noises.

Very quietly, I turned and went back to the toilet, made some small domestic sounds to calm myself, and then came back up the corridor pretending I knew nothing.

So there it was, one mystery solved. My connection with Max was no mystery to Jill: I was a *thief*, my music was the same as her uncle's because I had stolen it. She was only trying to defend her uncle's rights while the whole world went along with the artifices of a mysterious hack claiming to be the person he had mentioned, and never mind that I had abandoned every right to the music. She alone was in the right; her family, Peter, Dan, the police—everyone else was taken in by the ruse.

It helped nothing that I was the evening's guest of honor, cornered by attention I didn't want and couldn't avoid. As the Cunninghams had once attempted, the Sojourners all but dismantled me with a flood of polite questions. Dan seemed content to listen. I did all I could to make every inquiry an exercise in changing the subject, terrified this might only provoke his interest. Between his attentive silence and the keen interrogation of the rest, a sauna could not have caused me more perspiration.

At first, I had a grasp of things: I got Filipo onto his dear and nearly inexhaustible topic of the work of Kobo Abe, and Patricia to expand on her youthful wandering life with a guitar. Paul obligingly spoke of his previous nightclub work—"as a musician, not a bouncer," he specified with a wink—then rumbled on for some minutes about everything wrong with the construction industry, periodically interrupted by catty little asides from Tonya. Then things began to unravel again. Tonya divulged some banalities about her work as an accountant for S&T Investigations, delivered an ode on her love of harp, complained Richard did not have one in the house, and without segue or scruple brought up my work with Max. Penny let me query her about her special-needs students, but then eagerly pounced: "And how *did* you connect with Max?"

Oh God, what had I once told Peter? Or the Cunninghams? It was all I could do to insist my connection with Max began and ended with correspondence, and, struck either by inspiration or another gross miscalculation, begged them to tell me more about Max themselves. They responded with a seismic enthusiasm, recounting for me stories I already knew by heart, pulling out souvenirs and photographs I had visualized hundreds of times before, and feelingly describing their old friend's character in terms I could have dictated to them. I acted surprised, touched, intrigued in turn, all the time overacting a calm and grace I did not possess and that I frantically hoped would pass muster.

Richard alone produced a souvenir that gave me an occasion for something genuine. Wanting to show me some of his son's literary efforts, he brought out several old issues of the magazine *Flute Talk*. In most Max was no more than a subject, either in word or image, but in three he was an author. One article was a highly technical offering on orchestral level work, the text punctuated by bars of notation and its pedantic patois lightened by droll touches; a step down from that was another article on teaching beginning students, his specialty, titled simply, "Lessons From Beginners"; and the last, an unabashedly comic piece the editors had titled, "Did you hear the one about . . . ?" describing some of the misadventures a guest soloist could meet with.

The tone of each was transparent and light, and except for the academic offering, quite accessible as might be any well-written article by a master instrumentalist and communicator. But never once did he mention his career in music, nor his early training. There was no reference to his education, never a word of his participating in any competitions, not a single dropped name; any anecdote of the sort was penned as a third party: "It is said that . . ." "I was once told . . ." "There is a story of . . ." And yet they were his own experiences: he had deliberately disguised the source. Even in the last article his approach was so canny it was often impossible to tell he was speaking of things that had happened to himself. The biographical remarks were silent on all else: not a word of his profession, not a clue, and only the editorial sparkle of the *summa cum laude* that forever tagged after him like a youthful regret hinting at anything at all.

I had known of *Flute Talk*, of course; I had friends who were flautists, and I had seen issues before. It was what had inspired me to invent Max writing a few articles for it—and these were the articles. One of my flautist friends had once shared an hysterical story they had read in an issue, though without giving the reference, and I had incorporated it into Max's article on musical misadventures. There it was: the story my friend had told me had come from Max's article.

With the magazines in my hands, I had the overpowering, unsettling feeling, that I could not shake off, that I was meant to do something with it, but that couldn't be right—I already *had* . . .

I asked Richard, "Had he written for *Flutist Quarterly* also?"

"No." He gave a wistful smile. "He never joined the National Flute Association. But I did, and I received the *Newsletter*—the *Quarterly* as was—so he had everything I did, and all the benefits too."

I knew so much, I didn't need to ask a single question. These were the people who had known him best, and yet they could tell me nothing,

nothing about him I did not know far better. What was the meaning of a breach of privacy such as that, and where was the knowledge I needed most?

"You know," Richard was saying, "that work of his that was the same as yours—that's one of his greatest compositions. It was sheer genius." He jabbed his index finger in an open *Flute Talk*, twinkling at me over his specs. "I wrote a piece about it for *Musical Quarterly* before we knew about you; you should have been in there! If you've written the same music as a genius, doesn't that make you a genius, too?"

"Oh, dear," I crimsoned, "I couldn't be a genius. It's only that a genius like him could write simple music as well as complex. I couldn't begin to take myself that seriously."

"Still, Brinsel," persisted Richard. "That's what genius is, making the sublime simple."

"It's not all that sublimity crap," Dan objected. "Genius means you know too much for no good reason."

This was a definition of genius I could identify with. But as for the conventional meaning, I still hadn't seemed to convert them, and in fact the only other one who appeared to agree with me was Jill, who chose that moment to stand up and stalk out.

My world was not so simplistic as Jill's and I was wrestling with mysteries she would never have to deal with, but when it was announced that we were done talking about music and it was time to make it, I too could not stand any more and hurriedly excused myself to the toilet. There I sat in a heap on the floor for as long as I dared. Had I been able to think of a good excuse, I might have lingered . . . except for the floral towels, the braided rug, the quaint little pictures Rachel had put up, each object shouting its story at me. Had the Cunninghams, had the Sojourners, or Peter, all despised me as much as did Jill, it all might have been a bit easier, but there I was cranking out lie after lie under pretext of helping them, and they believed me, they *trusted me* . . . Feeling about as terrible as when I had left, I went back.

I had got as far as the main corridor when I was met by the corkscrew sounds of instruments tuning. I froze, fighting the urge to bolt out of the house. I stood there sniveling with my hand in my mouth and my gaze hit the portrait of Max and Ariel, those two faces indifferent of all else fixed on a future that never happened. "Help me!" I hissed.

Somehow, I got back to the living room and moored myself in a chair. We had arrived at the high point of the evening—music—but for myself, I simply hoped it could not get lower. For over an hour the Sojourners jammed, played musical games, told dreadful jokes, tossed off duets, solos and instrumental discussions, and I endured over an hour of dislocation, yanked from one memory of them to another, snapped out of the present by this tune or that remark and returned to the present at random. Twice I unthinkingly put out my hand to pick up a flute that was not there, and once thought I glimpsed Peter turning to look at me as if curious or puzzled. By the end of it I was exhausted. Never had I so little enjoyed such wonderful music or pretended so intently that I did, and when at last they wound down and stopped and it was over for a while, never had I been so relieved it was ended.

I craved solitude and space enough to strategize or at least think, but Rachel picked that moment for a call-up to the kitchen, and conscripted me, with Tonya and Patricia, to help prepare the meal. The kitchen was no help; and thinking proved impossible: feminine chatter ringed and prodded me, Rachel and Tonya smiling and tossing me lines, Patricia beaming at me and occasionally offering something warm and cheerful. I tried to follow their thoughts, to step from one word to the next with all the attention I could hold, frightened of tumbling into the surge of memory swelling through the silence between each sound. I touched each item I was preparing deliberately, carefully—the basket of rolls, plastic utensils, paper plates—as though they or I might dissolve into the air like a voice if I did not establish firm enough contact. The talk receded to scenery. It was a lovely summer evening but the light in the window failed me; it was night. The ambered stenciling around the kitchen, the voices filtering from the living room, even the lighting the same as it had once been at another time, or somewhere else.

Rachel had been on second shift at Anderson Memorial. She had volunteered to take it that night for a colleague who was ill. The day had started out well and gone downhill in the evening. She was just enduring it, waiting for the shift to end, when she was paged after midnight. A family emergency, the operator told her. There was a police officer to see her, and Mr. Serrev; she was to get her things because she was to go with them. She went down, wondering with a panic if something had happened to Richard or the girls or John. When she saw Peter waiting for her, haggard and gray, she forgot her father in relief and wondered in concerned irritation what sort of trouble her brother had got in now. They went to an empty exam room and closed the door, and Peter mentioned Max and something about work and trouble and then stumbled over the silence as though he had forgotten how to make a complete sentence.

Not two seconds later she didn't have to ask, it was all horribly plain: the officer, and Peter, here. His gray face, the seat, the silence. She had seen this a hundred times before; she had had to do this a hundred times before. Her heart went cold. She had been thinking, *If I don't say anything, it won't be real.*

The first thing she managed to say was *No*, and then, "What happened?" Then it was, "Does Dad know?" and "Can I go with you?"

Instead he had taken her home, and then he had had to go to Richard. To wake him in the middle of the night, with news like this.

"Peter, what brings you here at this ungodly hour? And with this fine gentleman? Come in," and he waved in Peter and his companion, down the corridor and to the kitchen. The tea service lay in the drying rack and Richard snatched off the cups and fumbled with the knob for the kettle. "I'm sure you could use some good instant joe . . ."

"Let's sit down, Dad, I have to tell you something."

"Is it . . . something bad?" Richard looked from him to the officer.

"It's Max . . ." He hated the sound of his own voice. "Richard, I'm sorry."

Peter had been sitting there, at the kitchen table, Richard, there, Sgt. Reger standing there, and I could still see Richard's stunned face, see his hands on the table trembling before the rest of him, the disbelief and shock as palpable as another person in the room.

Why remember that, when I had never written it down, when it had been only a smudge of information? Because it had been nothing more than a story? Or because I had . . .

Richard dropped one of his wife's china teacups and it hit the floor and smashed into a hundred ivory pieces speckled with roses; the impact was sharp and clear as a breaking window, and I was startled at how immediate the memory sounded.

"Brinsel, are you alright?"

Rachel had stopped stacking serviettes and was staring at me in pained surprise. Tonya had turned and glanced in our direction, and I realized everyone had stopped talking. Then I realized I had not simply remembered the sound of the breaking cup; at my feet, scrawled over the linoleum like an algebraic equation of stupefying complexity, lay the remains of one of Elisabeth Thompson's china teacups.

My heart seized into a cold lump—it was all over, I was caught out, the room would erupt in cries of "We know who you are, get out! get out!" Instead, for an instant that stretched into hours the kitchen froze in a silent tableau vivant, each of us standing immobile and dumb over the spectacle of bone china slivers spread like scattered petals on the checkered floor. Then Rachel noticed my shaking hands and moved towards me; the spell snapped and the room swung into motion again. Tonya went clucking sympathetically for the broom and dustpan and Patricia wet a few kitchen towels, and Rachel took one of my hands and squeezed it, her face as pale as I had just been remembering. "Brinsel, are you alright?"

"Oh, oh my goodness," I stammered, "I'm so sorry, I'm so sorry, Rachel."

"Are you okay? Are you alright?"

"I'm fine, yes, I'm so sorry," I persisted, trying to gather the pieces with my free hand, "let me just clean this up."

She leaned over and gently took my other hand. "Could I speak with you one moment?" she nodded towards the door.

Once in the hallway she fixed me in her most motherly concern, hushing her voice to a whisper. "Are you doing alright, Brinsel? You didn't answer us at all when we asked about the coffee, you just wandered off for a moment there. You gave me a little scare."

The photo of Max cocking a snook hung on the wall just over her shoulder. My head was still thick with a haze of unwelcome memories, most of them now not to do with Max at all. I looked up at Rachel, the professional mask of concern dropped over the panic in her eyes, and never had I felt so small and inadequate.

"Oh, I'll be alright . . . I was only remembering things."

She squinted, a frown tightening her face. "Is something bothering you? I mean, is something on your mind that's giving you all these headaches? You've always looked a bit tired, but in the last few weeks you've gotten positively peaked. Is there something we can do for you?"

"That's so kind of you, dear." I tried to unthread my snarl of emotions and reply with only one. "I've just had a lot of work lately, and I've been worried about the letters; there are so many boxes at home to go through, and my UK unit is still hard at it." The joke was feeble and she didn't smile. "I do so want them to be found."

"Sure you do, we all do. I just don't like to see you so beaten down. I mean, if there's nothing you can do but wait, like the rest of us, I'd rather you not take it so much to heart. I'd hate to have to admit you for exhaustion."

"I'll be alright, really; I want to do whatever I can for you. I can't tell you what it means for me."

Rachel squeezed my hand again, her brow pinching. "Oh, sweetie, it's enough that you're here."

It was a kind remark, the tenor of gentle, anxious thoughtfulness I associated so much with her, but for a moment, shadowed in her towering concern, I soured with resentment at being so small and frail within and without that I was constantly looked after and over or made the butt of a thousand patronizing snubs. Then, catching the fear in her eyes, shook off the feeling.

There was not much appetite left to me by the time Rachel announced the meal. We ate outside on the deck in order to enjoy the evening, but even in the midst of so much robust good company, I couldn't enjoy the food with the massive backdrop of Richard's house rising behind me and the lawn Max had mowed a thousand times stretched before me. Against the copse by the fence, the elderly apple tree where, aged eleven, like Puck or some extraordinary bird, he had perched with his piccolo and practiced for hours. The weight of so much useless, gratuitous knowledge pinned me in a silence that was so remote from the casual chatter about me, I might have been on another planet, and trapped there.

Dusk had crept in; fireflies were rising in the lawn as we moved back into the house and cleared away the dishes. I could still see the tiny dancing lights through the French doors as we settled once again in the living room. The sight was calming; I already knew the next round of talk would not be.

The group got down to business. This was the other side of the Sojourners—brainy exchange. It was a typical evening for them: the discussion quickly descended into a drawn-out squabble where Dan and Penny fought to score against each other, Paul and Tonya exchanged vicious shots, Tonya and Penny ganged up on Dan, Filipo threw in his quota of nervous, inappropriate quips, and Patricia tried to make sense of it all with vague leveling remarks. I was practically below Dan's radar; my only anxiety was Peter, enjoying the fracas from off side, his silence giving no clue as to the direction of his attention despite the fact that Dan had the floor.

Dan was by far the most voluble and, as ever, was directing the conversation without trying very hard. I wasn't sure what his act was to do with this time; at first it seemed to be the issue of disability—"You're all wheelchair challenged, that's what, you wouldn't know what to do with one if it fell on you"—then, egged on by Penny, it seemed to be manners in general:

"You can be honest without being rude, Dan."

"At my age I have earned the right to say what I think without fear of censorship. If that offends someone, is that supposed to be my problem?"

And became impenetrable to me again:

"It's meant to break the status quo."

"Sheesh, and whatever breaks it becomes it. *Plus ça change* . . ."

Freedom of speech was brought up. Dan objected that the matter was "clarity of speech. Some idiot went and confused communication with decoration." But "it" was no clearer to me than before. The function of diagnosis was dragged into the fray, and then the novelist Charles Williams; Patricia appealed to his remark that "difference creates energy." Rachel contributed: "And work. Did he mention it makes that too?"

"I utterly fail to see what is so different about giving the runaround. Get *off* the damn merry-go-round if you want to look at things different."

"It's *not* the runaround, Dan. It's finding better words to express what things really are."

Lynn: "Who's Charles Williams?"

I suddenly felt mildly useful, even superior, but before I could reply, John interjected, "He was a writer, Lynx. I haven't read him, but Jill reads those British folks, she probably knows something."

Penny and Dan drove on, impervious to other issues, or to any tendency towards ambiguity in their own.

"It's not about money, it's a refinement of language."

"Yeah, you tell me what's *not* about money. And dry rot is a refinement of wood. It's a disease of language, that's what it is."

"It's a cure for insensitivity."

"Like vinegar is a cure for a good honest cucumber."

"You are not even being funny."

"I'm not trying to be!"

The topic, or rather its failure to name itself, was driving me bonkers. I finally leaned over to Lynn. "What is it called now, what are they arguing on?" I whispered.

"It's political correctness," she whispered back. "You don't have that over there?" Before I could reply, her eyes lit up and she laughed. "That's right, you don't get political stuff!"

For half a second, taken quite by surprise, I felt only the sourness of being cheated out of asking a question, but just as quickly realized I couldn't remember ever telling her I couldn't understand politics. "Well, I don't, rather," I admitted, my face still burning with the question, "but . . ."

"Oh, it's not really about politics," she said hurriedly. "It's just about what to call things."

I was tempted to remark that the real issue would be *who* decided what things were to be called, but held my tongue. More than any play of semantics or taxonomy, Lynn's caginess seemed something worth my concern. Yet surely Max would not have spoken of me with her, whatever he had known?

When the evening's argument had reached a truce, Richard came over to me. "I thought of something else I could show you!" he gestured. "C'mon, you'll like this!"

Or had *Richard* known something? He was the one with the most connections, wasn't he?

"You've been looking a little lost," he said kindly. "I hope you're not worried about the trial?"

I was ashamed to recall that this was probably Richard's one overriding anxiety. "Ah, no, not really . . . er, well, a little, rather . . ."

"We both need a good distraction, don't we? What do you do when you're working on your art, and it's not moving?"

I stared at him in astonishment.

"You mean you never have any trouble?" He grinned. "Whenever I've got a project and I'm stuck, you know what I do now? I go look at pictures of my son. I thought it would at least distract you, and maybe even inspire you. And I think you'll get a kick out of this one . . ."

We were in the dining room, and I found myself standing before an unthinkable photograph hanging between the two cabinets at the head of the table.

A framed color print, two flautists standing together, casually dressed, holding their instruments. One was tall but well filled out—what the French call *important*—and jolly, with a round head and a deeply receded hairline around which sprang tufts of fine dark hair. Large hands holding a gold flute close to his ample chest. A warm, genial, very beautiful face, a bit pudgy. Twinkling, languid eyes. The other, thin and taller and wiry, very merry. A face leaner and more defined, gentle, with an ebullient smile. Haunted, deeply lined brown eyes. Strongly articulated hands. A silver flute cradled in his arms. They were laughing at something off the camera, their gazes going behind us towards the sideboard. One was Jean-Pierre Rampal. And the other was Max.

"Tell me, Brinsel, who is that?"

I nearly thought he had asked "*what* is that?" It was the question all the little hairs on the back of my neck were asking. For it was the photograph I had just written about in Max's letter, that I had, to the best of my knowledge, just invented.

"It is Jean-Pierre Rampal. And Max had met him?"

"Yes, quite a few times. They were great friends . . . He was an enormous encouragement to my son. It was he who told Max he must put his music to the service of the community." Richard took off his specs and began circling his handkerchief on the lenses as though he needed to busy his hands. "He told Jean-Pierre I was his father, and yet Jean-Pierre had not known who *he* was."

"Rampal knows of you?"

Richard laughed, rather hollowly. "Oh, yes, many people do. One of those grand distinctions." He pushed his glasses back on, blinking hard, and cleared his throat. "But Jean-Pierre hadn't known about *him*. And he ought to have."

He ought to have. For a single staggering instant my entire perception swung about like a Calder mobile, and I saw Richard through a gestalt I had since lost—*as my father*—and then was gone again.

"Yet wouldn't Max have said that some things are better than being the best—or rather than being known as the best?"

Richard glanced at me as though I had surprised him in a private conversation, the shade of incredulity and even guilt in his features. He put one hand over his mouth, then slowly rubbed his chin, looking back at the image of his son. At last he said, his voice closed with dignity: "Yes . . . that is how he was."

He half turned, rubbing his eye, and I stood there kicking myself for not keeping my mouth shut.

"Have you more pictures here?"

"I do indeed," he waved to the other wall, turning away from the photograph, "though it's not of Max, just something he owned."

I directed my gaze to where he was pointing, and there by the doorway, half hidden by the shadow of the cabinet, was one of the last pictures I expected to see. "Oh my!"

"You like it?" he smiled. "What do you think of it?"

I had lost all right to call anything *impossible*, yet it was impossible to prevent the tremor that started in my hands. This time I was standing before the intaglio of Saint Francis from Max's flat. "It's—it's—I thought I'd seen it somewhere before."

"It's possible. There's another copy at Saint Francis House downtown, perhaps you've been by there? An artist friend of ours made it some years ago. This copy was in my son's apartment for many years."

I could only stare at it, at that face with its blind eyes, all words stolen out of my mouth.

"You like it?" Richard repeated.

I turned and fled.

To my relief, Richard did not react. We returned to the gathering but, disturbed at my distress, he drew me aside and quietly apologized. To see Richard stricken with contrition for something he could not have caused was almost as piercing for me as seeing the unexpected intaglio had been.

The evening had collapsed about me, perspectives reversed, intentions turned seams out. I wrapped myself up in an enduring smile that could stretch no further. When the Sojourners regrouped for one last session, I spent my last energy not looking as miserable and whacked as I felt. The end came as it had to, at long last, but once more, I wasn't prepared.

"Our next number—I mean our last," Dan announced, "specially for those of you who felt the need to beat to death some cold cases, is a little canon in honor of our special guest, requested by Ms. Lynn Cunningham."

"Oh boy," cooed Tonya as the sheets came round, "some mystery music."

The phrase pricked my ears: "mystery music" was a game Max had played, sheet music with all identifying attributes blotted out, the object being playfully to teach them to identify by content, not label. I leaned over to Lynn to see it, took one keen glance, and sucked in my breath so fast I might have been socked in the gut. It was *On Caernarfon*.

15

dal Segno

At home I wrote feverishly, late into the night, everything I could remember of the evening. At the end I found myself in a wrath of almost twenty pages of typewritten notes and an empty teapot and a great muddle of hope and frustration.

The bewildering discoveries had been the worst of it: the matching articles, the appearances of the photograph and intaglio, more of my music. I could no more make sense of these than I could rewrite the idea of logic. Hearing the Sojourners play my music had been surreal—and this time it *was* my music, I had never attributed it to Max. He had scrawled "with permission" on the copied sheets—of course he had my permission, he had my every artistic permission, but how had he *got* the music? They had actually played it many times before, and once finished, a lively exchange had erupted over from where it could have come. Names of new composers were tossed back and forth. They commentated both the next thing to bang-on and breathtaking nonsense. I kept out of the discussion. So had Jill, who sat and picked at her nails the entire time. No solution was reached before we parted for the night.

The one thing about the incident that gave me any hope was the fact that if Max had disguised the source of any music, he would still have the untouched original somewhere. But where was it, and deuce, how had he ended up with it?

Back I went to the library, this time to try to dig up anything of my own works. There was no question that my music could be there; as for my books, in the letters I was writing and attributing to Max, I had made it sound as though the feat of unearthing them asked extraordinary persistence. Instead

I found a small collection, second editions, in mint condition. *Open Windows Press* in its stocky serif typeface on the uncracked spines. The acquisition date was 1988, and in three years they had never been checked out, perhaps not even touched. My publisher had no information on how they had got there. The librarian could tell me nothing. For a lead, it was as baffling as finding he had had my music.

Two weeks stood between meeting the Sojourners and the concert of Max's music. I spent it swinging wildly between desperate hope and belligerent frustration.

The desperate hope swung me very high. The thoughts I had thrashed out in the "conversations" with Max had toyed with the notion that something connected Max and myself. The only thing I could think of still was music. I hit the library again and made myself listen to all the music I could lay my hands on that he had heard in the last decade, the last year, the last six months of his life. I remembered volumes of heartache and trivial nonsense and mostly wept and drove myself and other patrons batty, and left exhausted and nearly empty-headed.

Surely, I had to find the *right* music; back in my office, I pored over the score Rachel had given me. If I had been able to write the same music as Max, all the time believing it was my own and I was merely attributing it to him in the course of a story, could it be possible that this same music could show me how I was to complete the letters?

When I had written *London Spring,* it had been in response to a meeting with friends. I had not had any intention to compose anything, and what impressions I had usually organized themselves into color and shape and line, not sound. But when I had sat down to work, the day behind me had coalesced into melody, and I recognized in it the form of all the delight and fellowship of the trip I had just completed. The title, which had offered itself, was oxymoronic, for there was nothing pleasant about the capital for me but the presence of my friends, and "spring" was nothing to do with tulips along the Serpentine. That spring could happen even in London was merely a happy irony.

Max had written his version of it under similar circumstances. Recovering from depression, he was on the way back from Sojourners one night in spring, and, walking along the river downtown, he had spontaneously begun whistling a tune that came to him, very simple, light and winsome. He was hearing it all the way home, and no sooner had he got to his flat than he went straight for some manuscript paper. The theme, for flute. The piano baseline. Parts appeared as if out of the air: violin, sax, guitar, another flute, bass, and each with a solo. *Variations on a Winsome Theme in D,* and, on a whim, merely liking the ring of it, he scribbled in "London Spring," intending to find a better title later. He was up until 2:30; he turned in reluctantly.

Two weeks later when he saw the Sojourners again, he presented his drafts and another idea to have a session to write words for it, and three months later they did. All of them, Richard, the Cunninghams, even Peter, gathered around a table in Richard's classroom. It had been an absolute riot.

I paced along the river walk south of Ashcroft Avenue, desperate and hopeful. This was where he had been when the music had come to him. Something had to come to me. I walked for hours.

I was at belligerent frustration by the following Sunday. The epistle for the second week in a row was exhorting us "to have done with falsehood and speak the truth to each other." Falsehood had got me into this and was keeping me in it gracefully. Speaking the truth was not among my better options.

As for the gospel, I was not listening in any way that could be described as devoutly. I heard the words "I will raise them up on the last day" and thought to myself that at least I should have some opportunity to knock his block off for having got me involved in this incomprehensible and unholy mess, even if I had to wait until the last day. The idea of swinging at someone in the midst of the general resurrection did not contribute anything towards my attentiveness at Eucharist. We sang *Amazing Grace* and I blubbered disgracefully.

The last rehearsal for the concert was two days before the event. I had declined, quite firmly, to attend the party for the premiere in the first week of August, insisting to Rachel it really wasn't proper that I go when it was their celebration. At any rate, Jill had been there also, and probably the last thing she wished was to see the *thief* of her uncle's music sopping up the glory with the players and board; I hadn't mentioned Jill, but Rachel, no doubt thinking along the same lines, and regardless of what justice was owed me as a co-composer, hadn't pressed the issue either. I didn't know whether I was angrier with myself for being so cowardly or angrier with Rachel for letting Jill's immaturity dictate the guest list.

To soften the refusal, I said I might come to the last rehearsal. But once again, my loss of nerve carried the day. I got only as far as the doors to the hall itself and there collapsed in a sick giddied heap, the sheer physicality of music mine and unknown and yet realized, the director's interruptions, Richard's interruptions, the lectures, the discussions, washing over me through the doors, enough to paralyze all my resolve. The thought occurred that I could go in and put all their concerns for an authentic realization absolutely to rest, a thought all the more laughable as I would have had to be dragged in. I must have looked as ill as I felt, for a staff member passing by asked me if I was alright, and one of the guards took the trouble to come and inquire if I needed an ambulance. I went home and thrashed the typewriter with my useless drafts, made a blizzard of them in the living room, and sat down in the mess and cried my heart out; I had lost my story, my hopes for writing, even my music, and *he had got everything*, all the credit, all the glory, and literally nothing I could do about it. I wasn't sure how much more I could take.

During the week, I spotted a marquee poster for the Philharmonic on one of the glass cases outside the arts complex. And there it was, a special off-season event, in copper yellow lettering on a blue and gray ground threaded with white lines of music: *This Gift: The Music of Maximilian Thompson. A Benefit Concert for Young Musicians*. I stopped and stared, crossed with ambiguity.

Max had never meant for his music to become something commercial. But he had never told anyone this, and it was beyond his control now. Everything he had ever made was now at the disposal of others; someone else had arranged his works, written the program notes, completed his CV. He had no more say in what was performed, was left out, how it was arranged. This music we had both written, which was also completely out of my hands, and forever.

What, I wondered, would Max have done had he seen it?

"Well, how about that," he would say, looking the bill up and down. "Someone did a lot of work to get this put together, I hope it raises a lot for those kids . . ." And would smile, shrug, and walk away, no more disturbed or interested than had the issue been sheep on a hillside in Wales.

Ms. Brinsel Thomas
Bwthyn Stella Maris
Strand Lane
Wimsey
Bristow Surrey
RH7 9JP
UK

M.M.= October 9, 1987
* Camille Saint-Saëns (1835)
* John Lennon ('40)

Dear Ms. Thomas,
I received your good letter a few months ago now, and a lot of work has kept me from answering . . . I hope, since you have taken to calling me by Maximilian instead of "Mr. Thompson," you will do me the courtesy of just calling me "Max," since that is what all my friends call me. I'm a big fan of my name, but no one should have to be addressed with a tag of ten letters and five syllables if he can have one easier to say.

    Thanks again for humoring me over poor Sgt. McC. I have been thinking about what you said in your letter about the difficulty of writing that sort of thing when you live in another country, and I wondered if I might not be able to help. I have some experience with this very thing, as I mentioned, and I could give you some ideas for stories in that vein if you are interested.

    I enjoyed very much what you wrote about making music with friends. I understand so well what you say about the creative collaboration and spirit of such being life-giving. I don't know where I would be today without the friends I have.

    You ask about Rampal. I guess the photo gave too much away? I met him many years ago now at one of those concerts I can't seem to stay away from. I was not in music seriously at the time, but it was with his encouragement that I got back into things. He is a jewel of a musician and human being. He has been magnificently supportive of my tiny little ventures in the world of music, something which touches me deeply, all the more so since I am Nobody in the world of music. It makes the photo I sent you all the more a scream. My nieces teased me they didn't see how I had the nerve to hold a flute in his presence, let alone play one, but I'm not afraid of very much. Life is too short for a luxury like that.

So, you want to see what kind of music I have? Well, for the most part, not published! I will scrounge around and try to find something presentable, but I fear I'll have to go begging. My dad has most of it, and he tends to hold onto things, and then misplace them. No doubt all will be uncovered at some future date.

Your letters are a treat for me and I am privileged to enjoy them, but also your friendship. What would the world be without music and art that aids sojourners and ties borders? Don't answer that.

in gratitude
Max Thompson

16

Segno

The 14 August. Evening. I dressed anxiously, paced, took off my shoes, sat down and massaged my feet. I went to get a drink of water. The door buzzed and I ran to throw on my shoes.

Rachel with a big smile, dazzling in a dark chocolate dress and tasseled tea silk shawl. "Ready, Brinsel?"

No! "Yes! Let me just grab my wallet."

We went down to the car; unnervingly, Rachel had me get in front, and herself squeezed into the back with her daughters, directing loftily to John, "To Armstrong Hall, James."

A pinched nerve jerked me or some static spiked my hand as I clinched the safety-belt; whichever it was, the effect was the same, I whapped the glass with my elbow and yelped and startled everyone.

"You okay, Brinsel?" John asked.

"Ah, ah, it's just nerves," refastening the safety-belt, twisting it around my arms and middle as though I had never used one before. "I'll be alright."

I spent the ride holding my elbow, fizzling inside, my stomach lurching around far more than was comfortable. The city sped by in the summer twilight, and all too soon John pulled into the multi-story car park behind the arts complex. Rachel led us through a locked door next the lifts and down a series of corridors; we emerged, to my surprise, from a door backstage, the corridor of the dressing rooms veering off to the left. When we came through the last door, I recognized, in reverse, the corridor that led through the reception.

"Alright, alright, you two," Rachel addressed the girls, both so effervescent with eagerness they were nearly bouncing, "go on. John, would you go with them and tell Alex we're here, and with Brinsel? We're going to find Dad and the usual suspects."

I was determined to brave the evening no matter what, but was already having doubts my guts could measure up to my intentions. The size of the crowd didn't help. From the road we had seen the river walk already filling with patrons, and now they were flooding the reception with great swaths of movement, color, and noise enough to entice a headache. Grand and imposing by daylight, the arts center under darkness took on mythic proportions, the reception vaster than I remembered, the reflections of indirect light in the nighted glass panels further confounding my sense of space and proportion. The repeated verticals of the panels of wall and glass with their contrasting values, the arced webbing of spars across the roof of the atrium, even the hidden mechanisms of the superstructure, all gave me the most peculiar impression of being in a colossal piano, as though a giant hammer could come crashing up unannounced. The sea of concert-goers in their dapperest and at their most poised, swirled around oblivious either of danger or significance. The show before the show would go on, in full swing, and everyone on stage.

We were next: Rachel pulled me into the scene and steered through the milling masses to one knot of coattails after another, making introductions. She knew everyone there was to know here; not only by default of being the daughter of Richard Thompson, but also as a premier sponsor of the orchestra and an honorary member of the board. I was introduced to almost half of them and several other staff, and I squirmed each time, either from the looks of polite surprise as though they had stumbled across an idiot savant, or the gushing effusions to meet a featured *composer* and never mind who. These people had heard Max's work and thought him a composer on par with Richard; but who was I? If I was not the villain and *poseur* Jill believed me, I was obviously a charity case, a sign of Max's beneficence. I was utterly out of my element, and beside Rachel's stately elegance, as small and inconsequential as a wren. I nodded and smiled at everyone with my paper smile, and each time their parting benediction was the same: "I hope you will enjoy it, Ms. Thomas."

"I am certain of it." I was boiling with anticipation, terrified with it; my sanity seemed to hang on the potentials of the evening. Rachel, excited as the twins and preoccupied as myself, noticed nothing, each time excusing us with a few uncomplicated courtesies and whisking me off to the next bagatelle.

And then too quickly it was time. I had never sat anywhere but the cheapest seats, and ascending the stairs to the boxes felt like entering forbidden territory. The Cunninghams' seats were an eyrie: a little room giving the illusion of a private showing, and the view onto the stage and the stalls below made me gasp. John and the girls had already arrived, Jill and Lynn at front, saving the next chair for Peter who had still to appear. Rachel ushered me into the seat above, handing me the program which had been placed in it, and sat beside me.

I was pulled out of my study of the program notes when Richard eased into the chair opposite; he grinned at me and said something, but I was so keyed up with tension I could not register more than the kind tone of his voice. The house was full, and a low ripple of applause signaled the orchestra filing onstage, setting up scores. I didn't dare look at the players closely and instead peered over the top of my program at their special guests, the Sojourners. None of them would have ever found themselves there but for Max—somehow, he had done that to all of us.

Just as the lights were beginning to turn down, Peter walked into our box, suited up as on a Sunday, and the twins excitedly directed him to his seat. He smiled at me as he took his program; for a split second, seeing him flip through it like a phone directory and turn his attention on the stage, bemused, I remembered that this was about his best friend, and then my anxiety took me under once more.

Warm applause below: a tall woman carrying a violin striding across the front of the stage—the leader of the orchestra for twenty years, Susanna Labinski, her presence snatching my attention like hunger. An instantly familiar master spirit in this milieu, yet every memory I had of her was merely something to do with Richard and especially Max being there amidst the players—Max onstage in workaday mufti or elegant blacks, aged eighteen or thirty-five, with flute or baton, possessing by skill and sheer communicative charisma an authority among his hundred-odd colleagues as though they were the back of his hand and his thoughts were theirs, a rapport so sensitive and finely tuned it was not unlike that which I had once wielded over them with a pen. I shut my eyes, hearing the air shine aloft the tuning note, sounding the spectrum of the hall's acoustics, the long echo of the tuning note from Max's first concert as a player or his first occasion conducting. I would open my eyes and see him shaking hands with Labinski, and then acknowledging the orchestra; he would have spent the afternoon taking interviews and writing reports and would slyly acknowledge Richard's presence in his opening remarks, but when the applause rippled up again and I looked, Labinski was shaking the hand of Richard's successor, Denis Marcelli, and Max was not there.

"Good evening, and welcome to this concert of the music of our very own Maximilian Thompson . . ."

I could hear Richard clearing his throat repeatedly. Rachel was already sniffing and wiping her eyes. I concentrated on the blossoms of light at the back of the stage, counting my breaths. Whatever happened, it had to help, it *had* to tell me something, otherwise . . .

This is it, Max, I thought grimly. *You owe me, now . . .*

". . . we present you *This Gift*."

The lights dimmed to their thinnest point and then winked quietly out. The seething whispering of the audience hushed.

I gripped the armrests for dear life.

The downbeat, and the orchestra leapt into life.

Symphony No. 2, *Striking the Colors*. I was still breathing, if chaotically, and they were beginning with "everything"—every instrument a color and every tint and shade a carefully chosen style of music, a brief sketch, the piece progressing up the spectrum, sounding in detail the entire tonal palette of the orchestra. He had stuck to every rule and then broken each one, reshaping it to make something new; it was in audial, illustrative form a masterful essay on music itself, and listening to it, everything I knew about music flew straight out of my head.

I remembered writing some of those lines myself, slaving over bars and notes until my head was insensible with them, and I remembered how I had written of Max seeing the artwork on color wheels at his nieces' elementary school and jotting down, with the simplicity of writing a grocery list, the same music. He hadn't composed so much as put down, note upon note, rest upon rest, the music that had come pouring into him from he didn't know where, the same way I had written down his life. It was happening in front of me, each note as I had drafted, that he had completed.

A gentle patting on my hand; Richard was beaming at me teary-eyed in the silence after the last bar. "Isn't it something!" he whispered thickly.

I nodded, unable to reply at all; then the first shrill slip of flute swirled into the hall. I forced my mind on the program notes as if I could hook myself into the words to prevent being flung into the ether.

Halil, Hallelujah was about flutes, a circling sinfonietta for flute and small orchestra. A plait of ribboned light almost entirely led by two flutes, the principal and Penny, two silver threads through the orchestra's warmer, denser weft. I saw the blackboard in Richard's classroom where Max had hastily chalked the notation and dynamics, just as they came to him, in the middle of a class. I saw the puzzled faces of his students when he turned back to them. But nothing more.

A piece written for Dan followed: *Gumshoes/You don't stand a chance*. The program notes to this piece betrayed Dan's collaboration: they gave very little away. I avoided looking at the musicians and instead watched Marcelli, his lone figure miming something like kneading or sculpting or painting on an enormous scale, hands and the whizzing stick describing a pattern on the air dutifully translated by the orchestra—but this was only one more useless game; he was the pivot at which all attention was fixed, and the arc of his every gesture relentlessly pulled the eye and ear back to that other audience he addressed. I could not escape it for trying—everything in the hall pointed back to the source of the sound that filled it, and when Dan was cued and his bow hit the strings, the sheer vibration seized my attention as forcefully as if he had grabbed my arm and hauled me from my seat.

In my mind, the sound splintered into innumerable memories of Dan, as if the notes had morphed into a spread of snapshots; but like the music to which they corresponded, they coalesced into an intensely guarded, increasingly labyrinthine mosaïc of clues and hints, spliced with ironic asides and discreet puns, disclosing a finely drawn portrait of Dan in the shadow of something exigent. Even the game of cat-and-mouse played with Labinski, scribbling a hopscotch of gold across every line, called up both Dan's character and a maddening urgency, some hint waiting to be noticed and apprehended. It was riveting, seething, edge-of-the-seat pursuit—the hopeless muddle of memories no less than the music—and true to form, both images and sound winked down a little hole at the last bar just as something was within grasp.

When I came back to myself moments later and glanced down at the program to see what was next, my breath caught in my throat. The title piece. Rachel leaned over, sparkling teary-eyed at me. Richard smiled and squeezed my hand. For an instant I remembered standing in Rachel's study with the drafts in my hands, knowing I had to give up every claim I had to it; and this was the result. Now, it had to have an answer for me . . .

Of all the pieces tonight, this one was the one I was most certain was my own and not his, the one my heart kept its rights over—and the only one publicly acknowledged that I had any part in. I knew every note and rest and nuance as if it were a story I had written and revised a thousand times; it was all singing inside me, and as though tapped into this frequency, with sureness and deftness the orchestra tossed up an edifice more lovely, more captivating to my ears than the whole splendor of birdsong, a palace whose every room they rendered in dazzling perfection even more wondrously than I had conceived it, ours to enter and enjoy. No sense of fear or loss, I did not collapse in a surfeit of memories—instead I was astonished by a commanding affirmation of life, promise, gift. Even the brief prose parts in the piece, the last remnants I could no longer call my own, filled me with joy and pride and satisfaction, and being there to hear it, I felt unexpectedly and unbearably cherished and valued and I wept.

Playing a Part 217

This music that we had both written was one of the very few of his compositions with original texts. It had been written for the writers of each piece to read their own parts, but for this arrangement, the prose was simply recited by the soprano and baritone performing, with solo accompaniments. They did not give the names, but if one knew the people, one could tell simply by the words and expressions the characters of the writers. Jill and Lynn had parts, as did Rachel and John, and Richard, and Peter. All of the Sojourners. Felix. Mishael. Max.

I had been hearing stories about him, remembering stories, for months. Everyone had something to say about him or could remember something he had said. I had been putting words in his mouth for months. But now I was hearing his own words. *His* words.

Max Thompson, the unliterary, whose chief grasp of poetry had been the virtuosity with which he handled a column of air he blew through a thin silver pipe—these were his words, not words I had put in his mouth.

> *In the spring once more*
> *the blue nights of open windows*
> *and music down the stair*
> *and stars and the shadows of trees*
> *on the silent street; new blossoms,*
> *and warm rain on face and arms,*
> *the wind plays the harps of the trees*
> *In the blue night, ultramarine*
> *the moon is chasing me*
> *And I look down on the earth*
> *I have never seen before:*
> *Open windows with stars*
> *in the arms of the trees, the wind harp*
> *in the rain of new blossoms, and*
> *the face of the moon shadowed*
> *on the ultramarine street*
> *and the blue night down the stair*
> *chasing me, I don't know where*
> *And music, it was always there*
> *in the hollow of the night*
> *we knew it as silence.*
> *And what gift is there better than this*
> *I do not know . . .*

The words rang up through the hall as though the music had vanished; they hung in the air like the long echoes of bells, their shapes gently dissipating, and I saw how completely they were his, not even something I could have invented.

The last movement, the finale. The other instruments withdrew one by one until only the flute and the piano remained, and then it ended quietly the way it had begun, the piano alone.

And that was all.

No memory followed, no revelation. I remembered nothing more. The music that had caused all the trouble did not have an answer. Only the world it had opened a door to, gentle and tranquil, remained; I needed answers, not peace, but there was nothing.

I had hoped and waited, hoped and waited, and there had been nothing, *nothing*. It was only music. It had no answers. It meant nothing.

I tried to breathe normally, the program wrinkling in my hands.

"Brinsel?"

Rachel had come up behind me and put her hand on my shoulder. She quietly sat down beside me.

I was sitting desolate on the curb that ran along the footpath before the hall complex, my face in my hands. The sound of the crowds on the pavement behind us was thinning. The interval was nearly over.

"You doing okay?"

After a moment I bobbed my head. She sighed and gently rubbed my shoulder.

"It's kind of like winning a gold medal in the Olympics, isn't it? And you didn't even get to come to the rehearsals."

I swallowed, queasy. I was nobody, nothing; a thousand working composers would have given their eyeteeth to be in my shoes that moment, and I wished it were them and not me.

"It's such a wonderful piece, too; I can't tell you how much the players have enjoyed it." A faint laugh, as though far away. "They've just been raving over it. I think it may even end up in their rep."

The evening was humid and close and it was hard to breathe. I closed my eyes and pressed my face between my palms, trying to decide whether to go back to the box or to sit it out in the reception.

"Max never . . ."

And after it was over? Then what could I do? This had been my greatest hope, almost my last hope.

Rachel sighed. For several moments I heard only the dull roar of the city, the trickling of the fading crowds. I opened my eyes and saw, through the lattice of my fingers, reflected lights bobbing in the black water of the river, enormous stars, connected to nothing.

"Well," she said finally, "I guess we should start heading back in . . . intermission's almost over."

Neither of us moved. A very faint breeze lifted the hair on my brow.

The bell sounded for the end of the interval.

"Thank you for being here, Brinsel." Rachel's voice quite small.

"You're welcome, dear," I said mechanically. I let go my face and gripped my elbows, imagining standing up and walking into the city. I imagined being at the cottage in Wimsey thousands of miles away. Anywhere, anywhere but here. "It's good to be here."

The crowds were nearly gone. Rachel sniffed and ducked her head. I took a deep breath and looked at my feet again, wondering how to tell her I didn't feel well enough to go back.

"You know," she said, her voice low. "I can't tell you how much it means to us you get to be here for this. I mean, Max never got to hear it, but as you both wrote the same music, and you made it possible for us to perform it, and you can be here . . ."

I raised my head and, after a moment, turned to her. She smiled tightly and gave my shoulder a small squeeze. The voice was Rachel's, and the face, but the eyes were her mother's, and the words were coming from somewhere else.

I put my hand on hers. "Let's go," I said.

Three pieces remained on the program. I would do it, I would listen to his music for him, for Rachel and Richard. I was weary to death with putting on an act, but I had to be pleased about it for their sake. All I could do was to endure the rest.

The Mad Conductor had already begun when we arrived back at our seats. I remembered first penning a synopsis, no more, of this piece years before, and I remembered Rachel showing me the actual manuscript in Max's hand, something I had imagined the sound of so easily but would have had trouble realizing on paper. It would take only twenty minutes to realize instrumentally: the orchestra would be compelled to disorder and compelled to reunite. Once, it should have been a delight to listen to Max's own *großer musikalischer Spaß*, but it was no longer a joke—what was so amusing with everything going wrong?

I simmered through the first few minutes, virtually the only part where everything went "right" in the most conventional way; even the music was conventional, very little to distinguish it from a modest if rather dull, slightly overdone compositional effort, and nothing to suggest things were about to come undone. I buried my attention the program notes.

"*This brief comic symphony, his third and last, falls into two parts as the man with the stick takes center stage. Scherzo on scherzo, or perhaps something more?"* Wry and witty, more of Dan's handiwork. *"Here is a man with a mission, and for a while, the musicians are willing to try to follow him. A mad genius, perhaps? Well, they have made up their minds by the time they reach the third movement . . ."*

The quirky directions had already begun, Marcelli demanding contradictory emphases and wild swings of mood, and the orchestra obediently, without displaying much understanding or enthusiasm, following him. Beyond that Max had written it for his father, I could not remember from where this piece had come, only that it had been one of the last things he had composed. But I could not even recall his notes; infuriatingly, incongruously, what rose before my mind's eye over and over was my name in his handwriting on that last scribbled note: *Brinsel Thomas has all the information I do and can help . . .*

Into the beginning of the second movement, the conductor's directions became even stranger, sending the tempo sliding crazily across the spectrum with great sweeping strokes. A brief jazzy episode while the orchestra attempted to match his tempo; I was remembering, disconcertingly, from a Christmas four years gone, Rachel telling her father, *Oh come off it . . . You've never been indeterminate a day in your life . . .*

I listened, lost, swatting off utterly incongruous memories of Max's last Christmas. It might have been the music itself, the layers that shuffled over each other like cards and vanished just as quickly, leaving nothing to hold onto, without points of reference or, seemingly, order . . .

. . . Jill mocking her uncle, *What do* you *know about writing stories? . . .*

. . . And yet I had to admit it was still fantastic for all that; part of Max's genius in this particular piece had been to compose something that, even while careening towards utter cacophony, might still be appreciated as harmonious, even melodious. It sounded an absolute mess, but a beautiful mess, and you couldn't help believing it was all going to come together in the end, though you had to wonder how it could be possible.

. . . Lynn asking him, *Was there ever* anything *you couldn't figure out?* . . .

I could see it clearly, knowing that underneath, everything was going as it should have gone, though on the surface it appeared matters were collapsing in ignominious ruin. It was a picture of an orchestra being undone, and just beginning to sound like it, too. It was the end of the second movement and perhaps the end of the piece; one could sense that the orchestra as a whole was having grave doubts about the conductor. Musicians turned and looked at each other bewildered; the music sagged, picked up, dragged, skittered.

Without warning someone marched up to the rostrum and leapt up the stairs into the light.

"Dad!" gasped Rachel.

"Grandpa!" hissed Jill.

"Richard," whispered John.

"*Yes!*" breathed Lynn.

Richard! Rachel holding her head in shock and Jill frozen, her hands twisted together. John looking blank as a slate and even Peter, the unmusical Peter, even he knew something atypical had just happened. But there was Richard at the rostrum, and, smiling graciously at Marcelli, he bowed and joined him.

Marcelli was stunned—so flabbergasted he froze, and the orchestra, unexpectedly, fell to silence, except for an oboe so wrapped up in the spirit of it all that it whined out *teee teee teeeeehhhee* into the dead stop, and then too ceased. Richard was suddenly the sole point of attention of twelve-hundred pairs of eyes.

He tapped Marcelli on the shoulder, straightened and jabbed at himself importantly, miming a baton keeping time, his smile hugely brilliant. Grasped the lapels of his jacket with an outrageous self-assurance and beamed as if to suggest no one in their right mind could refuse such bombastic presumption. And I knew from the way he leaned over expectantly and tilted his head that he was giving the orchestra and Marcelli a big wink the audience could not see.

"Rachel," whispered John, "is this supposed to happen?"

"Oh, God," she groaned, "what does he think he's doing!"

The meeting at the rostrum was becoming less cordial. Marcelli, playing along, puffed out his chest and glared archly up at the intruder, unable to look larger with Richard glowering a foot over him. A frantic and belligerent miming erupted from each. At last, Marcelli, in a magnificent hauteur, smacked the baton into Richard's hand and stormed off the rostrum, miming outrage. Richard watched him go with a grin, then turned with an almost menacing eagerness back to the orchestra. He cracked his knuckles noisily and shook out his arms with a flourish.

The players, trying to recover from the first blow, had their attention fixed on the baton, awaiting his next move; raising his hands slowly, he grasped it in both hands over his head and cracked it in two.

The sound slapped every musician there like an electric shock. Half the orchestra was gaping at him with expressions that were genuine versions of the affected disbelief they had shown through the first two movements. We could not see Richard's face but Dan, staring goggle-eyed up at his old friend, suddenly sprouted one of his devilish, manic grins. He touched his bow to his strings.

Richard shot a long, meaningful look at the musicians; I could just hear him directing something in a stage whisper. Then, hands spread wide, he jabbed the downbeat.

The music sprang up under his fingers and darted away. And suddenly I was hearing and seeing the piece *exactly* as I had once imagined it would be—written by Max for his father, and Richard playing the part to perfection.

The third movement began and so did the tug-o-war. He directed *fortissimo* to the cellos. They teased him with *pianissimo,* and then softened to a whisper. He wanted *pianissimo* from the bass woodwinds; they responded with an outburst of indignant hooting, the violas shadowing them in support.

While he strove to conjure the theme out of the violas, it ran away from him around the perimeter of the orchestra and stalled in the trombones, swelling, then staggered through the oboes and horns and leapt with abandon into the violins, finally possessing Labinski with an impassioned solo. Richard attempted to cut her off and was roundly scolded by the brass. The clarinets leap-frogged with the bassoons in and out of the theme. Richard, keeping time, tried to tie them off. He wanted a big sound from everyone. Everyone dropped out except the harp.

No matter what he directed he was defied: he wanted *delicato* from the violins, they gave him *delirante*. He wanted the orchestra to *crescendo*. They gave him *diminuendo*.

For several bars he was keeping 4/4 time and the orchestra went in 9/8. They jumped to 2/4 and he began conducting 5/4. His frustration and outrage were magnificent to behold.

And then the bottom dropped out at the end of the third movement—the entire orchestra leapt into free jazz. They jauntily, fearlessly took it away and Richard, to all appearances, lost it completely.

He swung wildly as if warding off a swarm of invisible bees. They were throwing the theme back and forth across the stage and Richard was in between, saluting now one side and now the other with the music always one step ahead, his efforts completely ineffective. The sound was wild and magnificent, a steam organ crammed with an orchestra; it was rag and then Latino, it went Baroque and in a few strides erupted into bebop. A conversation seething with drama and life was being shared across the entire orchestra to which Richard scarcely seemed privy.

And then, suddenly, at the coda, like arriving at the Great Gate of Kiev, everything came together—for thirteen majestic bars, conductor and orchestra responded to each other with the precision of obedience, painting an abruptly distinct, figurative image on the heels of a scurry of abstraction. Richard unfolded his most subtle gestures, eating up the part.

But it couldn't last—one by one the sections broke up and spun off their own ways, the orchestra splitting into four different time signatures. At the very point it seemed the music could only come apart at the seams, Richard threw up his arms as if in defeat—and every sound snapped to silence, the entire orchestra halted at a precipice awaiting his next move. Then he roared—one howl of sheer artistic angst—and the orchestra, section by section, falling in behind on his pitch and picking up volume until they had drowned him out. He swung at them with his fist and they flung the music back; then again, and again.

A wild and staccato flute solo, *burlando*, then joined by an oboe, and all the woodwinds. The orchestra muscled up behind them, mounting in aggression, and pulled out all the stops. Richard jabbed and swiped and parried. Three last fierce bars, and, almost in desperation, he made the cut-off. They responded.

A breathless silence, then the clatter of the cowbell knocked over. A hundred professionals in formal attire looked in the direction of the sound and hissed *"Shh!"* and Richard put his head in his hands.

For a moment nothing moved. Then he straightened and bowed deeply to the orchestra.

The gesture sparked the tension in the hall, and in one rush the audience crackled and exploded, rising and thundering applause. The orchestra rose and served him an enthusiastic klatsch. Richard turned to the hall, radiant. Then he put his hand over his mouth, and suddenly I put my hand over mine.

In that moment, sitting there beside Rachel, by Peter, those vibrant sounds I had just heard still ringing in my mind, the crack of Richard's baton, the symphony that had gone awry and worked anyways—in that instant the world receded and I gazed down from the balcony into the well of the auditorium and saw the stage as from a tremendous distance, saw *Richard*, who alone could have directed that symphony aright—just as I alone could have known that what had happened, would happen, that in one stupefying flash, I *knew*—

The audience was roaring with applause, whistling and even cheering. Marcelli was standing on the rostrum, his hand raised to Richard. At my side Rachel applauding intensely, tears in her eyes, and John and Peter smacking their hands together loud, strong. Jill and Lynn cheering shrilly and clapping, laughing with mad excitement. I suddenly realized nearly everyone was standing but myself, yet I couldn't seem to rise. I kept looking around me at those faces and those people I knew so well, petrified that I was watching them through a frame I could not reach through.

The silence settled again, the audience quieted, the concert continued. The twins nearly vibrating exhilarated out of their seats. John holding Rachel, who was crying. Richard at the rostrum, directing the remainder of the program. I was holding my head, trying to piece things together, trying to hold my thoughts together.

And it was useless; I had been distracted for a moment by an entertainment, but a joke was not going to help me. I let the last two pieces wash over me, drowning in them; they were only to do with Ariel, was not all his music to do with Ariel? She had started it. And there was Richard, so tall and yet so diminutive before that crowd, the light gleaming on his woolly head and highlighting the white ribbon of his waistcoat, shining in stars on the piano black of his shoes. He was bowing, the hall was exploding in applause, and the orchestra had become a shimmering of bows tapped on the desks, and he was leaving the stage, and it was over.

17

Max

I imagine that when other people wake up the morning following the premiere of their music, it is with something like elation or ecstatic relief that leaves one warmly satisfied and hungry for more. I woke up with a dread something like nausea, and it only got worse.

On Friday the air conditioning broke down and the humidity climbed up; at midday the wind died and the air thickened, stunned with smog and moisture. The heat settled in dense and smothering and immovable. Things went awry and people grew terse and edgy. Most people blamed the heat. I blamed Max. Never would I have had such troubles had his idiot whimsy not involved me in his problems. I burnt the breakfast porridge and burnt the turnips, and it was his fault. I ruined my favorite paintbrush. I missed two buses and an appointment. On the way back to my apartment block, the three yobs who took such pleasure in mocking my voice pursued me with crude remarks in even worse mock Oxford. It was all Max's fault. At home, the fan broke and I boiled over and tore up paper for half an hour.

My resolution not to say anything more to Max dissolved in a blaze of irrationality. I fumed culinary invectives at him in Italian, "unsanitary cook," "evil cook," "slop cook." I scraped together the scant Hawaiian I knew, but the most offensive epithet I could manage was an ungrammatical, unthreatening *pupule ōkole*. None of the usual German expletives seemed adequate to express my wrath and I hurled *Wagnerischer* at him, as untrue and meaningless as any actual obscenity. He won by saying nothing. This was too much; I would make him talk.

I stormed to the typewriter and snapped it on. I typed severely, "Hello, Max."

"Hello there, love."

I was in no mood for this. "Why is it you call me that?"

"Don't most of your close friends call you that?"

"Yes, but they're not American, and that's not an American endearment."

Even beside myself with frustration, he was still unassailable by my mood. Had I been able to impose on his voice my own exasperation, the reply would have been, "A bit negative today, aren't we?"

Instead, silence.

"I don't understand this, Max, I don't understand any of it. I don't understand what I'm supposed to do. You are not even helping."

"I couldn't really help you if I did everything for you, could I?"

"Try starting with helping me with something at all!"

"Tell me, Brinsel, when you are out doing your research and meeting people you know, do you tell them everything?"

"I do not."

"Why not?"

"Why *not*? Because then they would tell me nothing! Nobody could possibly believe me. I've got an idiot story: 'Hello, my name is Brinsel Thomas, and you're a character I invented. I know all about you. So, tell me about yourself.' I wouldn't be worth the time of day."

"So it's because you know everything that you don't tell them everything?"

"YES."

"What's the reasoning behind that? I mean, in less pragmatic terms?"

"Talk sense!"

"Please, Brinsel, it's important."

I swore baldly at both myself and the typewriter. "They couldn't be who they are and do whatever they need to if I got in the way with what I already know."

"I've had a challenge like that too."

I couldn't imagine what that meant.

"I don't understand this. How can I write these foolish letters? And what are they going to have that Peter can't work out?"

"And yet you told him why yourself. And it is true."

"What do you mean, I told him?"

"When you first met with Peter, you explained that we had corresponded. That I had shared all the details of the case with you in that correspondence in order to give you ideas for stories. That you understood it was actually something real when you learned about my death. And as we both told Peter you knew *everything*, he logically concluded that what he was missing is in those letters."

The man was a genius. "Fantastic, Max! Ruddy fantastic! So had I!"

"Then what's the problem?"

"I made the whole blasted thing up, that's what's the problem! It's all a lie! I DON'T know everything! And for it to make sense, I need to know what to write."

"Brinsel, *it is true*. You have everything you need already, in fact more than you need. It's a process of subtraction."

"Confound it, Max, I have given up my right to call my work my own, and I am almost ready to give up my sanity. What else am I supposed to give up?"

"Whatever it is that is keeping you from moving forward."

"Ignorance! That's what I've got to lose."

"It is something more harmful than that."

"What would *you* do in my place?"

"That isn't the issue here, Brinsel."

"Why did you say I knew *everything*, when that was only possible before? Now that I'm here, there's nothing I can know."

"Brinsel, it's not *knowing* that you need to be concerned with right now."

"How can you say that? That's the whole point of this! I don't *know* about the case. And you promised Peter I *did*. *I* promised him I did, simply on account of your word, your—" The bottom of the page edited my adjectival remarks; hissing and seething, I tore out the paper and jammed in another, "What on earth do you expect me to do? Write, and pretend I can magically present all the facts just as you had them? It doesn't *work* that way, Max."

Silence.

"Why, why is it I know so much useless information about you, when everything I need to know I cannot, I cannot possibly know? Why, when it's because of the investigation that I know any of this—isn't that the reason? Isn't it?"

"What if the investigation is not important?"

"Not important! Not important! What could be more important than this right now? Solving your case? Maybe getting some justice? Good God, Max, you of all people."

"What do you think is the most important thing here? You said that you trust the process when doing your art. Suppose, that like your way of approaching your art, knowing *facts* right now isn't as important as having *trust*?"

"Max, this is not art! It's an investigation, remember? The work *you* did? And is that not what I'm here for according to that idiot note you left?"

"Brinsel, please listen to me. I'm trying to teach you to ask the right questions."

Confound the right questions. Why could he not answer the questions I had?

I imagined strangling him; his character was constantly supplying me proof he deserved it. Only he had been well over a foot taller than myself and I should have had to stand on a chair. I would grab his smart alec neck in my teacup hands and try to throttle his thirteen stone with all the force of my six and a half. It would be like a mistletoe trying to bring down its tree. He wouldn't have raised a hand but would have stood there with that deeply puzzled, hurt expression, and asked, "Brinsel, just what is it you think you're trying to do?"

I typed, "Answer me one thing, Max. One thing. Give me an *answer*. How do I know all this?"

A pause. "Alright, but it's not the answer you'll want."

"Try me."

"Because you love me. Because you love us."

I was tried. "What is *that* to do with knowing about you or anyone else?"

"It's what can help you with this."

"Big help!"

"Brinsel, this is the truth. All your facts come of this. I can dress it up any way you like, scientific, philosophic, aesthetic, I can give it a religious job, whatever you need. But this is the heart of it, this is what matters."

"You tell me how that is to help with any of this!"

"When you wrote about us, Brinsel, what were you writing?"

I jabbed out, "Stories. Nothing but stories."

"Did you know ahead of time how they would go?"

"But what of all my other stories? What of everyone else's stories? Are they also real, just because they love them?"

"We were real before you loved us. And this isn't about someone else's stories, this is about you and us. My friends. Our stories."

I clenched my hands to keep from bashing the keys. "Then do I know about you *only* because I love you?"

"Brinsel, please listen to what I'm saying, please don't simply react. I have already told you how. That is what matters."

"Forget it! Forget it! Who cares what or how it is? I just need to know what to do! That's what ruddy matters! Tell me what I need to do!"

"Don't you remember only love can create anything?"

"But you told me I wasn't the one making anything up, that it was real without me."

"And it is."

"Then what is loving you to do with it??"

"What does love mean?"

"Would you *stop* playing semantics, Max, I cannot stand that. Can you not give me a straight answer for once?"

He wouldn't step out of character for one instant. And why should he? I was the one typing. He would continue to be intransigent and inquisitive and irremediably obscure until kingdom come.

"Can I ask you a question, Brinsel?"

Angrily, "You are always asking me questions." I bit my lip and threw out, "What is it?"

A pause. "For any other anxiety you have, you seem happy enough when you are with my friends. Why is it you are not so happy to talk with me?"

My heart sank. He was right. He had become my punch ball.

I took a minute to breathe more evenly. More carefully this time, I scrolled in another page.

After a few moments, I typed, "I'm sorry, Max. I have not been very kind, and I apologize." I stared at the keys, trying to keep the letters from quivering, my throat tight as wire. "I think the difference between you and your friends, I mean why it is difficult to speak to you, is that though I know what they don't, you know what I don't."

And that I can speak with them but I am not really speaking with you.

Silence. Then, "Brinsel, what's the difference between *their not* knowing, and *my knowing?*"

"That they don't know what you knew?"

"The difference is in you."

The letters deformed, wriggled, snapped back into shape.

"It makes you afraid, doesn't it?"

I closed my eyes. I lifted my hands and brushed them over my face and then held my mouth as if it might fall off. The wire of my throat tautened unbearably.

"In my position, you would be crackers not to be."

"You don't have to be."

I gulped a sob and typed quickly, "That is almost the least helpful thing you have said."

A long pause. Then, "Well, what can we do about this?"

And then it came to me, at last, the clearest, the most undeniable fact. There was no *we*. I was a fool, I was a *noof*. *I* was the crazy arse.

I depressed the keys as though each were an entire word. "*You cannot help me.*"

I was sitting there alone, in an empty room. Nobody could help.

"I care about what happens to you, Brinsel."

"Even if you did care, you could do nothing."

Silence. Somewhere inside me I could feel a horrible tearing.

"I'm not going to let you fall, Brinsel."

I threw my palm at the top of the machine as hard as I could. "It's too late, it's too late."

Silence.

"Can you live without fighting it?"

I pulled my gaze back from the ceiling. "Without fighting what?"

"Can you live with the question? Without having to know just how all this can be, and without understanding why? Please don't be angry. Think about it one moment."

I covered my face with my hands.

There was nothing to think about, nothing to look for. Without fighting it. It would come to that, giving up. I was going to live with yet another unspeakable, unanswerable question. I had no other choice.

I let go my face and reached for the keys.

The typewriter was off. Under the words "think about it one moment" was "*Non scrutatio, sed admiratio.*"

I could not remember typing it.

It was difficult to meet the post-concert elation in which I found Rachel on Sunday morning. Before Eucharist even began, she leaned over to me twice and commented radiantly on this or that aspect of her brother's compositions. She might have been propounding philosophical propositions for all that I registered her.

The music of the gradual psalm another of his infernal compositions. I could not escape his intrusive unhelpfulness anywhere.

Somehow, I found myself at the lectern. I pulled out my reading specs and stared at the page of the Epistles as if the characters were random squiggly marks on the page, undecipherable.

"A reading from the letter of Paul to the church at Ephesus . . ."

I couldn't make out the words, could only hear my voice breaking into disparate syllables and flying randomly into the air, glancing off the beams of the rafters and entangling in the whirling ceiling fans. I returned to my seat next to Rachel and tuned out, the color behind my closed eyelids steely gray, nursing what felt like a promising headache.

I heard only muddled fragments of the sermon. Felix spoke something of how . . . something and of bread and . . . something, and then I lost him. He was behind plate glass, or lobbing words over our heads that sailed into the choir loft without reaching me. Then it was over and he sat down, and the congregation knuckled under for the few moments of silence that followed.

I studied the frayed binding on the prayer book in the pew rack, my head clouded with gray shapeless distractions and squeezed by that throbbing cap of pain. I fiddled with the hem of my sleeve and fingered the ends of my scarf. I looked up into the chancel.

A man was standing against the wall to the left of Felix's chair. Tall, his head almost reaching the bottom of the hymn board hanging a few inches away. The sun through the clerestory windows cast scrolls of white light over his crossed arms, and the shine aureoled his figure in such lucid, commanding intensity that all else seemed no more than paper tracery, and he the most real thing there. He was gazing quietly into the chancel and I could see the calm features of his face and his head of brown hair in profile. Then, lowering his eyes, he turned his face fully to the congregation. His gaze did not wander but met mine and he smiled, simply, as with great pleasure, his entire face lighting up; reflexively, I smiled back. He raised one hand and touched his forehead, his mouth, then dropped it over his heart, like a signature, the sunlight ribboning his front and flashing over his fingers; he gestured into the chancel, turning his gaze back in the direction of the tabernacle, and I looked too. When I looked again he was not there.

Felix raised his hand to his nose and absently rubbed it, his gaze on the floor.

Someone snuffled a sneeze in the pew behind us and whispered, "Excuse me."

Silence.

The blankness of the wall by Felix seemed too obvious, the sunlight sliding down it in vertical white stripes.

Everyone was rising for the Creed.

Around me voices and movement; I had shrunk to a small, immobile point, frozen in the shocked confusion of something immense and unintelligible. All I could do was stare into the chancel, studying that empty space as if it said something.

"Brinsel? Are you okay?"

Rachel leaning over me with a frown of concern. All round us people were noisily passing the peace. I looked at her, first startled she was there at all, then that I was there.

"I'm alright . . . I just . . ."

"Do you need to go out?"

"No, I'll be alright, it's passed now."

And it was, though the dark blur of astonishment was still in me. The world presented itself to my senses in patches of disconnected sound and movement on a field stripped of pathos, even the pain gone, the only sensation that of a peaceful and absorbing silence. After Eucharist, Jill stalked importantly past us in the corridor, but Lynn paused until I met her gaze. She hesitated, about to say something, then checked herself, smiling in apology, and turned after Jill. Even Rachel was unusually quiet as we went to coffee, though she clutched my arm, not releasing me until she had settled me in a chair with some juice and a piece of bread.

It was then that I began to notice how far apart everything was—the chairs remote from each other, the far wall an inestimable distance away, even Rachel, hovering nearby, on the other side of some divide that the bread in my hands stood as a milestone to. Richard wished to read to me the reviews of the concert from the Sunday paper, but his voice reached me only as a sound like paper, flat and unsubstantial. As hard as I listened, his voice kept receding behind the faces about me: the expressions of interest, delight, curiosity, almost as distant as his voice. Peter, standing nearby with that mask of incomprehension and satisfaction, was the nearest thing to nowhere.

I had seen that face so often for almost five years, the lined gray eyes and the thin steel specs, all bluff gruffness when most at ease, and like so many faces I knew, forever dogged with old sadnesses. He had found his place in the world, but it wasn't a position of having and keeping; as with his profession it was so much constant searching and sorting. He was accustomed to having to look for lost things and knew that some lost things could not be retrieved, regardless how thoroughly or how diligently one looked.

My own search was almost over. There was only one place left for me to look.

It had been a drive across town for Max. For me it was a long bus ride choked with exhaust and fumes and countless faces hazy in the midsummer heat. It should have been about ten miles or thirty-five minutes, but all the measurements blurred together; I was going back three years, eight years. The ride dragged on; the bus jerked and stopped and lurched into circulation again, people stumbled off, boarded, grabbed defensively onto the plastic straps swinging from the ceiling. I kept looking round, wondering where they were all going, and if they were going to get there.

The face of the street changed from trim to rough as the bus progressed by fits and rushing starts. By the time we passed 100th Street all pretense collapsed under the weight of the poverty; except for a few newly constructed churches and carefully kept up businesses, everything was in disrepair. I pulled the cord at 130th Street.

The bus shuddered to a stop three blocks later, and, shaking as well, I disembarked. I turned down the next street. Halfway down the block, the pavement dipped at a drive between two brick buildings. I studied the area hawk-eyed, as he might have when looking for details, but not with his attention, nor even his patience and persistence. I must have looked about me five or six times before I could force myself onward.

The through street before me was not an alley but an actual thoroughfare, with streetlamps; it simply had no name. What made it most uncomfortable was the absence of windows on most of this side of the surrounding buildings. That, and the intersection of a narrow alley halfway down where a skip was parked.

You could hear and see the traffic on the main road, a few of the trees, and sometimes a vehicle would turn down this way to cut through to the opposite block. There were marked spaces for parking; people in the area parked here during work hours. Delivery lorries passed through. In the middle of the day it felt as innocuous as any other quiet street. He had been here in the middle of the night.

The 17 May. A Tuesday. He had risen at 3:30, turned out some Saint-Saëns on the piano after 6:00, and left for work at 7:00. Traffic through midtown was snared in a tailback. He mulled over two slippery jobs and six dull ones he was working on with other investigators and two he was working on alone; the rest didn't need mulling. Listened to the classical station and fingered out the music on the steering wheel, humming. Thought of music they were working on at Sojourners. Switched the radio to NPR. "Yes, yes, I can *see* you want this lane!" Arrived at their office at 7:35.

Mishael wasn't there yet, running late. Peter was already there putting things together. Their staff was trickling in. They met for the work of the day and got down to business.

Mishael came in; having a dreadful day already. Her employees had been late. Traffic had been awful. Asthma acting up. Did they need anything? Had anyone called?

Telephone calls. Papers everywhere. A happy conclusion in the morning work period. Mishael cheered up a bit. Max turned up the classical station all the way, conducting the music triumphantly with a pencil.

A visit to the police station to talk with some officers and pick up paperwork and drop off paperwork. Two interviews out.

Read new music for fifteen minutes during his lunch break and took two minutes to scarf down his sandwich. Made plans for ordering replacement parts for a student's instrument. Worried over a student whose instrument had been stolen. Jotted scores he had to bring for classes at the coming weekend. Scrawled notation for a psalm verse on the calendar on his desk.

Some business correspondence hastily dashed off and passed on to Mishael, though not among them a fictional conceit on my part: he scribbled a letter to me and posted it himself.

Peter left for the courthouse and to stop by another agency.

Two new clients came in. Two older clients came in. Four new clients telephoned. Everyone wanted instant results.

Max got to play phone tag. Then a protracted, intense phone call with someone else, perched on the edge of his desk, the receiver pressed against his shoulder and resting the phone on his knee, fielding inquiries from his staff with small, precise gestures.

Two hours spent chasing through a stack of records. Another hour on the phone, six different telephone directories and a list of numbers at hand.

A meeting with two interns. A meeting with Mishael. A meeting with the coffeepot and a newspaper folio.

The staff dispersed. Mishael packed up and went home, her day having got better: "Hey guys, t'morrow, t'morrow."

No music classes that night; they planned to work late. At 7:30 Peter went out to pick up something to eat and Max bent intently over his work. A night of surveillance ahead.

Sometime between then and 8:00 when Peter came back, he had scrawled the note which he left on his desk. And had gone out into the May night. Peter worked, waiting for him until 11:15. At that time not Max but Sgt. Lewis and Lt. Hutchinson arrived. And brought him here.

I stared at the asphalt. The brick walls. The skip.

I could see the police tape, the lights of the cars. I clung to the brick wall with my fingers.

I could see both things at once: the indifferent faces of Davis's companions. Peter between Riley and Sgt. McConnaughay, stunned to silence.

He had been followed. Davis had been watching for his chance. He could have gone another way. But would it have even mattered what street? He had been thinking, *In the morning, it will be out of my hands.*

Why mention me in that note?

This street led through to another, a shortcut that saved only about a quarter mile of walking to his car on the next block.

Who would guess there had been blood on this street?

Had he mentioned me, as I myself had told Peter, because he meant to tell him about me? He was sure it was finished . . .

But *why* mention me at all when I knew *nothing*?

And then why had he written, *if something comes up . . . ?*

Perhaps Max hadn't known. He had been going to come right back. The note wouldn't have mattered then.

It was about half past ten.

The first blows struck so hard and fast I could not breathe, smashed into the black and white of pain. Once more there was no one at all who could help, there was only the contempt so cold it hardened every blow until I lost coherence and place and time. My palms pressed on my ears protected nothing, prevented nothing, each noise shouting inside me and wrenching my stomach tighter so that I had to keep swallowing to stop the sounds from rushing out—I was going to be pummeled to unconsciousness and I was preoccupied I might be sick on the wall or the ground. I could not stop the whimper; he could not stop the sounds that were beaten out of him, and he had ignored the other sounds as I could not do. I saw him try to run and I saw him try to defend himself, and I saw him fail and go down knowing he would never stand again. He had thought, *Here we go again* and *This too shall pass*. And *Peter will say they've done him a favor.*

What had I said to Peter? . . . *I don't understand why he mentioned me, unless he thought I might be useful . . . I don't think he would have mentioned me otherwise . . .*

I leaned against the wall, breathing hard.

but I don't really know . . .

And yet I alone had known that when he went out that night, he would not be returning. Max had known nothing. Davis had only had intentions. I had known it as something that had already happened, and I had seen it as though I had been there.

Though he did not feel he could get up at once it was not as bad as other times and he thought *I'll give that a five*. That part was over quickly, and then he thought they would take whatever it was they wanted and leave and he could collect himself and go. Then he heard Edward Davis's voice, and he knew who they were. The next thing they did was to pull his arms out so he lay spread-eagled; when he struggled, they kicked him until he had to stop. He had not had any illusions from that moment.

When it had been fiction—when I had believed I myself had made it all up—it had not upset me to write it. It had been disturbing; that was only right. I had expected that, I had been prepared for that.

But it had not been fiction after all, it had not hurt like this. I had not been prepared for this. It was like two police officers arriving at my door one morning and asking me . . .

I saw two men; there were others, two perhaps or three, but I did not see them. I saw only the one who had every intention to kill and the one who knew he was going to die.

So little had been said; Davis had said all of it. His voice very low and soft. "I asked you to do a job, Thompson, a *job*, and you couldn't even do that right."

I had followed the scramble that Max's thoughts had become. He was overwhelmed with pain and the effort of breathing and of not being sick, and had not responded, not once.

"It's great to have a job helping folks, isn't it? You brought this on yourself. Who's gonna help *you*, huh?"

He was trying to think his way out of it, his mind whirling.

"I don't like taking no for an answer, you know, and I think you know a little too much about things that don't concern you. I'm going to get that file myself tomorrow. What are you going to do about it, huh?"

What *had* he been thinking of that work he had so recently finished, about Davis? Nothing, nothing at all . . .

Everything was seized in an immediacy and stillness and a clarity that burned his mind clean of everything but the moment itself, and then even his thoughts vanished into a luminous awareness, a presence, whole and so pure it was nothing more than himself, at last stripped free of all he was not. It could not have taken longer than the last thread of a second.

Initially he had groaned and it was one of the worst sounds of all; I was standing, feet pressed into the ground with my back against the brick wall, but his groan erased everything I could touch and as everything began to leave him I fell, feeling his last long fall to where the world, the entire world he knew, reports, bank accounts, electricity, weather, family, music, fell soundlessly away.

The other sounds were cold and impersonal and shot the darkness with even starker black and their indifference caused me to crash back into the earth he would never reach, the brick wall scraping my head and arms. I had not thought a memory could be so terrifyingly loud.

And that was all.

I slid down the wall and folded into a heap, my hand in my mouth.

I could not shut out the sight of his hands; violently red, nothing left of them. After the anguish and the astonishment the last look on his face calm, as though he merely had been surprised with news that he was to perform in five minutes, the unconcerned "oh," his mouth slightly open. Everything perfectly, astonishingly, incomprehensibly still.

The sky above the street impassive, a brilliant strip of china blue chalked with cirrus spanning the hard rooflines. That night it had been dim and far and pricked with stars. They were the last thing he had seen. He had left his eyes open.

They rifled through the tools in his bag and took what papers and recording media there were and threw the rest into the skip. They tore off his shoes and threw them in too, and not satisfied with that tore off his jeans as well. They might have done more but they became frightened, and they took his keys and his wallet, and fled.

I wanted to cry, but nothing happened. An old instinct to say the Commendation for the Departed rose up. I wanted to speak, but I could get no further than "*Depart . . . depart . . .*"

Two boys walking briskly by glanced at me in alarm and hurried past.

I was watching the scene that was no longer there, and I was watching myself sitting there, unable to tell if I was remembering it or living through it, or living through something else, somewhere else. "Max . . . I'm so sorry . . . *I'm so sorry . . .*"

The noise had not been unusual for this part of town. There was noise like that every night. Someone had rung the police. A police car had come through the neighborhood without seeing anything unusual. The second car had found him.

It had been a long, long, horrible night. Peter had gone to see Rachel. And Richard. He had been with the police very late and gone home and collapsed in a chair and stared at the wall until morning.

The note Max had left must have become a focus of activity very quickly. The subsequent investigations must have spread out at once, and with devastating ineffectiveness, for Peter above all. There had been no trace of me. *No trace of me.*

There was no trace of violence on the street. Even the air was calm. The sound of traffic in the city. Car doors slamming. Horns. People calling to each other. The long burn of the afternoon.

I didn't know how long I sat there, breathing.

I had followed his steps through the city and through all the places of his days I could go. This was where following him had led me, back where I had started almost five years before. There was nothing else, nothing.

Finally, I rose and dusted myself off. I walked north towards Jefferson Street where he had left his car and where he had been headed. I stepped onto the pavement, and fled.

I could no longer follow him. No one could follow him, no detective, no assailant, no investigation, not even I. He had slipped away from us all. He had resolved his last and greatest mystery, and taken all his secrets with him.

18

Myself

I couldn't write a thing for days.

For two days I knew little more of existence than the sweaty bedclothes and the unforgiving noise behind my eyes. To drag myself out of bed for aspirin or anything else was climbing a rock face that kept tilting crazily upwards and breaking off to shatter on my head. The world was white with pain and smelled rot black and mold brown. I didn't answer the phone.

On the third day I walked on mushroom legs across the room and sat at the typewriter and closed my eyes and, unable to write anything else, typed "the quick brown fox jumped over . . ." and filled several pages with it, trying to push the image of that still face and those unseeing eyes out of my head.

After that I lost track of several hours.

The heat broke that night in a pounding storm. I lay in bed listening to the rain hammering the street and thunder shuddering over the roof, and the last of my anger slipped away, and with it, my resolve.

As long as I could be angry, angry enough to write ridiculous conversations with myself, angry enough to go along with things, there had been a reason, and a way, to keep going. Now there was nothing. No explanation. My pretext had not been good enough. My pretext had been asinine. The game was up, and all the questions unanswerable.

On Sunday, John remarked concernedly on my haggard looks. Rachel, to my relief, was at work that day, though Lynn did an admirable job of mothering over me for a few minutes. Jill fled before me as though she had caught a whiff of the plague. I felt raw and unduly critical and could scarcely find it in myself to be anything resembling polite. At Eucharist the Old Testament lesson from Job on the day of reckoning, malefactors, and murderers made me ill, and I then had to read from Paul's epistle to the Ephesians on wives and husbands, or as Paul would have had it, husbands and their wives. All I could think of were the broken families and broken lives around me, and I was one of them. All I heard of the Gospel were the words, "Do you also want to leave?"

God, I prayed desperately, *get me out of this, I want only to go home.*

After all of that, there remained still the letters to finish.

And nothing had inspired me. There was nowhere else to research. I had witnessed all there had been of his life, all that I could uncover. I had heard his music performed—that music which seemed to be the one tie between us. I had visited the last place he had been on earth; if anything in his life, if anywhere could have helped me recall the details of that case, it ought to have been that street. Instead I remembered what had led me there in the first place, something I had not wished to, and something that could not help at all.

That was the only story about Max I had not written from his point of view; I could no more know or write what had happened to him after that, than I could know the facts of the case he had claimed that I possessed. I could not know him or treat him as a character after all.

I sat at my desk surrounded by shreds of paper from God alone knew where that had been there since Saturday. I could not even remember having torn up anything, never mind what it had been.

I had tried beginning the next letter just as I had begun the others. It would have been dated late November or December . . . there was the date, my address, the salutation . . .

But it was useless, sheer stupidity; as soon as I had said *letters* to Peter, *letters* had become *evidence*, and would be examined as such. Had I actually imagined no one would notice a difference?

The pile of "conversations" I had written to try to think things out and which had been largely unsuccessful. What good had it been to try to put words into Max's mouth when it wasn't real?

The temptation to write something absolutely damning of Davis could never be satisfied, since what was needed were the facts of a real situation. All I had were the few thoughts I had gathered on the case, in an attempt to make sense of things—assuming they, like the rest, were the real thing. And if they weren't?

The five letters I had written in Max's name; what would I have written in response to the previous one, and what would he have replied? I had been away from home for six months after that, and it should have been necessary to mention it. Surely it would be an easy matter to form a response to that.

Max would have begun the letter... he would have begun by saying...

Nothing came, not the smallest word.

I cleaned for several days. My rooms had never been so tidy or dust-free. It was beginning to look like Max's flat. I tried disordering things. Nothing helped.

I had one trick left in my bag.

I stared at the drawing of him beside the typewriter. Those eyes, that smile.

What had he been thinking when he mentioned my name? What on earth was that music to do with it? How could he have said I knew anything? The same questions I had been asking myself for months. I was no closer to an answer.

And all those photographs... he was not a character but someone real, someone I had no control over, that I never had.

I turned on the typewriter and took a deep breath, blinking hard.

"Hello, Max."

The room echoed with the tiny sound of the keys. The hum of the typewriter. The hum of electricity.

I waited.

"Hello, Max."

I could hear the blood rushing in my ears, my body's impassive static, thudding with each heartbeat.

"Are you there, Max?"

Of course he was not there. He never had been. He was real and he was dead. What could he do for me?

I could create a conversation with a character, I knew exactly what he might say in character, without even thinking, but Max had not been a character. It was one thing to pretend, but when you could no longer pretend...

"Help me, Max. *Help* me."

That flat silence. The dispassionate sound of nothing happening.

"I don't know what to do, Max. I cannot do anything else."

Silence. Nothing.

"I don't know what to do. I cannot do anything else. Do you hear me? I can't get the letters to Peter. I can't do any more."

Nothing.

What could this mean for the trial? Far worse, what could it mean for me?

"I cannot handle this, I cannot do anything. It's too much for me."

Brinsel has got all the information I do. But I didn't have, I couldn't.

What could that mean for Peter's trust in Max? His trust in me?

"I've failed, Max."

No words came. Nothing, utter nothing.

"I've *failed*, Max. I've ruined your case and probably the trial as well. You said I knew and I *don't know*, I don't know any of it. I can't *do* anything."

Nothing.

Did this mean I was responsible for it all, after all? That I had *caused* it all?

I had never had writer's block so profoundly. I ought to have been able to write a few words to make a dialogue. It was impossible, I was talking to myself.

"I've waited and waited. I've tried to let things come to me. It won't work. It's too late."

Silence. I stared at the empty white paper and the small idiotic black type. There it was in black and white, did I need it any clearer: I could do *nothing*.

"Are you going to help me now, that I've gone to the end of my rope? Are you going to help me at all?"

But he was dead. He couldn't talk to me, he certainly never had. He couldn't help me.

I couldn't tell if I was weeping for frustration or rage or grief and I didn't care.

"That's it then, it's done for. You, your case, the whole blighted thing."

Silence.

Max could do nothing. I could do nothing—I, who had once known so much, who had promised I could help, I was as good as dead in all this.

It would have to fall to Peter to do anything now. And somehow, I had to go tell him . . . tell him what? That I had lied? That Max had been mistaken—that *he* had lied? And *why*? What could such a pretext have been *for*?

Had he really promised to help? No, he couldn't have, I had invented that, had invented Ariel saying he would . . .

Of course, it was a game, it was all simply a game. Nothing more. I had not moved so much as a millimeter from the terrible place I had found myself in May. Nothing had been accomplished.

"Go on, then," I typed, because I was not talking to anyone but myself and it did not matter, "if you're going to do something, now's the time. There's nothing else I can do."

Nothing. Nothing at all.
I turned it off.

The only thing left for me was to tell Peter I couldn't get him the letters. I began to ring him more than once, but each time threw the receiver back in the cradle before anyone answered. What was the point of confessing—why bother say anything? I knew the truth; would I even stop at saying it was useless? Would I not go on and say it had all been a lie, that Max had lied and so... so had I? I could see the headlines already. *Lunatic British author charged with falsification in cold case.* I could write that article so easily.

How could my life have become so knotted up? All I had wanted was to write a story. Instead I had lost myself. I had believed—foolishly—that I belonged, that I was useful. Forget that the Cunninghams would be devastated by my duplicity. Forget that all of Max's friends would have every reason to mistrust me as much as Jill already did. Forget that Jill would loathe me more than ever.

How could I have ever thought for a moment Peter wouldn't ask for the letters—how could I have ever thought I *could* invent them? Because I had cared so much, I had wanted to salvage Max's integrity at the very point when it had been most threatened. And in doing so, I had jettisoned my own. My honesty for his. And what had been the point? We were both liars, and I would be the one to catch it.

September began.
I had been dreading seeing Peter that day at Good Shepherd; I was torn between dropping the entire thing at his feet, or saying nothing. I almost couldn't bear to look at him.

I wasn't the only one whose mind was elsewhere. The twins stroppy with the beginning of school. Rachel fretting over the twins and over something at work. Peter ominously withdrawn and silent. Even John unusually off keel, being sharp with the girls and impatient with Rachel. Eucharist could not quite reach me, or I could not get to it. I was watching the liturgy without being able to enter it, something projected on a wall with moving figures accompanied by meaningless voices and sounds. The passage from the epistle to the Ephesians all to do with persistence in prayer. My prayer felt stupid and irresponsible and useless as dust in my mouth. The Gospel a series of verses from the seventh chapter of Mark. *What does Mark 7:16 say?* Nothing. There was no Mark 7:16. I had looked everywhere, there was nowhere else to look. I prayed the same prayer I had the previous Sunday, that I had been praying all week. *God, get me out of this, I can't take anymore...*

Afterwards, Rachel had to go to work and the girls to class and Peter and John sat intense and preoccupied in a contained conflab at coffee. I had long since ceased to be an attractive novelty to the parish, but today it would have been welcome to have something to distract me. I sat alone.

It was Richard who noticed my lostness. He came and pulled up a chair by me.

I watched him studying his coffee in silence. Max's father. I could almost see his son there . . . though Richard never could have been Max. And yet now his presence, silent and for once, unimposing, spoke more powerfully of Max's than anything else around me.

He glanced at me and smiled. "How have you been, Brinsel?"

"Rather wanged out." I gestured, my hands describing a figure that meant nothing.

He smiled broader, as though I had told a winner. "Hard being an artist, I know."

"Have you been composing lately?"

"Yes, actually. I'm in the middle of something wonderful, I've been writing a blue streak since the concert."

At least one of us was. "What is it on?"

A mischievous smile. "It's a piece for flute and orchestra. I am calling it *The Superlative Flute*."

I laughed in spite of myself. "It sounds like a dessert."

"We'll put a big dollop of whipped topping on it," wryly, but I could tell it pleased him to have cheered me a bit. "And you? What have you been up to?"

"Oh, just little bits of this and that, really."

"Nothing in particular?"

Again, I flicked one hand opaquely. "Some articles, a bit of art, that sort of thing. It's been a quiet few months."

He nodded, pursing his lips with a thought. "I just began writing again after Christmas; before that, it was quite a while . . . And you'll be leaving us soon, now."

I made myself smile and nodded.

He was biting his lip; he cleared his throat. "I hope you've gotten the writing done that you came here for." And with a shrug, smiling as though we shared some affliction, "You know, it was Poulenc who said, 'Who can ever know all that lies at the secret heart of some works?' I mean, you know, you've been through a lot with us . . . I would love to see that story some day."

Ah, Richard . . .

"We've enjoyed having you here with us. It's not often we have visitors like you, and I appreciate meeting my son's friends. It's almost like having a small part of him, and with you, one we never knew we had . . ."

Please *don't say it*, Richard.

For a moment I thought he wouldn't; he turned away. Then, "I never really let go of him." His voice very thin and tight. "He had to fight me almost every step of the way, for his career, for his music, everything."

A long silence, thinly etched by the dull aural scribbling of everyone else talking.

"Perhaps," I ventured, "that was what made him able to do it at all. Perhaps he couldn't have done all that he had if he hadn't something to fight against."

Richard turned surprised eyes on me, his face sober.

I remembered him as he had been after Max's death. That singular grief he could not share with anyone, even with Rachel. Those terrible *if onlys*.

At last he replied, almost solemnly, "He and I were very much alike, always fighting for something, or with something . . . or against." He shook his head, his eyes unfocusing, and shrugged roughly. "You know, he'll be remembered for a bit, but it doesn't matter, none of it matters. You saw my studio, all my gleaming accomplishments. And," another helpless shrug. "I would trade all of it in a heartbeat, but I can't have him back, I can't . . ." He swallowed, biting his lip again. "He could have been so much, but I pushed him too hard, and I *lost him*."

He was staring at his hands, those big palms and the long fingers and fingertips calloused by years of plying strings. He had spent a lifetime and a career with those hands, making music, teaching, composing, conducting. I remembered those hands carrying his infant son, and nearly thirty-nine years later carrying his son's casket.

"You seemed to have found him, though, at the concert."

A very quiet smile. "I certainly understood him a bit better then. I finally knew what he had been after in that crazy piece; it was a joke, alright, and on me. He wrote every bit of that for me, me wanting to make it all go my way, just as he always knew. And when you don't have something you can manipulate, when you don't know what's next, what do you do? Think about it, can you interpret what you don't know, what you can't even extrapolate? Well, I was sitting there, and it suddenly hit me, this was one place I didn't have to know. I'd gotten it all backwards. You know, when I got up there, I told them straight, 'This one's for Max, now get it right!' And they did!" He beamed at me, twinkling in puckish glee. "Everyone would take their part, everyone would *do* their part . . . even Richard Thompson.

And it worked, don't you know." He nodded and leaned over and gently clapped one big hand on mine with a wry smile. "Maestro Thompson is not in charge."

It had taken Richard some fifty years to be able to say that. I smiled weakly.

"I'm glad you've been here, Brinsel. It's meant a lot, more than I can say. I accepted Max's career long ago, but the fact that . . . you had such a strange connection with him and his music, and even with his job, that's really helped me."

And I could be no more help.

I stood in the back of the church staring dully up the nave, up that lofted, sculpted space, to the Victorian jewel box that was the chancel. Its three arched windows thick with light: the healing of the blind man, the agony at Gethsemane, the Good Shepherd. Sunlight cast fluid mosaics of colored light across the marble high altar and the tiled floor. The central chancel window of Jesus the Good Shepherd seized the eye in a blaze of red and gold and white—not a limp Victorian dandy in philosopher's robes, carrying the lambs and herding the ewes, but a vigorous Fauvist laborer, young and beardless, attired for work with staff in hand and hat on head, going out to find the ones that had strayed: the Good Shepherd who had come to seek and to save what was lost. It was the same scene I had pictured a thousand times through Max's eyes.

Max had succeeded at helping so many people, but in the end he could not help himself and there had been no one to help him; in the end he had failed, and disastrously. He had lost everything, his fiancée and unborn child, his career and ambitions, his life. Even his last work had been lost and come to nothing. I had tried to help, but I could not retrieve what he had lost any more than I could the things I had lost. Nothing was found, nothing could be saved. I too was going to fail; yet once again, I was going to lose.

My gaze fell to the open baptismal font at my side and I saw my own face reflected darkly in its lucid pool, staring back at me with the disinterested eyes of one of my characters, and I startled away, alarmed.

And who was there to help me?

Labor Day. It rained on the parade. I stayed home.

The week proceeded in stultifying torpor. It was a matter of when, not if, I chose to tell Peter it was all out with the letters. Waiting seemed easier than the idea of telling him. Perhaps tomorrow, or the day after.

I picked up the phone and rang the station house. I needed to speak with Peter Serrev as soon as possible. There was a window on Thursday. Was there nothing sooner? This was Brinsel Thomas, and it was quite important.

No, Mr. Serrev was away on assignment and would not be back until Wednesday. If it was an emergency . . . No, Thursday morning would be fine.

Wednesday morning as bleak as Tuesday had been. I worked mechanically, insensibly, on a short essay on my experience of an American city for a journal back home. I scribbled, or made marks with a paintbrush, regarding my work from an unbridgeable distance. Everything I did as good as a waste. *Peter, I'm sorry, I can't get you those letters . . . I'm sorry, they don't exist . . . Peter, I'm sorry, I . . .*

Why did I bother fighting it, why had I ever tried? The truth would make itself known no matter what I told him. In the afternoon I walked out the door and propelled myself from one errand to the next, arriving back towards evening with typewriter ribbon and batteries and post picked up at the post office, and no appetite.

Everything went to its place. I unbound the post. A large packet with airmail stamps and Dai's loopy handwriting. I was going to cause him terrible trouble for his job. One good thing—he had sent the file at last. I could do a little work before packing up and going to jail. I tossed the packet on the table and sifted through the other post.

I went off to do other work in the kitchen, and it was late when I finally ripped open Dai's packet and pulled out the contents.

A letter from Dai in my hand, and beneath it, the file I had asked for. And something else.

Dear Brinswl,

I've finally remembered to send the file. Aren't you proud of me? It wasn't too hard to find. I just don't know why you insist on putting "writing" material in a file marked "receipts paid." Is this some sort of artist thing, or is it you've got a secret method of organization to keep blokes like me from finding stuff?

Now, a word about your mysterious projects, word being "variations on a theme," theme being "you make things impossible to find." You know, Swlu, that I will do anything for you, but by George when you asked me to find that infernal piece of paper you sent me on the Search for the blinking Needle of Cleopatra in the Haystack of Archaeology. There I was in your tiny loft, bashing my head on every beam I could find and no doubt scaring off all the pigeons on the roof with all the creative names I gave them. And all your cartons, NO organization, NO labels, everything in a whomping higgledy-piggledy most admired disorder, of every possible geological strata. She Who Must Keep Everything. Let me introduce you to my friend Mr Skip. If you don't come and clear out this—what's the artistic word, installation??—I just might invite myself over someday and toss the lot of it out the window to Mr Skip. School papers in the china! A crate of copper plates and books not to be budged till kingdom come! Pictures in your winter woolens! God in Heaven! What could she have been thinking, I ask. Nothing! I conclude, she wasn't thinking. Needless to say I didn't find Said Famous Paper THERE. Well, long short. In a little carton shoved up under the eaves I found a number of souvenirs of your trip three years ago. You were in such a state when you had your relapse, we just put all of that aside for you to look at later, and it doesn't seem you had ever got to it. One of us had thrown in some papers with it too and a big pile of post you never got to. I believe these are the letters you had asked me for; you hadn't ever opened them and I doubt now you ever saw them. You'll let me know about this? I'm all curious. There were just four, I'm hoping that's all there was. I'm sending them on straightaway for you. I hope they're what you needed.

And no, no further luck on the blessed and devoutly sought piece of paper you wanted me to find. You'll just have to look for it yourself when you come back; you may have a better idea of how to go about it than I.

Mur and the cubs send their hellos. Mallorca of course was lovely and sends its regards, I'll give you the unabridged version when you come back.

Ah! aren't you glad you've not got my job. Sometimes I envy you your quiet writer's life, your quiet artist's life. How do you bring it off??

Best love from your poor beleaguered
Dafydd

Very slowly, I put the letter down.

In the bundle of correspondence under the file were four letters from Maximilian Thompson. The first was postmarked 26 December 1987. The last was postmarked 17 May the following spring.

It was raining when I arrived at the station house.

The usual crowd, everyone looking damped down by the weather. I signed in and sat down and waited.

I had not been waiting long when Peter breezed through the security door and leaned over the counter. He straightened after a few moments, turned, and met my gaze.

This time I did not hesitate at the lift. Neither of us spoke on the way up. At his office he closed the door and gestured me to an empty chair before his desk, "Have a seat, Brinsel," rustling aside some papers on his desk, clearing folders and a telephone directory out of his chair and sitting down. Detective Riley already sat quietly in another chair nearby; he stood and pulled the chair back for me, greeting me with a nod and a twist of his face, and I tried to smile back.

There we were once again. Peter's hurricane-stricken office. The pictures of Max staring out from the wall. The sign that read *Lie in Wait—Truth Will Out.*

I looked at Peter and said, "I have the letters."

He gave a small smile and gesture that said, "Let's have them" and himself said, "Here we are."

I was grateful for the momentary courtesy of the chair, and tried not to shake as I drew from my satchel the bundle of correspondence, both what I had written and what Dai had sent. I handed it to Peter, and he received it gravely.

"Thank you, Brinsel."

I rose from my seat, and he looked at me as though I had interrupted him. "Please stay, Brinsel."

I sat, and without further comment Peter glanced the papers over and began reading them, handing each one to Riley as he finished it. Riley read them in silence and replaced them on the corner of the desk.

Peter passed through the first four very quickly. Then he dropped tempo, each page seeming to take an hour, his gray eyes flickering under his spectacles. He sat there reading, and I sat there with the fear of being caught out on a technicality flapping about in my chest, the questions *how* and *why* burning giant holes in me.

Peter's gaze was still razor intent as he went through the last letter, but I could see his hand trembling slightly. When he finished, he closed his eyes and sighed, heavier than relief. He took off his specs and rubbed the bridge of his nose, then simply sat there leaning on his elbows, hands clasped, and all I could hear was the rain.

Riley replaced the last letter on the desk and nodded to Peter.

"Brinsel," Peter's voice behind his clasped hands extremely quiet. He lowered his hands, not quite raising his eyes. "Thank you. Would you mind waiting outside one moment."

I got up, found the doorknob, and let myself out into the corridor. There were no chairs; I leaned against the wall, shaking so hard I could scarcely stand. I was still jelly-legged, my heart still in my throat when after several minutes the door opened and Riley came out with a folder under one arm. He offered his hand, and I clasped it. His wounded face smiling soberly. "Ms. Thomas, I wanted to thank you so much for your help, for being here. It's been good to meet you."

"Thank you," I said, pushing myself unsteadily away from the wall. "Is everything alright?"

His smile deepened and he nodded at the open door. "You can go on in," he said. "Peter's waiting for you."

He turned down the corridor, leaving me with the open door. The moment nailed me to the spot with terror. Peter didn't believe me, or he suspected fraud—he specialized in fraud investigation—or the letters weren't what he needed, or . . .

"Come on in, Brinsel," he said, seeing me in the doorway. He was leaning forward scribbling busily, his specs on the middle of his nose. "Have a seat, I'll be with you one moment here."

I lowered myself into one of the chairs yet again, listening to his pen scratching across the paper—he, writing, I being written about—until the sound became unbearable.

"Is it—is it alright?"

He paused and glanced up at me, and this time I saw his eyes were streaked. "Yes."

After several minutes he leaned back in his chair, staring at the desk between us. He raised his eyes and met mine.

The silence in the room burned. The slight noises that reached us from outside fell in it like kindling and made it roar: rain on the window, someone's radio down the way, someone noisily passing in the corridor greeting someone.

"Is it finished?"

Peter's face calm and deeply sad. "Yes, it is finished."

Then he did something I had not expected. He rose, and, coming round the desk, approached and tightly hugged me.

Then it was my turn to begin weeping. I had no idea how long I cried, sitting there.

He stood and handed me the box of tissue, and I took all of it. "I seem to do a lot of this here."

"It's not a bad place for it."

I did laugh at that, and he added, "I know you've been through a lot."

I said flatly, "You don't want to know."

"I know a little," very gently, but he had turned back to his desk. "I'd like to explain some of what we found, if I could, Brinsel, so you'll understand how it affects things. You deserve to know."

The world felt hazy. "You shall want me to assist at the trial."

"Yes." Peter rested one elbow on his armrest and propped his face in his hand. "Even though they were written fictitiously. You weren't entitled to that confidence, and it will have to be said for the record why you had it. The good thing is, he only gave you a puppet case, or rather *cases*, nothing that could possibly stand up in court, yet something that for my purposes, still looks and smells enough like the real thing. He was always good at finding loopholes and swinging them for all they were worth."

Somewhere in the back of my mind the words *fiction* and *nonfiction* stirred and began scuttling around as if to pull up a thought.

"And yet, the thing is, the missing information was not facts but direction. Max had been aware of something none of us had even thought of." He dropped his arm, shaking his head. "That's just the thing. There wasn't really anything *new* in the letters he wrote you, certainly nothing I hadn't already found. It was just arranged differently. We were asking one set of questions. He had been answering completely different ones. He knew what he was doing, and I did what I could to follow him, but without his records, I couldn't."

Asking questions. And looking at things anew. The disquiet of failing to recognize a known face joined the vague shape of half-remembered thought.

"And he was right, which was why things happened the way they did." Peter looked towards the edge of his desk again as if something were written there, his fingers drumming. "It could've happened differently . . ."

"Had he done anything wrong?"

"No, he didn't." He still did not look up. "The only thing wrong was that it happened."

I stared at his desk, tracing with my eyes the contours of papers into trails that led in and out of each other and diagonally led up the arc of Peter's tie to his chin. He pressed one finger on the bridge of his nose and I saw for an instant the clever young hothead who had pulled himself out of poverty and straight through university; then the gray hairs, the lines in his forehead, the unshakable weight of loss.

"Those infernal letters," he shook his head again. "You know, I just wasn't sure about all that for the longest time; I had nothing, nothing to prove you were what we were looking for. We couldn't find *anything* on you, nothing at all. That music of his, that was just about the first thing that spoke in your favor, as little sense as it made. It would make sense that he would know you through music, but I still couldn't see a correspondence like the one you described explaining how he knew about you or why he would mention you as a collaborator. I simply couldn't square that with what I knew of Max. Maybe it was him I didn't know."

He took off his specs and rubbed his eyes. "They certainly made themselves hard to find. You must have had a phenomenal collection to go through."

I shook my head. "David found them in a box in the loft, with some other things. I was quite ill three years ago, and I had put them away without paying attention . . . and quite forgotten."

Peter pushed his glasses back on. "David?"

"My brother."

"You have a brother, Brinsel?"

"I suppose there's a lot about me you don't know."

He looked at me thoughtfully. "What does he do?"

"Well..." my mouth gummed with embarrassment. "I suppose I could tell you. He's a communications security officer . . . overseeing traffic with the US for Interpol."

"Interpol, is that so?"

I nodded, coloring generously.

"Is that why you didn't want me to ask for help overseas to find the letters for you?"

"I hadn't thought it would be necessary," the words awkward as marbles in my mouth.

"Huh." He scratched his head. "Max and I worked with them once or twice. David Thomas, huh?"

"No," I said, knowing what was coming. "David Coomes."

"Coomes. I'll have to ask Parker if he remembers who we worked with."

I resisted the urge to tell him it was highly unlikely it had been Dai.

"So . . . You're married, Brinsel?"

I didn't have the energy to skirt the issue. "He is dead."

Peter replied gently, "I am sorry." After a moment, "Is that why you left Wales?"

"No. It's why I cannot go back yet."

"No?"

I lifted one hand and set it down in my lap, unable to make any gesture that could speak for me. "I—I couldn't be who I was, without him."

Peter tilted his head, closing his eyes and nodding.

The long silence that followed had the same sense of collapse as a deflated balloon, yet it was weightless, a relief, not failure. Then I realized why; I had not said *cannot*. I had said *couldn't*.

"Well," Peter was saying, "well . . ." He smiled. "Were the letters hard to part with?"

I shook my head. "It's only been so hard, waiting and waiting and not knowing how things would go. I'm so glad it's finished."

"For now, yes," Peter nodded, rubbing his brow, three years of grief etched in his features. "You've had a hard time, I know. Rachel's been worried sick over you. I pity the soul she worries over, they don't get any peace. But . . . you haven't been well, it seems, and I'm sorry it's been so hard on you."

The last twelve hours had turned the leaden dread pinning me down into a suffusion of butterflies, the little silvery ones that Max, innocent of the pox the cabbage white could be to a vegetable garden, had called "Ariel butterflies." I was sitting in a cloud of them, looking at the world through their glistening haze and utterly stunned by the sudden lightness and freedom. The long torment of what to do about the letters was gone; now there were new mysteries that preoccupied me, and I had even less idea how I could answer them.

There had been no difference at all between the handwriting of the letters I had penned and the letters sent on by Dai; they were all in Max's sloping longhand, with his funny curling Ds completely unlike my own, and apparently, even by the same pen. None of the papers were exactly the same; all of them were papers Peter would recognize, their regular office stock, the standard American letter. Max had not used their letterhead for any of them.

Each of the letters had been "business as usual"; friendly comments, bits of news and history, suggestions. He didn't seem to respond to anything other than things he had read in my writings or things already discussed, just as though writing to someone away traveling. Then "some things you can think about for a story, that could go like this . . ." They read like four very dense plot treatments, presenting the entire case point by point with his natural flair for the technical, just as if he had actually been sending me "some ideas you could use for a story," at the same time making each letter appear to represent a separate case, and never giving away that it might be real or even happening as he wrote. But for the topic they were exactly like the article he had written for *Flute Talk,* the same evasive phrasing, the same use of pretext—and in retrospect it stunned me that I had been handed a blueprint and, looking for something else, not known how to apply it—and this time he had been disguising himself and his information for far more puzzling reasons. Even more curiously, "It will take a while to get you all of this, and since you are so interested, I appreciate both your patronage and your patience." He had jotted down composers and musicians whose birthday fell on the day he wrote—the 4 April, Kvitka Cisyk '53, Ariel Chapman '50. The 17 May, Erik Satie 1866, Marcel Moyse 1889. He had written *MM*—Maezel's Metronome—by the date of all his letters; I had scribbled it on his letter of October for it had seemed the sort of observation he *would* make, but it was in fact, the very one he had.

The letter of December began oddly, almost apologetically, as if he had been distracted into writing it: "I don't do this sort of thing all the time, so you will pardon my long-windedness . . . from one artist to another . . ." This was the letter that mentioned a police detective named Riley who had suffered burns in a road accident recently, something Max had been preoccupied with at the time; ironically, this fact was only implied, not spelled out. Max had not referred to him in the context of his notes on the case but simply in friendship. About his "business partner Peter" he had said very little. What his business was he never mentioned. This letter had included "a little Christmas gift, well, by popular demand, from one artist to another"— a copy of his suite *April for Winds*. "I got this run up locally, so I didn't have to go beg my *Archivist* for stuff. I hope you enjoy."

The remaining letters were more composed, but all still had that distracted edge. The letter of February cautioned me not to mention these things to anyone, to be certain to change things around a bit if I actually did use them in a story, and to keep the letters in a safe place. They had been quite safe; they had been lost in my loft for three years. They, like everything else, had been *real*. And they had, as Peter noticed, been very open, very confiding. They contained no motive, other than a peculiar altruism that seemed to show little concern for confidentiality, for giving me so much information *gratis* at all. Only the letters which I had ostensibly written him could supply a reasonable motive—or the five letters of his I had invented. The letter of May promised, "I will get back to you soon about this and explain myself a bit better; there's too much work right now . . ." And then, "I have something to tell you which will surprise you, I think, but I wanted to send this first . . ."

Quite incredibly they were all addressed to my home, not to my publisher, but what most astonished me, beside the simple fact that he had written to me, was how perfectly they fit into the sequence I had begun, as if we actually had corresponded. How could he have written such letters, never having made my acquaintance? It was not as though there was anything about me in print that contained half of what he had written. Could he have possibly known of me, just as I had known of him?

And what would I have done three years ago if I had cleaned up after my relapse and found those letters, at the very point I had just been getting deeply into their lives and their stories? What on earth would I have thought? Letters from one of my characters?

It was nearly noon by the time Peter let me go. He would not hear of my walking home and had Detective Neilsen drop me off on her way somewhere. She drove with her calm velvet smile and I sat with my hands twisted together, still stunned. At my building, though, rather than simply letting me out, she got out and gave me a hug at the door.

I pulled myself up the stairs, the stairwell suddenly Dutch and each step a foot high, pushed open the door of my flat, and vacantly stumbled in.

And there I was. It was Thursday.

I felt utterly shattered. All I wished to do was go to bed and sleep for days, but I had some unfinished business.

Thankfully, the small domesticity of brewing tea had its gentling effect, and hidden in the woolen throw's embrace I felt myself unclenching. I leaned on the desk, temple pressed to the blue warmth of the mug wrapped in my hands, remembering, like a page torn from a book long lost, a childhood Saint David's Day and my paisley shawl pinned with daffodils. Time dropped quietly about me, erasing both features and distance like snow blotting a landscape clean, and I let it go.

I turned on the typewriter.

"Hello, Max."

"Hello, Brinsel."

I hurriedly drank some tea. My mind felt wide and clean and open and the words came just as quickly and quietly as they always had.

I put the mug down and tried not to think.

I typed, "It's all over, Max."

"That's good, Brinsel."

A long pause.

I typed, "I went to the street where it happened."

Silence.

"Max, I'm so sorry."

Silence; then, "You know all about that. So do I. You don't have to dwell on it."

"It hurts."

"And it will."

Well, what did I expect?

"But it's not forever."

"I wish it hadn't happened." There was so much I wished hadn't happened.

I was supposed to ask the right questions. I was waiting for the words "What good is that?" to come. Wasn't that the right question?

Instead, "I don't."

The words shocked as if he'd slammed a door in my face. "What are you saying?"

"I'm saying that I *see* now, Brinsel. I see the working of all things, and I see how it works! I'm *unable* to wish anymore. Yes, I still desire, but not that it hadn't happened; if I could desire that, I could not *see*, and I could not have the joy I do."

It had come so quickly and strongly I hadn't a moment to listen until the words ceased, then I read them, and read them again. I studied them hopelessly like a math problem, rereading until I had to cover my mouth with my hands, until the page jerked and bleared before my eyes. Then I put my head down on the typewriter, and I cried.

All the frustration, all the incomprehension of the past few months collided with the high of unbearable relief and further incomprehension of the past twelve hours. I wept until I was wrung to exhaustion, and I dried my face and blew my nose and drank some tea, still shaking. The typewriter was still on and patiently humming at me. The paper waited, holding those impossible words.

I reached for the keys. I tried to think of something to say. There was nothing to say.

Then, "Are you satisfied, Brinsel? Have I answered all your questions?"

I gulped some tea to try to stop shaking, bumpily set it down, and typed, "Max, how did you know me?"

A pause. "Do you want to know?"

"You mean you'll answer me now? Have I not asked often enough?"

"That wasn't what I asked. I *can* answer you now. But do you *want* to know? Because it may make things difficult for you later."

I hesitated. Then, gathering myself, I typed. "Well, confound it, yes."

"Jill told me about you."

I scattered. My throat squeezed to a thin point all the way to my fingers. "*What?*"

"I asked you if you wanted to know, Brinsel. You should know what that means."

Frantic, "Explain this to me."

"You know Jill writes, correct? And that she shared with me many of her stories? One of them was about a Welsh artist and musician named Brinsel Thomas."

My heart skipped more than one beat. It was not possible.

It was. It made sudden, perfect, horrific sense.

"But—but if—" The keys were sticking under my fingers, but words were falling over each other in their haste to get out of my head. "If you knew me as a character in one of her stories, then why did you mention me in the note you wrote, as if I were someone real? Why did you say that I knew all that you knew? How would you know that? And who would know who I was, except for Jill?"

"You remember the music I had of yours? When we wrote the same music? That was how I first found out, and I looked you up afterwards. I knew you were real. But I couldn't tell Jill that straight out. She'd never seen your music, never heard of you; she thought she had made you up."

The deluge had run off; blank spaces and unconnected words flickered through my head and I couldn't pull any of them into a thought. I typed, "That note you wrote where you mentioned me. I don't understand it. It's the cause of all this mess."

"And yet that's not the question you need to be asking."

He had said that I had all the information that he had, and he had been telling the truth. Numbly, I made myself type it, the only words which made sense, which did not make sense, "You did write to me."

"Yes, I did."

Silence.

"But . . . *why*? Who was I that you would write to me? That you would send me all of that?"

"I assure you I had a good reason."

"Please don't be coy now, Max. Tell me."

"My reason doesn't matter anymore."

"Doesn't matter! How could it not matter, when you wrote me so much information I had never asked for? Don't tell me that was logical!"

"No, but is that the only way of knowing things?"

"The only way of being able to prove them."

"Is it?"

I set my fingers on the keys but couldn't type the reply I wanted to make. Remembered music from the concert—his music—was painting radiant contrails of light and color and things for which there were no words through my mind; it was another answer, and I could not write it down.

Finally I typed, "But you hadn't known that *I* knew about *you*."

"No, I didn't. But I had a good idea that you just might."

"You, you," I sputtered, then typed it, "you . . ."

"Is it so surprising? Yes, I only knew that Jill seemed to know a great deal about you, and I could not understand how. However, there was still the matter of the music we both wrote. That said *something* to me. Don't think I was being unprofessional—music may seem to amount only to sounding air, and yet it's something that has to be *made*, and that means everything. Maybe you can't measure making like a fact, but that making gives the music its own significations, and very powerful ones too. It may have been crazy, but it was no crazier than Jill knowing about you. Because there is nothing made that is random or meaningless."

I tore out the paper so quickly I almost ripped it in two, simultaneously jamming in another.

"Then what about the letters that I've just written, which you supposedly wrote to me? What was the *point* of my writing any of them, if the rest were just going to come all along?"

"Brinsel, what did I just tell you? And what said the letters had to come all along? They came because you asked for them. I said I would do the rest if you couldn't, and I did."

"Then why hadn't you simply written to me to begin with, rather than just sending the information on the case? Why did I need to finish your correspondence for you?"

"Apart from that I was a horrible letter writer? I assure you I didn't do it that way for nothing."

"Well, why was it?"

"At the right time you will find out."

"What's wrong with now?"

"It's not what you need to know now. Please take my word for it."

I could not find a single reason why I should not be told at once, except that I trusted him. "But how could you have got my music? I never sent you my music."

"Why does it matter how I got your music? If you published music, it's out there. I ended up with it. What is knowing *how* going to tell you? Think, think! Right question!"

"But, Max, I never *wrote* to you."

"Brinsel, you are not dumb. You are a fine artist in any medium. When you don't think with your appendix, you think quite well. Why *would* you write to me? You didn't have any need to. The fact remains that *I* wrote to *you*."

"But I never knew about it!"

"But, but, but! Why would you? Did you need to?"

"Max, I never knew you had *written* to me!"

"Must you know *everything?*"

The remark halted the breathless staccato of the keys like a pencil jammed in the carriage, and I cringed at the poetic justice. I had not known everything; I had not known that Max had known of me. That Jill had written about me—that she *knew* about me, in the same unbelievable way that I knew about her.

"No, I don't believe I might. Perhaps I did not know everything about you after all. I could not even know about your case."

"You can't possibly know everything, but you know far more than you can *think*. You've been telling people for months now that I wrote to you. Perfect nonsense, right? But it was what happened. It was what I in fact did. Do you still think after that, and after everything you've experienced, there was no truth in the rest? That you were not free to say more?"

Try as I might, the words looked uncannily like a language I had never seen before. "I do not understand."

"What's an instrument, Brinsel?"

I knew this riddle, but why it was turning up here was still another. "A key."

"Do you know why all instruments are empty?"

I frowned, perplexed, but typed, "I do know."

"Is an instrument ever an end?"

"No."

A long pause. "You didn't get the sign, did you?"

My gaze slid searchingly from the paper to my hands and back again. "What sign?"

"At the concert. There was a sign there for you."

"There wasn't anything. I listened, I can't tell you how hard I listened. There was nothing there."

"Yes, it was there, I gave the cue."

"There wasn't, Max. There was nothing in *This Gift*."

"It wasn't *London Spring* that had your sign this time. And it wasn't simply in what you heard but also what you saw."

The tiny black words sat on the page with an authority I did not have, and I stared at them helplessly.

"What's a sign, Brinsel? I mean in music?"

"Something you return to, something that happens twice."

"So, what happened?"

I cast around, irritated. "*Nothing* happened."

"Do you suppose a conductor and a writer have anything in common?"

"What?"

"Did Dad ever really lose the orchestra in *The Mad Conductor*?"

What was that to do with anything? "I do not understand."

"Did he?"

"I certainly thought he did. It was just *buffo*."

"No, it wasn't just *buffo*. When have I made a joke and not meant something?"

"You meant it to be for him, you wrote it for him."

"Yes, I wrote it for him. He's a conductor. What does a conductor do?"

"Well, direct an orchestra."

"He was directing them, wasn't he?"

"What are you driving at?"

Silence.

"Did he, Brinsel?"

I was staring at the words and it came to me, with ridiculous clarity: the applause, Richard with his hand over his mouth, I with my hand over mine, and if, if I . . .

In the silence I could hear my breathing, and I scarcely seemed to be breathing.

"No!" I gasped. I typed, "You can't mean it!"

"Yes, I mean just that."

The bottom of the page. I crammed in another sheet without bothering to remove the first.

"It's not possible!"

"I'm not asking for your opinion, Brinsel, I'm just giving you the facts."

I was drowning in a cataract of insupportably huge facts. My mind numbed to a lump of frozen bewilderment at all the facts.

"Don't be alarmed. Remember, you didn't *invent* anything."

"But which came *first*, what I wrote or what happened??"

"Brinsel, listen to me. You didn't invent anything, you only wrote down what was, and you could do this because you were a part of it. You *knew*, but until you articulated it, it was not knowledge you could manipulate. Do you remember when you told Peter I had asked you about your music? You didn't think that I had actually had it, that it was there. But it was. And when you decided that I mentioned Dennis in the letters, and the photo of Rampal. You didn't plan on that, did you? But I *had* mentioned them, they *did* happen. That's what I mean. That's what I've been trying to tell you."

Silence, because I couldn't find any words to reply.

"Think about what you wrote in those letters, Brinsel, and about what we've been discussing all these months. The way you do art. That you can look at things differently. That you can change things. That you love us. That we have a connection. Did you know Peter looked up my library records after you told him about your writings? It's all there just as you wrote."

"Roamer," I began to type.

"The message for Roamer, you know, was really for you also. I never told him about you, Brinsel. He was pulling a useful trick on you to see what you knew. Maybe he's no Harvard grad, but he knows what pretext is and how to use it, just as you do. I wanted you to meet him so you could have at least a *pretext* for trusting that I knew about you, because you weren't picking up any of the actual clues. I wanted you to understand we are not so far apart as you think."

"But he knew I used a typewriter."

"Risky business, guesswork, but sometimes it's the only way to get things done, and he can put his money where his mouth is. He has an eye for detail and an ear for nuance, and he can bluff the face off a cliff. You know that for him, a *badger* is a journalist, someone who also types. And he knows I would be the one to give a name like that."

Silence so intense I could feel it like another presence in the room.

"Yes, you *could* have written the rest of the letters. It's not so impossible as it sounds; for someone else, not being part of this, no, but this is about you, and it would have been possible for you—in the same way, just as you realized, that only *Dad* could have really directed that symphony. The approach is the same—you must trust the process. That if once you write a story that turns out to be true, there is nothing that says you cannot continue witnessing to what is true if you happen to be within it. That you have to be on the inside to know what you know, but you have to step outside to write it. You're the only one who knows how I think, Brinsel, and you know without having to think twice what I look at, which questions I ask. Knowing it was real was your greatest challenge, but it would still all have come to you if you had let go. You decided you couldn't, and so, as I promised, I did the rest. You had two ways to trust me, both to write and to not write; you did a little of both."

"Max, I *gave up*."

"That's a kind of trust too. Sometimes it's worth even more, because you can hold onto something so tight you distort it. And the important thing is that you did what you could first; otherwise there would have been nothing for you to give up."

"But I *failed*. I couldn't do the right thing."

"Who's judging you, Brinsel? Not me, no. Do you think the right thing was only what you imagined it to be? And from where I stand, all that distinguishes failure from success is the refusal to love."

"Then what was all of this for? Why did I nearly have to lose my mind to get to this point?"

"Brinsel, I've made all my choices, I have no more work here, but you still do. You didn't have to nearly lose your mind, you didn't have to do anything. In other words, you didn't have to care one way or the other. But you did do something; you *chose* that."

"But what I chose was in fact what you did."

"That doesn't surprise you, does it?"

"Everything is surprising me. If you told me up was up I would be surprised."

"Brinsel, did you think you were alone in this?"

A tightness was pulling at the back of my throat. "But I never saw those things happen!"

"Do you have to *see* something to know it's there? To know it happens?"

I opened my mouth and closed it and sat staring at those words, the world and the universe infinitesimally expanding around me.

"Everything was given to you, wasn't it? And I shared in some of that too . . . I was given what you were, and I was able to give to you."

The words blurred and disappeared and I rubbed my eyes. "Why hadn't you told me all this to begin with?"

"And you would have taken it sitting down?"

No, I wouldn't have. I would have thrown the typewriter out the window. And got on the next plane to Heathrow.

"Do you understand now that it was important that you be here?"

"You mean for the investigation?"

"Oh Brinsel, that was the smallest part of it. What happened to all of you, and especially what happened to *you* was the important part, and, now, what happens to Jill."

"What *did* happen to me?"

"What am I going to do with you, Brinsel?" I could hear a smile in the words as though he were laughing. "Think!"

Nothing. I let the paper fall out of the machine and whipped in another.

"Tell me, Brinsel, when you began writing about me, what was that about? And did all that collecting, all that writing do for you what you hoped, as much as being here and knowing what you have to do with it now? With the reason you began with?"

I laid my fingers flat on the keys and stared at them.

Rachel, unable to talk about her brother for three years. Richard without Elisabeth. Max without Ariel. Even Peter without Eleanor. Max himself, his solitude, his silence about Ariel, and his death above all.

The intaglio of Saint Francis in Max's kitchen.

My fingers jumped up at the thought. "Max, you know about him."

"Yes, I do know."

Yes, of *course*. The small words filled the room and overflowed out the window, swelling until they saturated the world like light itself.

"And . . . and his case?"

"That I don't know."

The old frustration clutched at my throat. But he had never known anything either, *never*, it had never even been possible, it was just one of those things . . .

I typed, slowly, "It didn't do quite what I had hoped, not like being here."

"And you know, don't you, what this means?"

I bit my lip, feeling more tears, and typed, just as ambiguously, "What I must do with you, yes."

"Yes, and who is the only one who can help Jill do what she has to?"

My mouth and throat went suddenly dry.

"You know, too, that I *couldn't* have told you all this at the first? That you couldn't have understood it until you'd gone through the whole process—the process of *trusting* me, of trusting yourself to this? It is costly, yes, but there are costs more than worth paying, and this was one."

"For the letters?"

"For more than the letters. For the life of each of you."
Silence.
"Even . . . Davis?"
"Yes, Edward Davis too."
And he would know, now . . .
I typed, "Then what were those letters supposed to prove?"
"Didn't Peter tell you that?"
"He had said he hoped they would be useful in finishing your case."
"Were they?"
"They proved that you were right about Davis."
Silence.
I asked, "What were they supposed to prove to me?"
"Have they proved anything to you?"
Yes. They had. "That, that . . ." I couldn't write it. It was just truly beginning to sink in.
Silence. Several moments of it.
"You know, Brinsel, everything has its time, especially in music, and there are certain things that for the beauty of the whole, only happen once."
I had to wipe my eyes. "What are you saying?"
"That you shouldn't try talking to me like this again. I wouldn't answer. You'd just be talking to yourself."
"But," I began stupidly. "But . . ."
"But what Brinsel? Don't be afraid. I happen to love you."
"You loved Ariel."
"So I can't love my friends? So loving you means I love Ariel less? It's not like that. I don't have those limitations any more. Not even in regard to Edward."

It shocked out of nowhere. The cold revulsion froze me in a flash.

I snatched my hands as if the keys burned. The nausea I had felt at the jail back in a crashing instant.

The black text sat on the page bald and authoritative and I sat in my chair pale and furious and we stared at each other, frozen in deadlock.

I could stop and turn off the typewriter and let the matter end there—let it hang there—or I could reply.

I did not want to reply, to honor the remark with a response. I would simply sit there, outraged and righteous, until the world failed, as had all else.

The silence became unbearable.

"Why did you not hate him, Max? Why were you not even angry? Why, when he took the last thing you had?"

A long pause, then, "What's the real question, Brinsel?"

"That *is* the question."

Silence, clean as glass in sunlight. It was not an answer.

I insisted, "Why, why, when you knew what he was going to do, why were you not angry?"

"I didn't need to be angry with him, or hate him."

"But *why*? It's not as if you even forgave him! I *know* you hadn't!"

"No, I was free."

"Free from what? The obligation to forgive your enemy?"

"Free to not look on him as one. That, for us, is what forgiveness means, in the end."

Silence, silence as I had never heard it. It was exploding around me like light. I could not tell I was sitting in the chair, or feel the keys under my hands.

Something enormous swelled up within me and found words and exploded.

"How *dare* you," I slammed out. I smashed the top of the machine with my fists and the carriage leapt an entire line. "It's not fair, it's not *fair*."

I wanted to shriek and roar and leap up and hurl the typewriter out the window, but all I could do was sit there sobbing and hiccoughing, my hands in my hair, ridiculous and outraged and every wound open and burning. After all I had endured, after all I had been through, there was no defense left to me. And yet he had had none, either.

The face in the image of Saint Francis came to me. If someone had told or read him something—a tax form, an article—that he could not find out for himself, he had to entrust himself to the given information, he had never been able to say *That is not what it says, that is not true*. He had been lied to more than once, and yet he had never once said *It is not fair*. What was *fair*? Who was I to tell Max it wasn't fair, to accuse him of being unforgiving? And he would no more blame me than he would have blamed Ariel.

I dropped my hands to the keys.

"How can I help you, Brinsel?"

I remembered him sitting in his office year after year, patiently asking that question with the same timbre of concern, again and again. Calm and completely attentive, listening without forming conclusions, the brown hair and the pressed shirt and tie, and the hands that could make miracles with a flute, those hands simply clasped on his desk, listening with the rest of him.

I looked at my own hands, not seeing them. "I lost him."

"There is no proof of that."

"Who needs proof?" I snapped. "Who needs evidence? I am the proof."

"Brinsel, it's not even true. What was lost was not a person."

"Prove *that* to me!"

"Forget all that for a moment, Brinsel, what would he say about it? Don't *think*; that's not how you know it."

I was sobbing, but took as deep a breath as I could and let everything like a thought curl up and blow away. Whatever answer there was, was there in the pit of my stomach and hidden in my palms and behind my ears, it was unnumbered images lighting my mind that I understood without having to think twice. Music and pieces of music. Silence and darkness and color, every hidden place and every uncovered place, and none of it had words, not a bit of it a single, measurable fact.

All sorts of words were tangled up in my throat. I pulled out the page and scrolled in a blank sheet. I typed, amazed at how orderly and calmly the letters appeared, "I lost the life I knew before."

Silence.

"Are you ready for the life you are about to receive?"

It came moment by moment, one note, one rest at a time. Part by part, and sometimes, against all understanding, one knew it.

"This is as far as I can take you, Brinsel, you can go the rest yourself."

And when you did know it was the last time, then what did you do? A thousand thoughts and questions swirled up, and desperately I snatched at one.

"But why did any of this happen? Why you, me, why any of it?"

Silence, the gentle sound of a smile.

"Turn around."

The air quivered, the room electric. I let go of the typewriter, and turned in the chair.

The room lay uncurious and ordinary before me. I was still holding my breath, standing in the middle of the room, feeling the disappointment like a wound, relieved, grieved, inconsolable.

"Go look out the window."

The filmy rectangle of light approached me until it pushed the room away. My hands pressed against the sill and my fingers knit the curtain aside.

"Look, Brinsel."

Cars on the street, and the buildings, and trees. The street became the river and the buildings dwindled to trees. Clouds of houses, forests of them. People walking, there must have been billions, like notes, like distant stars. An elderly man carrying a book looked up at me and laughed and waved as though I were only a few feet away.

"I can give you a partial answer now, only partial, because it's only a partial question, and you don't yet know what more you could ask."

It took me fully a minute to realize I was not typing, that I was hearing the words just as I had always heard every voice, every strange music, seen every image or story or verse demanding to be translated into the language of earth, that came to me with that authority that could never be questioned because complete.

"Why is there music, Brinsel?"

The notes of people grouped and shifted, following some pattern invisible to me; the entire world so vast and evident in its giddying mystery that no reasoned certainty I had ever learnt could answer for it.

I said, "Because I couldn't exist without it."

Birds flickered past, crescendos slashed into the air. I thought I saw stars like notes speckling the sky and even the earth with its billions of notes of people, like snow, or sea spray, or shining points of sand.

"We all need each other, Brinsel, all of us."

"It's not an answer," the sharpness of my own voice startling me. "It's not enough!"

"It's a partial answer. Remember, questions and answers don't tell how much you know, they give away just what you don't—they give the coordinates of your understanding, you could say. What you're asking is a question that has no complete answer where you are. At the place there is an answer, there is no question."

The street below offered no hint of anything unusual, as if it had never been anything more than a street choked with noon traffic. I let the curtain fall. The typewriter seemed eons across the room, left there years before. But then I was there; I put my fingers on the keys as expectantly as a pianist, knowing, at last, I did not know what enough would be.

I typed, as slowly as I could, "Thank you, Max."

The words came very gently. "You're welcome, Brinsel." The space of a heartbeat. "Now, go, *galante*, it's your turn."

My turn to what?

"Max," I said. "Don't go."

Nothing.

The hum of the typewriter.

I realized he had nothing else to say and neither did I, and after a few minutes I turned it off myself.

19

Disclosure

The rest myself—that would be Jill. I was not looking forward to it.

But now I had time on my side, and the gift of new perception. On Sunday when I stood at the lectern for the Epistle, I glanced at the congregation and the nave and saw the world as new as the day, the light brilliant through the windows and spotlighting faces and shoulders and pews—faceting the familiar scene into an astonishment of flares of color and fingerprints of sun, tints and hues and nuances of light I couldn't remember ever seeing before, as though I had been given a pair of powerful lenses after a lifetime of short-sightedness, or the first time I had glimpsed through a microscope the unimaginable world that was always there but without the proper instrument, had been unable to perceive. Even the dusty smell of the open lectionary before me unearthed a stratigraphy of history written in motes, loam, water; the creaking of the lectern's wooden floor the voice of an instrument breaking open harmonics I had thought I knew and making the simplest note a palace of trembling and undiscovered sound that could be entered and explored.

Then, as the page came into focus through my specs, the words at once blurred and my throat tightened.

"A reading from the letter of James," and for a moment I could neither speak nor really see. I took so long to gather myself, I had to read it again, almost in disbelief, then pushed on: "Every good and generous action and every perfect gift comes from above . . ."

Emotion, but something much stronger than that, superseding that: gratitude, love. "Listen," Richard had said earlier, leaning over with a smile during the introduction to the Gloria, "that's his *Good Shepherd Mass.*"

I listened; through the rest of Eucharist the music held my attention in everything; it carried me straight through the liturgy, and sometime after the recessional I discovered I had been set gently down where I had started, and wandered to the fellowship hall in a daze. I could not speak about the events of the previous week; still, Rachel noticed something was different. At coffee she hovered near, holding a pastry in a paper serviette as though unsure what to do with it. She smiled at me and fatigue circled her eyes. "Were you out on Friday? I called, I had off and was hoping you had some time for a chat."

"That would have been lovely. What time did you ring?"

"Around eleven."

I rubbed my brow, remembering. "I *was* out, like a light, I think I slept most all day. That hasn't happened for ages." And then the next day I had gone out on a Saturday morning into a world miraculous and strange, and which I had never really seen before.

"A rough week, huh?"

"Yes . . . but now it's over, and I can rest."

"Ah," drawing herself straighter. Then, gently, "And how are you doing?"

"Well, I think," I replied, and paused. "It's as though . . . I woke up in recovery and they told me I was going to be just fine." There was only one small complication. "And you?"

Rachel smiled thin and sad, grief describing her face as if it were her mother's. "It's been a rough week. One of my patients died in surgery on Wednesday. Even after so many years, it doesn't get easier."

"I'm so sorry."

Still the sad smile. "I used to talk about it with Max. It's better than it used to be. It's helped to be able to grieve for Max."

A moment of silence and great peace.

Rachel shyly nibbled a corner of her pastry. "We're having a small birthday party for Dad on the twenty-first, and I wanted to know if you'd like to come. We'd love to have you there."

I couldn't help reflecting how often I had been present unbidden and unbeknown. This time, for her, it meant the inclusion of an unknown part of her brother's life into an intimate family gathering. For me it meant the date was set for my showdown with Jill. I hoped this could be done without reducing the party to shambles, but just how, I didn't have a clue.

The next two weeks passed in a strange calm. I spent them sketching, painting, writing small words and tracing reflected worlds as I walked through streets already fragrant with late summer, and sat in parks listening to the wind in the trees and wanting to write music like that.

I tried to think of all that had happened in barely four months, but it was still so close, so strange, and so mind-boggling. Mostly, I thought of Jill, of the two-year-old who had put her own shoes on herself and Lynn's shoes on her so that she had the left shoes and Lynn had the right shoes—for it had made perfect sense to her; of the six-year-old who had heard Zara Nelsova in concert and begged for a cello for Christmas; of the eight-year-old who had practiced like a fiend and wept to frustration over her mistakes until her uncle had stopped her and made her play "bow nonsense." He had taught her not only how to make music, but how to play with it. And on her own, she had begun to play with words and to write stories, one thing beyond all question she could do better than he . . . and I wondered how I could loosen her grip on that without causing her to lose it.

On the twelfth, the anniversary of Ariel's death, I thought of her and of how Max used to spend that day. It was the first time it occurred to me to pray for either of them, and abashed by my tardiness, I did so.

On the nineteenth, Richard Thompson turned seventy-two. The Philharmonic put on a concert of his own works which he happily conducted. Once again, I sat in the Cunninghams' box with Rachel and John and watched him lovingly woo the music out of the orchestra, this time, music I had not written, and which was wholly delightful to hear for the first time.

On the morning of the twenty-first I awoke in a panic. If only I hadn't known how Max had known about me . . . How on earth could I help Jill, knowing what I knew? Knowing what I did wasn't going to help me—how could it? And when, above all, if I was truly who I claimed to be, I could not know *why*?

I kept looking at the small color photo of two flautists—a pocket-sized version of the print that hung in Richard's dining room—that had fallen out of one of Max's letters. A note on the back, without other explanation, read in his scattered lettering, "Get a load of these two clowns, anything is possible!"

I had to trust that.

It rained warm and thundering through the morning; in the afternoon Rachel swung by to pick me up on her way back from the grocery, and we drove to the Thompson house under bright summer-end skies a stiff wind had picked clean of all clouds. Rachel was looking forward to a small family gathering with Dan and myself, and was completely at ease, chattering a mile a minute, and until my ears picked out the word "Eleanor," it was all just pleasant noise screening my tense silence. Peter's ex-wife Eleanor, Rachel explained, was the reason he would not be joining us; though they had been in touch for years, she had now asked to see him as well. The news was enough to lighten my heart. Anything could happen now.

My view of my own prospects was only slightly less hopeful by the time we reached Richard's house. My nemesis was not in sight, nor her sister. We followed the strains of an American football match to the kitchen, where Dan, Richard, and John were noisily packaging raw vegetables in tinfoil for the grill. I unloaded the grocery sacks and prepared the meats, gratified to have something to occupy my hands, and Rachel began pulling out bowls and measuring cups and ingredients to make the pudding.

Once, passing by the doorway that led to the dining room, which had a view straight through the house to the deck, I spotted Lynn and Jill standing over the grill, watching it smoke, and felt my resolve waver. Ready or not, the day pushed onward; the kitchen swirled with activity, the activity ebbed. Richard and John carted the prepared platters outside. Rachel brewed me a mug of tea and I received it with gratitude. I sat at the kitchen table with Dan where the Thompson children had had breakfast every morning and where Max had once carved a flock of fermatas. I traced them with my finger, listening to Dan reminisce of his career in investigation.

"I did that for so many years, Brinsel," he asserted. "I was a dick when we were DICKS. You know all those old detective movies? A load of crap. Now, *I* could tell you stories about what it was *really* like back then."

I asked, in a tone of perfect courtesy, "And was it really any less ordinary than the heap of bunk you just told me?"

"Ah ha!" he hooted, slapping his knee. "So, you're on to me, huh?" He went on, almost indifferently, "I was at our fine public library the other week, and I finally looked up some of your writings. They've got a few there; it seems someone made a gift of them in recent years."

I wondered who that could have been.

"At any rate, I looked at 'em . . ."

I made a small affirming noise, but he was waiting for me to ask, so I did. "And what did you think of them?"

"I thought they were crap," he replied cheerfully. "But it's nice knowing the person responsible for it."

Yes, Dan, the old studied hand of where to replace diplomacy and even tact with bluff dissembling—beyond question, he had not *read* my books. "Would you mind putting that in writing? I'd like that for my collection of reviews."

"Certainly. You see," with another smile, his voice becoming gentle, "I know I can trust you with the juicy details of my profession. I know you're not about to run off and publish all my trade secrets."

I was as humbled by this admission as I had been unmoved by the barb. But he wasn't finished.

"You see, Max trusted you with a lot when he gave you those letters. In all my years of work I've never seen a case like that; I've *never* heard of that happening, or a case turning out like this one has, and I'd thought I'd seen about all there was to see. But he still risked a great deal with those letters. He told you things about that case I wouldn't tell my mother's dog. He *trusted* you, and so I can too, completely. Because, Brinsel, you never did make a story of what he sent you."

I held my mug of tea a little more tightly. "No, I didn't."

"Because I looked, and I went after everything of yours I could get my hands on, far and near. I even spoke with your editor," nodding insistently, and bluffing or not, I knew better than to call it. "You didn't write a single word of that case, not a jot. He offered it to you, for reasons I don't know—I'm almost certain they weren't what he told you—and you held his trust."

Across the kitchen Rachel had changed the American football match to the classical station and was lost in a recording of Copland, beating the batter in time and moving and humming like an outsize hummingbird.

"It seemed to me Max was entirely worthy of trust."

"You are not a bad judge of character," he twinkled.

For some minutes the clatter of conversation and dishes together. Richard and John had returned; Dan had gone out. I retreated into my thoughts, sorting through a floodtide of memories, and returned to the present to hear Rachel say, "It's alright, isn't it, Brinsel?"

"Alright?"

"John just went to get the camera," she explained. "We wanted to capture you on film, so we can prove you were here."

"Oh," I said, meaning much more. "Sure, it's alright, sure."

"This one loves to look at pictures," Richard winked. "You should show her the collections."

Rachel brightened. "Want to see our pictures, Brinsel?"

"Oh yes, I'd love that."

She led me down the corridor to Richard's study, a narrow yet comfortable room of stuffed bookshelves and armchairs, ragged paphos vines in calcified pots and tall western windows. At a bookcase by the window, she slid open the glass door and indicated two shelves of albums. "All these here are ancient history, and these are from school . . . good grief, I haven't seen these in ages." She picked up an album, grinning. "I bet we're all pretty easy to identify, but feel free to bring stuff to the kitchen if you want answers. You're *in*, you know. Only family sees this stuff."

"Thank you."

She left me alone, leaving the door wide. Giddy with something like nostalgia, I stood stock still for a few minutes. It was literally a brown study; Richard preferred these auburns and chocolates and teas, and the whole room was wrapped in a dun warmth, a bit stiff, but not discomforting. On the tidy, mostly bare desk, a small silver frame circling a black and white photograph: a radiant twelve-year-old boy playing flute, an orchestra behind him. Behind the desk a shelf of composition manuals, bird books, ledgers. A color portrait of Elisabeth on the wall above, the frame heavy and large and old-fashioned. I found it poignant and strange to meet that gentle gaze, and felt quite shy of a sudden.

I thought of Max standing at this window, ten and lit by the light of a winter afternoon thirty years gone. He was deciding where and how to inter his flute so that no one would find it. They had just returned from his mother's funeral.

I pulled out a few albums without looking at the dates.

I heard John come down the stairs, then Rachel's voice muffled in the corridor, laughing, ". . . She's looking at old photos. I can see her going back and writing a story about him . . ."

In the middle of the room, two chestnut elbow chairs that had been the Thompsons' first furniture, beside them the silk poplin settee that had begun its career in the sitting room, its caramel cloth eroded in four great patches to the blonde harp-string warp. I set myself and the albums on it. Trying to mentally prepare myself for the hard work just ahead, wondering how and when I could manage it, and trying to pretend at the same time—I knew it—that I didn't have to do a thing. That in the end, "things simply unfolded"—or it was Jill, or it was Max . . .

He was about three or four and nestled in his mother's lap, gazing bewildered and shy at the camera; she had her arms around him and was beaming. Her eyes bright and youthful and untroubled in her lovely face; his, brooding and intense, though just as bright. I gazed in those two unsuspecting pairs of eyes from the distance of almost forty years, knowing the rest.

Black and white photos of Max and Rachel when very young. The two of them at five and nine with their first instruments—both violin. Rachel was smiling half-heartedly at the camera, resting the bow on her strings. She had been playing for not quite two years and her younger brother three months, and he already surpassed her. Richard had momentarily had his own Ruggiero Ricci, his own Jascha Heifetz, except for the small wrinkle that his son had no love for the violin. Max was staring off to the side, his expression too old for his face, his grip on the bow too tight. By age six he had taught himself Paganini's broken-string trick, and by eight, devised an entire suite of cheekily useless chicanery. Richard had said, "He needs an impresario." Elisabeth had said, "He needs a childhood." Richard had said to his children, "You will play this," but it was Elisabeth who had asked them, "What do *you* want to play . . . ?"

The arguments over their son ended with the advent of her illness. The last picture with her children had been a family photograph taken when Max was nine. He had just begun to study flute and his face plainly spoke of the joy this was to him as he held it cradled in his arms; already the pose he would have the rest of his life. His eyes were happily looking nowhere, grinning, his face slightly averted from the camera; that camera shyness too would follow him his entire life. Rachel stood beside him, thirteen and gangly and holding her oboe with more rivalry than affection. Elisabeth behind both, her hands on their shoulders, capable, prim, beautiful, something like fear in her eyes. Max had suspected nothing; Rachel had not yet known what was happening; Richard stood staring smartly at the camera, his face straight and giving nothing away. One last photo of Elisabeth, with Richard alone and both looking for once completely helpless; then she was gone.

After that came several pages of two adolescents growing up: concerts, family settings, holidays. Max as a po-faced student, alone in his world: twelve, with the musical and intellectual maturity of a professional three times his age, behind his gaze a universe of feeling unimaginable to his peers. Or simply as Rachel's brother: droll and absurdly clever and with more than a hint of mischief. Rachel, serious about herself and scientifically minded, appeared alongside him not very willingly. She had grown tall and prim as her mother and there was the echo of Elisabeth in her solemn face, her eyes, her long, straight hair. Richard appeared less often, and usually in the context of music; he had become music director of the Philharmonic and the work gave him a focus and poise he had not had before. It would have taken very perceptive eyes to recognize him as someone who had just had a large chunk of his life hacked away.

A newspaper photo of Max at sixteen, already grown tall as a pole, playing his flute and being coached by his father. His eyes attentively on Richard, who was speaking and gesturing with great energy. He was six months from graduating at Horton and one from successfully auditioning for the Philharmonic. I could read in that intense young face a question and an answer. *How can I possibly make him happy?* And, *I will never be able to make him happy.*

Footsteps, quiet yet incredibly loud in their statement, then the click of the door being shut.

I looked up from the album.

Jill stood near the door, her face the granite carving that holds both grief and rage in check. She took one slow step into the room and stopped.

Silence, enormous and suffocating.

"Hello," I made myself say.

The silence swallowed the sound as though I had said nothing at all.

Jill's eyes so flat and hard even the light from the windows did not catch in them. She was squeezing her hands into furious buttons and scarcely seemed to be breathing.

"Please come in," I tried again.

But I no longer had the asylum of ignorance that would have enabled me politely to return to what I had just been doing. I knew too much, just as she expected me to.

"Alright," she said, very low, but her voice so hard it cracked. "Who are you, and who are you really? I can't believe you've fooled Peter for this long. And all those other people working on the case. So who are you? Because I know you're *not* Brinsel Thomas."

I let the album fall shut. "I'm sorry," I said, "I don't quite understand."

A tremor rippled down Jill's form, her fingers kneading in her hands. "That's right, that's right. Well, let me clue you in. There is no such person."

I tried to think of what Max would do if he panicked before a solo, but all that came to mind was something to do with not locking one's knees. "Why ever not?"

"God damn you," she breathed sharply. "This has all been very cute, hasn't it? Some kind of lovely *game*," nastily pinching the words to imitate my voice. "You've been enjoying yourself, haven't you? You have put on *such* a good show. You act *so* well."

"I'm sorry, I d—"

"Oh, you're fantastic, really," she cackled, eyes glaring. "You are some kind of actress, some kind of actress. But I think we've had *quite* enough of this little game. I don't know who you are, but you don't fool *me*. Who are you?"

"Jill, I don't understand."

"You wouldn't, would you? What do you get out of this? You think it's funny, fooling the whole world like this?" The words collapsed into a hiss. "Where did you get my papers? Who gave them to you?"

"Jill, what papers?"

Her gaze and her contempt were as vicious as her uncle's had ever been when he lost his temper, as horrible as her mother's or her grandfather's. "That's right, play dumb. Of course you don't know. Perhaps it comes of taking yourself *too seriously*. You've really gotten into your role, haven't you?

Forgotten who you really are? But you don't fool me. I know you're not Brinsel Thomas. *There is no Brinsel Thomas.*"

I was so far out on a limb the leaves were coming off in my hands. The settee and elbow chairs encircled me like a child's fort, the last hold against the youthful rage that choked the narrow room like a thunderhead. Jill and I stared at each other and the space between us became a glacial impasse, glass-hard and forbiddingly icy.

I desperately wondered what I should have said had I not known. I frantically, fleetingly, wondered if she was right.

I blinked and swallowed hard, fixing my mind on one of Max's solos again and simply trying to be where my feet were and to breathe, and got first a finger-hold, then a grip on myself. "Jill, you've been very upset since I came, and I can only suppose it is because of my friendship with your uncle—"

"Don't try to change the subject. What does he have to do with *you?*"

I couldn't help loving Jill so much even now; she had incredible courage. I felt her life lay in my hands. And, if she had truly written about me, then she knew me just as well, and could anticipate my reactions . . .

"Your uncle had my music, Jill, and he had contacted me."

"Yes, and then I suppose he told you all about my story, didn't he?"

Brinsel Thomas could not exist for Jill save as a character, and consequently her uncle could never have written to such a person. Yet I realized in that instant how Max had known where I could be contacted. He had learnt the name of my publishers from Jill. He had discovered my *address* from Jill. That was how, where Peter and the police later failed, he had known where to write to, how he had been able to look me up and discover I was in fact the same person who wrote the music he had also written.

"What story is this?"

Her face crumpled in adolescent disgust. "You have got some *fucking* gall, you know that?" she hissed. "Do you *like* pretending to be an idiot? My story about Brinsel Thomas, that's what. As if you didn't know!"

I held out my hands. "Oh Jill, Max never wrote me anything about family. He never even told me we had written the same music."

"Who are you? Why are you here?"

"I came here to work on a story I had been writing. I didn't realize that I was sought after here. I didn't know Max had told me anything that others would want to know. I was supposed to do my writing and go home this month, and nothing else was supposed to happen."

"*What do you want from us?*"

"Nothing, Jill!"

Jill had been standing near the door since coming in; now, in one knifelike movement she invaded my illusory refuge, halting at the farther chair so that she became a towering shadow in the window. "I am so sick of this game. I am *sick* of your lies. I don't know who you are, but I know you are not Brinsel Thomas, and I intend to put a stop to this little game right now."

I blurted, "Will you listen to me if I explain who I am?"

She stared at me as if the act could remove me.

"I would like to tell you about myself. But I need you to listen, without interrupting. Will you give me that space?"

Silence, but I recognized the terror behind her fury.

"I promise to tell you the truth. It is what you deserve. But will you let me speak?"

I could scarcely believe the words coming from my mouth. What could I say that could thwart a wrath that seemed so justified? And which truth could I possibly tell her?

The silence transfixed the room like amber, nothing could move, no one could speak. Jill clamped her hands onto the chestnut rim of the chair and my mind instantly created a scenario of her hurling the object at me.

Instead, she lowered herself into the chair, gripping its wooden arms until her knuckles stood out in hard, white knobs. "All right," her voice quavering but still rimmed with steel. "So, tell me about yourself."

Time was up for making a rational choice. I took a deep breath.

"I was born in Bangor, Wales. I am forty-eight years old, and my birthday is 16 April. I have an elder brother, David, and a sister, Rhiannon we call Rye, who lives in a home for the severely mentally disabled. David works between Greater London and Cardigan, where he keeps his family . . ."

And so it all came out, the cold little facts that supposedly added up to the sum of me. How our parents had died in a road accident when I was still very young. How we were sent to live with our mother's sister in Dyfed where a dull and rather absurd childhood followed: our uncle a dry and unhappy man, our aunt a busy schoolteacher, our cousins much older and so more sympathetic than they might have been, but none of them with any artistic bent—and my sister Rye and I, the most artistic ones in the family, were quite bent in more ways than one. How a landed benefactor had arranged for Dai and I to go off to schools and so be off our relations' hands . . .

I babbled whatever came to mind, whatever crossed my line of vision as I looked over my life; I grabbed monuments and I grabbed strawflowers, laundry and old broken things and stuff and nonsense—things I would never have told a soul. I picked up anything I could find, and flung it at Jill, waiting for something to happen that would change my fate.

Jill sat and listened to this chaotic litany of loss and confusion with the same fascinated attentiveness she would give a piece of music, her expression melting from an adolescent's obstinacy to a child's bewilderment. She met the disclosure of the nightmare of my first marriage and its fatal end with a sudden look of horror, and, as if cued, something came to mind I didn't dare mention, didn't want to mention. I tipped out a heap of trifles and after telling her how I had once upset a jar of sodium hyposulfite over undeveloped negatives for my degree work, heard myself say, "And my second husband, he made it possible for me to live again, that I could come back to myself after the trial, he was everything, and he was murdered—"

The pink astonishment in Jill's face vanished as if I had hit her with a sack of flour, and I dropped the next thought. I wondered if I had insensitively said too much or if she somehow hadn't known that set of facts and its unforgiving fallout; then I heard, extremely small and strangled, "*You, you—*" and, more whimper than word, "*No.*"

The room stopped. Then the fury roared back into her and yanked her to her feet, paper white and trembling. "*No*, no, that can't be true—that can't have happened—"

"I'm sorry, it did happen."

"How dare you—it's a lie, it's a lie!"

"I'm sorry, Jill," now seeing, at last, where the lines lay. "This is the truth."

Frantically: "How do you know that—about my character?"

"Jill," I said gently, "I don't know about your character, I only know this is who I am."

Panic, real panic, animating her voice, "But how did you know all that about—Mr. Thomas? I never told *anyone*."

"I know because he was my husband, Jill. Because I was there."

"I—I don't . . ."

I had never seen such shock in anyone's face. This must have been what Sweigart and Neilsen and even Petrucci had seen, and how I had greeted Cathy.

"Oh my God," Jill sobbed, sinking into her chair. "Oh, my God . . ."

I said nothing, my throat pinching as though this could stop the tears.

"How does this *happen?*"

"I don't know, Jill."

"But it isn't real—"

"Jill, this is who I am."

I nodded at her; she was still gaping at me in a vacant shock I intimately understood. The door now stood open to the unanswerable.

"What if, Jill, it *is*, what if it is all real, and somehow, I don't know how, you simply know about me?"

A thunderclap silence. Her eyes fixed on me in wild bewilderment.

"What if," I said, struggling with the idea, "you know all these things because you love me?"

"Because I *love* you?"

"Because you love Brinsel Thomas. And by that I mean that while you care about what happens to her, you have let her be who she is, even when you've not agreed with it, and you let her make stupid choices, horrible choices, you didn't wrap her up and keep her from living, not because you wanted to hurt somebody, but because you respected her—I mean, that you *identified* with her. Is this not true? You love the characters you write about. And I am one who is not a character, but a real person . . . I can only imagine how extremely difficult this all is for you. It is difficult for me as well, but I do not want you to be unhappy; you are all dear to me, on Max's account. And you have been so unhappy because I have been here."

But I could not really have any idea how difficult it was for Jill, who sat there, only sixteen, eyes frantic and breathing as though someone had rammed her in the stomach; none of my "characters" had confessed themselves to *me*.

I said as gently as I could, "Jill, I have no explanation for your story or why it seems to match my life. I have told you everything I can. What you do with that now is up to you."

Jill's eyes no longer met mine; she had retreated completely, her expression hovering between white rage and black grief and her face almost gray with shock. She closed her eyes, cradling her head in hands that fluttered against her temples. Her voice when she spoke surprisingly calm.

"Go . . . go . . . I have to be alone, I have to be alone."

As quietly as I could, I went out, muffling the door shut behind me.

I paused in the corridor, listening to the noises of the house filter to me. The thick, ubiquitous hum of electricity. The stairwell clock flawlessly ticking off each accomplished second. Distantly, Rachel and John and Lynn in the kitchen; the clink of ceramic dishes and the electric staccato of a mixer. Their voices rising and falling and mingling, Rachel clear and carrying, John *basso*, gentler, Lynn warbling in and out between them.

No sound came from the study.

I drifted up the corridor to the living room. Sunlight mirrored off the back of the baby grand and caught me as I came in, and for a moment I saw nothing. The voices from the kitchen more faint here, and two other voices now discernable.

Through the French doors that cut the streaming light into slivers on the parquetry, I could see Richard and Dan sitting outside on the deck, chatting in the warm fall air. Two old string players, the old conductor and the old detective. Laughter. Gesturing. For several minutes all I could do was stand and gaze at them, thinking of Max and Peter, and Max and his father.

And now my fate, as it were, lay in his niece's hands, just as all of theirs had once lain in mine.

I did not hear Jill when she came in. I was relaxed in a wing chair facing the window, not quite dozing but not really quite awake; I had been thinking of Ariel, but was unexpectedly remembering, from a Christmastime four years gone, Max telling Jill in this very room *you've got a great brain all on your own, and your uncle'ld just get in the way*...

I opened my eyes to see her, tall and silent, standing a few feet from the chair. She had smoothed her hair and dried her face. We looked at each other for perhaps half a minute, each a closed book; then she lifted one hand and beckoned, and I rose and followed her out.

When I entered the study, I saw she had opened another photo album, this one with pictures of her and her twin from their childhood. She picked up the album and pointed to one of the photos of herself and Lynn together.

"This is how old I was when I began my story about . . . you." About nine or ten. "Then I kept writing and just watched things happen. You were doing what I thought I wanted to do, I didn't know about your past. I didn't know you were . . . I didn't know about your . . . your problem. Not till later. I didn't have any plan, at least not until later. Can you tell which one is me?"

I did not need a second to single her out, but for the sake of the part I had to play, bent over the album and studied the image. I put my finger on the page half questioningly.

"How can you tell?"

"Am I right?"

Her eyes searched me and then the page. "Yes."

"It's your smiles. Your sister looks like she's got something up her sleeve. You simply look happy."

Jill regarded the picture and leaned back again. "I'm not like Lynn, I don't play tricks on people." Her gaze glanced across mine and hastily dropped to the photo. "It feels like a long time since I've been happy like that. Max and I used to talk about all sorts of stuff. For a long time he was the only one I ever shared my stories with . . . He was the only one I ever told about Brinsel Thomas." A strong pause. "He was one of the best friends I had. I hated him for dying."

She stopped, staring at me through a flash of tears, and this time not looking away. "If it's really you," she whispered throatily, one hand rising as if to touch me, then wavering aside, "if it really is you . . ."

We sat there reading each other's faces in silence, myself alone in that peculiar, deathless silence of secrets I could never tell, behind that immovable glass of knowledge that I could never break, never pass through, but through which she, and she alone on earth, could now reach.

"I know almost everything about you." Her voice dispassionate. "Even things I never wrote down . . . like about Jim." She swallowed, pinching her hands together, and pushed on. "I know about how you used to look at the sea; I know what happened during your O levels that made you change your mind about your work. I know why you named your cottage what you did and who it was that inspired you. I know why you had to send Rhiannon away." She swallowed again, paling. "And there really is a place called Wimsey?"

"I hope so," I said softly, "because I have been living there."

We sat staring at each other.

"It doesn't bother you that I know so much about you?"

"No, Jill. I trust you."

"Why do you trust me? You don't know me."

And *did* I truly know her? Her honesty and resilience left me reeling. Were either of us delusional, our conversation could have no real resolution; that it was proceeding at all was evidence to me that she was speaking the truth, and believed I was, too. "Could I tell you a story? One I don't think you know."

Her eyes flickered but, after a moment, she nodded. "Go on."

"When I first began to write to your uncle, it was in response to a letter he wrote asking about my music. I had no idea at the time that he had sought me out because we had written the same music. It was Peter that told me that when I met him. Your uncle," I said, "became a friend very quickly, over the course of a few months. And then he did something I cannot quite understand. He offered to send me examples of the work he did with the suggestion that I could use it for stories. I did not know, though, that it *was* his work, for he never told me his profession, and spoke of almost nothing but music. Max didn't know me very well when he gave all that he did. Yet he trusted me—and he risked a great deal. He never mentioned you," I added, my eyes tracing her face as my pen had once traced her portraits. "Yet I feel I can give you the same trust. I owe it to him, and . . . I owe it to you. However it is you know what you know, I trust you with it." I tried out a sketchy smile. "What else *can* I do?"

Jill's eyes darted back and forth, never quite meeting mine but the light beginning to gleam in them again. "I don't understand this, *any* of this, but I believe you, I really do." Her voice fell on the words, breaking, but still they came tumbling out, fervent and honest as embers. "I was so hurt that Max mentioned you. I really felt betrayed, and I . . . I *hated* him for dying when he did. I was so upset that he had mentioned you, I was mad for months after Peter told us about the note about you. But I was really mad when Peter told us they had found you and you could help them. I was afraid you were just someone trying to take advantage of us, that you had known about Max's note and my writings somehow and wanted to swindle us, or hurt us, because Grandpa is so famous. I was afraid you were someone delusional like that woman who thinks she is Grand Duchess Anastasia. Everyone else believed you. But I *couldn't*, because I had *invented* Brinsel Thomas . . ."

I sat on the edge of the settee with my hands clasped together, feet flat on the floor, overwhelmed and listening as I had never listened in my life.

"You know," she whispered, the tears still in her voice, "all the time when Lynn was asking you questions, I knew she was just being herself and couldn't help it, but the problem was, everything she asked you was something that I had written about you, even though she doesn't know anything about it, and you sat there and said all of it exactly as I had written it, and it was just like you were rubbing it in my face. I mean, *everything* you said, *everything*, I *wrote* all of that. It was all *my* words, and I was so sure you had stolen them. I was so mad that everyone and especially Mom trusted you, and I was so afraid . . ."

I wanted to give her a tissue but couldn't move. "What made you decide to trust me now?"

She shook her head slowly. "For the first time I really thought, I mean *really thought*, what if you're telling the truth? . . . I was so certain that such a person couldn't actually exist, and even though everything Peter told us about you was the same as what I had written, I knew Max *wouldn't* have told Peter about my story—he wouldn't have told anyone. But I thought about it, and I've decided yes, you have to be telling the truth; I can't see how you could have known all that about . . . Brinsel Thomas otherwise, or especially things I never told Max. But the biggest reason I trust you is because I really do trust Max, that he wouldn't have told anyone about my stories without asking me." She searched my face. "I just don't . . . understand how this can be possible."

"Neither do I. We might not ever know."

"And you really are Brinsel Thomas."

Were there some confidences one had to break? If Max had broken his niece's confidence, it was because somehow, in telling me, he was returning

Jill's confidence to herself, because it was I that she had written about, and it was for me to return to her. Perhaps he had not broken it after all.

And, looking at Jill, I understood I *had* asked, for once, the question I ought to have asked, which was why Max had answered me.

I nodded. "Yes, that is who I am."

More incredulous than ever, "And you *really did* correspond with Max?"

"Yes, we did. It seemed nothing much at the time, though I am glad now it proved very useful. I hope Peter will let you see his letters someday. Your uncle was a beautiful man."

She whispered hollowly, "Were you in love with him?"

I couldn't help myself and smiled; daringly, I took one of her hands in my own, and she didn't resist. "It would have made a fine story, wouldn't it? No, it wasn't like that, not at all. Jim . . . when those things happen, you never forget them." I cradled her string-calloused sixteen-year-old fingers in my age-calloused ones, thinking of all the nights she had sat up *writing*, and then I couldn't stop the tears. "I never could forget Jim, or what he did for me. I did not choose how things ended or that they did, but I have chosen to remain alone. It's my friends that matter most now; and your uncle, one of those friends." I gave her hand a small squeeze. "You don't have to fall in love with every beautiful soul that comes along."

Jill was staring at my hands cradling hers, a contest to accept the fact as simply plausible still playing across her features. "Max used to say that."

"He knew what it was like, he did." After a moment, I admitted, "I have almost never spoken of Jim, Jill. I've not been able to. I've not *wanted* to. There was, however, one person I did speak with."

"You spoke to Max."

I nodded, too much of what had to be left unsaid in the word *yes*.

She said detachedly, "Max never spoke about Ariel, either."

This startled me; I feared she might draw that connection and ask me about Ariel next, but her thoughts drove on, rapidly rearranging the pieces of the puzzle and then snapping them into place in mute awe. "Max knew you were real, and he never told me. I gave him my stories about you, and he never told me he knew you were real."

"You were eleven and twelve, Jill, and you loved what you were doing. He didn't wish to spoil that for you; you might have stopped writing altogether. What you were doing was important to him just as it was important to you. I'm sure he believed that it would all come out sooner or later, when you were older, though he surely didn't bank on any of this."

"And that note about you?"

The note which had led to all this. If I hadn't known why before, and he hadn't told me, could I even know now? "I don't know," I said, but at the same instant realized, there being no more fear to spoil my questions, that I did—that Max would not have written anything carelessly, that having claimed I had the information in question, he had in fact made this possible, and that he had written this fact on that note *because he had intended to tell someone*—he had written it *to himself*. It had been the sign not only that he knew of me, but also that he would not keep this knowledge to himself any longer. He had been going to do what Jill believed he never would.

It hadn't been the question I needed to ask after all, since it was an answer in itself, and for the time being, there was nothing more to say of it. I shook my head. "You've been through so much," I said. "And I am not able to explain any of this either."

"I never could have imagined anything like this."

"Have you ever written a mystery story?"

Her face clouded again. "No. I asked Max for help a few times, and I even tried to twist his arm by . . . by . . . but he never told me what I wanted to hear, so I gave up. And then he died, and all that stuff happened . . . I found out more than I ever wanted to know about all that."

I squeezed her hand tightly, then let go and knit my fingers around my knees.

"*You* are my mystery," she said. The wonder in her face like someone seeing for the first time. "Does that mean my other stories are real?"

I hesitated a long moment, as though feeling the question carefully. "Perhaps, but perhaps it doesn't matter."

"How, after all of this, can it *not* matter?"

"Perhaps it isn't the most important question. I mean, perhaps the real issue isn't to do with whether they are real or not, but what you do with it if you find out. You have to decide what you're really responsible for, and to see that changes the shape of your choices. Which choice you make can effect something—it can especially change you." I added quickly, as though the thought had just come to me, "It could be a little like letting go of a dear friend."

Again, only that look that told me she was thinking of Max.

"You were quite close to him."

Her face spoke for her. "When Mom told us that he had been killed, Lynn went crazy. She was screaming, 'I'll kill them. Who did it? I'll kill them.'"

"And you?"

A silence. "I didn't do anything. Nothing at all." Her voice thin. "I guess it was shock, it didn't seem possible. Those things always happen to other people, like stuff you read in the papers. I never thought . . . It just hurt so much."

"Yes. It does."

"I wish it would go away."

"It's not forever, dear."

Her voice very low but steady: "If you hadn't been there too, I couldn't believe you."

I must have appeared more dejected than pensive, for after a moment she said thinly, "I owe you an apology; I've been an absolute bitch toward you."

"You've been an adolescent. There's a considerable difference. And, I think too, under the circumstances, you have been entirely within your rights. I have never proved who I am."

She pressed her lips together and glanced at her hands; then, "Well, I'm still sorry, I've made all this worse."

"I accept the apology. It's nice to know I can go home without my guts being hated out."

A wan smile flickered across her face and then was gone.

"I don't blame you for any of it. In your shoes I don't know if I could have done other. I know it's been extremely hard for you, for all of you."

She said with surprising gentleness, "It's been hard for you, too."

"Yes."

"Even after eight years?"

She did not know the matter was unresolved. "Sometimes it takes a long while. There were ten very good years before that, and some adjustments are harder than others." I was grateful she seemed to understand it had not been her doing; it had happened so long before she had written of it, she would never be able to blame herself.

"Are you ever going back?"

She had never lived anywhere but here; she must have enjoyed writing about my chaotic annual travels of the past few years, funded by Dai in an effort to keep me working and sane. But being an indigent, itinerant artist wasn't home to me, nor really was the cottage at Wimsey I had been trying without success to attach myself to. "I don't know."

She rubbed one eye with the back of her hand, still so young and fragile and overwhelmed with her own potential. Max's incongruous quip about those who spoke Welsh doing beautiful things because of the Welsh, I realized, had not been so incongruous after all, had not been about myself or any kind of art or Wales. It had been about Jill, about a secret they shared and hence a language *they* could speak together. His own barmy way of telling her that simply because she was skilled at one thing, she needn't settle for only that, that she could do anything at all. And she had understood.

She said again, faintly, the idea too astonishing to grasp, "And you *really did* write to him . . ." Her eyes wandered down to the album still open on the table.

I reached into my pocket. "Look, Jill."

Even after our conversation, she still gasped in shock when I unfolded the Welsh New Testament I had received at my marriage, worn and battered like me with everything it had been through. I untied the cord that held it together and placed it in her hands, letting her leaf through the pages to find the photographs—of my wedding, of my brother and his family, of Rhiannon, of Jim and myself, of friends—she knew would be there, the expression on her face beyond all words. When she had gone through them all, she sat with eyes closed, and sighed deeply. Gently, she let the book shuffle shut and tied it back together, and placed it in my hands. "Thank you."

"You're welcome, dear." I began to put it back, then, opening it, found a picture of myself and Jim, and pressed it into her hand.

She studied the small photo, gently touching it with her finger, neither Jim's lovely sightless eyes nor my own plain green ones seeing her. His mouth was open and he was laughing, but we were watching people who could never see us, hearing sounds that could only be imagined. Jill raised her eyes to me, awestruck.

"And," she whispered, "you really did have that dream about Jim looking just like the picture of Saint Francis . . ."

"My God," I breathed, frozen to the chair.

I could hear the voice of the piano drifting up the hallway; Richard's handling, Tatumesque. He was playing "When I'm Sixty-Four." Jill caught the sound too.

"I guess we should go out," she said, but neither of us moved.

After a moment she asked, almost shyly, "And you speak Welsh?"

Rachel's oboe had joined the music.

I nodded.

"Say something in Welsh."

"*Rhywbeth.*"

"What did you say?"

Dan's violin, and then his voice, unusually pleasant, carrying over the piano and oboe.

"Something!"

"I ought to have known that," Jill said with a small smile now. "I know what you're like."

I could hear a flute with the oboe: Lynn. The piano lost its Tatumness, ran a few dilute bars, then continued in its richer voice.

"And yet, perhaps there are a few things about me you don't know."

She regarded me intently, a smile there and not quite there. "What do I do now, with the story about you? I won't be able to work on it anymore."

I pressed my hands together, searching her face. "Do you remember when our house burned down and we lost everything?"

She nodded. "Yes, I remember that."

A great coil of laughter from the living room; only the piano and flute for a moment.

"We lost all of it, everything, pictures, records, instruments, all of his work, all of mine." Not the first time I had lost everything, but I did not need to mention that other time. "And then . . ."

She said, quietly, "You got on, you started things again, and kept working. Jim . . . called your new place Phoenix House."

I smiled, thinking of the jokes surrounding that one. "Thank goodness that one didn't go up in flames."

She echoed my smile momentarily, then sobered again. "But how can I do that, go on writing after this?"

The flute curled deliciously through the house and danced rings round the study; Lynn was fantastic, sparkling with life, amazingly rich and fearless. That quality of sound that made your heart leap and every nerve tingle. She had come incredibly far in only three years, her tone remarkably like another flute I seemed to remember hearing somewhere . . .

"I'll leave that to you."

"What a mess life is," she breathed. "I can't make head or tail of any of it."

We couldn't part neatly; this was life. Jill got up, saw herself in the bookcase glass, swore like Dan and ran out. I returned the albums to the shelf, then stood and looked at the picture of Elisabeth again, listening to the flute spiral around the oboe, now the piano, now the violin. On the opposite wall beside the mantel, a portrait of Max and Rachel and their father, from the concert for Richard's retirement. Father and son in black formals and Rachel in a deep burgundy gown and black tasseled scarf. They had performed a handful of pieces he had written for their instruments, and Telemann's *Concerto in B Major for Two Flutes and Two Oboes*, Richard taking the violin part. In the photo he stood between them, both he and Rachel looking at Max. And Max, thirty-eight, eyes tired and twinkling, for once without his instrument, for once smiling towards the camera. Their faces all so much alike, Rachel only slightly shorter than her father and brother, and nothing else in the picture to give any sense of scale. I smiled at them and went out.

By the time I reached the living room, the music had changed; Rachel had gone back to the kitchen, and whatever instruments had been taken out had since been put away. Jill and I held our détente like a closed book, leaving the room yet untouched by the ground that had shifted in another part of the house.

In the interlude that remained before dinner, we played a few rounds of the game I had once believed my friends back home had invented—"musical instruments," the game of musical chairs with instruments added, tooling off "Frère Jacques" in canon each time we stopped. At the first go off, I got the flute; I was dimly surprised to find the instrument so cold, but was so whacked and clumsy that my hands insisted on trumpet fingering, and I could scarcely make it whistle. There was too much giggling for anyone to play very well, and high spirits prevailed over musicality.

On the third round Richard ended up at the piano and the rest of us with instruments we weren't familiar with, by that point sounding like an ensemble needing to be put out of its misery with all haste. Richard smashed his hands into the keys after the first verse. "My God! Dan, do you hear that? I've had people audition for the Phil who couldn't play that well."

Dan nodded. "I know, but what can we do, Dick? They've all got day jobs."

"Fire the bums," Richard roared, hands already typing out the next line. "I want to form a chamber orchestra . . ."

One more round to go; when the music stopped, I was holding the triangle.

"Isn't this great?" Max had once enthused to Jill, brandishing the small instrument. "I'll be a triangle virtuoso. I can have all the corners on this market."

"One of the corners is wide open."

"Darn! I guess I have to leave room for someone else."

"Would you go ahead and *ring* it already, Brinsel?" Dan in his best mock-irritated voice. "Why is she just sitting there with that goofy grin on her face? I swear, you are just too much like Thompson for my health sometimes."

Laughing, I rang it for all I was worth.

The memory of the music we had heard while in the study kept returning to me, and as we sat down to the meal, I looked for a window to bring it up. It did not take long; John, who had been in the kitchen during the concert, joked about "When I'm Sixty-Four" and asked Lynn about the other pieces they had been playing.

"You were playing beautifully, Lynn," I finally slipped in. "I heard you from the study."

She laughed. "Thanks. How could you tell me from Grandpa, though?"

"Well, you were the one on flute!" I laughed in return. "It was *fantastic*, absolutely fantastic."

A sudden fall of silence around the table. All eyes lit on me, and not a hand moved.

Rachel with her fork in midair. She dropped her eyes in the direction of the butter, then to her plate.

Richard's gaze stopped on me, unblinking.

The air seemed to have gone out of the room.

Rachel finally, somewhere between disinterest and avoidance: "I was playing oboe, it probably sounds pretty fluty from the other end of the house."

Lynn studying me, her mouth slightly open.

Richard said, with the slightest difficulty, "No one was playing flute, Brinsel," and began eating again.

Dan, in a discussing-the-weather voice: "Look, just like I said, she's a ringer for the kid." He stuffed the vegetables in his mouth like a turtle. "He was always hearing things too."

"I heard it also," Jill jumped in sharply.

John's glance darted to his daughter, then moved to me. Rachel's stayed on Jill.

"Oh," Richard said, cutting his chicken into smaller and smaller pieces, "it's an old house, it's not so unusual to hear things sometimes. Been a lot of music here over the years."

"We did hear a flute," Jill's voice taking a razor edge. "We weren't hearing things."

"I'm afraid there *wasn't* a flute, Jill," said Dan, peering apologetically over his specs. "We can't get around that."

"You can't tell me I didn't hear what I did," she snapped, purpling, then scorned, "You detectives all want the world reduced to black and white. It doesn't work like that."

John, softly, "Jill."

"That's enough Jillian," Rachel, less softly.

"That's the only way you can do it in that business, I'm afraid," Dan replied, in the quiet voice used only in crisis. "It's just reporting facts. Your uncle would have said the same."

"This is life, not business."

I began to understand; Jill's world, her orderly and measured world, the one she could lay out on a page in words or music and preserve some illusion of control, had today proven itself as far less measurable than she had ever imagined.

"And where do you suppose I did my work, Jill? Business happens in the middle of life."

"This is different."

Rachel repeated, "Jillian."

"Is it? I don't think so."

"Then prove it, dammit!"

"*Jillian Elisabeth.*"

"All right, Jill, you want a demo, I'll give you a demo. No, it's okay, Rachel. Listen up, Lynn, you'll want to hear this." Dan put his fork down and counted on his fingers. "What's the problem here? What's going on? We've got two people at one end of a house who hear a flute. We've got four people at the other end of the house making music. We've got a piano, an oboe, a violin. Zip flutes. We've got one more person a few feet away who's not playing any instrument. We don't know where this sound of the flute is coming from—"

"It was coming from the living room."

"Those are our facts. That's what we know for sure. Now what? What can we say next? Was there a radio playing somewhere? Not in the house; the one in the kitchen was turned off. Was someone outside playing a flute—?"

"*It was coming from the living room.*"

"We can't answer those questions with the information we have."

"Mr. Malcombe," said Lynn quietly.

Rachel made a small noise and movement and John laid his hand gently on hers and she stopped.

"What sort of conclusions might we draw from just that, without knowing anything else? One: Nobody heard a flute. The two people who heard it had an auditory hallucination: they imagined it. Two—"

"We did *not* imagine anything!"

"Two," Dan ticked off on his fingers, that dry, wry countenance never twitching. "The sound of the flute was actually coming from somewhere else and merely seemed to originate from within the house. It is possible for sound to play tricks like that. Three—"

"Mr. Malcombe," Lynn repeated.

"Please let me finish first, Lynn. Three: since two people heard a flute and five people didn't, the two who heard a flute actually heard a sound that resembled a flute, perhaps the violin or oboe, or an air vent—"

Jill spat out an invective so sharp the air stung, clenching her hands into angry knots on the table. "I know what a flute sounds like. It was a *flute*. It was playing the same music you were! And even better."

"Four," Dan's voice never altering the slightest pitch, still calm and disinterested as though the topic were actually the weather. "There is no natural explanation for the sound of the flute."

Silence.

Rachel was staring from Jill to me.

"Mr. Malcombe," said Lynn again, still very quiet. "You're forgetting something."

"I am?" Dan looked at her now. "What is that?"

"Did the other five people really not hear a flute?"

Nobody stirred. Dan stared at Lynn, the light glinting across his specs partially obscuring his eyes.

Richard sitting frozen with his broken bread in each hand, eyes closed.

"I heard it," she said finally, softer than ever. "I heard a flute playing the same music, I heard it over the piano and over the oboe and you, and the sound was in the living room."

An even longer silence.

"Then," replied Dan at last, equally soft, "we have our answer, don't we? The answer is that there is no answer, not an answer we can be sure of." He picked up his fork again. "Excellent work, Lynn."

I realized I was holding my breath and slowly inhaled.

"But," persisted Lynn with the same evenness. "Is there a way to find an answer, even if we can't be sure of it?"

Dan studied her over his specs quickly, fondly, holding his glass midair. "*Non scrutatio*," he said, "*sed admiratio*." He drew a sip of wine and smiled at her. "You know what that means?"

She nodded. "That you can see more possibilities with wonder than with analysis. That observation operates under the principle of what is empirically provable, and wonder under the premise of possibilities that are reasonable, but, perhaps, not . . . not within the reach of reason."

Rachel's gaze swept from Jill to Lynn. John seemed to be holding his breath.

"And which one is more important?"

"Both, they work together."

Dan, with a small, deferential nod towards Jill: "You know, Jill, it was your uncle who taught *me* that."

No one said anything else about the matter. Dinner went on peacefully; John and Dan joked about the corncobs, Rachel snorted at Lynn's witticisms, Richard asked me about British barbeques. Jill said nothing.

Afterwards, she volunteered herself to help with dishes and I didn't get to see her again. I felt she avoided me the rest of the afternoon; it was no longer the same avoidance, though, and Rachel and John had both noticed it.

As for myself, it was Jill's sister I had to seek out next. I found her sitting alone at her grandmother's piano, pedaling to play very softly. Her eyes flicked up and she saw me; a smile blossomed on her face, and she dropped her gaze to the keys again. I took this as a welcome and sidled next to her on the bench.

For a while, only the gentle sound of the piano. I listened, watching her hands. Sheet music curled on the desk, the papers leaning towards her, but she did not look at it. She was playing from memory phrases from one of Richard's piano sonatas, pronouncing the notes spare and clipped and omitting the ties.

I asked, "Did you know about Jill's story?"

"Yes, I did." Her attention fixed on the keys. "But I figured out you were real enough. Max would never have mentioned you otherwise."

"Both you and Max knew?" A pause, and she nodded. "And Jill didn't know you had seen her work?"

One of her secretive smiles. "No. She doesn't share many with me."

"And it didn't bother you," I pressed, "that Max had said I was one thing and Jill said I was another?"

A flippant shrug; easily: "I would trust Jill with my soul. But she was just writing a story. Max was conducting an investigation. In that case, if I had to choose between believing Jill and believing Max, I'd take Max."

"Is the fact that there is a story to mean it is less true than the results of an investigation?"

Her fingers hesitated ever so slightly; she shrugged.

"Are you *truly* willing to believe," I said gently, "that something not within the reach of reason might be true, even when it appears impossible?"

Her hands stilled; she gave me a sideways glance, then continued playing, *ritardo*.

"Who do you think knew about me first?"

Lynn stopped playing, studying me as if I had suddenly lapsed into another language. "It wasn't Max?"

"I don't know who knew first, but I can say, without fear of error, that Jill knew most first."

She took her hands off the keyboard, eyes widening.

I smiled. "And all that she wrote about me . . ." I picked out a C and fingered the first piano piece I had ever learnt: *Here we go, up a row, to a birth-day par-ty . . .*

"Is it really true?"

"Yes," I said. "It is all true."

Lynn was silent, palms pressed against the keyslip. Then a marveling smile, noncommittal. "Isn't it funny how everything is tied together? You, Max, us?"

"Jill would say it's proof of the superstring theory."

Laughter. "She would, too!" Her fingers alighted on the keyboard and conjured up *Garlands for Rose*, one of the many pieces her grandfather had written for his wife.

"And yet you never let on that you had a foot in both camps."

"Max taught me that. Never show more than one card at once, he told me. I've been doing that a long time." Gravely, "I found that you have to be very careful which card you're going to show."

I fingered the edge of the fallboard as if looking in the gap for a word. "You made Jill quite angry by asking me so many . . . particular questions in her presence."

Lynn shot me a searching, fleeting glance; she leaned into the piano, just above its voice, in almost a whisper, "I had to, you know. I had to make her angry. She knows I always ask questions. And there you were, this strange person who had known Max—what would she have thought if I had said *nothing*?" Her hands paused in the middle of a phrase as if they had forgotten what they were saying, then continued. "I couldn't even do that. I would have looked like I knew too much. Jill believed—still does—that I never saw her story. It was easy to just be myself, but hard pretending I didn't know, one of the hardest things I've ever done."

"Well," I said, "you did beautifully."

She smiled a small smile like a new leaf uncurling; she closed her eyes, feeling the music, then opened them again, her gaze somewhere beyond the piano or her hands, perhaps not even hearing the music. "It was when I heard the flute this afternoon that I knew she was alright."

The piano pensively hummed *Garlands*, throwing long, sonorous sashes ornamented with rosettes of various sizes around itself and us.

Then she looked at me sidelong again, a question folded in her eyes. The very picture of her uncle. Her face was registering: do I, or don't I?

"So . . ." very slowly, tasting the word. She beaded three high roses with her right hand and moved slowly towards the center, improvisationally plucking their petals as she went. "So, when are you going to tell Jill that you know all about *us*?"

I looked at her in astonishment but, escaping my gaze, she reached up and pushed back the desk a few inches, peering down at the wires and continuing to play with her other hand. "You know," she spoke into the shell, quickly, "it isn't just reporting facts, it's which ones you put together, and how you do it, and why, and which ones you accept as facts—which ones you can prove as facts." She looked back at the keys, pulled the desk forward, and sat again. "Which ones you see and how you choose to make sense of them."

I waited, watching her.

"You know," she stopped playing and turned to me, all embarrassed, pleading smile, "I've felt for ages that you know a lot more about us than you're letting on."

It was my harrowing afternoon, or the relief of it all, or her earnest conviction—suddenly I began to laugh. "Supposing I did," I said, "my dear, what could knowing tell you?"

Lynn leant closer, all attentiveness. "*Do* you?"

20

A Loose End

On Monday, Peter rang up and asked to see me. He had a 2:30 window that afternoon and then had to be out of town; could I make it? I walked to the station house under the searing blue skies of early autumn; Sgt. Menendez buzzed me through the security door, and a few moments later I found myself standing at the lift. I stared at it for a good two minutes, arguing with myself, and finally hit the button.

I rode with my eyes firmly shut and bolted out at the third story. Peter's door hung ajar; I could hear his voice on the phone and waited in the corridor by the lifts, gazing at the pinboards, the posters of the FBI's Most Wanted, announcements. Someone was selling a car, someone selling a house. Someone came out of the lift behind me and walked whistling down the hallway.

I heard Peter ring off and, after a moment, he opened his door and peered out. "There you are, Brinsel, you're on time, I'm late. *Ploo sah shong*, as Dan says. Come on in."

He waved me to an empty chair, moving a stack of files from his desk to a side table. "I want to tell you a little how things cleared up. And I had a few things to ask you about." He settled into his desk chair. "So how have you been lately?"

"Very well," chuffed to bits I could be so honest at last. "It's so *good* to have this completed."

"You and me both. I'm happy to tell you first off that there is no question about Max's evidence. I can't tell you much that you don't know already, except that it did what it was supposed to and the trial is the least of my worries."

"I am quite relieved to hear that."

Nodding. "And it wouldn't have happened without your help. I've never seen anything like it in twenty years, and from someone I knew so well, or I should say, pretty well. It doesn't do me any good, but I wonder sometimes what it would have been like to have had his file. It was much, much bigger than we'd thought. Much bigger than *he'd* thought."

A long pause as he scratched his chin, staring at the barrow of paperwork that was his desk. Then looked at me. "What did you think when you received that first letter?"

I shrugged. "Some bloke with something to say."

"Did you ever make a story of the material he sent you?"

"I hadn't done anything with it. I had put it away and quite forgotten it."

"It would have been an extremely difficult story to write. It wasn't stuff you want to read about."

"I don't think I could ever have written about it."

A nod. "You don't write mysteries, do you?"

"Not detective fiction."

"And yet you told him he could send his ideas, and he sent you all of that."

"Perhaps he misunderstood what would be useful for me."

"It was certainly an area of great concern to him." A strong silence. More upbeat, "Well, even if you can't use all of that, maybe you can make another story now. I enjoyed your stories, Brinsel."

You almost were one, Peter.

"Thank you," I smiled. Peter, the detective who liked my stories, and Dan the detective who thought they were crap. Neither of whom had read them. "You were able to find them?"

"I can find almost anything," slyly.

Yes, he could. So could Max. Max, who somehow had got his hands on my music; it was going to haunt me the rest of my life. "Except . . . except me."

He said nothing, eyeing me, then nodded. "But there's a bit more to that, I found. I made some phone calls the other day and had a nice long conversation with Officer David Coomes of the Greater London Interpol unit."

My surprise leapt out before I could stop it. Peter smiled, a trace of that old grin.

"David was a little surprised to hear his sister was part of an investigation over the pond. We had a good talk about things, all sorts of things . . ." He hesitated, his mouth working awkwardly. "I'm very sorry about James,

Brinsel. I hope they'll be able to close that someday. I'm sorry you had to be part of this and have something like that in your past."

And yet it was because of that, precisely and only because of that, that I had become part of this to begin with. Something else I could never tell Peter.

"I was very sorry, too, to hear about the harm that was done to you previously by someone else. David was very frank about that."

"Thank you," I said, "for not saying his name."

Peter nodded again, his eyes very sad.

"You knew all this, didn't you? Ever since I first spoke with you."

"Yes, I did know. We needed to know who you were. But I still wanted to go about things the old-fashioned way, you might say. I wanted to give you that space. I wasn't afraid you would disappear, not after we finally knew who you were and could keep track of you. And, I felt, I owed you the trust of telling me things yourself."

"But, why had you waited until now to speak to Dai?"

"Did I wait, Brinsel?"

In the silence that followed, my mouth open, I read in his face what had happened just as simply as though I had written it myself. I closed my mouth.

"I did speak with David initially, after I first met with you, to let him know what was going on. And I told him I'd be in touch."

And Dai had said nothing of it to me because it was an investigation. They did not call him "Dai Can't Say" for nothing.

"I called him the other day, though, to ask about your medical and psychiatric records."

My records. There it was.

"You have had a horrible history in a number of ways, Brinsel, and I am sorry about that. It was the collapse that interested me, and which answered a lot of questions. I had suspected it, and I can understand very well how that happened. But don't imagine that I think less of you for any of it. If anything, all the more. If I haven't been sure about you, I have found you an extraordinarily courageous woman, all of which those records proved, and amply. If Rachel and John knew what you have been through . . . but, you know, I'm not going to tell them."

I made a careful study of everything I could see below the level of the desk and scratched my nose and fingered my lip, and finally looked at him.

"It doesn't bother you, that I'm ill?"

"Does it bother you?"

"Does it affect the investigation?" I insisted.

"I cannot see that it does, or even that it could matter. It's not as if you could have written any of those letters. It would be physically impossible, for one."

He smiled. I did not.

"I'm sorry, Brinsel," he said after a moment, misreading my silence. "I didn't mean that I suspected you of anything but the truth. There has just been so much strangeness in all of this." He glanced at his hands and cleared his throat. "David also helped clear up for me part of the reason why our initial search for you turned up nothing overseas. You won't have known about it, but he was actually part of the UK contact when we were looking for you. And this is where things get funny. Whoever was handling traffic at that time goofed royally, if you'll pardon the expression. They read your name surname first—Thomas Brinsel, not Brinsel Thomas. So that's who they went looking for. They did find three Thomas Brinsels—one is even a musician. But none of the poor guys knew anything. In the end, though, we abandoned that and kept looking over here; there was nothing in the case that could point overseas. David admitted to me he thought it was funny it was so like your name, but he didn't consider you at all, as it wasn't even the same name. You might have an idea why," he nodded at me expectantly.

"Because it was in English?"

Again the nod. "We were looking at an anglicized spelling of your name. For one, there is no *e* in the Welsh. Isn't this true?"

I nodded.

"And your books are only published in Welsh."

"Yes."

Peter was gazing at me with an old, solemn expression I recognized; I had also seen it in Dai's own face—Dai! With the closest possible contact, they still had not been able to find me. Somehow, I had fallen through the cracks. And Dai had known about Max . . .

"And all of that is why it has taken so long?"

"Well," he sighed, "it's like this, as Max would say: short staff, long song. We've had three people—Riley, Neilsen, and yours truly—working on this one, but it's been mostly yours truly. The bottom line is that the department couldn't give a lot of resources to a very cool case like that. Riley wasn't even sure what Max had wanted to tell him." He gestured, shrugging. "Nobody saw much in it. No one guessed Max had information as sensitive as that last letter showed. He was just a private eye; we've got a million of them running around out there. He wasn't the police commissioner. Not someone the world would miss."

I heard through his voice the sound of birds outside, sparrows chiruping on the window ledges, the burr of pigeon wings.

"That we've been able to catch up with it in only three years is something in itself; as you yourself know, these things can just sit around. But that's all done now," his voice lowering. "At least we had something to go on."

Another silence.

"I am just all curious about those letters," he went on. "For one thing, it was so unlike him to have such a thing as a correspondence at all. And then, they were so damned *odd*, they were just so . . . *calculated!* He'd do it, sure, if he had wanted to write a letter, but all the information he *gave* you, I don't know. Everything has a price tag on it; you know, almost half of our expenses were simply getting information. If it were even conceivable, *you* ought to have paid *him* for all of that."

Peter put his elbows on his desk and sighed.

"The thing is, it just doesn't explain it to me. He'd just give you ideas for a story? That I cannot believe," taking off his specs again and first pointing with them, then tossing them on his desk and throwing his hands widely. "Max wouldn't *do* that. He'd have something up his sleeve, something he wouldn't even tell you." He pressed his hands to his face, staring, and as he could see nothing retrieved his specs and pushed them back on his face. "But what?"

That Max *would* have had something up his sleeve could not surprise me. But I could not imagine an explanation to fit it. For the only things he hadn't told even me were that his niece had written a story about someone who turned out to be real—who turned out to be me—and that the music I had written, which he somehow had got, was the same as the music he himself had written. Peter knew about the one; I could not tell him about the other. And I could not see that either answered his question.

I worried my hands together. "Perhaps it was his way of saying he trusted me, that he trusted I would not jump to conclusions if he told me we had written the same music. For he never told me about that, and I should have found out eventually."

"That's some kind of price for your trust, if that's the case." A long, dense pause; he sighed again, rubbing his neck. "And no, that's too much like blackmail, not his stripe, either." He made a face. "Then there's this: what happened to *your* letters, the ones you wrote him? It's been driving me wild."

I quickly averted my gaze, but he was not looking at me for an answer.

"I know where they'd be, in that damned file that's vanished into thin air. That's what makes the *least* sense—he'd *never* misplace something. It had to be stolen, and it might be gone for good." Another enormous sigh. The creak of springs in his chair as he leaned back. "What I *want*, Brinsel, is to find something that connects you directly with that case, that would provide a logical reason why Max would give you information about a case he hadn't even completed and one that serious, something that would *entitle* you to that sort of confidence. Never mind that he wrote it as fiction . . .

"I think he must have taken a page from Jill," still shaking his head. "Him and literature did not go together. Did you know she writes?"

I said, aware of each word, "Lynn has mentioned it."

"It seems she's been deathly jealous of you, at least that's the only reason I could think for all the grief she's been giving you. I'm glad that seems to have been sorted out, Rach said things have calmed down. So, there we are . . . Very interesting letters, too, and even if you forgot about them, you remembered a lot of interesting little things from them."

His voice had picked up in a casual way that spurred in me an instinct to caution. "Yes," I said, "sometimes, details just stick with you."

"Those letters certainly showed him as he was. First he talks only about music, then he talks only about his job. He never figured out how to keep the two apart. He even wrote down musicians' *birthdays*." A shrug. "Well, well. And yet, of all that stuff, he never mentioned *my* birthday."

"Your birthday?"

"Yes, you seemed to know when it was, remember?"

I looked down at my hands as though they could inspire me and felt a violent flush spread over my face. "I don't know," I mumbled, "some things you just know."

"So that's the size of it, huh?"

It had to be; at least, it was the truth. I nodded, small and a bit sad.

That very shrewd look I knew so well. A long moment while he tipped his head back and studied the ceiling, then dropped his gaze and smiled again. "I was down to see Roamer recently, and I asked him if anyone named Brinsel Thomas had been to see him. Do you know what he told me?"

I had a feeling I knew.

"He said no." Smiling somewhere between casual and cunning. "So I asked if he had had any communications from me or anyone else during a certain week in June. And he said yes. He told me that he had received an old note from Max from someone sent by me. And, very curiously, even when I told him I had not sent anyone, he refused to tell me who it had been. He said it was between him and Max." He set his elbows on the desk and leaned forward, not taking his eyes off me. "Would you tell me, Brinsel, just how you came by that note?"

I opened my mouth speechlessly and then managed, "I cannot tell you how."

Peter nodded, his eyes narrowing. "I found something else which interested me." He shifted some papers on his desk, and, picking up a slim folder, handed it to me. "Can you explain this, Brinsel?"

I knew before I saw what was inside that I could not. "From where did you get this?"

"From Lynn."

"From where did she get it?"

"From Max."

"But from where did he get it?"

"Didn't he get it from you, Brinsel?"

I stared at my music helplessly, the missing sheets of *London Spring, April for Winds,* and *On Caernarfon.*

"Not this music," I squeaked, as close the truth as I dared go. "Not this."

"I admit I'm not too concerned about that," he said. "He didn't keep records of where he got music unless it was a gift, and if you had sent these to him, he would have noted it. What perplexes me is the transfers of copyright you made on two of these pieces. It's true they match his own works, and for God's sake, don't let Richard see *London Spring,* or he'll nail the copyright back to your shoes. I had *no* idea the entire thing was the same."

I was out in the rings of Saturn looking at all those black dots that were my music and didn't trust myself to look at him.

"But I don't know why you did that, unless maybe you thought you owed him something? There is nothing illegal in it, but I'm very puzzled that you don't say why. Unless, Brinsel, you gave his estate the copyright to the music you had both written, in payment for the information he sent you? And it would have been a bit late in the day for that."

"I wanted to remove every obstacle for his music."

"It was extremely generous of you," he said gently. "And I don't know quite how to say this without giving you the wrong idea, but you have reminded me of him very much in some ways. You, like he was, are very generous, and also very good at hiding things about yourself that can powerfully affect how others see you. I don't blame you one bit; I'd probably do as much in your shoes. David didn't mention it," he added. "Not until I called him last week did he confirm my own ideas."

I closed the file, my fingers sliding over the cover as though it would keep me from sinking into the hole suddenly yawning before me. He hadn't *just* found out, not from my records. "When had you noticed?"

He lifted hands and shoulders, nonchalant. "It wasn't a time, it was just small patterns. Then there was Rachel. She remarked on it because she thought I knew."

Rachel. Of course. Of course Rachel would notice, of course she would look after me for more than headaches, of course she would feel free to speak with me even about Ariel...

And, of course Lynn would be so open and confiding with me, would freely share so much... of course Richard could show his house and his studio to an almost complete stranger, and... of course John would... of course the Sojourners...

"You *knew*," I said shakily. "You *all* knew. You knew I was daft, and you told them."

"I do *not* see it that way," he retorted, "and if anyone else knew anything, I wasn't the one who told them. I didn't *know* until I saw those records, Brinsel, and I only wanted to see if it was true."

"You hadn't asked them to watch me, had you? Because I'm *insane?*"

"I only asked them to take care of you. David had said you were still rather fragile, and I wanted you to be able to have some sort of support. I couldn't be that support myself, as you know. And you know yourself that records like that are only designed to handle one angle of proof. I've found you mysterious, maybe, but not insane. Because there is a lot here I feel you haven't shared... would you like to?"

I could scarcely meet his eyes. "I don't believe I know what you want to know."

He opened his hands. "As I said, there is nothing illegal in it that I can see, only illogical, at least from the evidence we have. I know I cannot account for a great deal of this from the letters you gave us, or from anything you have told us."

Neither could I.

"If there were other letters, that might explain some of this, but it seems there weren't, and from what you've told us, and from what we've found out otherwise, I cannot even see how there might have been. I am still missing whole pieces of this puzzle that you haven't volunteered. And yet, apart from what it may have to do with Max, it doesn't appear to be anything connected with our investigation. If I didn't trust you so much—on Max's account, but also on my own—and if I didn't sense myself that you have some connection with him, this would be simpler for me."

He had lowered his gaze to his desk and I could not read his eyes.

The term "logical positivism" flashed through my mind and vanished like someone slipping round a corner.

"You've been quite a puzzle for me, Brinsel. I am bound to believe you simply on account of Max's word, and yet there is so much about you I can't explain, that your records can't explain, that David couldn't explain. I can't figure why, for instance, you were so surprised to *see* the music of yours which I showed you at our first meeting, when you had just told me Max had written to you that he had it. I've thought a lot about that. And unless you had something to hide—what, I couldn't guess—I can't think of anything to explain a reaction like that."

And what was I to think—what was there that could explain my music and Max's music? Yet what had Max done when he discovered *my* music—that *I* was real? When he had learned that the person in his niece's stories whom she believed she had made up, and the person who, he had discovered, had written an identical piece of music as he, were one and the same, that all the pieces—location, character, curriculum vitae, occupations, everything—lined up?

Uncharacteristically, he had written me a letter. A whole series of letters, concerning an investigation he offered, with the only intention we knew of, as ideas for a story. He had not been paralyzed by the dilemma of how or why, though that very question would have keenly interested him. If it had seemed impossible to him, he had not stopped at that; having exhausted all the facts he had looked at it again and considered other possibilities, wild possibilities, illogical possibilities. He had asked himself, *What if I'm not seeing it right? What if I don't have all the parts?*

He had asked himself, *What if Brinsel Thomas knows something about all this?* and, merely suspecting I did, had written *The Mad Conductor*, his illustration of both what and what not to do in such a case. It was illogical on the part of either of us to have acted on intuition, yet our instinct, against all reason, had been correct. For there in Peter's office, only some four months before, without a clue as to what I should do or what might be required of me, I had spontaneously, illogically, claimed Max had done almost the last thing I should never have suspected him of, but which beyond all expectation the facts had borne out. And there I sat in the same place, my hands twisted in a knot and a mountain in my throat that might have been my heart, staring at the face of Peter Serrev—Peter whom I knew so well and without the least shadow of a logical cause, knowing beyond all question that I never would explain any of it to him.

Peter was studying his hands. "But I do trust you, Brinsel. Maybe I shouldn't, considering how much you're not telling me, but there you go." His eyes met mine, the grief indelible as etching. "I am just stuck with this: on the one hand, Max's instinct was almost never wrong, and on the other, he was very careful with facts. He trusted you. And so I'm going to swing on that also. I have to let it rest that whatever was between you and Max has nothing to do with that investigation at all. Maybe even that I don't need to know, and that it would be better if I didn't."

He glanced down and so once more missed the look on my face. Again the voices of birds—the creaking of gulls, the explosive twittering of scattered sparrows.

Then, "You were probably wondering about the message from Roamer which you gave me." His face serious now. "It was very useful to me."

I found my voice, hoarse and distant. "I am glad."

And what if, rather than writing to me, Max had shared the case with Peter? What if my presence had never become necessary? Or what if I had arrived before Max had died? Would he have recognized me? Would I have intervened? Or done nothing? If I had published my story about them . . . If Jim had not been killed, or his murder solved . . . But these were useless questions indeed.

"I wish you could have met Max," Peter's voice far away. "He was quite a guy, even with that flute."

I had never met him, never. I had not realized it until that moment. I had seen his world through his eyes, and now that I was in it and he was not . . .

Peter looked at me and said nothing. I could read what was in those tired eyes the way I had once written it on a page somewhere.

He leaned over and clasped my hand. I remembered the terrible existential moment I had first shaken his hand months before; this was different. He smiled but it did not reach his eyes. "I know," he said, "I miss him too."

I pressed his hand reassuringly, and let go.

21

Thanksgiving

As I hadn't been able to extend my lease for only two months, the Cunninghams all but kidnapped me. I was given a room in the finished attic where I could see above the festive autumn trees and the tar-shingled roofs, and overhear every scrap of music rising from the rooms below. Rachel and John made every effort to make me feel at home. The twins took me under their wings and engaged me as tutor in both schoolwork and music. And we all kept an eye on each other.

Lynn and I had our secret to keep, and Jill and I had ours. Apart from the occasional display of knowledge of British culture, though—not least at Bonfire Night—she was doing a commendable job of letting go of her character Brinsel Thomas, and letting me be me. It was not a simple process; there were no scenes, but there were critical moments. Apart from Lynn, I was perhaps the only one who could see what was going on, and how hard it was for Jill; and unlike myself, she had to do it in the midst of the work of being a teenager, in the midst of nothing short of a family crisis. Misplaced items, short tempers, and outbursts of silliness became the order of the day, and nobody mentioned the upcoming trial.

When it came, the trial was my first experience of the American legal system—my first direct experience, for I had seen it often enough through Max's eyes. My part was mercifully brief, and in the end deemed moot. Perhaps that is the most remarkable thing about those few days in November so long ago now: the event itself was dreamily surreal, yet after months of merely calling up memories, one of them was actually happening.

With its almost liturgical choreography, its stock characters, predictable costumes, scripted lines, and unquestioned conventions it was all bizarrely like theater to my mind. The details escape me; I do not remember now the proceedings, the defense lawyer's arguments, or even the smell and look of the chamber. I remember mostly the people.

I remember Richard, Rachel, and John were there, and that we sat together in the gallery. That Richard was grave and silent and sat on one side of me. That John held Rachel's hand and sometimes she would hold mine as if to reassure me, and that Lynn came on one day, but her mother wouldn't let her get out of school after that. I remember a few others of Max's and Peter's friends came. Captain Petrucci stopped in on one day. Felix sporting clericals for the occasion and looking oddly officious. Retired private detective Dan Malcombe made himself a fixture, and doubtless disquieted the defense, and a few others, with his manic beady glares. I remember several people in the jury and one fellow in particular with bulging eyes I had once merely imagined had been there.

Peter presented with the prosecution. It was more than an ordinary trial for him, and for myself as well. Those few fevered days, ultimately unremarkable, ultimately inconsequential, captured in parentheses the justice I had wanted for myself and Jim, and sensed that we, in company with untold numbers of others, would never get on earth.

And what had I expected justice to look like in Davis's case? That his life would be ruined as well? He had already done that to himself. That he would also die? More pointless squandering, rectifying nothing; already I would never be free of him. And what of justice in the case of the original "Edwards," my first husband and another lifer, whose name I could not even say, and that other unknown person who had killed Jim? What was justice to mean without being simply canonized vengeance? None of us could have what we most desired, to have back what we had lost. But I understood, at last, what Max had meant about forgiveness. I simply could not tell anyone.

I don't remember what doubts there had been about the case. I do remember that not only Peter's evidence but the evidence the letters had brought, or led to, was the weight that tipped the scales. I don't remember all the other charges. I only remember that Edward Davis was found guilty of one count of intentional first-degree homicide and sentenced to life in prison.

I was not surprised; I had known, five years previously, that this would happen. What I had not known, had never expected, was that my actual participation lay between the problem and the resolution. I myself had had to become part of it first, present not merely as a fascinated observer, but present in person, and as myself.

I remember Davis never acknowledged our presence and I think refused even to notice us. He sat as he had the entire time, his face appearing only in phases when conferring with his attorney. If anyone there, anyone at all, could have shown him compassion, if anyone could have been an advocate for him, not in an abstract legal sense but in a personal and human one, it ought to have been myself. *The refusal to love:* there was my failure sitting there in handcuffs, there was the reason I had not been able to finish the letters. I had known about them all because of love, but him I did not want to love; I was not ready for freedom that real, and I knew at the same time simply by virtue of that, that I had accepted the care of him, that I was almost the only one who *could* care, and worse, that I did. I think it was only then that I realized what was happening, because I started to cry.

Afterwards there was a lot more crying, and hugging, and things got very muddled. I remember standing on the courthouse stairs and saying to Peter, "You did it!" And that tired smile, that tired and sad face, "We sure did, and we couldn't have done it without you." I remember arriving at the Cunninghams' with a migraine and having to go to bed early.

In the morning I woke with a clean head and a fresh heart, and for a long moment wondered where I was.

Then I remembered. Everything.

It was Thanksgiving morning.

I lay gazing at the ceiling for several minutes. The thin November morning sunlight shafting sideways through the dormer window. I remembered Rachel the morning after she had heard the news, three and a half years before. It had not been like this. Nor on that morning twenty-four years before when, alive beyond all reason, I had come to after being left for dead—and both myself and my unborn child had died, though there was evidence only for the latter—the casualties of a marriage I had not had the strength to leave and which consequently had reached its logical conclusion. Nor that morning, nearly nine years gone, when after a frantic night I had opened my door to find two police who asked, "We do apologize for disturbing you, but are you Mrs. Brinsel Thomas?" and I had known, on hearing that *Mrs.*, what it meant, and that I would scarcely hear it anymore. Who needed proof in that moment? Some things, you just knew.

I remembered waking up in my Thirty-Second Street bedsit on a morning late in May a few months previously and imagining a well-planned day ahead of me, on the menu an outing around town with Cathy to do some research for a story that had captured my heart.

The house quiet and still, the distant murmur of music; after a few minutes I scraped myself out of bed, pulled on my housecoat, and wandered down to the kitchen. It was still early, no one there yet but Rachel, towering over the table in her burgundy dressing gown and arms wrapped around her middle. Hair falling over her shoulders, fine threads of gray mingled with the nut brown. The classical station churning out the last few minutes of Dvořák's *Symphony No. 9* into the sunnied air and she gazing down at the front page of the newspaper spread out on the table. She glanced up when I came in. I smiled at her blearily. "Good morning, dear."

"Look, Brinsel, you made the papers."

I woke up about thirty more degrees. There on the front page, at the bottom, was a banner article about the trial. "After Three Years, Last Case Closed." A photograph of Peter hugging me outside the courthouse. I was smiling, though Peter simply looked dazed. We both looked exhausted. The caption read: "*Peter Serrev, former associate of Max Thompson, greets an unidentified woman outside the courthouse after the trial ended yesterday.*"

I blinked at the photo, fully awake.

Rachel laughing. "'*An unidentified woman*'! As if you hadn't even been a witness. Well, it could have been worse, they could have confused the two of us."

"What would be so dreadful about that?" I yawned.

"Oh, Brinsel." She dropped her head into my shoulder and suddenly burst into tears. "My stupid brother, *my stupid brother* . . ."

I hugged her and let her cry, nothing I could say.

Max was dead; there was no story that could be written to bring him back. It was really all over, and now it was about us.

"It's your first Thanksgiving," Richard told me over breakfast. "So work on an appetite!"

With the feast to prepare for, we were all set to work somewhere; I was assigned, rather absurdly, to the kitchen, but the presence of the twins softened my culinary ignorance. Lynn and Jill initiated me into all sorts of rituals of the day, familial and cultural, and I helped them prepare the snack trays that would be left out until dinner. Jill rhapsodized breathlessly, non-stop, about what Rostropovich had done in Moscow in August, and Lynn tried to interest me in the workings of small engines, and both educated me with a litany of American foods which were not quite the sum of their parts—ants-on-a-log and the like—which quickly blew into a rash of vicious punning. By the time Rachel came in, we were having a full-scale epidemic of laughter and the most dreadful runaway puns.

"Well, aren't you a bunch of cunning hams," she mimicked her brother. "Aren't you done yet? We've got guys out there agitating for food, and I'm ready to start on the bird. Your dad's waiting for you, Lynn, you're missing the game."

She shooed them out with their handiwork. Jill lingered in the door, the intention of hanging around inscribed on her face, but her mother pushed one of the trays at her.

"Go on, peaches, Grandpa's waiting for you. The concert's already started."

Jill threw me a small smile that said something I couldn't quite catch, but resignedly took the food and left.

It was incredible that the angst of the trial was over, though all of us were still a bit fuzzy and off balance; Rachel was rather raw and weepy but held herself together, her gaze constantly returning to a photo of her brother amidst the violets on the windowsill. The frame propped up one of the green arms of the aloe Cathy had given me, now living among the violets. We chopped and mixed and sautéed, and Rachel taught me how to stuff dates and make a *real* pumpkin pie—"Not like the recipe on the can!" The radio pouring out Rampal playing CPE Bach, Rachel creaming the sweet potatoes and merrily chatting about holidays past, I trimming a few pounds of brussels sprouts. And it came to me as unremarkably as though she had mentioned it that were Max there, he would be with us, helping with the food, and there would be music, and laughter . . .

Rachel was thinking of him too. She had been silent, listening to the radio, when she abruptly turned to me and all but stuttered, "And what am I supposed to do about *that man?*"

My fingers closed around the three sprouts I had just picked up and I couldn't meet her gaze at first, but at last turned to her. We looked at each other, our silence suspended against a radio commercial for insurance.

"Someday," I said, "I'll tell you what I did."

She pressed the back of one hand against her eyes and nodded, staring into the violets on the windowsill. For several minutes, only the radio announcer rhapsodizing about a recording of Piatigorsky to be played next. A sudden excited yell in stereo from the downstairs. The music of the Thanksgiving Day concert on channel twelve in the living room could just barely be heard; Max had conducted it himself at Taylor Theater four years previously. I had mentioned it in a story written only last Christmas, but the memory felt much older than that.

When the Thanksgiving concert was ended, Jill came looking for me. Rachel had gone to the living room to watch the parade with Richard; Lynn and John were still in the study pulling for their favorite team. I sat at the kitchen table, listening. Jill came silently and made no overtures; when I opened my eyes, I saw her standing in the doorway.

She was holding a large packet carefully wrapped in brown paper, the posture of a small girl hugging a book too obtuse for her years, but the face of someone who knew what it meant.

"I wanted to give this to you."

I did not have to ask what it was, and understood I could not refuse.

She stepped to the table and held the packet out to me, and, with the burning memories of receiving in them a handshake, a flute, manuscript sheets and a packet of letters, my hands took it, and held it, and it remained in them.

I still asked, "Are you sure you want to do this?"

"Yes," instantly, but firmly. A sliver of a smile, "I already know how it all turns out."

I had once thought I knew that too. And yet I had been wrong, I had been missing parts.

"It isn't in here . . . ?"

"No, I never wrote it."

I understood what she was doing. And my way had led me much differently, for there was no one to whom I could give my files.

"You know," said Jill raspily, "you really are just as short as I thought you were."

I smiled, but I felt large and blundering and shy and hugged Jill's gift with a helplessness I couldn't disguise, looking up at that tall girl who had just given me one of the most treasured things she had. "I don't know what to say, Jill, and I don't know how to thank you."

For a moment I thought she might burst out weeping. She drew a quick breath, blinking, a tiny, wry smile tugging at the corners of her mouth. "Just be grateful it didn't happen to you."

I quickly embraced her so she would not see my face, and she hugged me, her grip tighter than mine. When I trusted myself to speak, I asked her shoulder, "What are you going to do now?"

She drew back and studied me. "I'll write something else."

"That's the spirit," I forced the words out with a bravado I did not feel.

In the living room a fire perked in the hearth, and the open drapes framed the snow-colored afternoon sky veined by the bare limbs of trees. The parade on the telly was over, and we were trimming up for Christmas. I helped untangle long garlands of tiny white lights and unwrap heirloom ornaments from clouds of tattered tissue and pull the nativity figures from their shredded paper nestings, brushing them off with my fingers, while Rachel kept up a running commentary on each little item.

We were nearly finished, and quite ready for the feast, when Richard slipped out and returned with something tucked under his arm.

"This is for you, Brinsel." With the same sort of offhanded, purposeful indirectness his son would have had, he held out to me what he had brought, and I saw it was a cloth-bound book.

"Thank you," I gave him a smile in return, then looked at his gift. "Oh! Wherever did you find this?"

"I have my tricks," delighted and very pleased. "Open it!"

Somehow, Richard had got for me the new edition of Waldo Williams's *Dail Pren*. On the flyleaf he had written in his long graceful hand, "Anyone who speaks Welsh can surely do other beautiful things. To someone who helps fill the world with beauty. Richard M. Thompson." "Thank you, Richard," I said again, flushing.

"I've never heard Welsh," he said, "and I was wondering, if you would be willing to read us a poem?"

Richard got everyone to come sit and listen and, standing before them, my heart somewhere between my hands and my head, I read them Jim's favorite, "In the Days of Caesar," amazed at what I saw written in their faces. When I reached the end I paused, studying the words, then closed my eyes and felt out a translation. It was a moment before I realized I was crying. But I knew then, I just knew. Sometimes you just knew.

Jill knew also. She stopped me as I went to put the book away. "You're going back to Wales, aren't you? You can go back now."

I nodded. "Thank you, Jill."

She caught my arm. "I have to speak with you."

The urgency in her voice startled me. I could not imagine what else there was to say, but followed her down to Rachel's study. Jill's eyes burning as she sat and gazed at me a long moment.

"I wanted to tell you, I wanted to tell you what he said, the last thing he said—"

I nearly dropped the book. "Oh Jill, *don't*."

She swallowed hard. "I understand, but it's okay, it's okay."

"*Please*, Jill, I don't want to know."

Her face was desperate. "But it's so much to keep to myself, and I really felt you should know."

"Please," I closed one hand over hers, "keep it for me. Jillian, you know, don't you, how close we were, and yes, still are? There is nothing, nothing he could have said in that moment I would not already know one way or another—and I am certain the same is true for each of you in your uncle's case. But that you heard it, that *you* know, that is something for you alone."

She wrestled with this, frustrated, then nodded. "Alright."

It was dizzying; Jill knew much, much, that I did not know, by her own admission more even than she had written down, and did not even seem to realize it. And then I understood something that had not even occurred to me before, the most essential thing, no doubt, Max meant for me to tell her.

"Would you please do one more thing for me, Jill? Something even more important."

"What?"

"That you never speak of this matter to anyone, never to your friends, never even to write about it, not in any way. Never, do you understand?"

I was not certain she did, but I did not dare be even more direct. She nodded mutely at me, startled.

"Be very careful what you do with what you know. Knowledge like this can be unsafe."

She grasped my hand. "I won't tell anyone."

This would try her maturity like nothing else, yet I had to trust her with it; I could not tell her another word. Peter alone, having spoken with Dai, knew Jim's case was cold, and I prayed he would say nothing of it to any of them. My peace in this entire business had come at the cost of Jill's anger; now her peace, and her safety, would have to come at the cost of my frustration.

Richard gave the blessing at dinner. The meal was marvelous, and the conversation went without saying, everyone being themselves almost as though I weren't there. I had to keep pinching myself. It was almost like being at Dai's house at Christmas, only it was Thanksgiving at the Cunninghams, and rather than two adolescent boys arguing about the latest eisteddfod or the next thing at Newport or Manchester and Cardiff, and Dai light-heartedly flinging around quotes of anything and everything and Mur with her gruff wit so much like Peter's it was the mild and cheerful John and the blunt Rachel, Richard the big noise and yet every bit the *tad*, the *taid*, and two lovely young women at home with themselves . . . all of whom, it seemed incredible to think now, I had once known only as characters in a story I believed I had quite invented. I believe I missed Max most at that moment, when he should have been there to enjoy them, but it was only myself, instead.

I thought of waiting to look at Jill's file until I got back home, but it seemed important to see it on her ground first. That evening, alone and not feeling at all alone, I sat on the braided rug in my attic room, the brown packet in my lap, gazing for some time at the stars peeping through the window. At last I turned to Jill's gift, feeling its heft and the beating of my heart like two unbearable weights.

Under the bedside lamplight I unwrapped the brown packet and took out its papers, turning through them gently. Tiny pieces of my life jumped out at me in words and phrases I recognized at first glance. My life as written by a young girl, perhaps a bit simplified, perhaps even a bit trite, but still recognizable, and unmistakably mine. I had written about Max in first person; Jill had written about me in a rather omniscient third. As I had thought, though she treated briefly the misery of my first marriage and had been aware I was later a widow, Max would not have known of Jim, for Jill had not written about him until after Max's death—her way of dealing with his. When I had written about Max, I had needed a reason for such a pointless death; for Jill, there could be no reason good enough—and she had been right, for in itself such a violent event could mean nothing, nor could any meaning be given it—and so she had written of Jim's death just as it had happened, cruelly and senselessly. It was what she had not written that calmed the fear I had contracted earlier; if she knew at all who had killed him or why, she had not written it here.

Holding those sheets, I realized many of them were the same ones Max himself had read; I had written of him, and he had read of me, we had *both* been characters . . .

And what had made Jill first write about me? Memories of beginning to play violin and her uncle's jokes—those irreverent, disarming untruths for the sake of another point of view—about how horribly he played it?

Under that folder was another large folder, with metal clasps and cord ties and layers of re-taped typed labels. The cover was tied shut with red cord wound around Bristol paper buttons; the cord was taped down and an illegible scrawl wandered across the edge of the tape onto the folder. I stared at the folder, puzzled, then loosened the tape and the strings and the metal clasps, and opened the cover.

"Ohhh, no, oh *no*."

Max's handwriting. Pages of typed interviews. Reports. An entire dossier.

"Jillian Elisabeth Cunningham . . ."

The dossier. The file that had "gone missing" after Max's death. His niece must have wanted a piece of him to remember—and had picked it up in his flat, there where he had put it for safekeeping *in his music*, where even the police had missed it, never guessing . . .

Nobody had ever asked Jill if she knew anything . . . and why would they? What could she know?

In the very back, tucked under the concluding remarks, I found a small yellow envelope. A shred of Christmas wrapping was still taped to one corner; a gift tag: *To Uncle Max from Jillian*, clipped to the top. He had scrawled on the envelope: *Remv b4 flng.*

Inside were several sheets of lined notebook paper folded in half. Five letters. With uncannily familiar handwriting.

For a moment I couldn't breathe.

At Max's last Christmas, Jill had given her uncle a gift of three packets of her writing. One had been a Christmas story; a second, a chapter from another story she had been working on. I had not bothered with what the third was. Now I knew. Jill had written her uncle, in the name of her character Brinsel Thomas, five letters in my wire-brush handwriting, in pretended introduction and response to letters he would have sent Brinsel Thomas. Her familiar and pointed and creative way of trying to eke information out of her uncle for a mystery story—she had been poking fun at him, she had been *mocking* him; she had been saying: I know you don't write letters, and that you will never trouble yourself to do so, so I am telling you what I want in this way, and I am *flooding* you with letters . . . knowing he would have been "too busy" to reply to any such letters in the first place, but that her intransigence would nevertheless win her a response. He had not responded in the way she had hoped. Knowing I had actually existed, not knowing how to begin a proper correspondence and not wanting to forfeit a professional distance by doing so, he had sent the requested information to the real Brinsel Thomas. To find out if all the connections he saw between his niece's story and what he had learnt of me, and what he suspected of me, were in fact true, and to prepare me, in the best way he could have done, for the equally astonishing information that we had both written the same music.

The letters were exactly what I would have responded to those I had written in Max's name.

Dear Mr. Thompson, I was pleasantly surprised to receive your letter from Waterhouse . . . you ask about my artwork . . . the publisher of my writing, Open Windows, has the distinction of running such a small operation that we call it "publishing out of a hatbox" . . . You make too much of me, I am only a teller of tales and scribbler of featherweight fiction, and my work irrelevant . . . what of your music? . . . thank you for the delightful picture, and for clearing up the mystery about Rampal!

And the last letter, *Dear Maximilian . . . Your suggestions for stories would be most welcome and appreciated . . . I shall try to find a way to recompense you for the trouble if I can make any use of them . . . I shall send you copies so you can see what sort of damage I've made. Perhaps in return, you could share some of your music? . . . I shall be away this winter and several months next year and won't be able to respond if you should write . . .*

Beneath the yellow envelope was a long white envelope, unsealed and blank. Inside I found a sheet of the business stationery of S&T, covered front and back with Max's scrawling handwriting.

May 17, 1988

Dear Jill,
Well, here is your old uncle, writing the first letter you've ever got from him and probably the last because he just doesn't do letters, as you know very well. In my history I only have much experience with two kinds of letters; the one you aren't going to get from me, and the other is a bit too formal for these purposes. I'll try to aim for one of our nice chats and if I get too businesslike, just bear with me.

Your attack was very clever; it's taken me five months to think of a suitable punishment to fit the crime, but I figured if you had the gall to throw five of your character's letters at me (at once! geez louise! *is* that *how you carry on a correspondence??*) I could make you wait, and at least cough up one. I've been thinking a lot about your (Brinsel's) question for a mystery and I'll get to that in a minute. You know ignorance can be dangerous; knowledge can be a pretty dangerous thing too at times and pricey, not even the free stuff is really free. So if I give you any ideas you have to sit down and look at them carefully and not mess around. Got that?

I just spent a few months writing to a mutual friend of ours to try to get some information, sort of on an exchange basis, but I haven't heard a thing back yet. Sometimes, my work is like that. Evidently I'm not numero uno on their list although I suspect they may simply be out of town just yet—and, I strongly suspect, they already know all about the dish I've sent, and much, much else. Maybe I won't find out, though. Sometimes you just don't. There are lots and lots of unanswerable questions out there, real ones. Start with music. Make any sense to you? Blows my mind. I can cite you chapter and verse on everything from A to zyklus and explain it to pieces, play anything on anything I lay my hands on, I can do the figures for a million scales, analyze harmony and orchestration standing on my head, draw frequency wave diagrams to bring tears to your eyes, but it all means nothing when you get down to it and can feel it all over. I still don't get what it is or what it does, and I've been making music since I was old enough to spit. It does so many illogical, nonlinear things. And how does it do that? Well, before you add people to the equation, by math! It can express the eternal and timeless—and how? In time, only by time! We work mostly with measured music—but music itself you can't measure. Why?? Can't understand it for the life of me. And writing music—when it just shows up, just "comes to you"—well, how? (And what's behind the idiom "comes"?) Sometimes I think I know, but sometimes... Some stuff you aren't going to find the logic to and just can't explain and you have to live with not knowing. Even me. To this day I still ask why Ariel; but then, why anyone? It's like that. So you keep asking. Ask anything, don't be afraid. Piece of advice: if you can, find the real question first, and bear in mind the shape of your question may decide the shape of the answer you may get. (Form can determine, as in limit, content—think of your music). If there are no stupid questions, there are a lot of lazy ones and those that come with a judgment already in mind—that's not a question that comes armed with an answer, that's insecurity in a river in Egypt. Used well, the insecurity can be a fine thing, but stay out of that river. Find out what it is you're really asking, and don't stop asking; it won't be comfortable, it will be worth it. And maybe someday, who knows? You get an answer somewhere, somehow. Or maybe you start asking a different question. Maybe asking becomes more important than getting an answer, especially one you think you already know. Maybe you find out the questions aren't that important.

Salient point: I can tell you that some things are gifts and gifts belong to a different order of logic. You probably won't believe me as people don't normally call those insoluble things gifts—not, of course, unless they are of the variety to incite admiration, and the peculiar affliction of yours truly is a case in point—but I'm not interested in whether you believe me or not. I'm just giving you the facts of the case; provided you don't go break any laws (or hearts, I hope) what you do with them is your call. You're a responsible body and you've got a swell brain, like I keep telling you.

So, long prologue. Down to business. I don't know if I should do this; but, I thought, who knows? So suppose it's like this, your big mystery to write about: suppose there's this character named Brinsel Thomas, who is an artist and a writer and what-have-you and all, and suppose—just suppose, instead of being your idea, she's a real person? Then what? What do you do with her? And here's something else: what do you do when two people write the same music, the exact same, note for note, and they've never met or heard each other's music? Go to court? Talk it out? Give it up? What gives? I bet you could spin a good mystery yarn out of all that, and more interesting than anything I do at work. Believe you me, I get stories sometimes (and work with some real characters), but they're a different class. Reminds me I passed on to Lynn some mystery music I'd like to show you sometime, I think it would interest you. It's Welsh and you seem to be in your Welsh phase. I think you'll like it.

At any rate, this is the most pertinent thing I can tell you: like it or not, no investigation—whether you call it data analysis or score analysis—is ever resolved on complete or unconditioned facts, but on provisional premises, on information grown in a complex matrix of contingencies, most of all out of a *soup of comfortable prejudices you call your reasoning, and how you make sense of what you've got. When do you have enough facts to prove something? How do you know? That depends entirely on how much information you have and whether you believe it's suited to purpose and complete, and that can only be defined by the* limit *of your knowledge, even the limit of your imagination. If you're honest, you'll admit your knowledge is always incomplete. That being so, you have to conclude that faith, not facts, is the ground of all knowing—faith that you have enough suitable information, at the very least. Don't go blowing hot air with dictatorial interpretations, and don't go looking for wisdom from me when you're older for I have herewith made my deposit.*

I can hear you rolling your eyes at me, you're thinking this is "Lynn stuff." No, I haven't suddenly confounded you with your sister after thirteen years. This is about you, Jinx. What's it got to do with your question? Just this: you are sitting in the middle of the biggest mystery I know of. It's called life. As with music, there are precious few real rules, and more valid perceptual tools than are usually given credit. All the schemata and all the tools you were ever given to sort out the world or solve problems will be unfit for some of the things that come along. You have to trust that there really are other tools available to you, and they are perfectly valid. I think your character and your story could show you a thing or two there.

Remember what Chas Williams wrote? "No one can possibly do more than decide what to believe." Good ol' Chuck, he must have known something about not knowing, at least not being able to "prove" things. At any rate, not a good saying for my business but a good one for yours. What do I know about writing stories? Well, that you can't know everything, that stuff will surprise you, that you're never really in charge—big words from the guy who doesn't get literature, I know. And then there's life: more of the same. I can't do a thing with it but love of it what I can. I will never unravel people or life; as soon as you think you've got something all sorted out, up comes more evidence you can't even fit in. Me I'm not going to break my head over it. Got more pressing problems to solve, such as the ones that pay the bills. I just lost money on this last one, but it's one of those instances where losing is winning for someone else. Other good guys, I mean. I can live with that; I'll just eat spaghettios for a month (can't be worse than your mom's cooking, right?).

Well, enough chitchat, clock's ticking, it's quarter of eight and I've got to run off. I'll see you on Thursday for strings and Lynn for algebra and that darn horn. You'll both ace everything and I'll get a headache from all the racket; you'll turn into beautiful young women who break hearts left and right and make everything you touch beautiful and your uncle will turn into a grouchy old bachelor who plays like Moyse and will probably end up looking like him too. Alright, so I'll look like your Grandad, I guess there is some kind of familial resemblance.

I'd tell you to be good and not grow up too fast, but I don't like to ask the impossible. Try not to do anything I would, such as give your mom a hard time. My love to all, &c.

Max

So how do you like my letter? Will wonders never cease. Probably not as good as all your literary work but it's a beginning, right? (Yes, I've been practicing). Don't worry, I won't let it go to my head; I know my place, I'm a man of notes, not letters, see . . .

I sat unmoving, galaxies colliding inside me, staring at that handwriting long after the moon had slid across the dormer glass and Orion wheeled over my head, then let the file, all of it, gently close.

Coda

Nothing stays like a story, and it remains quite present to me even now. It is like no other story I know; I have to tell it to my great-nephews and great-niece when we gather together at Christmas. I even play Max's music for them. Dai just laughs and winks and says, "Now don't believe a word of it; your old aunt learned a new kind of tale when she went to the States, the *tall tale*." And of course they don't ever believe me. It may be something to do with the fact that Dai can't talk about his work; "Peter Serrev . . . now wasn't that the name of one of your characters once, Suhl?" I have even showed him their *photographs* which I now carry in my wallet: "What fine characters are these!" he teases. It may be something to do with the fact that the Coomeses and the Cunninghams have never yet been able to get together. "You've not ever met Richard Thompson!" the young ones once told me. "You're just making that up." And one year, these took it upon themselves to inform me, "If it's not a myth, it can't be true." "You have been reading *much* too much Tolkien," I replied. Then I come to the end and,

"And *then* what?" I am asked. For they still want to know. And I say, "Then we all went to our own homes, and life went on." But that is never enough for them, so I tell them the rest of the story. Or rather, a carefully edited version; I don't believe they need to know everything.

In the morning I look down the hill from the cottage where I now live, down a gray lane at an off-track farm, to see the running light that is the river at the valley bottom. When I look the other direction, the hills are dark as green glass, bald stone describing dark shapes against the sky, and the valley, bisected with the road that comes from the motorway, chalked with farms and swept with the shadows of clouds. From the front window I can see the flint tower of Saint Beuno's in the nearest village where I serve as Reader, the clockface and the weathercock on the town hall from the front stoop and, from the end of the lane on a mythically clear day, the distant peaks of Snowdon. One could fit it all on one of those graphic propaganda pieces called postcards; it is a bitterly bracing isolation and material poverty that nourishes my art, giving me the last refuge I needed to heal. The Cunninghams had been pleased to learn I was returning to Wales after so many years away, but Jill alone knew what I was going back to, and what fears awaited me. The worst is past now; now, I have found a place for myself, whatever remains unresolved. At any rate, it is home, and I am not leaving anymore.

It was Jim who, years ago, said that reading a story was much like being blind: where the world you could touch or hear, smell or taste ended, you saw nothing that was not mediated to you imaginatively. I think it may even be like being deaf, as well. It was he who told me I should write, and it is because of him, and Max, that I still do.

It was Jim too, who loved to say, "When de Chardin said all of life was in seeing, he wasn't talking about the *eyes,* you know"; Jim who was always fond of reminding me there is more, much more to the world than meets the eye, and of course, like Max, he was in a position to know. Jim, who, effortlessly at ease in a world he could not see, could never understand how I could be so clumsy as always to trip over his cane. "Where are you *going,* Suhl, can't you *see* me?" One act among many in the long Jim and Suhly Show, as Dai called it. "What if you had been a Thomas *too,* sweet? *Then* whose name would you have taken?" A very hard act to follow on some days.

I still have the letters he wrote me during our courtship, some in Braille that he had read aloud to me, for I read it so poorly, and some in his nearly impeccable typing. I still wonder at times how he saw the world. What was Jim's favorite color? I don't know; Jim didn't have a favorite color as I know them. Yellow was "a small bottle" or "a piece of granite," it smelled like "earth" and sounded like "a brush." Blue was "a bough of rowan," "a tuft of grass," "your voice." Sometimes he was even less specific: space was a mystery, distance was immaterial. Time only happened "when you are away from me." What did things *look* like? Jim only cared if it was I who told him. To him blindness was a gift, and he threw inside-out as well the narrow clinical world I had been branded and pinned in—so what if I heard things I could not see? He was always hearing things too, and perhaps, he suggested, it wasn't that I heard things, but that others were deaf. He loved the music of Art Tatum and Stevie Wonder; they made him "see it just." "They're not *black,*" he told me patiently, "they're *green* and *red.*" He saw my artwork by the music I wrote for him, that was also Max's. Whose music was it? I don't know. It may be the wrong question; and the question may not matter.

Rachel has a framed photo of me in her living room, taken the last time I visited: I am standing among the Cunninghams, comically small... how did I get there? I have the same picture in my studio, hanging among other inexplicable souvenirs. I have been adopted as a sort of aunt by the people I once imagined were my characters. They have their own myth of how this friendship began, and I have mine. Both, I believe, are true. Only one can truly be explained, at least as far as our understanding goes—which, really, isn't so far indeed. Beyond all reason, I am able to say I was *there*; I *was* there, but just how... well, I have no answer to that, and I do not really want one. I did not create Max, nor any of them, no more than Jill created me; we were each entrusted an extraordinary gift, and have had to decide what best to do with it.

I correspond now with Peter, with the Cunninghams and their daughters and Richard. Peter and Eleanor remarried not long after I returned to the UK; he became a police detective, as did Lynn. John is still a mechanic, Rachel has gone into music therapy. Richard, getting older, is toying with the idea of actually retiring. Jill, my youthful chronicler, writes—she sends me signed copies of her works—performs, composes, conducts, teaches. Her ensemble has toured Britain twice at this writing. I sent her, long ago, her uncle's letter; "I cried all over it," she wrote back. "I understood he was saying you were real and he was trying to get me ready for that..." And "yes, my writing folder included a file of Max's; I got it when we took the stuff out of his apartment. It must not have been important since he had it at home in a stack of music... As long as I didn't know what was in it, he was still there. I don't need it anymore..."

And they are still performing his compositions, not only in his hometown but all over the country now. I fear it was my fault. My rogue article on the flautists was picked up by, of all things, *Flute Talk*, and things took their course from there. "They are having trouble pigeonholing him," Richard wrote me, with evident satisfaction. And, "People keep asking for you." Fortunately, the co-composer of *This Gift* is reachable only via the Cunninghams, and Rachel very handily tells inquirers I am unavailable. Meanwhile, the royalties from the music now attributed to both Max and myself do a handsome job of keeping me solvent. Dai just shakes his head: "I don't know how you do it!" The Cunninghams and Peter are in on some of the joke, but the rest of it is all mine to savor.

I suppose in a few years, a few decades at most, he will disappear into Richard's shadow, thereafter to appear only in footnotes; they shall no doubt publish one of those anthologies to Richard's memory. I'll have to leave a contribution for it... but then, what could I say? His son, whom I knew best, will never get a book like that. "I remember," Jill wrote me once, "at almost the last lesson he taught me, that he said he only wanted one thing anymore, and that was to keep growing." Perhaps the simplest, most demanding desire, and the least simplistic. There is no way to tell how it will go.

I still live alone. Jim's case is still cold, and I suspect that shall not change, either. I have questions still; I am still learning to live with them. I live believing the truth of all of it shall out at some point; for the time being, everything is incomplete, everything constantly shifting—answers, knowledge, perception, even the questions. I wonder if we could bear it otherwise; perhaps not just yet.

I must be getting older; the last Christmas, I got asked, "What do they do when authors die?"

"What does *who* do?" I asked.

"*You* know, the people who write about *you?*"

"Oh, well . . . they write up a nice bit in the papers about how long you lived and where, and if you wrote something everybody knows about, they say how brilliant it was, or how dreadful—whichever they decided it was—and if you hadn't, they say you wrote some rather interesting books not much read, or something of the kind, and usually they say what a character you were and try to put a good face on it . . . and that's that."

"Is that what they'll do for you?"

"You mean, say I was a character and that my books aren't much read?"

"Yes."

"It's very likely," I only offered.

"What about when the *characters* die?"

"*Which* characters, now? The authors?"

"No, the *real* characters—the ones in the story. What about when *they* die?"

"You know," I replied. "I rather don't think they do."

Acknowledgements

With gratitude to those who played a part that made this possible. Take a bow:

Assistant Producer: Sheila Upjohn

Assistant Stage Manager: Suzanne Rhodes

Human Resources Coordinator: Sofia M. Starnes

Librarian/Archivist: Kathryn J. Corbett

Properties: Cynthia H. Montooth, Robert Selevitch, Golder Cotman, Aaron Ellis, Skipp Porteous

Sound: Lisa A. Wulf

Lighting: Alice Cromer-van Lennep, Patricia Nakamura, Shelly L. Hall

Special Effects: Michael Ida, Leslie and Denis Brown, Rhonda Strong

Run Crews: Frederick S. Roden, Janet Irvine, the "UK Unit," JoAnn Crupi, Alan and May Griffiths

And a special note of thanks for Rowan Williams's *Grace & Necessity*, which prompted me to finish what I had started.